PRAISE FOR *STARRY STARRY NIGHT*

"*Starry Starry Night* is a triumph of storytelling voice. Here, colonial history, fractured cultural space, and the sinuous complexities of kinship are each uniquely illuminated by the consciousness of a vulnerable child. This is a beloved book by a beloved author. This is Shani Mootoo at her most lyrical and intimate."

—DAVID CHARIANDY, AUTHOR OF *BROTHER*

"*Starry Starry Night* will endure. Shani Mootoo gives us a novel that is achingly alive, a portrait of the artist, a study of the languages instilled in us and the languages we must find, a living example of how art can breathe worlds, remembered, discovered, betrayed, beloved, shared, into life. As soon as the novel ended I wanted to begin again. This is Shani Mootoo's masterpiece."

—MADELEINE THIEN, AUTHOR OF *THE BOOK OF RECORDS*

PRAISE FOR *OH WITNESS DEY!*

Finalist for THE 2025 PAT LOWTHER MEMORIAL AWARD
Finalist for THE 2024 BIG OTHER BOOK AWARD FOR POETRY

"*Oh Witness Dey!* confronts the politics of belonging and reflects on how individual experiences—those crucial 'umbilical cords'—connect us to our common history."

—*LITERARY REVIEW OF CANADA*

"Grounded in sharp emotional insight and a keen understanding of the past, *Oh Witness Dey!* is frequently devastating and solemn, but at times hopeful, compassionate, and even playful as it shirks poetic conventions and leans into its unflinching momentum."

—*MAISONNEUVE MAGAZINE*

"*Oh Witness Dey!* calls its readers to think through our own family histories, to listen to our own voices and stories, and to ask questions of them so that we can examine ways in which to move forward in making the world a better, brighter place than it is right now."

—*PERIODICITIES*

PRAISE FOR *CANE | FIRE*

"Mootoo uses verse, space, and art to create the images and feelings here in the collection, to great effect: even the use of different colours of font, from light grey to denote something quieter to other colours for emphasis of a point, or to draw your eye to a specific part. Holding this book and experiencing the way the art is laid out on the page was a true experience by itself."

—*THE MIRAMICHI READER*

"The whole of Mootoo's artistic output informs and ripples through *Cane | Fire*. Employing the glittering detail and a mythic tone that characterizes her fiction, Mootoo has crafted a poetic memoir that reimagines her family histories, including journeys from Ireland to Trinidad and Canada."

—*QUILL & QUIRE*

"Mootoo's artworks, most of which feature some sort of collage and reassembly, shift the effects of memory, of line, of sound, of relation and amplify the transformative possibilities of these poems."

—*WINNIPEG FREE PRESS*

PRAISE FOR *POLAR VORTEX*

Finalist for the 2020 GILLER PRIZE

"The writing is subtle and emotionally compelling, and the reader is left to meditate on questions of the intersections of race and culture, sexuality and desire, and the past and present."

—*CANADIAN LITERATURE*

"*Polar Vortex* is an unsettling novel about how secrets always come back to get us—especially the secrets we've managed to keep from ourselves."

—*THE GLOBE AND MAIL*

"*Polar Vortex* is a richly introspective and sobering look at how relationships—and our perceptions of them—constantly evolve and affect who we were, who we've become, and who we might be, despite our best efforts to deny that power."

—*THE FIDDLEHEAD*

"Compellingly charts the complexity of human relationships, the illusions of memory, and the corrosive power of denial."

—*KIRKUS REVIEWS*

"Mootoo's subtle, thought-provoking tale stands out among stories of characters gripped by the past."

—*PUBLISHERS WEEKLY*

"*Polar Vortex* makes no compromises in conveying the grip of the past on its heady and sensuous cast of characters, all of whom sing their song, as if they were the frozen swans of Lake Ontario that Priya and Alex encounter thawing out after the polar vortex has finally passed."

—*QUILL & QUIRE*

Also by Shani Mootoo

FICTION

Out on Main Street
Cereus Blooms at Night
He Drown She in the Sea
Valmiki's Daughter
Moving Forward Sideways like a Crab
Polar Vortex

POETRY

The Predicament of Or
Cane | Fire
Oh Witness Dey!

SHANI MOOTOO

STARRY STARRY NIGHT

BOOK*HUG PRESS
TORONTO 2025

FIRST EDITION

Library and Archives Canada Cataloguing in Publication
Title: Starry starry night / Shani Mootoo.
Names: Mootoo, Shani, author
Identifiers: Canadiana (print) 20250205785 | Canadiana (ebook) 20250205793
ISBN 9781771669566 (softcover) | ISBN 9781771669573 (EPUB)
Subjects: LCGFT: Autobiographical fiction. | LCGFT: Novels.
Classification: LCC PS8576.O622 S73 2025 | DDC C813/.54—dc23

The production of this book was made possible through the generous assistance of the Canada Council for the Arts and the Ontario Arts Council. Book*hug Press also acknowledges the support of the Government of Canada through the Canada Book Fund and the Government of Ontario through the Ontario Book Publishing Tax Credit and the Ontario Book Fund.

Canada Council for the Arts
Conseil des Arts du Canada

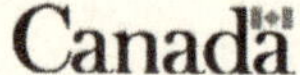

Book*hug Press acknowledges that the land on which we operate is the traditional territory of many nations, including the Mississaugas of the Credit, the Anishnabeg, the Chippewa, the Haudenosaunee, and the Wendat peoples. We recognize the enduring presence of many diverse First Nations, Inuit, and Métis peoples, and are grateful for the opportunity to meet and work on this territory.

For:
Vahli, Ramesh (Junior), Indrani, Kavir
xxx

The longer I gaze at the girl in the photo,
the more it seems that she is looking at me. Is this girl me?
Am I her?... The girl in the picture is not me, but
neither is she a fictional creation. There is no one else
in the world I know in such vast and inexhaustible
detail, which allows me to assert...

—ANNIE ERNAUX, *A GIRL'S STORY*

THE MOTHER: When you're a kid, you're in your
own world. You don't realize what's going on around you.

—CÉLINE HUYGHEBAERT, *REMNANTS*

You don't want those fingers, skin all chipped up, razor-like flecks slicing your own skin, fingers that even in a soapy lather exude the odour of garlic, you don't want fingers and hands like that bathing you, the same hands you'd witnessed pull and, with one swift twist, wring the neck of the chicken that had looked, wide-eyed, straight at you, pleading for one terrified second when it suddenly understood what was about to happen.

On an early morning she'd come upstairs, having just showered in the workers' downstairs bathroom stall—floating off her is the scent of the big, jagged bar of mottled blue soap, its lather running down the concrete wall of the stall, turning it slippery with thick streams of grey-blue slime. She smells like that soap. And gasoline. Chicken blood. Wet feathers. Garlic. All those odours, right there, when she tries to hold on to you to shower you. You struggle to get away, but she makes you sit on the peerha that the carpenter made and painted bright green just for you—and she tries to ladle water over your head.

Water sputtering out of the low shower tap onto the pale green bathroom tiles sounds like the wings of a headless bird beating the hard floor of the shed out in the back.

Her long braid glistens like asphalt after rain.

You bawl for Ma to come and save you.

SELVON STREET

ONE

Barlow grips my arm with her soapy hands; I can barely look in her eyes—when I do, even for one tiny second, I see in them the ruby-red water gushing-gushing down the sloped open gutter on its way out of the yard, under the backyard wall, and *fwooooshhh* into the municipal gutters beyond.

Give your grandmother a little break, child. She have other things to do. Stop getting on so. Let me bathe you.

I scream, tug, and pull.

But what wrong with you, child? Behave, na.

What can Ma be doing that she isn't bathing me? How can she allow this to be happening? I just have to keep pulling away long enough and Barlow will give up. I just have to scream until I feel the pain and the scratching in my throat. I will become hoarse, and later—when I'm clean and dressed, my hair still wet—Barlow will make the lime-and-honey drink she says will soothe my throat, and she will stand there and watch me sip it.

I like lime and honey together, but not lime—and not even honey—by itself. If I let a piece of lime touch just the tip of my tongue, the inside of my mouth curls up and twists, and saliva comes from all under my tongue and at the sides of my tongue and from the back of my throat, and tears run down my face, and all of me—my arms, my feet, my back—every part of me gets squeezed up, tight-tight-tight. But in the lime-and-honey drink, honey wins over twisty lime. The lime still tastes just a little twisty in the drink, but it doesn't make me pull inside of myself like what happens to snails when Sheldon and Colin sprinkle salt on them. I don't like honey by itself either, because even though it is supposed to be sweet like sweeties from Mr. Tang's shop, it still makes my mouth a little scratchy after I swallow it. It's too-too sweet. So they are good together, lime and honey. I want to drink all of it, but she doesn't let me. She says I will get a tummy ache. So I can only sip some of it, then she takes it away and puts it on a shelf and puts a saucer over it so ants won't get inside the cup. But when she is in the bedroom area cleaning the rooms there, I can climb on a chair and reach it. So I don't really mind screaming until my throat is sore. The louder I scream, the sooner she gives up, and Ma comes in to take over. By the time Barlow can't take it any longer, she'll be soaked from her head all the way to her bare feet. I wave my arms to try to stop her from holding on to me, and I kick my feet about and she gets even wetter and wetter. Steups, steups, steups. All the time she is steupsing. Steupsing isn't nice. And finally she lets go of me. Her large dark hands turn off the tap, and she stands up.

Look at how you have me. You wet me up good. Look at my dress. You are trouble, yes, child.

She wipes her face and her arms with my clean towel. She leaves me standing in the bath, naked and wet, and marches out of the room. She has been told not to leave me unattended because I could slip in the soapy water and hit my head on the tiles and maybe end up in hospital or die of a broken head.

Maybe now Ma will fire her. I grip the taps and try not to move about, but I continue to sob loudly. I pause for a moment to listen, then I cry out some more. I pause again and listen. And then, there is Ma in the doorway.

Tut tut tut. What is all that noise about?

Ma kneels on the wet mat on the other side of the low tiled wall and holds out her arms. I fall into them, limp. I heave and sob, squeezing my eyes tightly to get whatever tears I can out of them. She smells like paratha roti and then, when I turn my head into her neck, like cream of wheat. Her housedress is drenched fast as she wipes tears and water from my face, but she doesn't steups or scold me or pull away, and with her soft plump hands, her long fingers and clean nails, she begins the slide of soapy water all over my body. She tells me what she is doing, so I can be prepared. Like when she's about to dribble the water on the front of my head, to close my eyes and hold my breath. The warm water trickles from the ladle onto my head, then down my face, like a long slow waterfall. I stick out my tongue and lap the warm water. And it rolls down my neck, onto my shoulders, and down my back. I open my eyes and, through the beads of water on my lashes, I see her—she is blurred, but it is her, it is her—and she takes the bar of pink soap that smells like roses from the edge of the nearby sink and rubs it into the white washcloth that sits in her open palm. She takes her time. The bathroom fills up with roses. She is looking at what she is doing, not at me, and I am left standing on my own. I know I won't fall because she is there, but still, I stand very carefully. She puts an arm around my waist and steadies me while, with the other hand, with which she holds the limp warm rag, she bathes me. First my shoulders and then down my arms. She pulls and pushes the cloth gently up and down each arm—I offer each to her—holding my hand with one hand and the other lightly rubbing soft, slippery rose on the inside part of my elbows. She lifts my arms and passes the washcloth across my armpits. She pokes a finger into the cloth and makes a kind of tent, but then she closes the tent around the finger and uses the dressed-up finger to wash behind my ears. Then around and around inside my ears the finger goes, and when she tickles inside my navel with it, I wriggle about and laugh, and she smiles. Not just her lips, but her eyes smile, too. And her cheeks. I love my ma. She holds the cloth under the running water and the rose soap slides off. Then she wrings the cloth and the water hits the tiles, ragged and loud. Ma is strong, and pretty like a bunch of pink-and-yellow flowers. She soaps up the cloth again, and now the scent of roses is too high. It hurts my eyes. But I am not trouble for Ma, so I try not to make trouble for her. I stand strong, taking care not to fall, and she runs the cloth along my thighs, which I push out toward her, and I bend into her and grip her shoulders with both my hands to steady myself and offer her one leg, then the other, and she rubs the cloth over my knees, then behind them and down my shins and on my calves. She takes hold of my foot and passes the cloth quickly back and forth, and my feet curl in, just as if they were tasting a piece of lime without any honey. I giggle and try to pull away. She tells me not to wriggle like that because I might slip and fall, and she, too, is laughing as she says, If you fall, what would Ma do, eh, baby? A laughing matter will turn into what?

I know the answer, so I say, A crying matter.

And she says, proud of me, And we don't want that, do we?

I giggle. Mm-mm, we don't want that, Ma, do we?

She turns me around, and the cloth drags heavily down my back and across my bum. There, through the thick wet pile, are her hands. She doesn't let soap go in my eyes, but when Barlow bathes me, Barlow puts soap in my eyes.

*

When she, Barlow, and Polly clean shrimp, I help. Polly showed me how to do it. First, you pull the head off. The head is ugly. Stiff black strings wave around on the head. Ma calls those antennae. The strings have beads on them that are maybe eyes. You have to be very careful because there are parts on the head that are hard and sharp and will stab you if you're not, and your finger will bleed and you'll need a bandage. It will hurt a lot.

But I know how to be careful now, so I can pull the heads off without getting stabbed.

I think the shrimp in the big blue basin smell like how the bottom of the sea smells to other creatures great and small who live down there. I like that smell. It is also the smell of the blue sky over the sea, and the sun shining down on the sea and sand on the beach. All of that comes mixed up inside the bag of shrimp Polly buys at the market, and then when she empties the bag out into the basin, that mixed-up smell escapes and takes over the kitchen and enters my nose. It's very loud, but I close my eyes tightly, and when I do that, I see the sky and sea and sand, and then I think about the holidays. First there is the long drive from our house, number 39 Selvon Street, San Fernando, all the way to the house in Mayaro. Mr. Monty drives one car, with Polly and Frank in it, and Pa drives the other car, the blue one, with Ma and me. We go through the town, then over the hills, past cane fields and through coconut groves. When we arrive,

Ma gets out of the car, stretches, and says the same thing every time: Hm, look at this place. Trinidad pretty for so, eh? And I answer, Yes, Ma, pretty for so.

At the house in Mayaro, Pa always wakes up before me, and when I go downstairs to look for him, I find him standing on the veranda. He just stands there and stares past the beach, at the sea. I lean against him and look out. Birds called frigates fly high-high-high up, making slow circles or just sliding across the pretty blue sky. Early in the morning at the seaside, it gets very hot, and even if I wear my bathing suit, and even if there is a breeze, my skin gets sticky and salty because sea breeze has salt in it. You can't see it in the breeze, but you know about this because you can taste it if you lick the skin on your arm. And the sky is so bright that if you look up at it for a long time, your eyes will hurt. It looks as if you could see right through the blue, but all you see behind the blue is more blue, and there are just a few clouds, thin, like smoke, as if they don't belong up there.

Pa calls Frank and points to the coconuts in the tree inside our property. I see nice yellow ones on the other side of the fence and point them out to Pa. But he says we can't pick coconuts from trees that are on the other side of the fence because they don't belong to us.

Those nuts, they ready, Frank?

I cleanin' crab for Miss Polly, boss. I'll climb just now and see. One or two look like they might be good. They mightn' have jelly yet, but them will still drink good.

He looks like a spider or a monkey, or some kind of animal, gripping the tree with the soles of his feet and with his hands—the cutlass in one of them—and he hoists himself up in spurts, and it looks as if he is pushing the trunk downward with his feet, and when he hacks the nuts off and drops them all the way down to the ground, we have to make sure to stand far back so they don't fall on us and crack open our heads, and then he slides down really fast.

Pa watches past the fence of our yard, past the coconut trees on the other side, past the beach, and studies the sea that sparkles like tinsel on a Christmas tree. When he sees the fishermen's boats coming into shore, he calls out to us that it is time. Ma leaves whatever she is doing and puts on a big straw hat that has the word *Barbados* embroidered in green raffia on it, and she and Pa and I walk down the sandy path to the beach. They don't wear shoes, but I have to because the sand is too hot for my feet, and besides that, there are sharp things like broken shells and twigs in the sand that could slice right through my feet, and sometimes there are even pieces of glass from broken bottles that people who are bad, because they don't care about other people, just drop and leave right there, just like that. Pa uses bad words when he talks about people like those ones, but I am not allowed to repeat the bad words. Polly and Frank follow behind us. Polly carries a bucket, and Frank brings his cutlass.

The people who are holidaying in houses along the beach come out at this time, too. Some of those people are supposed to be white. That is what Ma says. But they are not real white. White means like paper or clouds, or a white shirt like one of Pa's. Ma says that what I am saying is true, that I know my colours, but that is just what they are called, white people. I keep looking at them, but I don't see the white. I told her they look more like the chicken's skin after Barlow pulls out all of its feathers. Ma said, Shhh. Don't say that. Just listen to me. They are white. That is what they are called.

I keep looking at them, and she holds my shoulders and tries to turn me from them. She tells me, Stop staring, that's not polite.

When Ma is busy watching for the boats to come in, I look at those people some more. Their hair is not like ours. Ours is black, and theirs is the colour of dogs' fur. But not all of them. Some have hair that is yellow like a doll's hair. My friend Sita has a doll with skin that looks a little like theirs, and yellow hair. It is true, I know my colours. If you go close to those people, you can smell coconut ice cream. Ma says they smell like that because they rub something on their skin called suntan lotion that will help them to get brown like us; it is the lotion that smells like coconut. Some of those people wear dark glasses, but they are not blind people. Ma says they wear those because the sun is too strong for their eyes.

Some of the people on the beach are like us, and Ma and Pa know some of those ones. Everybody says good morning to everyone else, and some people come and talk to Ma and Pa, but the ones with the dark glasses, whom Ma and Pa call white, mostly just nod and give a little smile and some say good morning. And then everyone stands back, waiting for the fishermen to come ashore.

And the people who live in the village also come. Some are like us, but almost all of them are like Mr. Monty and the rest of Pa's factory workers, and those ones are called Negroes. Those people don't stand back. They go right down to the edge of the beach where the small waves break, and they shout to the fishermen—they know their names—and to each other as the boats come in. Some of them help pull the boats up the beach and pull in the seine. There are many children, too. Some of them have very dark-coloured skin, and some are lighter, and some have curly black hair, and some, their hair is almost red. *Red and yellow, black and white, we are perfect in his sight.* Those are words from a song Pa sings at night when I sit on his lap in the hammock there or back home on the veranda. I want to play with the other children, but they always turn and run off when I smile at them. I run behind them, but they run faster, or stop and turn and stand with their arms folded, looking at me as if they are going to fight me. I asked Ma why they don't want to play with me, and she said it is because they don't know me, that they are a group of friends by themselves. I don't understand. If they stop and play with me, they will know me and we can be friends. They don't wear shoes like I do.

Then it all happens so quickly. There are the seine ropes and the big net and so many men, those from the village and some of the older white boys who are there for the holidays, all holding two lines of ropes, and everyone starts pulling, leaning backwards, pull, pull, pull, the heels of their feet digging into the sand, the rope moving from their hands backwards into the hands of the men behind, and then as the net comes in, there is a lot of rope falling on the sand behind all the men. It isn't easy, as if the sea doesn't want to let them have the net or the fish. Pa doesn't help, but Frank gives Polly his cutlass to keep for him and he goes down to help, and some boys who are my height, too. There is a lot of excitement now.

I tell Ma I have to go and help them pull seine. But she holds my hand tightly.

No, you stay right here with me. You see any girls there? Girls don't do that kind of thing, baby. You stay right here.

But I am strong. I can help.

She holds my hand now with both of hers and my hand hurts.

Just let one person trip and fall, and everyone will fall, one on top of the other, and there will be a big accident. You stay right here with me, let Ma keep you safe.

Then the net comes in and so do all the big corbeaux and seagulls, and suddenly in the waves that break on the shore and scatter all the way up you see all these jumping fish, big and small, and everyone is pulling large fish out of the part of the net that has reached the sand and they are handing money to the fishermen. A fisherman in a wet red jersey once tried to give me a little pink-and-silver-striped fish, and Pa came up to him and said something to him in the hard voice he uses when he talks to Mr. Monty and the other workers in his factory across from our house on Selvon Street. I didn't understand what he said. The man steupsed, dropped the fish back into the net, and turned away from us. I felt sad for the man and didn't like that Pa didn't let him give me the fish. He was kind and Pa was rough.

When all the fish have been removed from the net and the fishermen are dragging it up the beach to hang it to dry, I run to the water where the other children are. Pa always tries to follow me wherever I go, but I run in between the other children so he can't get close. We try to catch fish, too; when the waves near the shore break, the water looks soapy, with lots of bubbles, and it spreads all up the beach, but you can see little fish swimming in it, but then the water slides back fast-fast into the sea, faster than the fish can swim and they get left behind on the wet sand and you see them struggling to get back into the sea. That's when we run after them and try to catch them, the little yellowish, silvery fish with big bulgy eyes, but they jump as if they have legs like frogs—jump, jump, jump forward. They are faster than we are. Then, when a new wave comes and breaks on the shore again, the fish move even quicker and disappear into the deeper water. Once, one of those children spoke to me, but her voice was so soft I couldn't hear, and I had to go close to her. She was pretty. She asked my name, and when I told her, her eyes got wide. Hers is Ang*e*la and mine is An*ju*la. She smiled. Me, too.

On fishing days, there are men high up the beach near the coconut trees where there is an old rickety table. They clean the fish there for the people who have bought them, and they throw the stomach and intestines and the heart and the ugly gills and liver for the birds, and the corbeaux walk and hop in between people, grab the guts, and run down the beach with the pieces flapping in their beaks, or they fly up onto a branch of a coconut tree and eat there. Then there is that smell of the bottom of the sea, the waves, the sky, the sun, the fish and blood, and all the people coming together and talking and shouting. And that, without the coconut ice-cream smell, is the smell of the kitchen on Selvon Street when we're cleaning shrimp.

*

Ma, Barlow, and Polly sit around the table, and while they work, they talk. Barlow knows everything that's going on in the neighbourhood.

Standard Distributors truck. You see it? It pull up by Fatty house, the truck there idling a good fifteen minutes, wasting gas for so. She buy Hoover washing machine. Who give she money to buy expensive thing so, I don't know.

Ma answers, Miss Fatty working hard years now, yes. Washing everybody clothes by hand in the back there. Hanging up clothes to dry. Ironing in the heat in that little one-room house she have there. She must have saved up her money. That is all. She is right to put her savings into her business and expand if that is what she is doing. That is her business. Not anybody else's.

Polly only speaks about food. It had jinghi in the market this morning, madam. It have salt fish in the fridge, madam. We should use it up, madam. You want curry jinghi and salt fish for lunch tomorrow, madam?

While they chat, I listen quietly. I help them to look for tiny stones in the dry peas and rice, too. I am a good helper.

*

The front room is our room. That's where Ma and I sleep. We hug up tight-tight because the Boo Boo man might come when Ma has fallen asleep and try to take me away. Barlow says the Boo Boo man lives in the white tower down the road, with the half moon and the star on the top. When it begins to get dark, he looks out his window and wails. Barlow says this is to warn children to behave themselves, otherwise he will come in through windows and under doors, and he will rip them from their families and take them away. Ma says that is not true, the man is singing, not wailing, and the tower is in a building that is like her church, but this one is called a mosque. She says that the words of his song call to all people to come and pray to God. He is a good man, she tells me, and I should not pay attention to Barlow. I ask her why she tells me sometimes that I must listen to Barlow, and sometimes that I should not take her on. She rubs my face with her hands, pulls my head closer into her chest, and says, You are too smart for your own good. I ask her why she doesn't go when he sings, and she says because she already goes to the other church. I will never tell Ma that Barlow sometimes tells me that Ma doesn't know what she is talking about, that the man in the mosque *is* the Boo Boo man and he will come and take me away if I misbehave and don't do as she tells me to. I told Ma to tell Barlow not to come back to our house, but she said we need Barlow, that if Barlow goes, who will help Ma? Barlow is a good person, she says, and I should learn to laugh at some of the things she says instead of getting frightened, or crying, about them.

*

Ssshhwa-ssshhwa, ssshhwa-ssshhwa. Barlow is in the shed in the backyard sharpening the cutlass. There is a coal fire in the shed. The shed is on wood stilts, open on all sides, with a galvanized iron roof. On the fire is a tall pot full of water. She returned from the market earlier, a basket heavy with vegetables in one hand and in the other a live chicken she held by its wings. Its legs were tied together with string. She put the entire chicken in an empty bucket while she sharpened the cutlass, and it struggles inside the tight space, clucking loudly, then softly, then frantically.

Then, the cutlass hidden behind her back, she pulls out the chicken and holds it by its wings, so its body drops down heavily, stretched out. It is suddenly quiet. She lays it on the ground, its head hanging over the drain, then she steps on its belly with her foot and the chicken's eyes bulge and dart about. Then Barlow brings the cutlass from behind her back and lifts it high and with one swift motion she drops it down *thwack*, and it goes through the chicken's neck and hits the concrete, and she has to saw a little to separate the head from the rest of the body. The head lies on the ground with eyes wide open and its beak panting. I stoop down to look at the head. The top beak is pointy. I can't see any teeth. It slowly closes its eyes. It has eyebrows with long hairs. And those red things on top of its head and under its chin. I pick up a stick to turn over the head, but Barlow shouts at me not to touch it, and she runs over and scoops it up. She doesn't have to shout but always does. The body twitches and she has to hose down the blood that's squirting all over. Then she lifts the headless body by its still-tied feet and dunks it up and down in the big pot of boiling water. The flames under the pot leap high and sputter noisily when water splashes on them. The water in the big pot turns red and the air smells dirty and sad.

Sita lives in the house across the street. Sometimes she comes to play with me. She is not allowed to go upstairs inside our house, but she can play in the yard with me. If she is here when Barlow is killing and then cleaning a chicken, we collect and sail feathers in the thick red water flowing down the drain.

I save the longest feathers to make a headdress, so when my cousins and I play cowboys and Indians, I can have a costume, too. Colin and Sheldon say they are the cowboys because they are boys. They get to have holsters around their waists with guns on both hips and wear cowboy hats, but I never get to wear anything other than my regular clothes, and I always have to be captured and tied up and sometimes I have to die. With a headdress I will be stronger and can stand up to them.

*

Sometimes, early in the morning, the moon is still in the sky. The morning moon is thin, so thin you can see through it. Even before the sun rises high and makes everything too hot and melts the moon, the big blue trucks begin to leave the yard of the ice factory. I stand on my toes on the peerha and haul myself up on the veranda ledge. The ledge is always wet from dew. I can stay like that for a long time, even when my arms get tired and my tummy hurts from being pressed against the edge of the ledge. Pa doesn't immediately notice I am leaning across the ledge and looking at the men below because he is busy talking to them. He calls down to the foreman, who nods back up to him. Pa doesn't sound like my Pa when he is talking to those workers. There is Pa with me, Pa with Ma, Pa with Barlow. Pa with Uncle Sonny, Pa with the foreman and Mr. Mohammed the accountant who works in the office downstairs, Pa with the fishermen on the beach, and Pa with his friends who play cards with him at nights. So many Pas and they all have different voices and ways of speaking.

The foreman hands out papers to the drivers before they leave the factory. On the truck beds are blocks of ice bigger than a car. The blocks are covered with crocus bags that are already wet because the ice is melting, and it isn't even hot yet. The drivers back the trucks out of the factory and turn them around in the middle of the road. On mornings, the road belongs to Pa and to his workers and to these trucks. Just before the drivers drive away to deliver the ice to houses and businesses all over San Fernando, they look up in our direction and put their hands to their foreheads, but Pa doesn't wave back. He makes such a small motion with his head that I don't think the drivers below could see it. Once, when I was leaning on the ledge next to Pa as he looked down at the drivers getting ready to leave in the trucks, I put my hand to my forehead like the drivers do, in what Ma calls a salute, and Pa hit the back of my head with his hand and pulled me down from the ledge. Sometimes, as I lean over, looking down at the trucks being moved about, he puts a hand on my back, or he grips my clothing at the back of my neck, as he watches what the men are doing and talks to them.

*

Barlow swizzles our eggnogs with the whisk that looks like a wire fist. Ma leans against the doorway between the breakfast room and the kitchen and watches Pa drink from his tall, fat glass mug. I sit next to him and drink my eggnog from a mug exactly like his, only smaller. His smells of rum, mine of nutmeg. It is like drinking sweet custard. He calls Ma madam. She calls him boss.

Polly drops aloo pies into the hot oil. The smell of the flour in the oil fills the air and mixes with the taste of the eggnog, and

I can't wait for lunchtime to have aloo pies. When Polly makes aloo pies and roti and bakes bread, flour gets on the floor and all over the counter and on some of the tins and containers there. She and Barlow quarrel. Barlow says she is not working for Polly and shouldn't have to clean up after Polly.

Barlow sucks her teeth a lot. She smiles with Ma and Pa, but when they are not around, she steupses loudly at Polly, and more softly at me. I have tried to do it, but Ma slaps my arm and tells me I must never do that again, it is not a nice sound and nice children don't make those kinds of noises. I only do it to trouble Ma. I like it when she runs after me to hit me. She never hits me hard and sometimes she doesn't even hit me; she just pulls me to her and hugs me too tightly and laughs. Well, not really *too* tightly. I like when she hugs me like that.

Polly is plump, like Ma. I think that must make her a good person. She has gold teeth, more than Barlow has, but I don't think gold teeth are pretty.

Barlow's skin is darker than Polly's and than Ma's and mine. It is as dark as the furniture in the dining room. She is always saying mean things to Polly. She says, You come from the bush or what? Polly doesn't seem to care. Polly laughs a lot.

*

After lunch it gets hot. Even when I am not sleepy, Ma makes me lie down with her. She pulls the cord to turn on the fan. It wobbles, and she says, One day that thing is going to fall down, yes.

I'm supposed to sleep. Sometimes a lot of cane ash floats through the air. It lands on the curtains, the dresser, the floor, even the sheets on our bed and the pillows. I rub the little pieces to get the ash on my fingers, then I put it on my forehead to make a mark like the one the pundit has on his head. Ma doesn't like me doing this as it gets dirty black ash all over everything.

The galvanized roof pings as if someone is pelting it with stones. And the wood ceiling creaks as if someone is walking around on it, sometimes even running fast on it, like a person, or maybe a bird or a rat. The music and the singing from the cinema near the library is so loud it's hard to fall asleep. Sometimes you can even hear the men in the movie shouting.

The maraschino-cherry thing that grows on Ma's arm is round and big and smooth, like a glass marble. I want to suck it, but she won't let me. I play with it, though. I touch it and squeeze it and try to roll it, but it's attached to her arm. The skin on her arm is always cool, and I like to rest my cheek there. When it's hot like this, the khus khus in the cupboard with all the new table linen and sheets smells strongly. I like it but I also don't like it. It's so strong you keep smelling it and that makes it hard to sleep, too. When Ma falls asleep, I pull the cherry thing, twist it a little, and she wakes up and hits my hand and tells me it hurts when I do that. Sometimes I pretend it is a lucky marble and if I can only twist it off or cut it with scissors, I can maybe go downstairs, outside, across the road, to the far corner where some of the boys from the neighbourhood play pitch, and with my own marble I could be like them. I would win all the pitching games because the marble on Ma's arm is a lucky marble.

When she has a headache, I rub her head for her with Limacol and her head gets better very quickly. I think if I crush baby aspirins in a teaspoon and put it in a glass of Limacol, then add condensed milk and Vicks VapoRub and maybe some salt, and she sips it, and I put the rest on her head, her head would never hurt again. I can already be a doctor. She says she'd like us to try that remedy one day, but only when her head is really bad, and it hasn't ever been bad enough, she says. When I feel sick, she lifts me and rubs my head with Limacol, too. She sometimes gives me an aspirin in a spoonful of condensed milk. The condensed milk makes me feel better.

*

I don't like going to Miss Sybil's school. All the juice bottles are lined up on the window ledge and the sun hits them and makes them warm and the whole classroom smells like old sour orange juice, like when Barlow doesn't wash my juice bottle until the next morning when she has to fill it with juice again, and even after she washes it, I can still smell the old orange juice. The sour juice smell from the bottles on the ledge goes all over the classroom, and sometimes when I am falling asleep at night that smell creeps, like a dream, into my nostrils. And another reason not to go to school is the mangoes. Outside the classroom door, ripe mangoes fall from the tree onto the ground, and they get stepped on—the boys like to smash them with their shoes and then slide on them. Their shoes and socks get yellow mango on them and their legs, too, and sometimes the boys slide on the mangoes, and they scream and laugh and fall and get the mango flesh and juice all over their clothes and bodies, and Miss Sybil hits them with the ruler. Big black ants crawl all over the mashed-up rotten mangoes. They move slowly as if they are drunk, like Frank when he is drunk, and they stand on their back legs and rub their front legs together. When it is hot, the mangoes on the ground start to bubble and they push out the biggest sweet yellow smell ever. It's a nice smell but so sharp and big it can make you feel as if there is no air to breathe and makes your head hurt as if mangoes have filled it up and nothing else can fit in it, and this makes your tummy hurt, too, so I told Ma I didn't want to go back there because there makes me sick, but she told me not to mind, because all children have to go to school, which means I have to go to school, too. I asked Ma why I have to go, and once she said it was because when I get big, I might want to go and study to be a doctor like my daddy, and that one day your mummy and daddy will come and she wants them to see how smart I am. I asked her whose mummy and daddy will come, but I didn't understand what she said. Sometimes she says more things like that, and when she does, her voice changes and her face changes and she looks as if she isn't really talking to me but to someone else, and I don't understand what she means.

I like when Ma hugs me. Her skin is warm, my Ma's, like under a blanket. She smells different from Pa. Sometimes she smells like the powder on her dresser. He smells like eggnog. I wish I didn't have to go to school. I would rather stay with her and go to church with her. She likes to go to church. She goes a lot—every Sunday morning, and then some nights during the week. Sometimes I go with her.

*

Sita's mother and father are shorter than Ma and Pa and they are fat. She has a brother, Chandra, who is the oldest, and she has four sisters, Sumira, Vena, Geeta, and Preeti, all older than her. The outside walls of their house and the inside walls and the floor are all made of the same wood, and they are all unpainted. It's old wood, and some days the wood smells a lot. Like the rotting wood the gardener packs around some of Ma's plants at the front of our house. Some days it is a stifling smell, like old dust. They sweep the floor inside their house with a cocoyea broom. The whole house can fit in our drawing room and dining room together.

I can go over and play with Sita. I am not supposed to eat or drink anything from her house, but I do. If we stay in the kitchen, no one in my house can see me there drinking juice made from oranges or limes from trees in their yard, or sweet-drinks, because their kitchen is at the back of the house, and although they call it a kitchen, it is a very small unpainted room and is very dark and there is no fridge or stove in it, and the sink hangs on over the window, on the outside part of it. They have a pommecythere tree, and Sita's brother, Chandra, picks the bright yellow fruit that are so big I can't even close my hand around one of them, and he peels the smooth hard skin with his pen-knife. He cuts small slices for me, and we stand behind the house and bite into the sour, juicy, crunchy flesh that makes my mouth tingle and my eyes water, and we nibble away at them right to the spiny seeds. If a spine sticks between my teeth, one of Sita's sisters pulls it out with her fingernail or she might have to slide a piece of thread between my teeth to get it out, but sometimes the thread makes my gum bleed and it hurts, but only a little, and they get scared that Ma and Pa will find out and be angry with them. The sourness makes my mouth overflow with spit, and then Chandra holds my face in his hand and takes his time wiping the spit off my lips and chin with his fingers. Sometimes he puts his finger in my mouth and tells me to suck off the juice on it. Sometimes, too, he gives his mother a big bowl of pomme-cytheres that are not so ripe and she makes chow for us. I like the saltiness and all the little pieces of garlic and the lime juice and the green pommecytheres together, and she puts in a lot of bright green shadon beni that we pick from the backyard, too, and that gives it a perfumed taste. The lime is sour, but I don't mind it in the chow. They make two bowls: one for Sita, Sumira, and me that has no pepper, and another bowl with bright red chips of bird peppers they pick from one of the pepper trees in their yard, too. When the others eat the chow with pepper, their eyes water and their noses run, and they make sounds like they are trying to suck cool air into their mouths, and they say things like, Ogodogod, it hot-hot. Pepper real hot today, boy. Hot too bad.

If I eat too much, I get a tummy ache, so I can only have a few pieces before they move the bowl away from me. But the rest of them eat the whole bowl and then they fight for who can drink the salty sour juice at the bottom. Ma knows when I eat chow at their house because I smell of garlic, and even after she brushes my teeth, I can still taste the garlic. She says, Ent I told you not to eat when you go over there? You must listen to me and not be so harden, darling. You will get sick. Did they used boiled water in the chow? You don't know, do you?

Chandra has little birds in cages. They are called peekoplats. Sita says he keeps the cages in his room at night because they are competition songbirds and very expensive and people steal such birds. But in the daytime, they hang from the galvanized eaves of the house at the back. They hop about and whistle a lot, as if they are whistling songs, maybe to each other. I think they are trying to decide how they can escape. I want to help them, but the cages are too high.

The toilet is outside in the backyard, far from the house. It is in a small wooden house that is only that one room. Cut high up on the door is a little opening, like a window, and on the back wall there is another opening, but bigger, but neither has glass in it, or anything to open and close it, so there is always a little breeze coming into the room, and a little bit of light. Before I go over to their house, Ma makes me go to the toilet at home and tells me that if I have to go again, to let them bring me back home. I am never allowed to cross the road by myself. The room has only a box that is like a bench with a round hole in the seat. There is a peerha for children like me, and you climb on the peerha to reach the seat, and you sit over the hole and it's scary because you can fall in. You don't flush because there isn't a chain to pull or anything like that, and the room always has a big, big smell, like a fire that hasn't yet caught but is about to, and it makes my nose and my eyes burn. Whenever I go to play with Sita and her sisters, it is the toilet I look forward most to visiting. One of them has to come with me so I don't fall into the hole. They hold my hand as I climb up on the peerha and sit on the seat, and even when I look up at the little opening in the door that is like a window and try to breathe the outside air, the toilet smell is always there. But I don't actually use it as a real toilet, because if you do you have to clean yourself with pieces of hard newspapers that are stacked up in a pile on the seat next to you, and the paper is too hard and doesn't bend easily.

Even though it's dark inside the deep hole, if you keep looking for a long time you can eventually see far down. Sita said no snakes live there, but I think she's wrong. Once we found three snake eggs under their house. Her brother said they were lizard eggs, but I am sure they were snake eggs. Sita and I remained quiet and very still and looked at them for a long time, waiting, but they wouldn't hatch, so I broke one to help it, but it was still too young, and it just looked like a tiny-tiny chicken egg, except grey and runny. We decided to cook one and took it to her mother in their kitchen, but her mother got angry and told us not to touch those things because they are dirty, and she screamed at the older children and hit one of them because they weren't looking after us.

Chandra pulls my pants to my knees and touches me down there. But I'm not supposed to tell anyone about that. He smells the way the chicken does just after Barlow has chopped off its head. I tell him I have to go and play with Sita. He tells me Sita will only be my friend if I play with him first, and he pulls my hand and holds it inside of his pants and my arm hurts, and it feels very hot there and he keeps my hand there for a long time. He keeps a big sausage in his pants, and he always wants me to touch it. I don't like it, but he gets very serious and makes me frightened, so I do what he wants. Then suddenly he moves my hand away, but he holds on to me and tells me, Remember, do not tell anyone about this game. This is our special game. I don't play this with anyone but you. You are special.

I don't care. He is not special to me, and I don't like it or how he smells. I don't tell him that Uncle John also told me not to tell anyone about the same things. But I like being underneath their house with Sita. It smells like snake and lizard eggs and old mould and dust and dirt.

There are pieces of old broken furniture stored down there, and when Sita and I play there, we look for treasure in the mounds of old broken things.

*

Pa takes me to see movies at the Indian cinema. We walk there. We walk and walk and walk and walk. We walk in a straight line until we reach the corner by Mr. Tang's shop, then we turn the corner and go up the other street, and first we pass Mrs. Khan's house and then we pass the mosque. I look up at the tower, but there isn't anyone there. At the top of the tower is a pole and on top of the pole is a piece of the moon—Pa says that shape is called a crescent—and there is also a star. They are painted gold. And then we pass the market. There are always people sweeping the floor and hosing down the sidewalk in front of the market. It smells bad here. Like animals and blood, and sometimes it smells like Sita's toilet, and like rotting fruit and vegetables. And then we pass shops that sell baskets and plastic basins and metal buckets and oil tablecloths and rubber slippers. We never go into any of them. And then we get to the cinema. Pa buys me an apple and a handful of grapes from the man outside the cinema. All through the movie I smell the colour of apple on my hands. It's like a red perfume. The people in the picture don't speak in English. There are words below the picture, but I can't read them. There is always a good man that I like and wish I could be like; he is always the best-looking man, and he smiles and sings and dances and people like him a lot. Not all the people. He has to fight some of them, but he always wins, but before he wins, he gets a big cut on his forehead and has to wear a bandage and then he hugs the pretty girl, and both of them close their eyes, and sometimes tears run down their faces, and her mother bends down to touch his feet, but he doesn't let her go all the way down. He makes her come upright and then he hugs her, and the girl's father puts his hands together as if he is praying and the man does that, too, and they hug, and everybody is happy. During the intermissions Pa goes to the parlour at the side of the cinema and he brings me a red sweetdrink and a bag of round sweeties, all different colours. I don't save any for later, I eat all of them during the movie. I put one between my teeth and press down just a little and the outside cracks, like the shell of an egg, and inside is delicious chocolate. He always gets a coconut for himself, and mauby.

Then Mr. Monty comes in the car to pick us up when the picture is over. And we go to Man Ten restaurant and Pa buys barbecue chicken and chips to take home for him and me and Ma. He watches me eat, and he gives me more and more and more, and then I get so full, and he touches my stomach to see if all the compartments in my tummy are full, and if there is an empty shelf in my tummy, he is able to feel it, and so I have to eat one more spoonful. He touches it again to see if I filled up that spot, and when it is full, he pats my head and tells me I am his favourite of all the children. I like when he does that.

When Ma and Pa's friends come to visit, they tell me to do the Indian dancing like in the movies. I sing *dil deke dekho, dil dekho, dil deke dekho*, and dance. Pa says I can become an Indian dancer, and I will be a better dancer than any of the ones in the movies. He and Ma and the other grown-ups clap and laugh and tell me to do it again and again.

*

I draw chickens and dogs and horses and Ma and Pa and me. Pa gives me a lot of paper to draw on when he is at his desk working. He likes my pictures. Ma says I'll be an artist when I grow up, and Pa says I'll be a doctor like my daddy. I don't know what he means by that. If I am a doctor, I can make Ma's headaches go away. I can be a doctor who is an artist. But Pa doesn't like me to play by him when the workers from the office downstairs or the ones from across the street come to talk to him. I mustn't touch his papers or his ruler, or turn any of the knobs on the radio, not even the one that makes the sound get louder or softer.

Before we go to bed, Ma wipes my neck and inside my elbows and under my feet with the warm wet washcloth. She puts baby powder on my tummy and back and under my neck, and then puts my pyjamas on me. Then she takes me to Pa, who is sitting in his white-and-red rocker on the veranda. I sit on his lap, and he rocks the chair. He doesn't do the things Uncle John does when he makes me sit on his lap. I want to whisper in Pa's ear and tell him what Uncle John does to me, but I mustn't because Uncle John says Ma will die if they ever find out, and Pa, too.

Pa sings. He never goes to Ma's church, but he knows all the words of the songs from her church. His voice is so soft, so different from the one he uses in the daytime when he talks to the workers. In the evenings there is always lightning, and even when there are no clouds, you hear thunder rolling far away. Sitting on Pa's lap, I am not afraid.

Pa shakes me, makes me sit up, and points. He tells me, Make a wish, darling. Quickly. First star of the night. Wish for anything. Before the next star comes out. He says I mustn't tell anyone what I've wished for, because if I do, my wish won't come true. I think he makes wishes, too, and I want to know what they are, but he mustn't tell.

He hugs so tightly.

Jesus loves the little children, all the children of the world, red and yellow, black and white, they are precious in his sight. He sings the words into my hair. I like that one. And the one that goes: *All things bright and beautiful, all creatures great and small, all things wise and wonderful, the Lord God made them all.*

His shirt smells like Vicks, and his face like bay rum. I don't like the *rock of ages made for me let me hide myself from thee* song. It is sad. He sounds sad when he sings that one. I press my head into his chest, I turn and kiss his chest—not his chest actually, but his shirt—I look up into his eyes, I touch his hand. But when he sings that song, his face gets so lonely, even though I am there with him, and he looks as if he is seeing something I can't see.

When he sings the other songs, his voice, the rocking, and his smell that isn't like anyone else's make me fall asleep.

I awaken just a little when Ma comes and takes me from his lap. She takes me to the washroom, lifts me onto the seat, and goes *psssssssuu* with her mouth, and I do a weewee. In the front room, she lifts the mosquito net and sets me down on our bed. I don't open my eyes; I just feel everything she does. She gets into bed next to me and hugs me.

I wake up and I see the moving things on the wall. The light from the street lamp outside comes in the window and shines on the wall, and dark shapes move about against the wall. Sometimes they move very quickly, up and down and sideways, and sometimes it looks as if they are not moving, but if you stay still and close your eyes just a little and peep at them, you will see them move. Ma says they are just the shadows of the branches from the neighbour's coconut tree, but I think they are the Boo Boo man Barlow talks about. Ma just wants me to go to sleep so she can sleep, and she is big so the Boo Boo man won't try to hurt her, but I am little, and he can take me away if I am not touching her.

She hugs me and softly hums. I play with the special marble that grows on her upper arm, like a cherry bright and shiny, and I try not to fall asleep, but eventually I do. I awaken when it's still dark because I need to go peepee. It's so quiet—no cars pass in the road, even the dogs are not barking. Ma takes me, but she doesn't lift me anymore because I'm getting to be a big girl. So mostly now, I stumble alongside her with my eyes closed, one of her hands holding one of mine, the other ushering me toward the washroom.

*

Sometimes it is the sound of Pa and his friends slapping cards down on the table or exclaiming over the game that awakens me. When I am awakened by those sounds, I know at once that Ma won't be in the bed with me. I know she won't even be in the house, because on card-playing nights she goes to services at the Open Bible Church.

I go to church with her some Sunday mornings; there's a lot of singing and clapping hands. They sing the songs that Pa sings to me when he and I sit in his rocking chair. Everybody rocks on their heels, with their eyes squeezed shut. Many people shake their heads as if there is water in their ears. They shout *amen* again and again. They stand on their toes and stretch their hands high over their heads as if to touch the ceiling. But I have never gone with her to nighttime church.

When I hear Pa's friends and the cards being slapped on the table, I crawl out of the bed and crouch low so the Boo Boo man can't see me, then creep quietly out of the room. I run down the hall, through the drawing room and the dining room, and into Pa's bright room, where he is at the table with three other men.

And I stand at his side. Blue cigarette smoke hangs in the air, and the room smells of whisky. There are always four of Pa's friends there, but only four people can sit at the table and play at a time, so one of them stands and waits for his turn.

Pa shoos me back to bed. I tell him I have to go peepee. I am distracting him, he says. He says I'll make him lose all his money, and the other men then tell me to stay, and they laugh. I have to wait until that game is finished, Pa tells me. I whisper for him alone to hear that I can't wait—because it's true, I can't wait. Uncle John comes on card-playing nights, but he doesn't always take his turn playing. He just stands and watches the others play. He comes around to me and says he'll take me to the washroom. He lifts me up in his arms. I don't like how he smells. He kisses my cheeks, and I don't like that, too. But I am not supposed to let adults know when I don't like them. Nice girls and good children don't make other people feel bad. So, although I want to wipe away his wet kiss on my cheek, I don't, but it feels as if something dirty, like snail spit, has landed on me. He stands there with me and waits to see the next hand played, then he carries me to the washroom. He pulls down my pyjama bottoms and lifts me onto the toilet seat. He makes the long whistling sound between his teeth. Just like Ma and Barlow do. And I go. He wipes me with toilet paper, then wets the washcloth hanging off the sink railing and looks at me down there and then wipes me there. He carries me back out and, as there aren't extra chairs in the card room, he sits on the couch in the drawing room and lifts me onto his lap. He tells me to try to sleep as he bounces me on his knees. He clutches me against him. He massages my legs, and his fingers wiggle inside my pants, and he tells me that massaging me there will help me to fall asleep. He asks if it feels good. It didn't the first or the second time. But it's all right now, but I don't fall asleep because he shakes me too much. He takes a dinner-mint candy from his pocket and opens it for me as he whispers in my ear that it's a game only he can play with me, and I mustn't play this game with anyone else, ever. I mustn't tell anyone, he tells me, that he and I play it. I haven't ever told him about Chandra. He sucks the mint, then puts it in my mouth. If I tell anyone, he says, Ma will get very sick. She might even die, and no one wants Ma to die. Pa could die, too, so I must not tell him either. He takes me back into the bed. He tells me to put my tongue out and he puts his mouth around it and I feel his tongue on mine. His breath is hot and smells sour and also like the dinner mint. And he tucks me in. The ticklish feeling remains, and yes, I think it helps me to fall back asleep.

*

Uncle Sonny and Auntie Stella, Diane, Savi, Sheldon, and Colin come to our house to visit us, but Pa doesn't like us running through the house, so while he and Ma and Uncle Sonny and Auntie Stella remain on the veranda, we go down in the yard and play. Diane and Savi swing on the swings, but they are always looking at boys passing in the road and trying not to let the boys see them looking. This is silly and boring, and I don't understand why they like doing this, so Sheldon and Colin and I go under the house, where the office is and where some of the trucks are parked. We have to be quiet when we're under that part of the house because Pa does not want us down there, and it's right below the veranda, where he and Ma and Uncle and Auntie are sitting. It is very dark down there, even in the daytime, and it feels as if the trucks will suddenly begin to move, or as if there are men hiding behind the trucks who will creep out and snatch us. Below the house smells like oil and gasoline and wet crocus bags. A latticework fence bars off the garage from the yard at the far side of the house. Through the latticework you can see a low red-painted corrugated iron fence, and above the fence you can see the neighbour's house, with a window that faces our side. We tiptoe there and look through the lattice to see if we can see past the window into the dark room. These neighbours are not people we are allowed to talk to. Once, we asked Pa why, and he said it is because he said so and that we are to do what he says and not ask him again. We're not even supposed to look in their direction. They are Negroes, like the ones at the beach. Once when we were peeping through the lattice, trying to see into the window, we realized there was a man in the dark room looking back at us. We ran away from there so fast that I slipped on grease and got my clothing and my hands and legs dirty. Ma and Auntie Stella cleaned me up, and Uncle Sonny quarrelled with Sheldon, and Pa fired the watchman, because he should have been paying attention to where we were. But the next day, the watchman came back to work. He brought coconut rock cakes for Ma and red-and-white-striped sour cherry candies for me.

I go to Sheldon and Colin's house to play also. Sheldon is older than me and Colin is younger. I am in between. When we play cowboys and Indians, only they are allowed to have guns. They say I can't have a gun because I am the girl. They pretend to lasso me, and I am supposed to let them catch me, and then I have to kill myself or they shoot me dead. If I don't die, they just keep shooting and they're very noisy. *Bang bang bang bang bang.* Both of them, even though I am older than Colin. I don't like this game because I'm not supposed to win, just get shot and fall over and die. But it's their house, and Ma said I mustn't mind, I just have to play whatever they want to play. Once I folded my arms, closed my eyes, and stood very still. I wasn't going to play with them unless I could be a cowboy just that once, and I wanted a horse. Sheldon decided Colin could be my horse, but not for long, and then I had to be either an Indian they were hunting, and I had to die when they shot me, or I could be a girl they had to rescue from bandits. Colin knelt down, and I climbed onto his back. He crawled around and I had to hold on tightly because I kept falling off. Because we were laughing and making a lot of noise, Auntie Stella came onto the veranda where we were playing and saw me on his back and she yelled at me, pulled me off him, slapped me on my arm, and told me I was too big to have climbed onto the back of such a little boy.

*

During horse-racing season, Pa goes to Barbados almost every weekend. Ma and I go with him sometimes. We travel there by plane. The air hostesses know Ma and Pa, and they like me. They give me gifts. When the races are over for the day, Pa comes back to the guest house, and he and I go for a walk on the beach. I try to catch the crabs that are running on the sand, but they always get to their holes first. Pa points out the blue-and-purple jellyfish washed up on the beach, so I won't step on them. The long strings wrap around people and sting them in the water, but they are not easy to see in the sand, and if you step on them, they can still sting you.

I don't like when he goes to bathe in the sea. He leaves me in the shallows with Ma, and he goes so far, right up to the biggest waves, and dives into them as they curl, and he disappears into the water, and then the waves crash down, and it takes so long for me to find him out there in the water. I scream and scream and keep looking, and Ma thinks that is funny.

When he comes back, he lifts me high out of the water and walks further into the sea and tells me there is nothing to worry about, he would never let anything happen to me or to him or to Ma. He stoops down into the water with me and lowers me into it. It's deep there and my feet can't touch the sand, but he holds and lifts me a little as swells or waves roll to us. Sometimes waves crash right on us, and water gets in my eyes and stings, and he spins a bit and I feel as if he'll tumble over, but he doesn't let go of me. As we walk back to Ma, he bends and cups seawater in his hand and pats the top of my head.

*

Pa hasn't closed the bathroom door fully. From where I am in the bedroom, the tap sounds like it is singing. I can tell what he is doing by the noises he is making. He opens the cabinet door. I smell bay rum. When he comes out of the bathroom and into the bedroom, he doesn't notice me sitting in the middle of the bed. From the top of the dresser next to his bed, he takes a tortoiseshell comb and pulls it through his hair. He opens the drawer and I leap up, standing on the bed. He tells me to get down, I will fall. I tell him I want to see what is in the drawer and he tells me there's nothing in there for children—go outside and play.

I sit back down on the bed and wait. He closes the drawer and leaves. He pulls the door but doesn't shut it, so I slip out and tiptoe past the bathroom. In the backroom, which is his upstairs office, he's already in his swivel chair, spreading the newspaper on the green ink blotter on the desk. He presses a ruler on the page and pulls it down as he reads. He underlines words with his red-ink ballpoint pen.

Then he folds the paper and pushes it aside and reaches for the large green ledger. He opens it, flips through it, then runs his forefinger down a page.

He calls out and asks where his egg is. Barlow says, Coming, boss.

I wait until she brings it, and he reaches behind him and switches on the big radio mounted on the wall. Then I get my peerha from the side of the bed and carry it to his dresser. It isn't heavy, but I have to be careful not to drop it and make a big noise.

The wood handle is smooth. It isn't easy to pull the drawer open using the handle. It opens just a little and then sticks. I put my fingers inside and pull. One side comes out more than the other. I try to pull the other side and then the first side, and I do this again and again. I'm not being quiet, but he's still listening to the radio. Then the drawer suddenly comes out a bit, and I almost fall backwards. I can smell all the things that make him smell the way he does. I smell his hair oil. I put my fingers inside and do it again, one hand in one side and the other hand in the other side, and I try to pull both at the same time, and the drawer slides out a little but then it sticks again. But that's OK, because I can see everything. His Vicks inhaler, pretty Barbados dollars in a gold clip, his white handkerchief. It smells of bay rum. A box of matches. I won't touch those because he doesn't like me playing with matches. There is a dirty hairpin—it has a curl of hair around it and dust clings to the hair. I won't touch that. There are safety pins, too, and paper clips, and a blue jar of Vicks VapoRub. I want the jar. I'll ask him to give it to me when it is empty. There is a blue stain, like blue ink, on the bottom of the drawer. There are pennies, too. But some of them are stuck to the bottom. There's a penknife. If he sees me holding the penknife he'll shout at me. And quarrel with Ma about it. The blade is stuck, it's too hard to pull it out. I want to sneeze, but I mustn't. Here is the bottle of hair oil. It's oily. My fingers smell like his hair now, only stronger. I wipe my hands on my shirt. Here is a jar with a drawing of a tiger or a leopard on the label, or maybe it's a jaguar. It's orange with black stripes. I know I am not supposed to touch that bottle because it will burn my skin. It has a gold lid. I use a pen to push the jar around. It has many sides. A stamp is stuck to the side of the drawer. And here is a box that is hard to open. It springs open and the back part that opens the lid pinches my finger. It hurts, but I didn't make a sound. My finger has a red bit on it now, and it looks like it's going to bleed. I squeeze it, but it doesn't bleed. It hurts. His tie pin is in the box. The box snaps shut loudly and I'm ready to jump off the peerha, but I hear him coughing and clearing his throat. The blue glass Optrex eye-bath cup and his cigarette holder are there. And a brown bottle with beads that look like tiny chocolate balls but smell horrible, like old fish. The tin of Phillips' Milk of Magnesia is in there. And a nail clip. I will use the file inside the nail clip to dig out the stuck pennies—but suddenly there is a long scrape of his chair. I drop the nail clip and push the drawer in, but I can't get it to budge.

I push, lift, shove. The washroom door squeals open, closes. His weewee hits the water. I wriggle this side a little, shove again, pull, shake it up and down. The dresser trembles as the drawer jerks shut and a bottle of pills on the top tumbles as the toilet flushes. I kick the peerha under the bed and slide under with it and lie still. I don't breathe. He hasn't come into the bedroom, but I stay like that until he leaves the bathroom and goes back into his office.

*

Pa and Ma are taking turns talking into the telephone. They can't hear the person on the phone well. Pa keeps saying, Say that again, I didn't hear the last part. They are almost shouting because the person they are speaking to also can't hear them well. They take turns speaking and each one says congratulations to the person on the phone. Ma says, Papa and I are very proud of Suresh. Pa takes the phone, and he says, So we have a doctor in the family now. Ma has the phone now, and she says, You're sounding very far away, and she laughs, but it is as if she is shy. Pa takes the phone again and is writing down things the person is telling him, then he hands the phone to Ma and goes to his desk in the backroom.

Ma puts her hand around the phone and whispers into it, All your bills are paid up? Don't let Suresh leave any bills unpaid, you hear, Vij?

We can send a money order if he needs to settle up any debts.

No, no, I'm not worried, just want to make sure.

Then she pulls the dining room chair to the wall and lifts me onto it. She says, Vij, I'm putting Anju on now. She puts the phone to my ear and says to me, Say, "Hello, Mummy." She and I hold the phone. I don't say anything, but a woman says, Anju? Hello, darling. This is Mummy. Can you hear me? I try to give the phone back to Ma, but she holds it firmly and tells me again, but sharply now, to say, Hello, Mummy. I whisper, Hello. The woman says something. Ma tells me to say, I love you, Mummy. I say no and push the phone away. She speaks to the woman and says, She is shy. You heard her? She said hello. Don't worry. As soon as you come, everything will go well.

TWO

I am alone in the bed when I awake. I hear Ma and Polly and Barlow talking but not their words. There is a whirring sound on the veranda, too. I call for Ma, but she doesn't come. I call as loudly as I can. Still, no one answers. The sound of the whirring slowly comes nearer. I smell something sharp. It can only be Frank polishing the floor. I get down from the bed and go to the washroom by myself. When I finish, I pull the peerha to the sink and climb on it to wash my hands. I use lots and lots of soap and blow soap bubbles into the air.

It is Frank. The two round brushes at the end of the long pole he pushes and pulls across the floor spin and whir in opposite directions. Frank doesn't smell of rum this morning. Perhaps because all I can smell is the dark reddish-brown paste he spreads on the floor as he goes along. When he sees me, he stops long enough to bend down with his big happy smile and clap his hands at me and ask me if I am excited about something or the other. I don't think he is drunk, but I still don't know what he is speaking about, so I run away to the kitchen. Ma turns to see me and presses me to her body. She asks in alarm why my shirt is soaking wet and if I've gone by myself to peepee. She says, How many times I tell you not to play in the water? Now is not the time for you to be getting sick, you hear? All these years I am trying my best with you, and is now you going to go and make trouble for me? She takes me back into the bedroom and changes me, but she does it with more haste than usual. She doesn't stay long brushing my hair and doesn't play patty cake, patty cake with me as usual. Her haste makes me want to rush about, too, and I begin prancing in circles around her. She gets stern and holds my shoulders hard and tells me to behave myself, but I wasn't misbehaving and don't know what she means. I suck my teeth like Barlow does, and she raises her hand to hit me, but she stops and pulls me to her and hugs me, kissing my head. She is crying. It's as if I make her cry all the time now. She looks at me, and her eyes get full of tears. I don't know why. I hug her, and I want to cry, too. Still she says, Look, behave yourself, please. I begging you.

Everyone seems upset or busy or excited. Nothing is making sense. I feel excited, too. People are coming to stay with us. Not my cousins, but people I don't know. I think they live in a faraway country, with lots of big waves and fish and ships between them and us. There are two children, but they are smaller than I.

Barlow makes breakfast and I have to eat it by myself because Pa is downstairs in the main office with his workers. Usually when he and I eat in the breakfast room, there is nothing on the table but our food and salt and pepper. But today there is a high pile of clean, pressed, and folded laundry—sheets, I think, or maybe curtains. He would be very upset about that. Pa likes everything tidy.

Barlow stands next to me while I poke at the scrambled egg. She won't feed me a spoonful like Pa does and allow me to run around the house and return for another spoonful until the

plate is clean. She says the floor is too slippery, I will fall, and she doesn't have time for all of that horsing around today.

Pa doesn't usually go downstairs to the office so early. When he comes up, he gives me a stack of paper that is blank on one side, crayons held together with a rubber band, and a pen with knobs you slide to get nibs with different-coloured ink. He will not draw the X and O game he taught me. He says I have to sit like a good girl and draw pictures. When I ask Polly to show me how to draw a boat, she steupses and laughs and says she don't have time to draw no boat. She says, Everybody busy, child. You can't see that? You life changing just now, and you still don't know what coming your way. I don't envy you. Stay there and draw quiet. You always drawing so nice. Draw what you know.

*

Ma is baking a sponge cake. She puts icing on it. She made chocolate fudge yesterday, with nuts in it. Polly made sorrel this morning, and when it cooled, she funnelled it into whisky bottles. The house smells of cinnamon and ginger, like Christmas. I want a cup of sorrel, but everyone is busy, so I decide to get it for myself. I open the fridge and it is packed with food and bottles of sorrel and ginger beer. I try to think: Is it Christmastime? No, there is no Christmas tree, no presents being wrapped, no black cake. No ponche de crème was made. So, what is all the commotion about? Polly rushes at me and pushes me away from the fridge and asks if I am looking to make a mess for her in the kitchen. She pours a glass of sorrel for me. The smell of spices in it, of the same little cloves and of the sticks called cinnamon that she puts in cakes, is strong. But it isn't yet cold. When I ask her to put ice in it for me, she tells me to leave the kitchen and drink it just so. I stand in the doorway, sniff the perfume in my glass, and pretend to just drink my juice, but I am also looking at everything and trying to listen and understand why there are so many tins of sweets and cakes on the counters. Someone has brought a large paper bag full of pholouries and sahinas wrapped in waxed paper. Polly finishes one of her tasks and goes to the package. She breaks off a tiny piece of each and tastes it. She twists her mouth and shakes her head to mean *no*. She says in a really soft voice, Hmmm. It need something. They didn't use the right flour for this, na. It need salt. She twists her mouth and says, Like they never hear of jeera, or what?

She transfers them to two biscuit tins and puts those on top of the fridge, pushing them toward the back.

The phone rings and Ma answers it. Everyone gets very quiet. Polly and Barlow come rushing to the wall where the phone is mounted. Ma shoos them off, telling them to go down to the office and tell Pa to come quick-quick, we are getting a collect call. But she calls me and, with one hand holding the phone and the other trying to help me, tells me to stand on the chair.

She is shouting as if the person can't hear.

You where? How long the ship stopping there? Oh-ho. OK, we better hurry up, but just a moment, let me put her on. I'm putting the phone by her ear. Talk now, Vij. Talk loud.

Ma puts the phone by my ear and tells me to hold it. There's the same woman's voice saying my name. I want to give the phone back to Ma, but she shakes my shoulder hard and whispers to me to behave myself and speak up. I say, Hello. The woman says something. I say I am six years old. She says something again, but I still can't hear. I say, I go to Miss Sybil's school, but the woman doesn't say anything. Or perhaps I can't hear if she is saying something, so I push the phone away. Ma says to the woman, You hear how big she is? You will be surprised. She can be a real chatterbox when she is ready, but she isn't accustomed to the phone. Wait till you come, you'll see. Anyway, this talking is going to cost plenty. Papa and I, we're coming to meet all of you. Sonny and Stella will come in their car, too. You must be returning with plenty luggage, not so? It will ride in both cars then. Save all the talking, you'll be here in no time at all. You better go now, you mustn't miss the ship, darling.

She pauses, then says, But of course, we bringing her. Well, yes. That is true, she had just turned one. Five years ago. No, no. Don't say that. We did our best and loved every minute of it. No, darling, we did it for you and Suresh, but it was—I mean, she, she really is our joy. Shhh. Don't say any more. And we're ready to meet Tara and Anil. They'll get along, don't worry. Everything will work out. Look, I'm passing the phone to Papa. Tell him the time the boat is arriving and which dock and all of that. Talk to Papa now. Bye, darling. Tell Suresh safe trip. Ba-bye, bye, darling.

Pa and Ma talk, and I understand there'll be a lot of luggage. So, people are coming. But who are these people? Their names are Mummy and Daddy and there are two children to play with. My cousins Diane, Savi, Sheldon, and Colin call Auntie Stella *Mummy* and they call Uncle Sonny *Daddy*, and that is because Auntie Stella and Uncle Sonny are their parents. I don't call them that; I call them Auntie and Uncle. I don't understand why I would call these telephone people Mummy and Daddy.

Ma calls me to go out on the veranda with her, and although I am getting too big, she pulls me to sit on her lap in the rocking chair. I see Sita and her sisters on their veranda across the road and want to go over to play with them. Ma doesn't usually sit in this chair. It's Pa's chair, and whenever he is in it he makes it rock, back and forth, back and forth. She holds me so tightly. I want to go and play across the road, but I also don't want to leave the house. There are so many things happening. I might miss something.

*

On the back stairs, Frank is poking the eyes out of the dried coconuts with the tip of his cutlass. The coconut liquid squirts out of the eyes. He empties the nuts into a jug. He smashes the hard shell with the handle of the cutlass, and it shatters. Polly scoops up all the pieces and, with a small, pointed knife, she prods hard chips of white flesh out of each piece. In the kitchen she grates the little chips into a basin. I am not allowed to touch the grater. She adds water to the basin and sets it on the counter. She lets me stir the chips and water. Later, she presses all the liquid through a strainer, and it now looks like milk. She puts a pot of that milk on the stove and adds condensed milk, but I am not allowed to stir that. She leaves some of the condensed milk in the tin, twists off the sharp metal lid, and hands me the tin with a small spoon.

Polly takes the coconut milk down the stairs to Frank, and I follow her. At the foot of the stairs in the backyard, I stoop down on the gravel and watch Frank pour the thick white milk into the metal bucket inside the ice-cream maker. Then he packs chunks of factory ice inside the well around the bucket and sprinkles handfuls of salt all over the ice. Then he stands up and dusts his hands off against each other in the air and winks at me and says, Frank is a magician; he can turn liquid milk into heaven. I ask, Heaven? He says, Watch me good. He turns and turns and turns the crank handle, and it makes a big crushing noise as if it doesn't want to do what he wants it to do. He looks at me like he's dying of exhaustion. He says, Is no joke to make heaven, you know. He makes me laugh, and when I laugh, he holds his chest and stumbles over as if he is dying, and when I laugh again, he pretends to look sad and says, So you will laugh if Frank dies? And I say yes, and then I say no, and then yes again. He opens a plug and lets water run out and then he packs more ice and salt. When the handle gets so stiff that he can't turn it anymore, he removes the bucket from the barrel and takes it upstairs. As I come up the stairs behind him, he tells me not to trip and make him lose his job. He is not allowed to touch our food, so Polly scoops the freezing-cold ice cream into large containers, covers them, and stacks them in the freezer. I climb on a peerha and run my hand along the rim of the bucket that is in the sink now and scoop up melting ice cream and chunks of the sweet coconut. A few times I get a mouthful of horrible salt and have to spit it out. Polly says, When your mother was a child, she wouldn't eat ice cream unless it was coconut and your Ma had made it. She would lick the rim, just like you doing. You take after her, yes. I whisper, It is heaven. She shakes her head and says, You listening to Frank. I try to picture Ma licking the rim and I giggle. Then I realize what Polly said doesn't make sense. She doesn't always make sense, so I don't take her on. I don't take her on, but something is making me frightened, and I'm not sure what it is. I feel as if I need to ask a question, but I don't know what the question is.

While I was outside watching Frank, Polly made sugar cakes with leftover grated coconut. There are so many strings of ginger and chips of cinnamon bark when I bite one that I spit them out. Polly pulls my arm hard and tells me to stop spitting all over the place like that. I press what is in my mouth between the roof and my tongue, and all the sugary coconut flavour seeps out in a juice that fills the back of my mouth. It is so sweet that it makes my throat itchy. When the mass of it becomes too much of a mush and I begin to gag, Polly hits my upper back with the palm of her hand and makes me spit it all out into her hand. She asks if I am trying to make trouble today. She wipes my mouth hard with a dishtowel and tells me to go and play outside in the yard like a good girl. I go instead to the low table next to Pa's desk. There is a small chair there for me, so I can sit next to Pa and do drawing. I draw a picture of a face. It's a lady's face. I colour it, then use my yellow plastic scissors to cut around it, and I make a dress for her and arms and legs, and cut those out and glue it all together with a glue stick and the glue gets all over my fingers, but I don't let Polly see. I just wipe my fingers, again and again, on my shirt until all the stickiness comes off.

From Pa's rocker I watch Frank wipe all the jalousies. While he does that, whistling softly like a bird, Barlow cobwebs the room and almost hits Frank with the long stick. She likes to tease him and tries to make him get vexed, but he never does. I never hear him quarrelling with anyone. When Pa gets mad at him for not coming to work, or for coming late, or for spending all his salary on rum and not giving his mother any money, he just covers his face with his hands and cries and says how sorry he is. He whistles and I know the tune. It is one of the songs he sings when he is in the street at night and is drunk, about a girl who has brown skin and a baby and someone is going away on a fishing boat and won't ever come back. I think it is a sad song, but I like when Frank sings it. He doesn't sing the words inside the house, and his whistle is very soft, only for me to hear, I think. When he's finished with the jalousies, he cleans the glass in the windows and all the mirrors. Then Ma brings the curtains that had been on the breakfast table. He climbs on the ladder and Ma hands them to him, one by one. She asks him about his cousin and about his mother. Frank loves his mother more than anyone in the whole wide world. She has many orders for coals from a few restaurants, he tells Ma proudly. That means, I know, that the whole street and sky and all the houses will be hidden by the billowing white smoke from her fire, and the wood she burns to turn into charcoal will cause the air to smell sweet and chalky.

*

Polly sets out dinner on the table and covers it with cloths. Before she leaves, she says she'll come bright and early tomorrow morning. Ma tells her not to be late, not to disappoint her. Polly laughs and says, Why I'll do that? Is a big day. I coming early-early, it have so much to do tomorrow self. Don't worry. Everything will be just like how it used to be.

Barlow showered downstairs and put on her clean dress. She leaves, too. Frank is the last to leave, promising he won't get drunk tonight. He says he has no money to buy anything anyway. Pa tells him he will pay him at the end of the week, as usual. Frank laughs and says, Yes, boss, I wasn't meaning anything, you know.

*

Sitting on the couch in the living room, Ma looks worried and tired. I sit next to her and lean against her. Although I saw Frank cleaning the furniture, I do not let my hands touch the seat, as this is where Uncle John likes to sit. I lean hard into Ma. She whispers to me to just shift a bit, that I am pressing too hard against her. I pinch the keloid cherry on her upper arm. She grasps my hand and holds it firmly in her hand and brings it to her lips. I whisper in her ear that I love her. She puts her hand on my cheek and stares at me for a long time. She looks serious. She licks her lips and looks as if she is going to say something. It takes a long while before she kisses my forehead and says into my hair, Tomorrow you're getting new children to play with. I ask her why Frank polished the floor, and why Polly was making so much food that she made the kitchen and the whole house get hot and was sweating and quarrelling with me. She turns me to face her and says in a low voice, and very seriously, Because your mummy and daddy are coming.

I don't understand. She doesn't say anything. I don't know why, but I want to cry. I don't. I just wait. She says, You have a little brother and a little sister. They are all coming. You will meet them soon. Don't worry. You'll understand everything later. You'll understand better when you get big. Her voice is strange. I think she is crying, but I'm not sure. The only times I've ever seen her cry are when she and Pa quarrel, when he doesn't come home some nights. But he and she were talking nicely with each other today. He was very soft with her and with me and even with the workers. I wrap my arms around her and put my face in her neck. Her neck is wet. Suddenly she gets up very quickly, moving me aside, and heads to the washroom. It will be nice to have a brother and a sister. I wonder how long they are coming for. They can come and visit us. That would be nice. But not for too long.

Pa tells Ma he wants all three of us to sleep in his bed together tonight. He wants me close to him.

It is hot, but I like to sleep with both of them. He snores.

*

Ma says to Barlow, No, I will bathe her today.

She asks Barlow, You pack up the sandwich and the juice yet? The drive long. She bound to want something to eat and drink before we even reach halfway. And put the little things for Doctor and Miss Vijay in a separate tin. About three sahinas each. And some cake slices for the children. Make sure and put serviettes.

Barlow can look busy and alert even when she is just standing still. But I think she also looks worried. Ma says, Irene reach? I'm hearing her downstairs, not so? Today is not her day to iron, but she said she will come anyway. Everybody so helpful and I am grateful. Give her the red top with the sailor neck and the blue pants to press. Anju like that outfit and I want her to feel comfortable. And give boss shoes to Frank to polish. Give him Anju's shoes, too, and tell him to wipe them good. They might need a little white polish, but make sure he don't soak them. You know how his hand can be heavy. Mr. Suresh coming back qualified, so now you will call him *Doctor*, or Dr. Ghoshal, not *Mr.* Suresh.

Polly, season the goat good. Don't let it be fresh. Use plenty lime. Doctor like his goat season with rum. You know where to find the key for the cabinet? Lock it back good—and hide back the key. You know Frank; if he get inside that cabinet, he will sit down right there and we will come home tonight and meet him there self. Mr. Sonny and Miss Stella will likely eat with us tonight, too. So make enough for all of us. Don't let us run out of food, eh. And take out the black cord from the shrimps—I don't want it showing. And don't put too much curry in the pumpkin. I don't want everything tasting like curry-curry. Remind Frank to go by Mr. Tang shop and get two mix case of sweet-drink. Make sure he chip up enough ice; they will want their drinks. And he still has to climb the tree—tell him pick four coconuts. Give him the new jug with the red-and-yellow flowers. I hope he don't break that jug. You know how he can be careless. And remind Frank for me: from now on it is not Mr. Suresh, it is *Doctor*. Miss Vijay remains the same as always, Miss Vijay. Barlow, come. Help me with the front room. I want to use the new sheets from Mrs. Khan, and the new bedspread. You remember to wipe down the blades of the fan?

Ma is on the phone. She is talking to Auntie Putoot. Auntie Putoot is Pa's sister. I'm not supposed to be listening to big people's conversations, so I lie on the couch and use my crayons to draw Ma talking on the telephone. I can tell they are talking about me. Ma is saying that I am like her own child. I think she means I am her *only* child.

Maybe we were wrong, Ma is saying, but how do you explain this to a little child? It was I who feed her, bathe her, change her diaper, clean up her vomit when she sick. I can just look at her face and I know when she ready to sleep, when she not feeling good.

What she is saying is true. I am a child, but I already know these things. She doesn't have to explain any of this to anyone. But she sounds sad. Maybe she doesn't like doing all these things?

Who else knows what food she will eat and what you can't get near her mouth? Ma says. I go in the car with her to Sybil's daycare and I go to pick her up. She goes everywhere with me. And every night I sleep with her. Every night she sleeps in the bed with me. I turn in the bed, and even if she sleeping she will turn, too.

She says, Everything will change. I don't think it should happen too fast, but once they reach, I will have no say. She will have to get used to them.

I think she isn't talking about me anymore. I have to use the black crayon for her hair and her eyes and for the telephone, but the tip has gotten flat and I can't make small lines with it anymore, only fat ones. Ma is talking about Pa now. She says Pa is behaving himself these days. That is funny. I didn't know that Pa can misbehave. Only children misbehave, not Pas.

*

Anju, don't make me hoarse today, please. Come. I'm calling you. Why you only prancing around so much today for? Come let me brush your hair. I am going to put ribbons in your hair today.

Because I said so.

Listen to me.

Settle down right now and let me dress you. You want them think we didn't care for you?

Let me take a look at you. You looking nice. Go and sit on the couch and don't move from there. We leaving just-now-just-now. Uncle Sonny and Auntie Stella left their house already. They'll get there before us.

Wait, come. Come back here, come and give Ma a hug up before we go.

*

No, no. Don't put that food in the trunk. It's too hot back there. You want to smell up the trunk? Anju will surely want a sandwich and I don't want to have to stop the car. Put the basket on the back seat. Come, come, let us get going. I don't want that boat to reach before us.

Eh-eh, the front steps sweep? You notice if Frank sweep it? How I forgot to look and see? Lord, I hope he didn't forget it, yes.

THREE

I don't like crossing the bridge over the Caroni River. The river flows very fast. There is something that sticks out of the water, and branches flowing down the river get caught on it, and the water swirls around it and it looks as if it is moving forward and backward at the same time. I ask Pa what that thing in the river is and he says it is him. That he fell in and died. Ma asks what chupidness he is telling me. I hit his shoulder and tell him it can't be him, that he is in the car with us, but he says no, the thing in the river is him. I don't like when he does that and I cry and tell him I don't want him to drown, I don't want him to die. I ask if the thing in the water is an alligator, and he answers, No, it's me. Ma pulls me back toward her and whispers to me that Pa is playing with me, look at him right there in the front seat. She asks, How could he be in the front seat, talking to me, and be in the river same time, too? She tells me to stop crying, I am messing up my face.

When we get off the highway, we are all quiet in the car, and Pa hums very softly. The mountains ahead are green, but I want to sing with him. I know the words, because he sings this song when he rocks me on evenings. While he hums, I sing. *The purple-headed mountains, the rivers running by, the sunset and the morning,* and then Pa sings these last words together with me: *that brightens up the sky.*

He looks back at me, smiling.

And then we see the lighthouse up ahead. Ma removes the two ribbons and pulls the rubber bands from my hair. She brushes out my hair, and Pa passes her his comb, and she makes a part down the middle. Then she makes a ponytail on each side and ties back the ribbons into bows.

Mr. Monty lets us out of the car at the pier, and he drives away to park the car. We walk around a building, and Ma says loudly, Look. Look it there. It arrived. We just in time. Or we late?

There is a huge white ship, big as a house—bigger than a house. Pa takes my hand and is pulling me, so I have to run to keep up with him. He checks a paper in his hand then his watch, and says, We not late, they just placing the gangplanks. But we'll be late if we don't move faster. Where Sonny? They not here yet? I told him not to keep us waiting.

*

There is a large crowd of people, and there in the crowd are Auntie Stella and Uncle Sonny. Colin and Sheldon aren't with them, or Diane and Savi. People are lined up along the railings of the boat on three levels. From where we are, they look very small. They and the people on the ground are waving. Ma points. Look them there. Look, look. They coming down, she says, and her voice is squeaky. People are walking down the two gangplanks. Ma is laughing and crying at the same time. Look. She bends to me and points. See where my finger is pointing? See the lady holding the little boy? And the man with the girl in his arms? Look, the girl is waving her hand. Ma waves and continues pointing, but everyone on the boat and on the wharf is waving, so I don't know to whom she's been waving.

Once the passengers reach the ground, they disappear into a building. Only the people who came off the boat can go into that building. All the men and women are wearing hats. Pa and Uncle Sonny squeeze through the crowd and get close to the building, but there is a metal barrier separating them from the boat people. Ma, Auntie Stella, and I remain in one place, away from the crowds. We wait and we wait and we wait. It is hot and Ma keeps wiping her face and her neck with a handkerchief. Then the hat people begin to come out of the building, a few at a time. They have to walk down a steep ramp to the grounds of the wharf. Soon the crowd splits up and they form groups around the arriving people and there is a lot of hugging and crying and laughing and so much shouting—not angry shouting but happy shouting. But then there is a woman who is crying loudly, and now it seems as if she fainted, and the sno-cone man comes running from the pavement with ice from his cart. I am trying to see what is happening, but a lot of people surround the woman, and people are telling each other to move aside and give her room, and I can see somebody fanning her. Then we see Pa and Uncle Sonny shoving their way swiftly toward a man and a woman who each hold a child in their arms. Ma and Auntie Stella walk hurriedly forward, Ma pulling me by my hand, and when we all meet up, the woman puts down the boy, who grabs her leg and won't let go, and Ma and the woman hold on to one another for a long time and cry—both of them—each one wiping the face of the other with their handkerchiefs. The man puts down the girl, and he stoops down and says hello to me. The girl comes around to look at me. She is smiling, as if she knows me. Uncle Sonny says, Say hello to your daddy. I stare at Uncle Sonny, and before I can slide myself behind Ma, the man reaches toward me, holds my face between his hands that smell like cigarettes and kisses the top of my head. He is very gentle. The woman reaches out to me, to hold me, I think. Auntie Stella tries to push me forward, saying, That is your mummy, Anj, say, "Hello, Mummy." I slide behind Ma. Ma says to her, It's OK. It's OK. Don't cry, Vij, give her time.

I don't know why, but it is as if I am two people. One is real, and that one is there with them all on the ground, wanting to know everything, and the other one got shy and scared and wanted to hide behind Ma, to be back in the car, back in our home. That other me can hardly hear anything. I am hearing and seeing, and not hearing and not seeing.

Uncle Sonny directs us all to the exit where we are to wait. The little girl is shorter than me. Her hair is very short, but there is a lot of it, and it is curly. There is a bow in it. She isn't shy. She smiles a lot. She didn't mind having to kiss Auntie Stella even though they have never met. She says to Ma, My name is Tara, and Ma says, Is that right? I'm pleased to meet you, Tara. The little girl doesn't even know Auntie Stella, but when Auntie Stella holds her hand out to her, she takes it and doesn't let go of it. The man from the boat carries the little boy in his arms, and Auntie Stella and the little girl walk together. They are talking to each other. The little girl talks in a funny way. Ma and the woman from the boat walk hugging each other, and I hold on to Ma's dress and try to keep up. When we reach the cars, the man gives the little boy to the woman, and then he leaves, taking Pa and Uncle Sonny and Mr. Monty with him. The man walks in front of them, heading toward another building. He walks fast-

fast-fast. Pa, Uncle Sonny, and Mr. Monty look as if they are trying to walk fast, too, but they can't keep up with him. Auntie Stella, Ma, the woman and the children, and I stand by the car and wait for them to return. Auntie Stella wants to know what the boat was like, if the room was comfortable, if the sea was rough, how the food was, when was the last time they all ate, if the children liked being on the boat. The woman answers her questions, but she keeps looking at me, and I try not to look back at her, but I let her touch my head.

Ma and the woman talk and then they cry, and then smile, one after the other, and even at the same time. It is confusing. Auntie Stella keeps bending or stooping down to speak with the little girl. Every time the girl answers a question, Auntie Stella seems amused and alarmed and asks her the same question again or another one, just to hear her speak, I think, in her funny way of speaking. The girl calls Auntie Stella Auntie and Ma Mama, like the woman does when she talks to Ma. She is pretty. Auntie Stella and Ma must have said so a million times. They forgot, it seems, that I am here. Ma talks to the little girl, then to the woman, then to the little girl. I cling to Ma's dress and to her hand. She keeps trying to touch the little boy's face, but he turns away and buries his face in his mother's neck. She wraps her fingers around mine tightly.

I don't want to like the little girl, Tara, but I want her to speak to me. Everybody likes the way she talks. So do I, but I think they are paying too much attention to her. The boy is very small and thin. He won't take his face out of his mother's shoulders. The man returns with a stroller and a couple of small bags, and the boy is eventually strapped into the stroller. He hates it. He struggles to get out and cries. He just keeps hiding his face in his hands or turning his face to the back of the stroller and crying. Ma bends down a hundred thousand times to ask if he wants juice to drink, if he is hungry, and to point out things to him. He won't answer any of her questions or look where she is pointing. From one of the bags, the Auntie Mummy lady removes a very long belt that has loops on it. She stoops down and arranges it with various straps over the girl's body—over Tara's body, that is—and when she stands, she holds the long strap of the belt tightly. Tara seems quite happy like this. She no longer clings to my aunt but moves about on her own, unable to stray too far off. Her hair is like a big messy cloud on top of her head. Mine is just straight and my ponytails fall all the way down my back. She looks like a doll from another country.

Soon there is a terrible rumbling of carts and trolleys coming our way. Uncle Sonny is leading Pa and the man, who carries a briefcase and papers in his hand. Mr. Monty shows the porters who are pushing the carts full of suitcases and trunks where the car is parked.

Pa looks at the arrangement of the belt around Tara and sternly says to the woman—to the Auntie Mummy, What is that? That is a leash? That is not for children. I don't like that. Take it off. He is quite stern, and everyone becomes quiet while the Auntie Mummy lady undoes the thing Pa called a leash. Uncle Daddy says it is common practice, that the girl is used to it, that everyone does it where they came from. Uncle Sonny says, Not here; no one does that here; it doesn't look good; that is for dogs. Pa says, Better to take it off and put it away. Uncle Daddy bends down and removes the leash and holds the smiling girl by her hand.

*

To my surprise, some of the luggage that arrived with the family was brought up from the cars and put in the bedroom that belongs to Ma and me.

Polly has stayed at our house late tonight, to heat up the dinner and serve it. She and the Auntie Mummy lady hug, and Polly cries even as she is smiling, but not the lady. She hugs back Polly and at the same time laughs at her for crying. Polly shakes Uncle Daddy's hand shyly and pinches Tara's cheeks. Tara gets annoyed by this and pulls away, saying to her, Don't do that. Her words are so funny, the way she says them, so sternly, as if she is not a child, and that makes Polly laugh. Polly tries to take the little boy from Uncle Daddy, but the boy turns his face away, grips Uncle Daddy's neck tightly, and sobs without any tears falling down his crumpled-up face.

Uncle Sonny and Auntie Stella eat dinner with us at the big dining table. There is a high chair for the little crying boy. He stops crying when he is given a plate with a piece of roti, which he rips up, as if it is a piece of paper, and he flings pieces on the floor and drops more on the tray of the high chair and on his clothes. He eventually scrunches bits of roti in his fists and tries to eat them from behind his fist, in a backwards way. The girl will not eat the curry, but she eats mounds of roti. Polly cuts slices of cheese for her and wraps roti around the cheese, and the girl eats it all. Polly looks as if she's just done the most important thing ever.

At the table Uncle Sonny says to me, When your mummy left Trinidad to go and study in England she was a princess, you know. She didn't know how to do a thing for herself. She never had to lift a finger when she was here. Well, when your daddy met her in England on one of his breaks from school, she dropped everything, her studies and all, just like that, and next thing you know, she was getting married and moving to Ireland with him. My sister—your mummy—had to do things she never did before, she had to learn how to cook, clean house, and wash clothes even.

He laughs but no one else seems to find it as funny as he does. Uncle Daddy smiles and says, We'll make up for that soon enough; there isn't anyone more perfect.

Auntie Mummy rolls her eyes at both of them and shakes her head side to side like when you're saying no. Then Uncle Sonny, Pa, and Uncle Daddy begin to talk about cars. Uncle Sonny says he will take Uncle Daddy to look for one as soon as he's ready. Uncle Sonny's car is a red sports car called a Jaguar, like the big cat, and there is a very small silver-coloured statue of the jaguar on the hood of the car. Once I tried to see if it was possible to remove it, and he slapped my hand and shouted at me and asked if I was mad or what. Their yardman has to wash the car every day. The Auntie Mummy lady says all they will need is something small to get around in. The Uncle Daddy says, Well, let's see how it goes.

I want to ask the Auntie Mummy lady if she ever had roti before, so I get really strong inside of myself and I say, Excuse me, Auntie Mummy, do you like roti? And everybody laughs, and I feel happy that I said something funny. Before the Auntie Mummy lady can answer me, Auntie Stella begins to explain to me that the woman is Ma and Pa's daughter and she is Uncle Sonny's sister. I think then, if Uncle Sonny is my uncle and she is his sister, then I am right, and wanting to show that I am a smart child, I say proudly, So that makes you my auntie? Auntie

Stella laughs—but it doesn't sound like her usual laugh—and she says, But seriously, you all didn't explain it yet?

Uncle Sonny stops talking with Pa and Uncle Daddy and turns to me. He points to the man and says, This man is your daddy. You are to call him Daddy. Looking still at me, he points to the woman and says to me, slowly, as if he is a teacher in school, Listen. Listen good. Let me explain something. This woman, my sister, is your mummy. You call her Mummy. Just Mummy. She is not an auntie. She is your mummy.

I am looking at him because he seems to be speaking to me, but I can still see everyone. They have stopped eating and they are all looking at him, and at me.

He is saying, Your mummy and your daddy were living in another country while your daddy was at medical school in that country. Ireland, remember? Understand? You were their first child, and you were born in that country. Then they brought you here and left you here with Ma and Pa, who are your grandparents.

He is about to carry on, and Ma says, OK, Sonny. That is enough. He says to her very sharply, No, let me finish. And he carries on, Now that your daddy has finished his studies, they have returned to live here. *They* are your family. Tara is your sister. Your younger sister. And this boy here, this boy who likes his roti, he is your brother.

He gathers the three of us children with a circle of his finger and says, You, all three of you, are Ma and Pa's grandchildren. Got it?

Everyone else remains serious. I didn't mean to stop listening, but maybe he was speaking too fast, and I didn't understand everything, but I say yes. He is angry, I think, and my *yes* is very soft. I don't know if they heard.

He points to the woman again and says to me, What do you call her? I whisper, Mummy? Then he points to the man and says, And him? I say, Daddy. Tara claps her hands. I look at Ma, scared. She looks at me with a sort of smile, not her usual smile, and nods.

Why didn't Ma help me with all of this before they came? I wonder. I would have made an effort to remember their names, and I would have impressed them all.

But something is strange. I think I heard but maybe I didn't. I think I understood but not really. My tummy hurts, and my ears are hot. I feel as if I don't have ears and want to touch the sides of my head to check, but I can't lift my hands off my lap.

The woman I am supposed to call Mummy says to him, OK, Sonny. That's enough. He sucks his teeth, like Barlow does, and says, You all have no idea what you are doing. Auntie Stella is staring at him. Her eyes are open big, and her lips are pressed together tightly, which is what she does when she is angry, especially with him. He pushes back his chair and says he is going to get coconut water. When he reaches the kitchen, no one has spoken and he calls out, Anybody else want? No one answers, and he sucks his teeth again.

Pa asks me and the two little children if we liked the food and if we want anything more to drink, another glass of sweet-drink perhaps? But Ma says, in a really low voice, They will wet the bed; better not to have any more to drink.

After dinner, when Uncle Sonny and Auntie Stella leave, Tara and I go into the kitchen with Polly, and we play at Polly's work table, but I don't know what we play. Polly keeps asking Tara questions. She asks her the same question over and over, and when Tara answers, she laughs and says things like, But listen how nice she does speak. Ma and Pa and the people I am supposed to call Mummy and Daddy go on the veranda, but far from where we are, and are talking for a long time. I leave the kitchen and am going out to the veranda, but Polly calls me back, but not before I see the woman Mummy being hugged by the man Daddy, her face in his chest. He is stroking her head, and Pa's hand rests on her back.

Not long after, Ma and the Mummy lady—or just Mummy—go into our room, taking with them Tara and the crying boy. I follow, but I stay by the door and watch. They get ready for sleeping and Ma lifts both children up, one at a time, and puts them to lie down in our bed. She pulls down the mosquito net and tucks it in around the bed, with just one side open. The Mummy lady gets into the bed. The windows are open, but there isn't any air in the room. It's hard to breathe. But then I am all right because Ma doesn't get into the bed with them. She takes my hand in hers and walks me to Pa's room, where he, and the two of us, will sleep in his bed.

*

The following day, the family is there, all day. And the next. And the next. Daddy—that's what Pa told me, again, to call the man—leaves our house very early most mornings, and he usually returns late in the evenings. Sometimes it's the other way around—he leaves in the evening and comes back in the morning. The night shift, they call it. Uncle Sonny and Auntie Stella visit often. They enjoy hearing stories about deliveries of babies, the stitching up of heads of people who were hit with a cutlass in a fight, and car accidents.

When they are alone, Pa and Daddy sit on the veranda, he in the rocking chair and Daddy in a sofa pulled from the living room. They drink whisky from a blue bottle. The label says it is blue but that's not true, the label is black, and it is the bottle that's blue. I used to think that was funny, but now I keep wanting to knock the bottle over. I imagine it falling off the table, the whisky spilled all over the floor, the whole house smelling of whisky and the fibbing bottle broken. But I won't do it. I don't want to get into trouble. Especially in front of Tara, who is always good and whom everyone makes a fuss about, especially because of what they call her accent—the way she pronounces words, how she sounds when she speaks.

Pa and Daddy talk a lot about cars. And Pa tells him he wants Tank—that is Mr. Monty's name, but I am not allowed to call him that—to take Pa and him for a drive in some new developing areas where there is good land for sale.

Pa doesn't rock me to sleep like he used to. He doesn't even really rock me anymore. But sometimes, when Daddy is doing a night shift at the hospital and Mummy is getting her children ready for bed, I go and climb on him in the rocking chair, and he sings very softly so only he and I hear. When he sings softly, his voice trembles. *All things bright and beautiful, all creatures great and small, all things wise and wonderful, the Lord God made them all.*

FOUR

We sleep now in Pa's bed with him. There is less room, but I like the heat that comes off his back and how he smells—it is of his underarms, a hot and special smell. Pa doesn't eat popcorn because the kernels get stuck in his teeth, but he smells like popcorn, not like the taste of it but just the smell when it is being cooked. No one else smells like him. Not even Ma. She smells sometimes like roti if she has been in the kitchen when Polly is cooking, but almost all the time she smells like perfume, like a whole bunch of flowers, red ones and yellow, pink and white ones.

Every day after lunch, the lady I must call Mummy takes her children to the room that belonged to Ma and me, and she lies in the bed with them, and they all take a nap. I have stood by the door and peeped at them a few times, and some of those times she knew I was there and invited me to join them in the bed. Of course, I don't go. Ma says it is all right if I lie down there with them, but I prefer to nap lying next to her in the big bed in Pa's room.

There are no shadows at night on the wall in Pa's room. Sometimes, when there is no moon, it is so black in there that I don't know if my eyes are opened or closed or, if I hold my hand up, how far it is from my face. In the morning, out the big window that stretches the full length of the wall is the big old mango tree with its fat trunk and spreading branches and dark green leaves that just about block the view of the barracks. That is what Ma and Pa call the neighbours' house, the barracks. There is a short concrete wall and the latticework between them and us. Those are the neighbours we don't talk to. Maybe they are bad people. Or maybe Ma and Pa have a quarrel with them. Growing on the branches of the mango tree are ferns and plants that look like pineapples, but they aren't pineapples. They have a funny name I can't say, but Frank knows—or maybe he just pretends to know. Some of the plants have long roots that hang all the way down, as if they are trying to reach the ground so that they can grow there.

I don't like going out into the rest of the now noisy house. I don't want to have to play with the little girl, and to see how much Ma likes her, or hear Ma and the woman talking. So I just stay in Pa's room. Sometimes I place the peerha by the window and step up on it and try to see through the branches and leaves of the tree. There are lots of chickens over there in that yard. They chase each other and make a fast *buck-buck-buck* sound and bob their heads and peck at the dry white gravelly ground. There are children next door, too. I have counted five, all older than me, I think. They are noisy, they laugh loudly and shout, and Ma is always saying she wishes she could tell them to be quiet, especially on afternoons when people want to nap. I mustn't let Ma catch me looking over there. Once she came up behind me and shook my shoulders roughly and asked if I was peeping at the barracks children next door. I told her no, I wasn't, and she shook me again and said, How many times I have told you not to go staring at people? But I would rather be over there now than here with these new people in our house.

*

Poor Frank. He drinks bay rum and gets drunk a lot, and when he is drunk he sings. He stands under the street light at the corner and the light shines down on him and makes his pale skin look yellow. Tara and I hide behind the banister, peeping just over the ledge so we can see him. We put our hands over our mouths to stifle our giggling, but sometimes we let out a giggle that is loud enough to make him look up right where we are, then we duck down fast behind the banister. I think he sings to us. Some neighbours shout at him to shut up and go home. He sings, *Oh bring back, oh bring back, oh bring back my bonnet to me.* I think it is supposed to be *my Bonnie*, but he says *bonnet*. And he bends down and slaps his knees and cries, and he hugs himself and wails and rocks from side to side. Then suddenly he is up and bright, singing about the brown-skin girl who has to stay home and mind her baby. Sometimes he jumps up under the street light as if it were carnival time and he was in a band. He even points up to us and begins laughing shyly, and he shouts, You laughing at Frank! Frank know all the verses, you know! What song you want to hear? Tell me. Frank is a starboy.

The watchman comes out from the factory hitting his baton in his open palm and tells Frank to go home, but he enjoys Frank's antics, too, and leans back, one foot against the wall, and watches him.

*

Ma says she isn't sleeping well because Pa's bed is too small for the three of us. She says it is too hot with three in it. But I have a solution. I tell her maybe Pa can sleep in the middle room—because no one uses it, except Polly sometimes, but there is the room under the house, which Polly can use, so the middle room can become Pa's room now. She reminds me that a foldaway bed has been put for me in the front room where the new family now sleeps, and I can help out by sleeping in that foldaway bed. I haven't forgotten about the foldaway bed. But that is a bad idea. If I awake to go to the washroom, I'll have to walk all the way down the hallway, in the dark, and wake her so she can take me. She says Mummy will take me just as well. I have another, better idea. The foldaway bed can be brought into Pa's room, and he can sleep in it. She must have stopped listening to me, because she doesn't answer me, which is all right because I don't want to talk about that anymore.

It seems to me that the family is just staying and staying with us. As if they are living in our house, too. The front room no longer smells like khus khus grass from the cupboard with all the linen, or of the Limacol I rub on Ma's head. Or the powder she puts on after she showers. Rather, it smells like the man, Daddy. Sometimes when you drive by one of the sugar factories, you can smell molasses and bagasse burning, and he smells sugary and hot like that.

Even though I explained everything to Ma, sometimes they all still try to get me to go and sleep in the front room, and I have to shout to try to get them to hear that I don't want to do that, and it is only when I begin to cry—to cry really loudly—that they stop and let me go into Pa's bed. But I have begun to feel that the problem is that Ma and Pa don't want me in their bed with them anymore. And I think I have also begun to cry a lot. I don't mean to, I don't like to, but it just happens.

And Ma is spending a lot of time now with Mummy. They never stop talking and are always busy doing something together.

The dressmaker has been coming regularly to the house now, and women relatives and friends come to meet Mummy, who they all exclaim has become so grown-up, like a real English lady. Mummy says, But you know, we were in Ireland, not England. And Ma looks at them apologetically and says to Mummy, Well, you know what they mean. Those aunties speak about me, but they wait until they think I am busy playing with Tara or the children they brought with them, and then they begin whispering, and my name is repeated many times.

*

Pa likes Tara. And she likes him. But she doesn't even know him very well, and yet the other day she asked him to give her money. He looked at her and opened his eyes wide and said, But how old are you, darling? You are just five years old and asking for money?

She frowned and answered him as if he had asked a silly question. Yes, I need it because you can't go to the store without money. I have to go to Mr. Tang's shop. I need to buy a book of cut-out paper dolls.

I was glad he said no, that she should wait and let her mummy take her to the toy shop. But she just begged and begged, and I know Pa well enough to be able to tell, when he said it was a waste of money, that he was annoyed. She folded her arms and stared at him as he said there were so many toys all over the house, everything scattered all over the floor, that one day somebody is going to trip over something and fall and hurt themselves. I nodded in agreement. Tara turned her back and walked away, but I followed her. She is brave. She slipped into Ma and Pa's bedroom and pulled open Pa's dresser drawer. She removed his eyecup and went into his bathroom and filled it with water and put it to her eyes. Her eyelashes were beaded with water and water was running down her face and she went to Pa and made big crying sounds. He held her face in his hands but then he laughed. He called Frank and gave him some money and told him to take us to the shop, to hold our hands tightly, and buy us whatever we wanted. She got her way, but that was now OK with me because I would get something from the shop, too.

We walked on either side of Frank on the sidewalk down Selvon Street. All the way to the corner shop Frank was smiling, and one minute he was whistling a tune I didn't know, and the next singing what I think was a song from an Indian movie. We swung our hands in his. Tang laughed when Tara spoke to him. He loved the way she spoke. She chose a cut-out book, and he gave her a handful of sour cherry candies. His sister Mary parted the curtain to their room at the back and came out. She doesn't usually come out, but she did this time. To see Tara. She lifted the part of the counter that is like a door and came around and asked Frank, This is the one from abroad? She stooped down and looked into Tara's face. She stood and went back behind the counter and returned with a packet of salt prunes, a packet of fudge, and a packet of sweet red anchar and handed them to Frank. She never did that when I alone went with Frank. On the way there I had planned to buy a packet of fudge and a new roll of green caps for my toy gun, but I changed my mind. I wanted, instead, to show Pa that I was good at business, just like him. I wouldn't buy silly things like candies or toys or books, things that are a waste of money. Rather, I'd turn that money into even more money, as I'd heard him advising Daddy and Uncle Sonny to do with their incomes. Investing, he called it. I told Mr. Tang I wanted a dollar bill changed into pennies. He wouldn't do it at first, but I got upset and held up his other customers by pouting and beginning to cry. Frustrated with me, he counted out one hundred pennies, saying, Grandpa going to vex with me. What I do to deserve this?

There were now so many pennies that he had to put them in a bag, which was too heavy for me to carry, so Frank had to carry it back home for me. Frank didn't sing on the way back. He, too, was upset with me. When I got back and showed Pa how I'd invested his single dollar bill and turned it into much more money, while Tara had simply lost all hers, he became quite angry, first with Frank, then with Mr. Tang for having done what he said was "real stupidness," and then with me. Later that day, he sat me down with a piece of paper and a pen and tried to explain something about dollars and how many cents there were in a dollar, none of which made any sense to me.

*

Sometimes I feel lonely. But when I do, I don't even want Tara's company.

Tara is sitting on Ma's lap, and Ma is touching her hair. I go to the back stairs and sit down on the top step. No one comes to look for me. I can hear Ma and Mummy; so much talking all the time, but not to me, only to each other.

I go down the steps slowly and keep looking back. No one comes behind me.

I go all the way down, then underneath the house, and still no one upstairs calls for me. It is Saturday and the downstairs office is closed. Frank is doing his work somewhere else on the property. His friend Clydie is sitting on the concrete floor, leaning against the office door. He is probably waiting for Frank. Clydie doesn't work for us. When he sees me, he sits up and calls my name. I don't answer him. He says, What they do you, child? What have your face so? He tells me to sit down and tell him what happened. He smells like dirty old hair. He stretches out his hand toward me and I don't mean to, but I put mine out and I really don't mean to, but I let him take it. He pulls me closer. He says, What happen, somebody do you something? Sit down next to Clydie. And he pulls me down next to him. I don't want to be close to him. He smells like the beggars who come for rotis and a shilling on the first Saturday of the month. He asks where Ma is, and where Pa is, and where my mother and my little sister and Barlow are. He asks if I like having a sister now. Then I see that he is pulling down the zipper of his pants and I begin to get up, but he holds me back with one hand and with the other hand takes out his big pee pee, just like Sita's brother's pee pee that I used to think was like a sausage. I try to pull away, but he holds my hand tightly and pulls it onto the pee pee and the pee pee grows long and big and he shakes it and it gets sick and vomits and makes a strange smell. I am scared and want to leave, but he holds my hand, squeezing it so hard that it hurts. I want to cry, but I don't. He says I am his best friend, that he likes me more than he likes anyone else, but that I mustn't tell anyone that, or about what he showed me, and then he hugs me. I get so scared, because I also wondered if Uncle John would get angry with me, too.

And I wonder if Uncle John and Chandra know Clydie. Sometimes, everything, everything in the world, smells like Clydie.

*

I would like to play with Tara, but she plays with dolls and pretends a doll is a baby and she is feeding it, burping it, and then putting it to sleep. I don't like that game, but I agree to be the daddy who goes to work and works hard all day, has meetings with his workers, then comes home tired. She sets the table and puts dinner out for me.

But she and her parents and the little boy have been staying with us too long. Even when we are in the car going shopping or to visit relatives in the north, Ma and Mummy just keep talking and talking and talking as if they are the only ones who exist. We all sit in the back seat and Mr. Monty sits in front by himself and drives. Ma takes one window and Mummy the other, and Tara always wants to sit next to Ma. I don't make a fuss. I just sit quietly next to Mummy. I try and relax and be calm. I don't cry. Not on the outside. I do try my best to play with Tara.

*

Tara didn't ask if she could play with my Scottie. Scottie was on the chair in Ma and Pa's room, and she took him out without asking if she could play with him. I didn't even see when she did that.

She is on the veranda with my Scottie and her big yellow teddy bear. Standing where she can't see me, I watch. Scottie is sitting at my little table on one of the children's chairs. Her bear is opposite, on another chair. She is singing that song her mother sings to her and her brother Anil.

If you go down to the woods today you're sure of a big surprise, if you go there's lots of marvellous things to eat and wonderful games to play and the little bear and Scottie are having a lovely time today.

Those are not even the correct words. She still doesn't know I am watching her and listening. She is kneeling at the side of the table, which she has set with a plate and cups and saucers from her tea set and is making Scottie and the bear drink tea. I worry that there is real water in the cups, and that Scottie will get wet, and his fur, when it dries, will get stiff and will smell, but there isn't anything in the cups. She's just pretending.

She should ask if she can play with other people's toys. Scottie is mine. I can go over to the table and just take him away. I wouldn't be wrong. I'm not selfish. It's just not right to take something that belongs to somebody without asking them first if it's OK to do that. But if I take Scottie away, Tara might get upset and cry. Then Mummy and Ma and Pa will come running to see why she's crying, and they'll get angry with me even if I explain why I took Scottie back. They will tell me that I mustn't be selfish—even though I'm not being selfish. They'll say I have to learn to play with others. But I know how to play with others. It's others who must learn to ask if they can play with someone else's things. Mummy will lift Tara and I will be left on

my own. But Tara doesn't cry so easily. She won't even fight me. She'll tell me she's sorry. Then I'll feel bad that I took him back. I'll have to take him and go into Ma and Pa's room and stay there. But for how long will I have to remain there? The day will be long and lonely. I better not take him away.

I shuffle my feet by the door, and Tara looks over, and when she sees me, she gets up and runs to me. She holds my hand and leads me to the other side of the table. She tells me to sit down and join the teddy bears' picnic. I tell her Scottie is not a teddy bear. She looks surprised and it takes a while before she says, But we can pretend he is, and you and me, we are teddy bears, too. Would you like a cup of tea?

Before I answer, she is already pouring me a pretend cup of tea. I don't like her. I tell her there is real coconut fudge in the cookie jar and I can get some for us, and we can have it as part of the picnic. She is so happy that she makes me happy even if I don't want to be happy. I get the fudge and bring it back and we take bites for ourselves and pretend to feed Scottie and Bear, too.

*

The office downstairs is closed for the weekend and the lights down there are off. Tara, Sita, and I are downstairs playing catch. It's fun because in the dark downstairs it is a little scary. I didn't know Clydie was down here. When I see him, I run into the backyard so that Tara and Sita run behind me, trying to catch me. It is bright out here. But behind us I can see Clydie standing by the back stairs. Sita and Tara spot him, too. His zip is undone and his pee pee is out of his pants. He is holding it and we see it and race to the stairs, which is close to where he is, and the three of us almost trip over each other trying to get past him and upstairs. Tara is laughing-screaming, both at once. Sita doesn't come inside, she stays at the top of the stairs. Tara runs into the house, laughing and yelling that Clydie is showing off his pee pee. I am scared. Ma comes running out and Mummy screams for Frank to come here right away. She yells at him to get Clydie out of the yard. Ma is so angry that she spins Frank around and pushes him hard. He almost falls, and she shouts really bad curse words that we are not ever allowed to say. Mummy screams that Clydie is never to come near this house or her children again.

I put my hand up a little to tell Sita to stay where she is. Mummy is shaking, and Ma and Barlow are saying it is best not to say anything to boss and to Daddy or to Uncle Sonny. Let Frank deal with it. Then I pull Ma and ask her to call out to Sita's brother Chandra to come and walk her back across the street. I go and climb up on the bed in the middle room and I stay there for a long time, because I am afraid. I think if anyone looks at me, they will know things I don't want them to know, and I don't want Ma to die, or Pa. They can't die.

*

Daddy takes us for a drive in his new car. It smells like Ma's handbags, and like Pa's leather belts. Pa likes the car. It is bigger than his.

Ma has come for the drive, too, but not Pa. Daddy and Mummy sit in the front, Anil on Mummy's lap. Ma, Tara, and I sit in the back. We drive by houses built near the sea. Daddy drives slowly, and he and Mummy keep saying how nice it would be to live so close to water. Not far from there is the Mosquito Creek. There are other cars parked along the seawall and some people have gotten out of their cars and are standing or sitting on the wall. A man is fishing. The sun is going down and the sky is orange and pink and so is the sea. Daddy gets out of the car, but he gets back in right away and says there are too many mosquitoes out there. The tide is rising, and some waves slap the wall and the water splashes over and runs right across the road. It looks as if it can sweep our car away. I am sure I feel the car move. I ask if anyone else did, too, but no one did.

Daddy says he doesn't want the salt water to ruin his new car, so we leave and he drives to where there are vendors' tables with flambeaux lit all around them, so many you could smell the kerosene. Women are roasting corn on coal pots, and men are selling coconuts and oysters. Daddy asks what each of us wants, and when it is my turn, I look at Ma, and she pokes me and says, Answer your daddy. While still looking at her, I ask in a soft voice, Oysters?

Daddy hears, and he answers that that isn't a good idea, there have been cholera cases at the hospital and the Ministry of Health has issued an advisory about oysters causing cholera. I want to say that Pa always bought oysters for me, but I can't because Ma isn't supposed to know. Daddy points to the mangrove swamp on the other side of the road and says, Look over there, it's in water like that that you find oysters. See how dirty it is?

We all turn and look at the water. It is dark inside the swamp, and the water is deep green, almost black.

The skin on my face gets hot because I feel bad for asking for something dirty, and also because it means Daddy is saying bad things about Pa, that Pa gives me dirty things to eat. I want to tell them, and to say that Pa would never give me anything bad. But I can't give away our good secret. Daddy suggests something, but it is suddenly as if I can't hear, so I just nod. While we wait for him in the car, I take quick glances at the mangrove swamp. There are probably water snakes and caimans in there.

But just because Daddy is a doctor, it doesn't mean he knows *everything*. Especially about Trinidad. He hasn't even been living in Trinidad for very long. Pa is older than Daddy, and he knows more. He would never let me eat something that would make me sick.

Before Mummy and Daddy came, Pa used to take me with him on afternoons to football games in Skinner Park, and at halftime all the spectators would rush down from the stands to the back of the stadium and there we'd line up and Pa would buy oysters. The oyster man would open the oysters with his knife and slide the oyster meat into a glass, and then he'd add his special red sauce to the glass and he'd ask Pa if he should put pepper in mine. I don't like pepper, so he'd stir mine and hand it to Pa and Pa would hand it to me, and then the man would open oysters for Pa. Pa would eat his right from their shells, with a lot of pepper sauce on them. I'd sip the juice that was salty and limey and garlicky and had ketchup and shadon beni in it. The oysters were soft and slippery and tasted like the Mayaro wind and like how the river near the sea smells. I wouldn't chew them, just move them about with my tongue, all slippery and slidey, and get all their sea flavour out by pressing, and then I'd swallow them whole. I never ever got sick. Then, when the football game was over, Pa and I would go to the coconut vendor. The man knows Pa. Pa wouldn't even have to tell him what he wanted or what to do. He would hold a coconut in one hand and with a cutlass in the other he would swipe off the top of the coconut and some of the water inside would squirt out. I can't hold a coconut and drink from it like Pa does because they are too heavy for me. So the man would borrow a clean glass from the oyster vendor and he'd pour some coconut water in the glass for me, and then he'd cut the empty nut when Pa was finished drinking from it, and he'd scoop the meat of the coconut into my glass and slice off a piece of the shell for me to use as a spoon.

Maybe Daddy also wouldn't buy coconuts from vendors. He can't be right about the oysters. Otherwise I'd have died already.

We are still waiting for Daddy in the car, and I am not really moving about a lot and yet Ma asks me to please settle down. Mummy turns back and tells me to climb over the seat into the front and sit with her. I say no and move over closer to Ma and am about to sit on Ma's lap but Ma nudges me away, so I just lean against her. Mummy gets really quiet, and Ma reaches over and touches her on her shoulder. Mummy smiles and laughs and talks a great deal with Anil and Tara, but she doesn't with me, and that's why I don't want to go in the front with her. Whenever she looks at me, she looks sad, or maybe annoyed. I don't understand why she wants me to sit next to her. But I don't like to make people sad, and I don't want to make her angry. I don't know what to do. I am afraid of her. I don't let her see me looking at her.

When Daddy returns, he hands me a roasted corn on the cob. I don't like roasted corn because the black bits get stuck between your teeth and down in your gums, and it is really hard to get them out.

*

Miss Sybil's school is not a good school anymore. That's what Mummy said. And Ma didn't say anything. So Tara and I are going to Miss Mason's school now. The school belongs to a fat woman whose skin is like naked chicken's skin, which means she is from the white race. People come in different races, but everyone is precious. Like in the song, *red and yellow, black and white, they are precious in his sight*. There are many children in the school who have the same kind of pink skin that is white, like Miss Mason's. Miss Mason smells like powder that has perfume in it. When she is far away from you, it smells OK. But when she walks right by you, it is as if it goes into your brain through your eyes and nose and ears, and it is as if you stop hearing, and it makes you want to throw up or faint.

There is a horrible boy at the school. His name is Mark. He kills insects. Catches butterflies and pulls their wings off, and he pulls off dragonflies' wings, too. He takes the legs off grasshoppers, and once during lunchtime, when the teachers were having a meeting upstairs in Miss Mason's house, he killed a big toad. It wasn't even bothering him. He called the other boys to see, and he chased it with a stick until it reached the pond and then he cornered it in the pond and poked it and poked it until it popped. The toad did nothing to him, and now it will never come back alive. When Miss Mason saw what he did, she gave him and the other boys the ruler, ten times on each open palm, and they had to stay after school for half an hour and clean the teachers' desks with soap and water and a rag, water the plants and clean the blackboards, and then each one of them had to write one hundred times, *I will not harm any of God's creatures, great or small, ever again*, and they had to leave the writing there for us all to see the following morning. Another time, he stomped on this snail that had brown and white rings on the shell. It was huge, as big as my fist, and pretty. Inside the shell was shiny pink. The guts were yellow and there was green stuff oozing from it and the crushed shell pieces stuck to its insides. I hated Mark for doing that so I went and hit him and he tried to fight back so I pushed him and he fell inside the pond and Miss Mason came and shouted at us and she asked all the children to tell her what happened, and when they did he got the ruler and was sent home in the middle of the day and he didn't return for three days.

How beautiful that snail was, and how quickly someone was able to kill it so it died and wouldn't ever live again. If there was another snail waiting for it to come home, that snail is probably still waiting and doesn't know what has happened.

*

Mummy says my teeth are all rotten little stubs because Ma and Pa and Polly and Barlow and everyone have all spoiled me and given me too many sweets. I am not allowed to have as many sweets as I used to before these people arrived in Trinidad, and almost no more sweetdrinks. Mummy brushes my teeth for me now, not Ma. When she holds my face, her hands feel very soft, and she is gentle. There is a cologne on the dresser that was Ma's dresser, and she puts it on every day after she showers. It's a nice smell. But I feel as if I am doing something wrong when I like her smell. I don't want to like anyone's smell but Ma's.

Sometimes I want to be by myself. I pretend my pillow is a horsey and I ride my horsey and, pressed against me down there, it tickles and tickles and then makes a different kind of tickle that is bigger than all the other ones, and I get a nice feeling all over my body and it makes me forget how unhappy I am.

Mummy is going to have a baby. Tara and Anil will have another baby sister or baby brother. Tara presses her ear to her mummy's tummy and talks to the baby inside and everybody thinks that is cute and funny.

*

Ma says I can't go out with her so much, that I have to stay and play with Tara and Anil. She doesn't bathe me anymore. Sometimes she used to come under the shower with me and we'd bathe together. Now, Mummy bathes Tara and me together. She never gets under the shower with us, though. She scrubs my knees and elbows hard with a pumice stone until they turn red and sting. Sometimes Barlow bathes me. I didn't used to like Barlow's fingers that smelled of garlic. But I don't mind it so much anymore. Tara doesn't like Barlow to bathe her. She screams if Barlow tries to undress her. She says Barlow is rough. It's true.

*

Ma and Mummy are on the veranda. They're going through a suitcase of crocheted tablecloths and doilies that Mrs. Khan, the woman who lives next to the mosque, has brought to our house. In the suitcase is a small pretty pink-and-white doily. There are many shades of pink in it, the darkest at the centre. It is like a flower. I want to touch it. No one seems to see I am standing here, so I put my hand in the suitcase. But Mummy slaps my hand. It isn't a hard slap, but Ma would never do that to me, especially in front of a visitor. And Ma doesn't even say anything. I go into the drawing room and sit on the couch. I think of Clydie and wish I could go downstairs and find him there and then that same thought makes me feel even sadder, as if I am a bad person, and it all makes me want to throw up. I call Ma. She says, Just now, Anju. But just now never comes. Mrs. Khan has left, but Mummy and Ma are still on the veranda. I call Ma again. Nothing happens. So I call again, but this time very softly, in a whisper. She would not have heard me, of course, I know that. They just keep talking, talking, talking.

I go into the middle room and lie on the bed. When finally Ma comes and sees me in that room, lying on the bed that Polly takes a rest in sometimes, she asks what's wrong, don't I know I'm not supposed to be in the middle room or to lie on Polly's bed? I whisper that I have a secret. She asks, What is it? I pull her and she comes close and puts her ear to my mouth, and in the tiniest voice I say that Uncle John told me it was a secret and I was not to tell anyone. She moves back and stares at me as she says, Mhm. I whisper that I am scared to tell her. She says, What is it? What did he tell you? I can't hear you, Anju, speak louder.

I ask if she'll die if I tell her and she says not to be foolish. I ask her to promise she won't die, and that she won't tell anyone else. She steupses, holds me by my shoulders and looks into my eyes, and says, Tell me, Anju. What did he tell you? Did something happen?

I say he put his hands inside of my pants and rubbed me there and said that if I told anyone she'd get sick and die. She pulls back from me as if she got an electric shock from touching me. Then she pulls me up to her chest and tells me that she is not going to die. She rocks me in her arms, but not gently like she usually does, and then very sternly, she tells me never ever to say those words again, that I am not ever to tell anyone what I just told her. And that if he ever comes to the house again, I am not to go near him. She holds me so tightly, and then, even though I am heavy now, she lifts me and carries me into Pa's bed. She lies hugging me, but only for a very short while. Her body seems shaky and unsettled. It feels as if she doesn't want to be there, lying down with me. I feel ill. My tummy hurts. I should not have told her. Eventually she gets up and says only, Stay here, and leaves and goes out into the kitchen. I listen for a long time. There is shoo-shooing but I can't make out the words.

I fell asleep, awakened because footsteps were coming nearer and I smelled Mummy's cologne.

She sits on the edge of the bed and hands me something wrapped in tissue paper. It is the small pink-and-white doily with the very dark pink centre. I don't want to take it from her. I don't know why but I want to cry. It is so pretty, I want it.

*

Daddy and Mummy went for a drive by themselves. They just returned and Daddy is in a good mood. He calls us all, including Ma and Pa, onto the veranda and says, Kids, and Tara looks up to the sky with her eyes closed and says, Really, Daddy, we're not goats. Everyone laughs. Well, everyone but me. It's not funny. It's true: we're not goats. Daddy taps her on her head and says, That's right, darling. What are you? Are you a kitten? She laughs, and Mummy says, OK, enough. Daddy is trying to say something.

Daddy's eyes are wide, and he looks happy as he carries on: So guess what? Mummy and Daddy have good news. Before he tells us what the news is, Tara is jumping up and saying, We're getting a kitten—no, a dog, we're getting a dog. Polly comes and stands in the doorway. Ma jerks her head to tell her to go back inside, so she steps back a little but stays where she can hear.

No, we're not ready to get a dog, or a cat. One day maybe. Now listen. We have enjoyed living here with Mama and Papa. He looks at them and addresses them. You've been very good, putting up with all of us. But it's not right for us to be abusing your generosity. Then he looks back at Tara and me, and he says, Soon you will have another little brother or sister to play with, and there'll be six of us. So today your mom and I went searching and we found a new home for us. In three weeks' time we're going to move into a house of our own.

Behind my back, I count on my fingers and see that there will soon be five of them, not six. But I don't bother to correct him.

Mummy says in a low voice, as if to her parents, Well, not our own. We're not buying it.

Daddy says, No, you're right. We're renting. For now. Give me some time. You'll see, in no time we'll have our own house. One day. And this is a step in that direction.

He stoops down now to speak directly to Tara and to Anil. We'll be sleeping at nights in another house, but we'll always come back here for some of Mama's delicious meals, won't we, Vij? He looks to the doorway and says, And Polly's cooking.

Mummy says, Yes. Of course. In any case, this is only temporary. It won't be long before we find something else.

Daddy continues talking to Anil and Tara. He glances at me as he speaks to them. It's a very nice house, with a big yard for little children to play in, he tells them. Tara jumps up and down and says, And a dog. A dog, a dog. Daddy says, One day, not right away. Don't you want to get used to your new home first? She grabs her father's hands and tries to get him to swing her around and she begins to repeat, again and again, Can I have my own bed? Mummy tells her to stop, and to be quiet, that Daddy is still speaking. But he doesn't have any more to say.

For the rest of the day, I walk through the house, looking at everything as if it were the first time I am seeing it. I don't say this out loud, but I think that, finally, Ma, Pa, and I will soon be alone together in our house again. I feel a tiny sadness, because every morning now, when I wake up, I look forward to seeing Tara and playing with her. We go for walks sometimes—Frank takes us to Mr. Tang's shop to buy sour cherries, and more pop-up books or ones with cut-out paper dolls. Sometimes he walks with us on the street in front of Miss Fatty's house, and she calls out to us and gives us White Rabbit candies. Then we keep walking until we come to the cemetery. We can't go into the cemetery because the entrance gate is locked, but we stand outside and look through the iron railing at all the white tombstones. Some have flowers on them. There is a tall cross and a painted figure of Jesus Christ on the cross. There is blood in the palms of his hands where the nails went in, and red blood falls down his forehead because there is a crown of thorns on his head. Frank holds our hands tightly at the railing, and he stares at Jesus and his lips move, and sometimes he cries.

*

At home Ma and Mummy come down into the garden, and we follow them. Ma shows Mummy her orchids. Tara and I find a place where we can dig little holes in the dirt. We open the tap and fill a cup with water, then fill the holes with water and stir and stir until the walls of the hole fall in and the earth is soft. Then we take handfuls of the wet dirt and knead it as if we're kneading flour. We pinch bits off and make baskets with handles and fill them with clay eggs. We set them aside to dry.

Now Mummy stands watching Ma clip dead roses off the bushes. Ma loves her roses. She wraps moss around the stems, covers the moss with plastic, and ties it with string. She is doing something called *propagating*. They are speaking in low voices. Ma is saying, But that is the way they are. You know that. You have to take the good with the bad.

Mummy says, I know. I know. He is perfect. Everyone loves him. That is the good. And all the women, too. That is the bad. I don't know how long this is going to go on. I mean, it isn't even five months since we returned, and it is no different than when we were in Ireland. I don't know why they don't leave him alone.

Ma answers, Well, you can't blame the women, Vij. That is like making men out to have no will of their own. Look, there is no one else to blame but them, the men. They are the ones to blame. They are all like that. They don't know how to keep their zips up.

There is quiet, and then Mummy says, You mean Papa?

Yes. I should know. It went on for a long time. You were a child the time he went away for almost a year and then turned up like it was nothing. He came up the back stairs, he nodded to me, and went straight in the room. Just so. As if it was nothing.

He changed his clothes and came and sat down in the office, and started turning the pages of the ledger, like he had never left. To him nothing had happened. But you were too young.

I was young, but I knew. I remember. I think of it often, actually. I don't want that to happen here. He brought a doll for me.

Eh, eh, but you well remember.

You didn't say anything. At least, I don't think you did.

What you will say?

Tara and I are not speaking. If we are too quiet, they will know we are listening, so I tell Tara we should make lots of eggs today to bury for the archaeologist to find. She says, All right, and we go back to sculpting and listening.

Ma laughs and adds, I did speak to him. I remember. I asked him if he wanted me to heat up food for him.

I don't know if I can do that, Mama.

Ma stands up and faces Mummy. Tara and I stay where we are, stooped over our baskets, eggs, bowls, and teacups. Ma's voice is sharp but still low.

You will. You have to. You are lucky. Take it from me. In the end I was lucky. I *am* lucky. Look at all of this. Both of us, we both lucky, Vij. In any case, what options do you have, if you don't want to be on your own? I don't mean financially. Papa and I can do that. But even women need company. You know what I mean. Try to make the best of it, Vij. He is a doctor. You couldn't do better. He will provide for you and the children well. You have the children to look after. My advice is: take care of yourself, the children, wherever you make home, and make sure you meet his needs at home. He will always come back.

Mummy answers, Mama, I can't believe you are telling me this. I never thought it would be like this.

I never really understand when they are talking what they mean. It's as if they leave out a lot, but still, they seem to understand each other. But I can tell by their voices how they are feeling. I think Mummy is unhappy. Mummy and Ma don't like the mess our clay baskets and eggs make on the dresser, so now we dig holes and bury them so that when archaeologists dig up our yard, they will find our baskets of eggs and will know about us.

*

Uncle Sonny came over this morning. I heard him and Mummy and Daddy whispering, so I crawled under the dining room table and listened. He said they should have already put a stop to—well, at first I wasn't sure who he was talking about, but then I realized it was me—they should have put a stop to me sleeping with Ma and Pa. That I have to sleep with Mummy and Daddy in the front room.

This doesn't make sense. I sleep with Ma and Pa. That's where I sleep. Why would he think I should go into the room with those people?

I don't like him anymore. He talks with them about me a lot. Sometimes they will all be looking at me, their faces serious. He seems to always have a lot to say about everything. Some days ago, I heard Daddy say to Mummy, in an angry voice, but softly, that he, Uncle Sonny, may be her brother, but that he, Daddy, is her husband. I think Mummy should tell Uncle Sonny that. I don't let them know I'm listening. Nowadays, when he talks about me, Uncle Sonny sounds drunk, and his face looks like a pot of soup that is being stirred. I think sometimes he is crazy.

I don't understand why everyone is changing so much. Ma only hugs me when she and I are alone, and then she kisses my face so much, and even though I love when she does this, I have to tell her to stop. Now, at nights, Pa puts Tara to sit on one knee and me on the other, and he sings to us. I don't like it. She leans back against him as if he belongs to her, and I sit on the edge of his knee.

*

The church music is playing on the neighbours' radio. That means it is Sunday morning, Ma will be getting ready to go to church. I want to go with her, so I run to the front room and get my sailor outfit off the hanger in the cupboard and dress myself quickly. But even though I was hurrying, when I go out to show her that I dressed myself and am ready to go with her, she has already left. I run to the veranda and call for her in case she has gotten no further than downstairs. I look for the car but don't see it. Perhaps Mr. Monty has driven her. From where I am, I can see the back gate; if she is walking instead of going by car, she would have passed through the front gate, but she'd still have to turn the corner and pass this way. I shout and, although I don't mean to, I am crying. Then I just scream her name. I lean over the veranda and try to see past the neighbours' overhanging mango tree, but I can't see far enough up the road. I scream and scream and scream, *Ma!* It is clear now that she has gone without me. How could she have gone without telling me, without saying goodbye or asking if I want to go with her? I turn back into the house and through my tear-filled eyes I see Pa and Mummy and Daddy are all there, right there from where they would have heard me calling for Ma. They are not looking at me. The newspaper is on Pa's lap, but he isn't reading it. He is staring at the floor. Daddy's legs are crossed; he is pulling up the sock on his upper foot, rolling it down, pulling it up again. Mummy has a hand covering her mouth, she looks upset, or worried, or maybe she is about to be angry. I stand in front of them, but they are not looking at me. Can they see me? I kick the wall. With a fist I hit it. Mummy moves her hand from her face. She places both hands on the armchair and holds it as if she is about to push herself up, but she doesn't get up. She pulls her lips into her mouth. Still, she won't look at me. None of them, not even Pa, will look my way. No one will help me.

I go to the middle room, and although I know I am not supposed to, I lie on the bed. I will wait here for Ma to return from church. The mattress is very thin, and you can feel the springs in it. I pull the thin pillow down and bunch it up between my legs and play horsey. It feels good. There is someone by the door. They are peeping between the door and the wall. It is Mummy. I smile because I am feeling better now. She doesn't smile back; she rushes into the room and tells me to stop that right now. Her voice isn't loud, yet she sounds as if she is shouting. She grabs the pillow from between my legs and says, What dirtiness is that that you're carrying on with? Don't let me ever catch you doing that again. You hear me? Answer me.

I try to nod, but now I can't move any part of my body. The room has gotten almost as black as if it is nighttime.

She throws the pillow to the top of the bed and walks out of the room, pushing the door wide open. I move closer to the wall and lie right up against it. Polly's towel is on the bed, folded. I pull it and cover myself. I want to put my hands between my legs, but I don't. I don't want anyone to die.

*

Uncle Sonny and Auntie Stella and my cousins have arrived. On Sundays they have lunch with us and we all eat at the big table in the dining room. Ma has returned. I haven't come out of the middle room to see them. Colin comes by the door and looks in. He whispers my name. I don't answer. I don't even look at him. He goes away.

I wait and wait and wait, and then, finally, Ma comes into the middle room, and I begin to cry. She hugs me to her chest and says, Don't mind, baby. Don't mind. Stop crying now. How many times I have to tell you you mustn't come in Polly's room? Everybody is outside. You don't want to play with Sheldon and Colin? They asking for you.

I ask why she didn't wait for me. I tell her I was calling her but she didn't answer. She says, No, you weren't calling me. I never heard you calling.

But I did call. I was screaming. I want to scream now to see if she can hear me. But I don't. She takes me to the bathroom and sponges me off, then changes my clothes.

*

The house is full of people. At the table, everyone is talking all at once, there is so much noise. But I am not going to speak with anyone. If they don't hear me when I speak, then I won't speak. I don't look at anyone. I am hungry but I won't eat. I used to sit next to Ma, but now, when I try to sit next to her, Auntie Stella says, No, darling, you're sitting here, next to me on this side, and look, see? Tara is on your other side. I've been waiting all day to sit next to you.

Ma looks at me, and when she nods I know she isn't asking me, or saying it's OK for me to sit where Auntie Stella is telling me to sit, but rather her eyes are telling me not to make a fuss and to do what Auntie Stella tells me to do. Auntie Stella asks if she can cut up my chicken leg for me. I shake my head to say no. She pulls her hands away from my plate quickly. Tara puts a piece of her coconut bake on my plate. I break off a tiny piece and put it between my lips. Tara asks, or maybe she is just saying, It's delicious, isn't it? I don't answer. I don't like her. But as soon as I think this, I also think, She is my only friend at the table. After lunch, Auntie Stella takes the car keys from Uncle Sonny, and she drives Diane, Savi, Sheldon, and Colin back to their home, but Uncle Sonny stays.

The house is quiet. Tara is on a chair in the living room, reading. Anil is lying on the couch. He looks sleepy and is sucking his thumb as if it is the nipple of a bottle. This is just about the time we all go for a nap. Pa has gone into his room, and I am waiting for Ma. I want to lie close to her and I want her to hug me up. But I have to wait; today is Polly's half day, so Ma and Mummy are finishing cleaning up the kitchen. Uncle Sonny still hasn't left, he and Daddy are talking on the veranda. They are drinking whisky.

Then Mummy leaves the kitchen and calls her children to come with her into the front room for their nap. Uncle Sonny comes into the living room and tells me it is nap time, to go and lie down with my sister and brother. I don't like the way he tells me—he's become hard with me. I head toward Pa's room, but Uncle Sonny grabs me and throws me in the air. It usually tickles when he does this, when I am coming back down in his arms, and I would laugh and scream and he'd laugh and I'd tell him, Do it again. But I don't want to play this game with him today. And it seems like this time is different anyway. Everything is upside down today. This time, when he catches me in his arms, he brings my cheek right to his lips and he kisses me. And he tells me, speaking into my cheek, that I have to start sleeping in that room with Mummy and Daddy and my sister and brother. His face smells like whisky. I try to wriggle out of his grip, but he holds me even more tightly. He isn't laughing now, and his grip hurts. I don't mean to, but I am crying. Daddy is standing by the door to the bedroom area and watching. He tells Uncle Sonny that it's OK, to let me do whatever I want to do. But Uncle Sonny is still holding me, so tightly that I can't move. Ma tells him to put me down. But Uncle Sonny is like a drunk man now, his face gets all squiggly and he tells Daddy to go inside the bedroom. Daddy goes. I can't see Ma. She is behind Uncle Sonny, and I can't move in his tight grip. Then he throws me over his shoulder and follows Daddy into the bedroom. This is horrid. I scream, loudly and then louder, because I don't know if they are hearing me. He puts me on the bed next to Tara, who is lying down next to Mummy. Tara is looking at me, she looks afraid. Her thumb is in her mouth. She doesn't suck her thumb. Or maybe she does only when she is in her bed. She slides her hand just a little under my body. I am no longer crying, but it is as if all of me has gotten stiff. Uncle Sonny tells me very sternly to be quiet and to stay there. But there is no air in this room, and I can't breathe. Daddy lies down next to Mummy. I can't move. I am frozen. Uncle Sonny is standing by the bed. He won't leave. The room smells different from when Ma and I used to own it. These people are supposed to be leaving, Daddy says they are going to leave, but it is taking a long time for them to go. I decide to quietly disappear into the sheets and wait for this man who used to be Uncle Sonny to leave, then I'll get up quietly and I'll leave the room without anyone knowing, and I'll run to Ma and Pa.

He turns and walks to the door, and my body begins to relax. He opens the door, exits the room, and pulls the door in behind him. But then I hear the door being locked from outside. I leap from the bed and run to the door and try to open it, but I can't. It really is locked. I bang on it. I call Ma and Pa. I can't breathe. I hear myself calling Ma and Pa, but I don't know if anyone else hears me. I bang and I shout. At least, I think I am shouting. The people on the bed don't move. They seem to have fallen asleep. I scream. I know I am screaming, because I can hear myself. I bang on the door until my hands hurt. I lean on the door and slide down on the ground, at the foot of the door, kicking it, kicking and kicking. How are they sleeping? I press my face to the floor to try to see under the door, but I can only see a bit of the floor outside the door. I curl up and press my knees against the door, I straighten out and lie against it, as far away as possible from the bed. I press and press myself, thinking I can become the door, or somehow move right through it. I think I am crying still, but now I, too, can't hear my own voice.

*

The most wonderful thing has happened. Tara and I spent the day with my cousins, at Uncle Sonny and Auntie Stella's house. I was afraid of Uncle Sonny, but he took us to the ice-cream man and bought cherry ice-cream palettes for all of us. And now he's brought us back home. And this is the wonderful thing: the family's suitcases, the trunks they came with from Ireland and lots of boxes, are all at the back door, and two of the workers from the factory are taking them downstairs and placing them on the bed of one of the smaller trucks.

Tara is excited. She is skipping around the boxes and bags, hitting everything as she goes. She stops at a basket in which is packed her big yellow teddy bear and some of Anil's toys—his trucks—and a blackboard Pa gave us. I look into the box to see if my black-and-white Scottie is in there. It isn't. In a high voice Tara asks, What's going on, what's going on? And Daddy pulls her and me to him. He stoops down and explains to us that they are going to the new house and they will spend that very night there.

I too am excited, because this means they are not going to be in our house anymore. The blackboard is half mine, but that's OK. Tara can have it. I am about to get my room back and I will now be able to sleep in there with Ma again. Daddy asked me several times over the last few days if I'd like to go with them to the new house. That way, he said, Tara and I would always be together. Each time I said, No, thanks. He asks me now again, why don't I come and spend the first night with them in the new house? Ma holds up a little bag, offering it to me. She says, Look, I packed an overnight bag for you. Your pyjamas are in here, and a toothbrush, and your colouring pencils. Just go for the night.

I take the bag from her, open it, and shake everything from it onto the floor, and I say no. I remember to say, Thank you. No, thank you.

*

The house is quiet, and we are back to how it used to be. It's very quiet. But every so often Anil's and Tara's voices rise up in my head. Hers is excited and asking questions, and telling me to do things this way or that way. And Anil's is doing what Barlow calls yehn-yehing. It's as if their voices are ghost voices, and that is all that remains of them in our house. Maybe I miss Tara.

I sit on Pa's lap in his rocking chair. He hugs me tightly and plays with my hair. He points out the first star of the night and, as always, tells me to make a wish. I mustn't tell anyone what I wish for, but we have our house back to ourselves so that means wishing on stars works. He sings softly. I fall asleep, and when Ma comes to take me from him, I hold on tighter and feel my heart begin to speed, until I realize it is my Ma; then I turn and grab on to her.

FIVE

We are on the way to visit Tara. Mr. Monty is driving. I am taking her cherry candies. We have reached Marabella and are going very slowly because of the traffic. Ma says the traffic is *heavy*, but I wonder how she knows. You'd have to put it all in a bag and put it on the scale to know if it is heavy, like Polly does when she is weighing flour or sugar. That is a good joke; I will tell Tara about it when I see her. We pass a cinema where, close to the road, there are many vendors' stalls. The ones selling coconuts have jitneys behind their stalls with mountains of coconuts on them. And some sell raw oysters, too. I look at Pa to see if he is watching the oysters piled up on the tables. I wonder if he will ask Mr. Monty to stop here. But he isn't watching them. I can feel the salty slipperiness in my mouth. But no oysters for us anymore. There is a man selling bottles of mauby, too. I just look at the bottles and the taste is in my mouth. Licorice, cloves, sweet. Sometimes, after the football match, Pa would buy mauby instead of coconut water from a vendor man at the park. The mauby man would open a bottle for Pa and he'd pour some in a glass for me. The men by the stalls would take a long drink and then say, Aaah. I would say, Aaah, too, but softly. And the vendor man would say things like, Boss, how your girl-child does like mauby so? Not so, this is what you call a man's drink?

Maybe mauby is a vendor drink that Tara's daddy would like because it comes in a bottle. I want to suggest we buy a bottle to take for him, but I don't.

There are too many people walking on the sidewalks—they pass us because the line of cars is moving slowly. The walking people look hot and tired. Some carry baskets full of vegetables, and those baskets are probably heavy. You don't have to weigh them to know this. You can tell by the way they walk, passing their basket from one hand to the next, putting it down, wiping their forehead with a cloth, then picking the basket up again. They do everything so slowly. It's because of the heat. Beggars come to the car and tap Pa's window and put their fingers inside the open space. Pa shoos them away and rolls up his window almost to the top. He tells Ma to keep me away from the door and not to let me roll my window down. Mr. Monty can keep his window down, though, and he has one hand on the steering wheel, the other arm hanging out the window. He keeps sucking his teeth as the taxis swerve in and out in front of us, and they stop every minute in the middle of the road to let out and pick up passengers. Farther along, vendors are making rotis on coal pots. I can see the flames through the little window in the coal pot. They fan the flames, and themselves. The smell of the burning coals and the ghee on iron tawas makes me want to eat one of their rotis, but Ma never buys food from roadside vendors.

I can see the silver Guaracara River bridge now. I hope they don't live on the other side of the bridge, because if we have to cross it, we'll be in Pointe-à-Pierre, where the Texaco refinery is. There are big silver tanks with ladders running up their sides, and all around are giant silver pipes like climbing frames, and thin tall chimneys taller than the tallest buildings you've ever seen, but out of those chimneys come flames—not smoke but real fire. Orange-and-red fire, and sometimes even blue. When you drive near to one of them, you can even hear the roar of the fire rushing up through the chimney. Over there, on that side of the bridge, it smells terrible, like gas and rotten eggs, and I always get a headache when we cross the bridge, and always, always, always feel like throwing up. Ma knows I get sick in Pointe-à-Pierre. I don't want us to go any further. I want us to turn back and go home now. I begin to cry, and Pa turns around and asks me what stupidness I am starting up with, that we are not going into the refinery, and in any case, whenever we go to Port of Spain we have to drive through that part of the island and I don't complain, so why am I making such a fuss now? That's not true. I do complain. I look to Ma and whisper that I don't want to go to those people's house anymore, that I want to go home. She shakes my shoulders and she hits me, not hard, but it still hurts, not where she tapped me on my shoulder but in my heart, and she tells me to behave myself, that we will not go into Pointe-à-Pierre, we will turn off the main road well before the bridge.

I slump low and lie back in the seat. I don't want to look out at anything anymore. I just look at my shoes. I want to eat the sour cherry candies. But they are in a basket in the trunk with bananas and apples. I rest my shoes on the back of Mr. Monty's seat and I push. He turns and looks at me, he shakes his head at me, and then turns back to look at the road again. Ma hits my legs and tells me to sit back in the seat properly. I keep my legs on the back of the seat, but I don't press anymore. I won't look at her. She reaches over and pulls me onto her lap.

Just before we reach the bridge, the car turns off the main road onto a side street. There are a few houses when we turn onto this road, but none up ahead, and it is scary, because there are dark green mangrove trees on either side of the road, and you can see the sea. If we keep driving, we'll fall into the sea. But we're turning off this road onto another street I couldn't see before. It is narrower and has many potholes, some of them very large. I can't see the sea anymore. On both sides an open drain runs all along. There are a few houses—very small and low, like Sita's family's house, each with a little veranda in front but no fences around it. Long boards reach from the roadway over the drain and onto the land with the houses. I wouldn't want to go to those houses because you'd have to cross the drain on those narrow sagging boards. I sit up and look carefully, troubled that Tara might now be living in one of these houses. We turn again, onto another street, and here there are no more houses, just a long, long, long stretch of road with a mangrove jungle on one side and tall unruly bush and wild trees on the other. It looks as if the road is just going to end at a wall of jungle that seems to grow onto the road itself; it is so dense you can't see through it.

There is a small bend in the road, and suddenly, through the trees, I can see a tall yellow house, a concrete house on white-painted concrete posts.

A high chain-link fence surrounds this house. Daddy is making his way from the veranda down a long steep set of stairs. Mummy has come through the front door onto the porch, holding Tara's and Anil's hands, leading them, very slowly, down the stairs. Daddy opens out the two sides of the big metal gate, and Mr. Monty drives the car in, onto the concrete paving beneath the house, and parks next to Daddy's car.

When we get out of the car, I am shy. Ma pushes me forward and tells me to kiss Mummy and Daddy. Daddy smells of cigarettes. I give Tara the sour cherries from the basket, and she wants to kiss me. I let her, but I don't return the kiss. The yard is big, just as Daddy said it was, but not like our Selvon Street yard, which has, in the front, Ma's beautiful rose bushes, poinsettias along the silver fence, an arbour with a creeping fern and pink-and-white anthuriums beneath; there are no flowers here, no pretty plants, just grass everywhere, and it's not even nice grass—it's knotgrass. It's what grows in Sita's backyard, and that's what she calls it. It spreads out flat, but with long leaves.

Pa and Daddy walk around the yard, and Mummy shows Ma the door to the maid's room underneath the house. The maid's name is Maureen. We haven't met her yet. Tara tears open the plastic bag with her teeth. She gives me one of the round, hard, sugary, pink-and-white-striped candy balls and puts one in her mouth. I put mine in my mouth, too. Tara's eyes flutter and her face is all scrunched up. They are so sour and so sweet that my mouth becomes like all the parts of a rose, first like a tight-tight bud that doesn't want to open up, but it's also filling up with sour spit, and then it feels prickly, and then the sourness goes away and sweetness comes like an open flower.

Tara wants Ma to come upstairs and see her room. She is holding on to Ma's hand. I meet up with Pa and Daddy just as Pa says he will send one of his men bright and early tomorrow morning to cut the grass and tidy up the yard, and to clean the open drain at the front of the house.

There is a long set of stairs at the back of the house, too, painted red, but it only has a railing on one side. Maureen has come down those stairs partway and bends to see us. Mummy introduces her to Ma, and Tara says to her, This is my sister. Her name is Anjula, but we call her Anju. You can call her Anju, too. Maureen waves to me.

We use the stairs at the front that have railings on both sides. The veranda at the top of the stairs is very small, with only two chairs on it. I wonder where everyone will sit. Standing on the veranda, you look across the road and all you see beyond is a deep green mangrove jungle stretching far into the distance. Between this house and the sea, there is, it seems, nothing but flatness, swamp, and mangrove trees. You can't see any buildings, or electricity or telephone poles or lines. It is almost evening, so the sky is yellowy blue, but still it is blinding.

I wait until everyone has gone inside, and when no one is watching, I go back out onto the top of the stairs and climb on the railing of the banister. I lean over—careful first that nobody sees me, and second that I climb up no higher than the middle railing. Bending forward and looking as far as possible to the right side of the house, beyond more mangroves, I see some tall trees that look like mango and pommecythere trees, and between the branches and leaves the tops of the chimneys from the Pointe-à-Pierre oil refinery. Red-and-yellow flames shoot up and pulse out of them. There is a faint smell of bad eggs. I can feel my stomach somersault. I am about to go inside the house and tell Ma that I want to throw up—that perhaps we need to leave and go back to our home now—when I feel someone's hand on my back. I turn and see the maid, Maureen. She says, Careful, but she doesn't pull me off. Her hand remains lightly on my back, and this tells me I can stay there and look out. In an instant the smell goes away with a strong breeze coming in over the mangrove, making the jungle move as if it's doing a slow dance.

Tara has a bedroom, and she sleeps in that room all by herself. Her bed is as big as the one in our front room. There is a jalousie window in her room with louvres, and on its exterior, mosquito netting. I wonder what she can see through the window, but I don't want to go inside the room.

Ma tells Tara I will come and spend the night here with her sometime. I know that is not likely to happen, but I don't say anything. I wouldn't want to be there without Ma. Tara's parents are thin. They don't have soft, big, round tummies like Ma's and Pa's. And they're always correcting children. It's as if we are always doing something the wrong way. Hold the knife in the other hand. Don't wave the fork in the air. No elbows on the table. Close your mouth when you're chewing. Offer others before helping yourself with food. Say thank you. Say please. Say excuse me. Don't interrupt—but if we didn't interrupt, they'd never listen to us. We have to shout, Excuse me, a thousand times before they look at us, and then they say, Can't you see the adults are speaking?

*

Ma asked me if I didn't think it was a good idea to go and keep Tara company sometimes, especially since Tara doesn't have anyone to play with and I am her older sister. I used to be able to talk with Ma, and if she asked a question, I could answer. But I am learning that not all questions grown-ups ask are meant to be answered, at least not truthfully, not saying, that is, what you really think. They ask a question in such a way that they are already telling you the answer, what you are supposed to say, by the way they ask it. *Don't you think it is a good idea?* means it *is* a good idea, and if you don't think it is, then you don't know a good idea from a bad one or you are being a troublesome child.

When I didn't answer, she said that since Tara and I go to the same school now, it would be easier for her, and for Mummy, if the driver could take us from—and bring us back to—the same house. She said that on weekdays I could go to Tara's house after school, we could do our homework together, and then I could stay by her and Pa on weekends. Tara could come with me, too.

But I didn't have to think. This is a very bad idea. I didn't say this out loud, but for a moment I wondered if, instead, Tara could live here with us—with Ma and Pa and me. I could say it like this: But isn't it a better idea if Tara comes and lives here with us then? Maybe Ma would laugh at how smart I am, but lately she isn't in a laughing mood. I feel weak, as if I have no muscles anymore, and I think she feels weak, too, but it's more as if she's very tired.

If Tara did come here to live with us, I'd have to make sure she never went over to Sita's house. I don't want Chandra to do to her what he used to do to me.

But even if she lived here, she would not play with me anyway. Not in the ways I like to play. She likes to read and to play with dolls—she doesn't like to play cowboys and Indians or to try making fires by rubbing stones or pieces of wood together. I haven't been able to make a fire doing this, but I want to keep trying, and it would be very nice if she tried with me. She can't make kites, and even if I made one for her, she isn't interested in learning how to fly it. I don't understand this. They are so beautiful, and when you're holding the string of one that is high up in the sky and the string tugs at your hand, it's as if the kite is speaking to you in its language, telling you all about the sky and the clouds and everything it is seeing when it looks down to where you're standing. I try to explain this feeling to her, but she just smiles and nods. She doesn't like to run around or play catch and hide-and-seek with Colin and Sheldon. She says they are boys. That they are too rough. Once when she asked me to play doll's house with her, I told her I didn't like playing with dolls or playing house, and she said, Why not? You're a girl. Girls have dolls. You can have one of mine.

She thinks I am a girl. Everyone thinks I am a girl. But when I grow up, I will be a boy, and Colin and Sheldon will let me be the leader. Tara doesn't play with us, so she doesn't understand that girls get captured and die.

I have this feeling that I am not going to get anything that I want. More and more, it seems to be this way. Everything is confusing, but I'm not sure if I am the one who is confused, or if everyone else is confused.

*

Pa says I am causing a lot of unhappiness all around. I am making Tara sad, and Mummy and Daddy, too. I ask if he and Ma are sad. He says they would be happier, in truth, if I were more helpful.

Ma and Pa never used to say these kinds of things to me. Before, when I cried, they did what I wanted them to do. Not anymore. Now I have to think hard, and very fast, about how to answer.

I tell him I will be more helpful: from now on, I will eat all my dinner until my plate is completely clean, as if the dog next door had come over and licked it all up, and I will also help clear the table. I will put my shoes side by side by the back door. I will not make any noise when he is trying to sleep, and if Colin and Sheldon and Tara are here, I will make sure they are all quiet, too. He kisses my head and rubs my cheek with the back of his hand and says I can be a helpful child by spending a few nights of the week at Tara's house. He says if I love them, I will do what they are asking me to do and try to stay with Tara for at least two nights in a row. They wouldn't love me any less if I spent time over there. In fact, if I helped out in that way, Pa says, it would make them love me even more. Which means they don't already love me as much as I thought they did.

*

Ma's words are: Sometimes a person has no choice and has to do what they are told. But just because a person has no choice doesn't mean they are happy or willing to do what they are told to do. You just have to fill your chest up with air, don't let it out, don't look left, don't look right, just keep your eyes down on the ground. And don't say anything. Definitely no crying. That doesn't work.

So I spend a night there, in the Marabella house, sometimes. Even though I do like being with Tara, my mind is almost always on Selvon Street.

I draw and colour and we play snakes and ladders and checkers. Sometimes we play hide-and-seek, and when it's my turn to hide, and she is getting close to where I'm hiding, instead of letting her find me, I jump out and scare her and we both run around screaming and the two of us, just the two of us, can sound like the schoolyard when it is full of all the children during recess, romping like wild horses. That is what our teachers say, that we get on as if we are wild horses romping and neighing.

You can play with others, do what you are told to do, and laugh and speak nicely, but all of that comes from the outside of

your body. Inside you feel the sadness coming, and you try but you can't stop it, but you mustn't show this. That's OK, because that way you don't make others unhappy, too, or make them angry.

Her parents can be very strict sometimes. Especially her mother, Mummy. Once, we had to decide which of us would get the first turn in snakes and ladders. We were sitting at the kitchen table in their house, and Mummy was behind us with Maureen preparing dinner. They were talking to each other, not paying us any attention. We began to do the *eeny meeny miny moe* rhyme, and when I finished the second line of the verse, I got a horrible surprise of a shove and a slap across my head, and there was Mummy stooping down staring at me, telling me very sharply never ever to let her hear me say that word again. I was too stunned to answer, but I didn't know what she meant. Tara asked, Which word, Mummy? And Mummy hesitated and whispered the word. Why, Mummy? asked Tara. Everybody says it. And her mummy said, It isn't a good word. It's not nice. It's a very bad word. Tara was about to protest, and very loudly Mummy snapped, Because I said so. Don't ever let me hear it come out of your mouths again.

She was really angry. I didn't understand why. We, my cousins and I, always say that poem when we need to decide who wins or loses a turn in a game. Tara and I just sat at the table quietly. We didn't continue with the game. I was even afraid to make noise packing up the board, the counters, and the die. Maureen began to wash the dishes, and I was happy the water was running so loudly. Mummy carried on making dinner. She and Maureen were quiet now. I watched Mummy. Her face was very strict. Then, after a while, she came over to us and stooped between Tara and me and said that instead of the word she didn't want us to use, we should say *penny*. Then she got softer and said, Let's say it together. Eeny meeny miny moe, catch a penny by its toe. Tara said, That's silly. What's a penny? Pennies don't have toes. I said to Tara, Let's just do it as she says. And Mummy said, As *who* says? I said, You. She said, Yes, but who am I? I asked, Mummy? That's right, she said, and explained, You don't refer to adults as *she*. *She* is the cat's mother.

We began to giggle. It was as if Mummy had gone crazy. Pennies with toes and cats' mothers—we didn't even have a cat. But over my laughter, even though there were tears in my eyes, I said, Let's just do as Mummy says.

When Daddy came home from his new office in Marabella—he only works at the hospital in San Fernando sometimes now—Mummy told on us. He said he wanted to have a word with us. Whenever he says that, it means there is something serious, no laughing matter, he might even be annoyed with us, and we are probably about to get in trouble. It was about the word we are not to use. I held my arms tightly against myself, clasping my fingers behind my back, and tried to look like a statue. But he wasn't annoyed. He was nice and just explained why the word we'd said was a bad word. He sat on the floor and had Tara sit on his lap, and he coaxed me, too, to come down on the floor with them. I slowly brought myself down and sat in front of him. He asked how our day was, but I don't think he was listening to our answer. He did not comment on what we said, but rather, holding Tara's hands in his, began to talk to us slowly, saying we must have noticed that there are, all around us, different kinds of people—like Maureen, like us, like Mr. Tang in the shop by Pa. We are all different because our skin colours and hair are different. I wanted to say, Yes, I know, red and yellow, black and white, but I just let him speak.

We are of different races, he said, but our differences are superficial, which means they are on the surface, not deep, that is, and therefore not important. All people are the same. We all have brains, hearts, tummies, and although the parts we go to the bathroom with might be different for boys and girls, basically everyone from all races are the same. Tara giggled when he said this last part about the bathroom. I thought about Chandra and about Clydie, and I didn't laugh. He made a drawing with a pen on a white piece of paper, of the outline of a person, and he drew the brain, the lungs, the heart, the tummy, the part called a liver, and all the bones in the arms and legs, and he drew ribs, too. He asked what colour was the person in the drawing? I asked if he wanted coloured pencils, but he said no, he wanted us to tell him what colour the person was, just as he'd drawn it. I understood then what he was saying.

So colour, he said, is superficial. But people can be unkind and can treat one another badly all because of superficial differences. Some of the biggest problems in the world are when people from one colour group, or race, treat those of another badly. The word we are no longer allowed to use is what is called a slur, which is the same thing as an insult, and is meant to be very hurtful. It has been used to be unkind, even hateful, to Negroes. It is a way of showing hatred to a single person or to that entire group of people. When he said that, Tara and I gasped and said we'll never say it again and we apologized for having said it earlier. I wondered if Maureen thought we hated her when we used it, but she didn't show any hurt. Then Tara said, But what about pennies, pennies don't have toes, and he started to tickle her, and I leaned back, jumped to my feet, and ran off really fast because I don't like tickling. I asked him later why we have to say *penny*. Why not something else like *wave*, because at least waves have undertows. He repeated the rhyme using *wave* instead of *penny* and talked about the music of rhymes. He showed how *wave* was too short a word to sound good, so we decided to say *current*. Eeny meeny miny moe, catch a current by its toe, if it hollers, let it go, eeny meeny miny moe. That's what we and our friends say now.

*

I again have no choice—but this time it is supposed to be for two nights in a row.

Daddy sits at the kitchen table writing notes in a large book like Pa's ledger and smoking a cigarette. I sit here, too, drawing a picture on the largest sheet of paper I ever drew on. Mummy bought it for me, and a tin of coloured pencils, twelve of them, at a store she said was an art shop. She said Pa told her I liked to draw. I draw a picture of the house they live in, the fence around the house, and the trees all around. I like to draw fences because the wires of the fence twist together to make diamond shapes, so in between the poles you just have to repeat the diamond shape almost a hundred times. You have to use a grey-coloured pencil for the fence. I have an idea. I will give this picture to Mummy. I draw twelve mosquitoes in the sky—for this, a black pencil—and then I put mosquito coils—the darkest green in the tin—with smoke coming out of them, four of those, one in each corner of the paper. But Mummy thinks they are flies. I ask, Would you like to guess again, and she says, Bats? That's close but not correct, I say. I stare at the mosquito coils to give her a hint, and then I put my hand in one corner and slowly unfold my index finger to sort of point at the coil and the smoke, but I don't think she sees what I am doing. She tries again, and says, Are they birds? I nod. She looks pleased.

When Mummy is out of the room and Daddy gets up to get himself a drink, Tara reaches over and takes his lit cigarette from the ashtray, puts it to her mouth, and blows on it. He sees and shouts at her to put it down, but he is laughing, too. She doesn't put it down but is about to blow on it again. He takes it away from her, sits back down, and pulls Tara up onto his lap. He asks if she wants to learn to smoke, and she excitedly says yes. He explains how to do it and then puts the cigarette to her lips and coaches her along. Suddenly she is choking and spitting, and her eyes are watering, and she jumps off his lap and says that that is horrible. He asks if I want to learn. I don't, but he insists I try. I put the cigarette between my lips and instantly begin to choke. It is bitter, or maybe sour, and it is as if there is a fire in my mouth. I retch and throw up on the kitchen floor. Not like real vomit, but just a lot of watery, frothy spit, and my eyes burn and are overflowing with tears—but I'm not crying, and my nose is all mucusy, running like a tap.

Daddy laughs, as if it is the funniest thing he ever saw, and Tara says, Let me try again, let me try again. He gets serious and says no, that's enough, and that smoking is a nasty habit, and we mustn't put his cigarettes in our mouths ever again. We ask why, if it is a nasty habit, does he smoke. He says only foolish people smoke. You can get addicted to it, which means you keep wanting it and have no control over wanting it. And smoking a lot can make a person sick. Tara says, But you don't get sick, and with his cigarette in his mouth he tousles both our heads and says foolishness is his sickness. He gives us cups of Coca-Cola. He is quiet for a while and then says that we are sisters and I am the older sister. I already know this and don't know why he is saying this, but it makes me shy. Then he comes by me and wraps his arms around me, which makes me uncomfortable, and he says I must look after Tara, and after Anil, too, because Anil is my little brother. He tells me he is very happy I am spending two nights with them. I hadn't realized Mummy was by the door to the kitchen and stood watching. She tells him we are bound to wet our beds, drinking just before bedtime.

*

On the morning of the third day, I am ready. I dressed and put my little clothing bag together, and another bag with my drawing book and the colouring pencils. When I was drawing the picture of their house, I thought about tearing it out and giving it to Mummy. I thought about it several times, imagining her being so pleased with the drawing, but even happier that I made something for her. I thought about it again last night, in the middle of the night when I couldn't sleep. But when I woke up this morning, I decided it was better if I took the drawing for Ma.

I am not sure if Mummy will drive me, or Daddy. I keep waiting, but it doesn't seem as if they are getting ready. Maybe Mr. Monty is going to come for me? I don't want to make a fuss, so with my bag on the couch in the living room near the front door, I just stay quiet and wait and watch.

The phone rings, and Mummy, in the kitchen, answers it. You can tell it is Ma from the way Mummy is speaking. I know they are discussing how I will get back home, as there is nothing else for them to talk about. Mummy just keeps saying, Uh huh. Uh huh. Uh huh. That doesn't go on for long at all, and then she comes into the living room and tells me that Ma isn't well, that Mr. Monty is taking her to the doctor. She says that Ma asked her to tell me that she'd like me to stay here and play with Tara for a little while longer and then she'll come and pick me up later.

I keep my two bags packed and ready. I don't want to play downstairs, where we are allowed to run about and scream as much as we want. I ask Tara if she wants to read. She says, But you don't like reading. I ask her to give me an interesting book and maybe I'll like it. I follow her to her bookshelf, on which are many books that all look the same, with nice but similar covers, and she runs her fingers along the books thoughtfully. She picks one. This one will help you to love reading, she says. There are pictures in it. The story isn't long and the words aren't difficult. You'll really like it. It's about a girl and she is adventurous. She is like you. We sit on the long couch in the living room from where I can see my bags, she reading and so quickly absorbed that within seconds she is almost lying on the couch, no longer even aware that I am next to her. I read the first page, but I am listening to the road and wondering what the doctor will say is wrong with Ma, how she is feeling, and what if she doesn't feel well for the whole day? She'll need me then.

After lunch, I ask Mummy to phone Ma and see if she is well yet, and ask when she is coming. Mummy says there is no point calling as Ma is probably still at the hospital. I ask if the doctor sent her to the hospital. Mummy says she made a mistake; she meant that Ma is probably still at her doctor's office. I ask why Ma didn't just go to Daddy's office; she wouldn't have had to wait there. But Mummy doesn't answer. She bites her lower lip a lot, especially when you're trying to tell her something and she isn't paying you any attention. She is always thinking about something else, but she doesn't ever say what it is she's thinking about. Sometimes Tara says, Mummy, what are you thinking about? And she answers, What is in my mind is for my mind only, none of your business. But other times, when she's not happy with us, she says in a very stern voice, You want me to give you a piece of my mind? I don't answer, but Tara sometimes puts her hand over her mouth and bends her head down and shakes her head and says, Oh, no-no-no, and that can actually make Mummy begin to laugh.

Time as long as a skipping rope laid out flat on the ground passes. Carib grackles dart across the living room window, one after the other, from the left to the right. You can know they are Carib grackles and not anis because of their long, pointed beaks, and because they have bright eyes the colour of yellow sour cherries. Frank told me that. Frank knows all the birds. He'd know them all here. A small flock of black-and-yellow birds flies past. I think they are bananaquits. Even as they fly, you can see the white under their necks and the stripe above their eyes. People like to catch them and put them in cages. I hope these won't get caught by anyone. Frank once told me they are easy to catch because they like people and trust them. He said, If you put a piece of banana in your hand and open it out, one might come and sit on your hand and eat from it. I lean back against the couch, watching a seagull lazily gliding, rising higher and higher until it is out of view of the window.

I must have dozed, because suddenly I hear Mummy speaking on the phone in the kitchen. Tara's book is flat on her lap and her head is against the couch back, her eyes closed, her mouth wide open. She reached her hand over—I don't know when, I didn't feel it—and is clutching the edge of my shorts even as she sleeps. I sit up and gently push her hand away; then I get up quietly and tiptoe to the kitchen door. I wasn't quiet enough because Mummy has turned and sees me. She watches me for a few seconds, then, using her curled fingers, calls me to her. She says into the phone, Here she is, and hands it to me. I put the receiver to my ear, but I don't say anything. Ma says, Anju darling, you there? I turn my back to Mummy slightly and put my hand around the mouthpiece. Ma asks how I am. I whisper that I am waiting for her, that I am ready to come home. She asks if I am not having a good time. From the side of my eye, I am able to see Mummy standing there. In a soft voice I say, Yes, but I want to come back to take care of you. She laughs and tells me I am a sweet child, and that her illness isn't anything to worry about. Before I can say anything, she adds that even though it is nothing serious, she still isn't feeling all that strong, she is tired and needs some rest. Right now, she says, she isn't able to take care of me. Whispering, I say, But I will take care of you; I will put Limacol on your head for you and let you sleep. I could lie next to you and read a book while you sleep. I am having to swallow a lot, and some of my words aren't even coming out. I want to say, I love you, Ma, but then I'm glad I didn't say it, because I might have made a mistake and said, I love you, Mummy, which I remember I was once, a long time ago, supposed to say into the phone. She says she just needs total rest and she will take tablets the doctor gave her and I mustn't worry. I don't say anything in response, because I am wondering if children can get what some adults get, the thing called heart attacks, because I feel as if my chest, where my heart is, is very tight. She is saying something, but I can't hear her. I tell myself sharply, as if Barlow were speaking to me, but inside of my brain for no one but me to hear, to behave myself right this minute. And then I hear Ma say that when I do come, I can put the Limacol on her head. I say, Tara gave me a book and there is a girl in the book, and she wants to learn to fly planes, and even though she is just a girl she got her licence to be a pilot. She says, Mhm, that's nice. I wait and then she adds, In any case, in truth, there is another problem, which because her head has been hurting her so much she forgot all about: the car broke down just after Mr. Monty brought her back from the hospital. I say, You mean the doctor. She just says, Yes, and carries on, saying that Mr. Monty has taken it to the mechanic to get it fixed and I'll have to spend that night with Tara, and then, tomorrow, please God, she'll see me.

Three nights. Three nights in a row. I don't say anything. I think Ma is still speaking, but it is as if my ears have stopped working. Mummy is speaking to me, and her voice sounds as if there is a bag over her head. I think she is saying for me to let her have the phone. I keep it at my ear, but she takes it out of my hand.

Those are words that Barlow usually says: *Tomorrow, please God.* So when I say my prayers tonight, I, too, will say, Tomorrow, please God.

*

The next day, Ma and I speak on the phone again. I need to let Mummy take care of me, she tells me. Again.

I knew it. I knew this was how it was going to be. I want to fall down right there, on the ground in the kitchen, and kick the cupboards. I want to pull out the drawer with all the knives and forks and dump them on the floor. But I don't think anyone can tell that that is what I want to do. I just quietly ask, Why? Why can't I come back home? Are you still unwell? In a firmer voice than usual, she says, Anju, darling, please don't give any trouble. Do as I say. For my sake. For your Pa's sake. Look, when you get older, things will change, you will understand more, and then you can do whatever you want. But not now, OK?

*

I don't remember how many nights it has been now.

I don't know why, but I tell Ma I drew a picture for her and that by the afternoon she should be feeling better and Mr. Monty should come for me. Even as I tell myself to stop talking, to be quiet, to not be so silly, words come out of my mouth: I say that I will be a good child, I won't make any noise, I want to come home, I repeat that I made a drawing for her. She says perhaps the drawing would be a nice present to give to Mummy.

In my room, making sure no one sees, I tear the paper with my drawing on it in half, put the two pieces together, and tear those in half. Later, when no one is in the kitchen, I will go to the garbage bin and shove it under stuff in there.

*

I am still in Marabella. I don't remember why anymore. I have lost count of how many nights it has been. Selvon Street seems so far away.

I look out the window in Tara's bedroom every day, hoping to see Pa's blue car, Mr. Monty driving it toward our house with Pa in front beside him and Ma in the back. But I just end up looking at the trees. There are so many birds—kiskadees, bananaquits, semps, all day flying in and out of the trees. There are peekoplats, too, like the ones Sita's brother Chandra keeps in cages, but these ones are free. I wish I were a bird.

Ma and Pa are giving me away.

MARABELLA

SIX

Tara tries to hug me when I'm sleeping. I don't like it.

I dream I am wetting the bed, but I wake up and walk by myself to the bathroom. At my house on Selvon Street, there are three bathrooms upstairs. There is only one here. It is between Anil's bedroom and Mummy and Daddy's. Mummy says she can't live much longer in a house that has only one bathroom for so many people.

I don't go back to bed right away. I make sure Tara is still sleeping, then I go and stand behind the curtain by the window. I open the louvres, pulling them downward slowly so their squeaking doesn't wake anyone, and I scan the yard to make sure no one is down there. Then I angle the louvres so I can look out at the jungle on the other side of the fence. Crickets sing—that's what Maureen says they do, they sing—and at night there are a million-million of them singing, all at once. It's a chorus. I try to make their singing sound—not at night, but in the daytime—but I am not able to. Even when I use my plastic whistle, I can't make it. But something in the jungle does have the watery sound that my whistle makes. I wish I knew everything there is to know.

If there isn't a moon, it is black-black-black outside. The leaves move about in the breeze, and sometimes something will fall. It could be a coconut, or a mango maybe, or papayas. Sometimes there is a low, slow whistle, four notes. It could be a human being calling to another person, both hiding in the bushes, pretending to sound like an owl or a potoo bird, waiting for the right time to crawl into our yard and break into this house. I don't know which it is, person or night bird, so I crouch back a little behind the curtain.

Things screech, and grunt. Sometimes a scream. An animal, I think. Maybe a rabbit, or a monkey that got caught by another animal and is being killed. People say roosters crow like alarm clocks, early in the morning, but I know they crow all night long—and even in the daytime. Moths fling themselves against the wire netting on the window, right near my face, frightening me. The sulphur smell is strong at night.

Making sure the sound of the rusting metal does not awaken Tara, I slowly angle the louvres upward to watch the sky. There are millions and millions of stars, some so close that you want to touch them, some far away, and some so tiny they are smaller than a grain of salt.

Even though the appearance of the night's first star is long past, I wish from one to the next, playing a game I made up called musical wishes. But I am not sure wishing works anymore. Maybe a person is only allowed a few wishes, because there are so many other people who also have things that they want—like Pa, yes, but Ma, too, and Tara, and Sita and Sheldon and Colin. And Frank and Polly and Maureen. And Mr. Tang in the shop on the corner. And the people who live next door to Ma and Pa. And all all all the people we pass when we drive through the towns.

When the moon is big and round and full, there is a kind of blue light over everything and you can see the black shapes of trees, especially the shape of the palm tree and the coconut tree branches. And you can even see birds, owls maybe, or maybe they are bats, flying across the silvery-blue moon-sky.

This house, the yard, the lonely area with all the bush around us, would be a good place for a Boo Boo man to hide in. I don't think I am being a good child. I am giving trouble because I don't want to be here. There isn't anyone here to protect me, and yet no Boo Boo man has ever come for me. Ma is right. Barlow's Boo Boo man isn't real.

*

Tara doesn't like playing with guns, but sitting on the back stairs, I show her how I can take the roll of caps and pull it out into a long strip and how, when I hit each little brown mole on the strip with a big smooth stone, it goes *clap*, the same loud noise as when I pull the trigger of my gun. She takes some of the rolls of caps from my bag and bangs all the moles, one after the other—*clap clap clap clap clap*. It gives off a smell of burning sulphur and paper.

But Mummy does not like us playing with the gun. She takes it away, and the caps, and gives us bottles of soapy water and flat things like plastic spoons with a hole where the bowl of the spoon should be. You dip that into the bottle and then blow on the hole and that's where lots of bubbles come out, one tumbling on top of the other, some float up into the air, six, nine, a dozen single bubbles shimmering in the colours of the rainbow. They don't make any sound.

*

Chicken doesn't come from the smelly, noisy market with all the vendors anymore. Mummy goes to the supermarket across from the Marabella cinema to buy all the food and vegetables. I like going there with her—it smells like old, rotting onions. The good thing is that Maureen doesn't have to kill and clean the chickens. They come already plucked of all their feathers, headless, too, wrapped tight in plastic and frozen hard. It's so heavy and hard and cold, if one falls off the counter onto your foot, it could break your bones. If you sniff the package, it smells like old freezer ice, but still, I just have to see the lump of stiff featherless body sitting on the counter in the kitchen, and the smell of singed feathers and wood fire fills my nose and brain, and my body remembers Barlow's hands bathing me, smelling of garlic and raw chicken.

I don't need anyone to bathe me now. When I had my last birthday, I became seven, but that was a while ago. I have to wait until my next birthday, when I get bigger, and then I will go back to Selvon Street to live with Ma and Pa. It takes so long to become eight. Even though I can dry myself, Maureen likes to wrap the towel around me and rub me down. She takes the length of my hair in the towel and rubs the towel full of hair between both her hands, until my hair is almost dry. It's rough and yet it always feels gentle. Rough and gentle, both at the same time. When she does it, I look at her and her eyes are soft, but she does not look at mine. She is thinking of something, or someone else. I don't mind. On days when there is no school, after lunch, when we are supposed to lie in bed and take a nap—Maureen, too—I get out of the bed quietly and tiptoe all the way out through the kitchen, down the stairs, across the cracked grey concrete, to her room, and I turn the door handle as softly as I can. As soon as it's open, I call her name so she knows it's me. She doesn't open her eyes, she just moves over closer to the wall and calls me with her fingers curling in and out and patting the bed beside her. Her bed is small, and the mattress is thin and lumpy. She puts her arm around me. I don't sleep, but I listen to her breathing. She snores sometimes, and I lie still as a book on a desk.

On weekends Tara and I go over and sleep at my house, too. She never seems to mind coming over. I sleep in the back-room with Pa and she sleeps with Ma in the front room. I don't like Ma to sleep with anybody else, but I am not allowed to make a fuss anymore, so I just go into Pa's bed. It smells like eggnog under his neck, and he hums while he pats my back, until I fall asleep.

*

The mangrove across the road is so dense that, even though I know it is green-coloured, it looks black. In my tin of coloured pencils there isn't such a black that has that greenish feeling in it. Or a green that has a blackish look. When I draw the mangrove, I colour it black, then try to colour over the black with green, but it doesn't come out the way I want it to.

Even though this house is very tall, from here you can't see any other houses, or any buildings except the refinery chimneys, but I don't think chimneys are buildings. Beyond the fence on either side of the house, and at the back, there is all that bush and lots of trees—I know guava, breadfruit trees, sapodilla, and the tall coconut trees. I have counted three different kinds of mango trees in the jungle—there are Julie, doodoose, and starch—and there are breadfruit, dongs, sour cherry, papaya, and banana trees.

The mango trees must be very old because the trunks are fat, and you can see vines with big leaves winding up the trunks and along the branches.

They bear a lot, a lot, a lot of fruit, and the branches get weighed down so low that if I were in there, I might be able to reach some of them. Attached to the trunks, and to the branches, are fat ugly growths, almost black in colour. These are ants' nests. You can see these nests, too, on the coconut tree trunks, and sometimes on electricity poles on the side of the road. There are palm trees inside there, too, grugru, and cabbage palm. The yellow-and-brown cornbirds have nests in the tallest palm trees. All day long, large bird after large bird will swoop in and disappear into the long neck of the nest that hangs down and looks like a sock with a cricket ball in it, and then, out of what looks like a tear in the nest, they will reappear, and with no struggle at all, slip out again and fly off. I stand at the window, one eye on the road, the other gazing out at the land, imagining getting to the fruit before the birds do.

*

One good thing about Tara's house is that the drain has baby fish and tadpoles in it. Mummy has gone shopping and left us with Maureen. Gordon the yardman is hosing down and scrubbing the concrete paving beneath the house. From the veranda I see he has left the gate open. Tara wants to work on a jigsaw puzzle, but I'd rather play outside. I tell her it's no fun being at her house, and if we are just going to be cooped up inside, then I want to go back to my house on Selvon Street. She looks at me for a long while, her face blank. I can't tell what she's thinking and I begin to feel silly. But she leaves the jigsaw puzzle and steps ahead of me, making her way down the back stairs. I grab a knife from the draining board, cut a chunk of cheese that sits on a plate on the counter, and run down the stairs behind her. She's standing there, her back to me, with her arms folded tight. She has an annoyed look. I pull a clothespin from the line and break out the metal spiral piece from the middle. From my pocket I pull a balled-up length of thread and begin to untangle it. She turns her head to watch me but remains with her back to me, and then she spins around, comes over, and takes the tangled thread from me. She pulls at it until there is a length I think will work. I tie it to the metal spiral and pack a tiny piece of the cheese around and onto the metal. Gordon glances at us, but he doesn't stop what he is doing. We walk past him and out the gate. He doesn't call us back. Even when we are on the road, no one calls us back. So we go down a little way, and still no one tries to stop us. And then we reach a good part of the drain.

Tara doesn't want to try, but she stoops, her hands clasped in front of her knees, and she watches. I throw the line into the thick, blue-black, oily water. Grasses on the edge of the drain hang down into it and are covered in the tarry sludge. Little eyes come to the surface, nibble at the cheese, but whenever I yank the clothespin back, no fish has been caught, and the piece of cheese is lost. I do this a few times, until the whole chunk of cheese is gone. Tara says, We're feeding the fish.

A car in the distance is approaching. It's Mummy's car, coming toward us. We run inside, as fast as we can, up the back stairs and into our room. She's not going to be happy. Her shoes clop swiftly toward our door. She pushes open the door hard, rushes at me, and hits me on my head, telling me that I am the eldest, I am supposed to look after Tara, not encourage her in my bad ways. I want to ask why she assumes that I encouraged Tara and that Tara is so innocent. But two things. I don't want Tara to get in trouble, and second, I did encourage her, not the other way around. She tells us we are not to leave the room for one hour. She does not want to hear any talking or whispering. We are to be silent. Read a book or do some homework. Do something constructive. Mummy is quarrelling with Maureen. I am frightened. I didn't mean for Maureen to get in trouble. I try not to cry when I whisper to Tara that I am sorry, but as soon as Tara tells me not to cry, tears come out and roll down my face. She says she liked seeing the little fish in the drain. Whispering behind her hand, she asks if I think there are big fish in there, if maybe one day we can catch a big one and Maureen can cook it for us. First I say, Mummy would be so angry, but you wouldn't get in trouble—I would. Then I ask, You would eat something that comes out of that dirty, smelly water? She covers her mouth with both hands and gasps, and then I don't know why, but she stares at me and starts to laugh. I keep asking, What? And each time I ask, she laughs more. She makes me laugh. I cover my mouth, too, hoping Mummy isn't listening, but she bangs on the door from the outside and shouts, What did I tell you? You want to be in there all afternoon? We stop short, listen, and then we laugh again, but no sound comes from our mouths. We roll on the bed; then, lying on our backs, we thump the bed with our feet, and tears of laughter that are silenced behind our hands run down our cheeks.

*

The coconut trees in the jungle look as if they are racing each other to reach the blue sky with the big puffy white clouds that move so fast that if you block out everything else in your sight and look only at them, you feel dizzy, as if you, too, are moving and might bump into something. I am not afraid of Gordon. He knows the name of every single tree you can see from here, and when he says them, it sounds like he is gargling, or singing in a strange language: mahoe, teak, balata, l'epinet, fat pork, gasparee, wild grape, bois bande. He looks out at the jungle, just like how I look out at the stars at night, and he smiles when he names them—except I don't know stars' names. He tells me that birds and bats eat the fruit of trees that are far from here, and as they fly, they do a poopoo. Their poopoo has seeds in it, he says, and wherever those seeds fall, they will take root—that's how you say it, they take root—and trees will grow wild and bear fruit, wild fruit.

There are snakes here, too. And they come into the yard. Whenever Gordon sees one, he kills it with his cutlass. One time there was one in Maureen's room, and I'm sure that even if we were in the town near the cinema, we would have heard Maureen screaming. I ran down to see what was going on. By that time, he had come out of her room with the headless green snake dangling over his cutlass, and he was laughing as he went toward her with it. She screamed at him, using bad language. I inspected it. It was thin like a vine, shiny, green like a lime, and long—if it were stretched out on the ground and I lay down next to it, which I'd never do, it would be as long as me—and underneath, it was yellowish white with sort of rough lines across it. It was headless, dead, but its body wasn't as limp as I had thought a dead snake's would be. It made a stiff green figure-three shape over the blade of the cutlass. It might have been dead, but it looked like it was moving. He flung the cutlass but didn't let go of it, and the snake slid off and was tossed far over the fence.

And the bats, yes, lots of bats. Sometimes they dart into the house in the evening, and everyone ducks and hides and screams, and Maureen takes the long cobweb broom and pokes them out of the corners where they hang upside down. Mummy is always saying she can't live in this area anymore with all these insects and animals. She isn't happy here. She says she doesn't like it that she and her children are living in a house where she can't even have her brother and his wife over for a sit-down meal. There is no dining room, only the dining table in the kitchen. It is a small house, much smaller than my house on Selvon Street. They should have stayed there, but Daddy wanted a house of his own, a little privacy, and that's why they moved. This is what I understand from all the pieces of conversation—or maybe they are arguments—that I hear but am not supposed to hear.

Pa told Daddy the area is too quiet, too lonely, and Daddy mustn't wait too long to move us to a better area. Daddy said, Of course, but as you know, Rome wasn't built in a day. Even though he wasn't talking to her, Mummy answered, Oh, so you intend to build Rome, I suppose. It wasn't really a question. He said, We'll see. We'll see. Mark my words.

Pa told him not to worry about money. Money is there when the time comes.

*

The last time Pa was here, he said the town's borough council should have the land beyond our yard cleared, because, he said, it is a breeding ground for mosquitoes and, therefore, for malaria. When Daddy said that the entire swamp, which meets up with the sea almost a mile out from our house, would have to be drained to take care of that problem, Mummy said, And while we're waiting for Rome to be built, we will all die of malaria.

Today a truck arrived, full of manure, and the driver backed into the yard and then made the bed of the truck lift so the manure slid out onto the grass at the side of the house. Then some days later, Mummy came home with the trunk of the car full of plants—marigolds, zinnias, geraniums, and gerberas. Gordon dug up the grass near the edge of the concrete, and he mixed the dirt with the manure and made a garden bed that looked to me like the dirt over graves in the cemetery. And Mummy pointed out where to put all the plants and he planted them. On evenings, just as the sun is going down, she waters them. They are all growing well, and the bed no longer looks like a grave. But it doesn't look like the front of the Selvon Street house either, with Ma's rose garden, the fence of poinsettias, and the arbour of anthuriums and climbing ferns.

*

Mummy teaches me many things, like how to set the table. We always have to have napkins—paper napkins if we're eating curry or barbecue, and cloth for everything else—and I must fold them into a perfect triangle—all the sides have to line up properly so no edges stick out. It takes a long time—and you can't place the knife and fork and the spoon just anywhere, or the juice glasses—everything has a place of its own. And when I do it all correctly, especially when I do it without her asking me to, her face gets soft and she says, Un-huh, very good. I am trying to be good.

Anil and Tara spend a lot of time in Mummy's room when she is there, and they lie in the bed next to her. Sometimes they lie on top of her and they even fall asleep like that, and she wraps her arms around them and closes her eyes and maybe she falls asleep, too. I never lie with them on that bed. Well, one time, when Mummy and Daddy went to Port of Spain for the day, and Tara and Anil were having their after-lunch nap, and Maureen was in the kitchen doing something, I couldn't sleep, and I tiptoed into their room, went to the bed, and touched it. Then I sat on it. Then I lay back and then pulled my feet onto it. I put my head on Mummy's pillow, but it smelled funny. I rolled over to Daddy's side. It smelled funny, too. They don't smell like Ma or like Pa. I got up quickly and smoothed the bed and ran out of the room.

She doesn't really touch me unless she is brushing my hair. Maybe if she called me to lie there with them, I might. If she were to hug me, I might let her, but she doesn't, and in any case I'm not sure if I'd like it.

Usually, when they are in there, I stand by the bedroom door and watch. Sometimes I make myself go in, and I sit in the white wicker chair at the side of her bed while Anil and Tara romp there or just lie next to her. I jump on our bed with Tara, but not on Mummy and Daddy's bed.

Her tummy is so big, it looks as if it will burst. She goes to the hairdresser lots. She says she doesn't want, when the time comes with no warning whatsoever, to have to go to the hospital looking like she doesn't take care of herself.

*

Someone called a rep, a man from a drug company, gave Daddy a box of cards. They are the size of the kind of cards Pa plays with, but there are pictures on them that Daddy says are famous, made by artists who lived a long time ago in England, which is a country on the right-hand side of Ireland. He gave the whole stack to me because he knows I like making pictures. Everyone says I am a little artist. But Tara and Anil wanted me to share. I like the ones with trees and rivers, so I kept those and gave Anil one with a boy who looks bored and is dressed in a blue suit and is holding a big black hat with a feather in it. The boy is wearing shiny blue shoes, a kind we don't have here in Trinidad. And I gave Tara all the ones with women and girls doing things like swinging on swings and holding lanterns. There is one of a girl in a white dress with a pink sash. It is the only girl-one I wanted. That girl has brown hair, and she has on a pink hat, pink like her sash, and the hat has long pink flowing ribbons. The sky in that one has lots of yellow in it. But the yellow looks good. It is as if the girl is standing in the sky. I wish I knew her. When I look at her picture, I feel like the starboy in the movies Pa used to take me to see. If I were a starboy, I would wrap a pink sash around my forehead to heal the cut I got when I was saving her from being attacked by wild animals in the jungle. We would be friends. I wanted that picture, but Tara really wanted it, too. I think she wanted it because she knew I liked it. But I didn't want to fight, and when she set her face up to cry, I let her have it. Sometimes when she isn't around, I go in her treasure box on the dresser and look at that one. There is another one I like a lot by a man named John Constable. The trees in his picture are not green like avocado trees, or like mango, or pommecythere trees. They are coloured like the mangroves late in the evening, very dark, almost black, but still green. And there is a cart with horses in the river. And a black-and-white dog. He doesn't make the sky blue, but it has many colours in it, like white and grey, but many, many kinds of whites and greys. I try to draw like him and colour my pictures like that one, and I put a tiny bit of yellow in my sky like in the picture of the pretty girl, but John Constable is better than I am. When anyone looks at my drawings, they always say, You're getting better and better at this. And I answer, Practice makes perfect.

*

I laugh when there is something to laugh at. But Daddy is always saying I am such a serious child. He tells me jokes to try to make me laugh. He is always asking me, Are you OK? I don't like when he asks me that; it makes me want to tell him that I want to go back to live with Mạ and Pa. But they might think I don't like them or Tara. I never know what to say, so I make myself do a big smile and I nod to say yes, I'm OK. I am trying to smile more, even when there is nothing to smile about, and especially when I don't really feel happy.

Daddy doesn't work at the hospital much anymore, but when he does, it is mostly at night and on weekends. His office is on the main road, on this side of the bridge. When he comes home from work, Mummy doesn't seem very happy. It sounds as if she thinks he is staying away from the house too much. He laughs at first, and she gets more upset. It's always like this. She begins to cry and he laughs, but when he laughs it doesn't seem like real laughter, and then he gets annoyed and tells her to stop nagging him. They go in their bedroom, and even though they close the door, everyone can hear the shouting, and Mummy crying. I want to barge into the room and to get taller than he is, and tell him he should come home in time to eat dinner with us because on afternoons she showers and dresses and puts on her makeup and then she just keeps going out on the veranda, looking over the banister, down the road, coming back in, and then minutes later, going out again. Over and over. She says, at least at first, that we have to wait for him to eat together, as that's what good families do. By the time we are allowed to sit down and eat without him, our meal is no longer hot. It's dry, or soggy. I want to tell him that if I were her husband, I would be good to her. That means I would come home on time for dinner. If she were my wife, I might even surprise her and come home sometimes for lunch since my office is so close to the house. I would say he should let her go with him to the office sometimes, and she could be near him and could tidy up the waiting room, or his papers, or line up the drugs in the sample cabinet so they would look neat and tidy. But then I get upset with her, too, wondering why she waits, and makes us wait, too, and I think she should go out and enjoy herself. I think these things, but I don't know if I can really say them. I don't want to be rude to these people. In any case, he plays with us and tells us jokes, and I don't want to nag him, too. But when I grow up, I don't ever want to be as weak as she is with him, or as strong as he is with her.

And I'd like to be able to tell him that people shouldn't laugh at other people, especially people who love them, when they are crying.

*

When Mummy and Daddy are not here, I sit at the table in the kitchen and I think. Maureen peels oranges to make juice and she always gives me half an orange to suck. She tells me I think too much, that I am too young to worry so much and should lighten up. One day, she said, you will see that you have life good, better than most. I don't know what she means, and why she thinks I worry. Maybe thinking is the same as worrying. Then we shouldn't think. But I like it. No one knows what is in your mind and you can imagine all kinds of things. For instance, if you want a horse but can't have one, you can imagine what it would be like to have a horse, you can give your horse a name, like Ivanhoe, you can brush his coat, give him sweet-smelling grass to eat from your hands and feel his warm spitty tongue when he takes the grass, you can imagine yourself riding Ivanhoe really fast, bouncing on his back, your legs pressing against his body, riding up into dry hills where there are no other people, but you might see someone, like the girl in the painting on the card I had to give to Tara, and realizing she is in danger, you and Ivanhoe race to her and save her from, say, being bitten by a big snake, or bad people who have pulled off her pink sashes and tied her to a tree with them. She gets on the horse behind you and holds on to you tightly as you and Ivanhoe gallop away.

Maureen's room downstairs smells like mosquito coils and sewing machine oil, but there is no sewing machine there, so I think it's something she puts in her hair that smells like machine oil. It is much brighter than Barlow's room downstairs on Selvon Street because this one has a big window, and outside the window there is no wall or house with neighbours, but the view of all that wildness. I like to be in there with her, even with the machine oil smell. When the baby comes, Maureen will sleep upstairs in the middle room with it and with Anil.

SEVEN

We're going to Selvon Street to have Sunday lunch with Ma and Pa. I didn't eat breakfast this morning. I didn't want to get so full that I wouldn't be able to eat whatever it is Ma is making for us. We go there almost every Sunday for lunch. As soon as we arrive, she'll give us aloo pies. Or pholouries. Or maybe pommecythere chow. I am hungry just thinking about it. And Polly, she will hand us glasses of sweet Milo's with crushed ice in it. Ma would have gone to church early this morning, but she should be back home already. When we get there, the house will smell of stewed or barbecued chicken and of callaloo with crab in it and, if you can separate the smells out like I can, of angel cake.

We are moving slowly all along the way to Selvon Street so we can take in the houses decorated with stars of Bethlehem on the roofs, and on the balconies with strings of red and green bulbs, lit now even though it is daytime. There are red, green, and gold pompoms hanging from the eaves of many of the houses. One house even has a large blow-up Santa on the roof. In faraway countries that are very cold, Santa wears a lot of clothes and enters people's houses through the chimney on their roofs, but it is hot here, always, so we don't have chimneys because we don't have fireplaces. But it's still exciting to see him there in his red clothes—he will be boiling hot dressed like that here—and with the big red bag overflowing with presents flung over his shoulder. But Christmas isn't the only big thing happening. Before Christmas day itself comes, the country's general elections will take place, in a few days' time actually, so signs are tied on people's verandas with the initials of the party they are supporting. DLP. PNM. ANC.

We will soon go by the famous crèche. From some people's home radios come snippets of religious sermons, and choirs singing Christmas carols, and church songs I recognize from when I used to go to the Open Bible Church with Ma.

Because it is election season, there are also cars and trucks driving throughout the neighbourhoods, with many people on the truck beds waving flags and beating pots and bottles with spoons, and they dance and wave their hands in the air. There are public address systems mounted on the roofs of the trucks and on the cars. One minute there is music coming out of them, but it's not Christmas music. It's mostly calypsos they are playing. Mummy says it is a pity the election is so close to Christmas, because you can't listen to Christmas music in peace these days. And the next minute, the music stops, and a man's voice, tinny and loud—so loud that his words are distorted—addresses the neighbourhoods: *This is the voice of the Democratic Labour Party. Your candidate for this area is*—and they say the name. Then another one says: *This is the voice of the People's National Movement. Your candidate for your area is*—and there is a different name. And another: *This is the voice of the African National Congress. Vote* ANC. *Your candidate is*—and a name. Each one plays a few bars of the party's anthem, and often the candidate for the area gives a speech. Even when they are far away from the street we are on, we can hear them. People have come out on their balconies or all the way out to their front gates to listen to the speeches coming through the loudspeakers. When there is music, Daddy dances in his seat, his shoulders keeping the beat, and when he reaches the trucks and cars with the speakers, he brings the car almost to a crawl. Mummy doesn't like this. Some people wave to him and call out, Ey, Doc, come and join us! Mummy says she is very uncomfortable and needs to get out of the car. She rubs her huge tummy as she says Ma and Pa are waiting for us and he needs to take a different route. But there is another loudspeaker voice in the distance, and he drives off looking for that one, too. Even though none of them can hear us, Mummy whispers urgently, What are you doing? No, no, no. I mean, Suresh, really, come on. We'll be late. I don't want to go down there—we'll get stuck behind them.

Daddy says to her, with a smile, I don't intend to be behind them; we won't be too much longer, have a little patience.

She steupses. He slaps her thigh lightly, rubs it, and says, This is new, darling, we're on a cusp here. Who knows, but if what we're hearing is true, independence is around the corner. This election will be our most important one ever, you know. Aren't you glad we've returned to Trinidad just in time? Lighten up a little, na. Don't you want to know what's going on?

Mummy looks through the window, away from the scene of cars. Daddy says, Oh, come on, pet.

That should have sounded as if he were pleading, but it sounded more as if he were saying she was being a wet blanket. He often tells her she is a wet blanket, which isn't a nice thing to say to someone. She doesn't look at him when she says, Fine. Do whatever you want.

He has become a different Daddy. He looks strange, almost wild and excited, and even though he is in this car, it feels as if he has left us and is with those other people out there. When we ask him what's going on, he tells us that each group is explaining why people should vote for them and not for any others in the upcoming election, and that they are also encouraging people to register to vote. He says that if the PNM gets in, Eric Williams, a man who is a doctor but not a real doctor like Daddy, and who is the leader of that party, will become this country's first prime minister. He turns back to look at us. He winks at us and says, Independence. Before the end of next year.

Daddy has explained what it means for a country to gain independence, and it sounds important and exciting, but I'm still not sure if I can say what this will mean for Tara and me, or Ma and Pa. Mummy says, Yes, let them cut the strings to England, and this place will go to hell.

Eventually Daddy drives away from this area, and we reach the house with the crèche on its lawn. A couple of other cars have stopped, too. We must stay in the car and look out, and when I ask why we can't get out, Mummy says, Because I said so. Daddy turns and says to us softly, Just do as Mummy says.

My favourite parts are the lamb and sheep. They are almost as big as me. If we were to get out of the car, we'd see the baby Jesus's face. There is Christmas music coming from the scene, but we can't hear it very well from inside the car.

Then, close to Selvon Street, a truck has come up behind us. On the truck bed is a crowd dancing to the beat of carnival-type music, but their music isn't being broadcast through a public address system. It's quieter, as if they have finished for the day. Daddy keeps looking back in his rear-view mirror. He sits upright, almost against the steering wheel, and a smile broadens on him. He's slowing down, trying to see the people standing on the bed of the truck that is now so close that if he stops they might hit us. Suddenly he waves his hand out of the window to stop the truck. Mummy looks back and, almost hysterical, shakes her head to say *no*. She says, What are you doing? Don't be crazy. I don't like this. Please, Suresh, I've had enough now.

As Daddy opens his car door and steps out, Mummy calls, her voice high and shaking, Suresh, what on earth are you doing? Get back inside. You're going to make a spectacle of yourself. Daddy remains standing in between the open door and the body of the car, and waves to a man at the front of the bed. The truck moves out to pass our car but comes to a halt at our side. The man, a man who looks white but not totally, calls out to Daddy by his first name. Everybody else on the truck is dark-skinned, but there are no people like us, no Indians on the truck. Daddy says, I just want to wish you the best, man. I'm with you. I'll be voting for you in the election. The man replies, Come and join us, Suresh. We need people like you. I'll give you a call. Give Vijay my regards. He ducks down to try to see Mummy, but Mummy is looking straight ahead.

They drive on, people in the truck waving to Daddy, as if, having been approved by the candidate, he is a friend. He gets back into our car, looking as if he has just won a prize. Mummy immediately says, So, what? You want to get involved in politics now? You're voting? You are not taking any damn call from him to join any party. Those are not our kind of people. I won't be a part of any of this.

Daddy says, It's such an exciting time, darling. We must take part. This concerns us all. Don't you want to be part of it?

She says, And I suppose you do.

It's not a question.

Daddy says, He sent his regards to you. Did you hear that? That was lovely of him.

As the caravan passes, the people wave to us, too. I half smile and half wave back, hoping Mummy doesn't see.

*

On Christmas day, we arrive at the house early. Ma meets us at the top of the front stairs. Merry Christmas, darling, she says to each of us, and tells us how pretty we look all dressed up, and then she touches Mummy's tummy and hugs her, and Daddy kisses her on her cheek. Pa comes out holding a drink with ice in it for Daddy. Polly comes and takes a basket of presents and food from Daddy. We run to see the tree, and Pa calls us back for hugs and pulls out from the pockets of his pants packets of sweets for each of us. Christmas music is coming from the radio in the back. *Angels we have heard on high, sweetly singing o'er the plains*, and *O Christmas tree, o Christmas tree, how lovely are your branches*, and *O come, all ye faithful, joyful and triumphant*. Mummy knows the words to all the songs, and she sings them softly, smiling a lot.

Before coming here, we opened our presents in the Marabella house. Tara and I got bicycles with training wheels on them from Santa, and Anil got a tricycle. Mummy and Daddy gave us clothing and books and games. Maureen got money from Mummy and Daddy, and we gave her cards that we made, and a handbag that Mummy bought and we wrapped.

Under the tree at Selvon Street are more presents, but we're not allowed to touch them until our cousins arrive. We play with the ornaments on the tree, trying to see the presents, to see which have our names on the tags, but without touching them.

When they arrive, Aunty Stella, with a big smile, says to Mummy, But look at you! It's coming any time now, you know. You're catching up with us. You ready for number four?

And now we can open presents. Tara and I get one from Ma and Pa, just one for both of us, and it comes in a box that is almost as big as we are. We rip off the paper as everyone else watches. It is a dollhouse. There are two bedrooms in it, a kitchen, a living room, and a bathroom with a bathtub. A plastic bag comes with the house, and in it are tiny people: a man, a woman, a boy, and a girl. There are beds, a fridge and stove, and some pots and pans. We both also got clothing from Ma and Pa. Someone else, I'm not sure who, gave me a stethoscope. While Colin rolls his new little trucks across the floor, I go around and listen to everyone's heart.

Mummy looks happy. There's a lot of drinking and loud, happy talking. She is having her favourite, ponche de crème. We can't have any of that because, even though it's like eggnog and has healthy eggs in it and is sweetened with condensed milk, it also has a lot of alcohol. But today we can have perfumed sorrel, as much as we want, and it's daytime, so no one can say we will wet our beds.

Daddy is explaining why he thinks it's not a bad thing at all that the PNM got in. Pa asks, So who do I owe allegiance to now, our Queen or this Williams? Those people, he says, will take care of their own kind, not the Indians, you know. We are on our own from now on. Mark my word. He seems worried. I'm not sure why, but he says something about the country going to hell. Daddy tells him not to panic, he'll still have his Queen as the country will still be in the Commonwealth. Uncle Sonny says, Suresh, boy, you sounding like those politicians on the radio; you not thinking of getting involved, are you? Ma answers Uncle Sonny before Daddy can. Well, why not? she says. Your grandfather was with the West Indies Federation before it broke up, and that was all about independence for all the islands. So why not your brother-in-law?

I see Mummy looking at Ma and slightly shaking her head, in the no direction, for no one else but Ma to see.

I don't think Daddy would be so happy if Trinidad and Tobago were going to hell. So I am not worried.

*

Daddy says nobody barbecues chicken like Polly. She says to him, Eh eh, so this is what you call bar-b-cue, Doctor? I always hear 'bout bar-b-cue, but I didn't know is that self I making. But I good, oui. She likes when Daddy compliments her, and he does it a lot.

There is so much food on the table, and so many of us, that the card table is brought into the dining room and pressed against the big table in there. I can eat Ma's Spanish rice and pigeon peas all day long. And the pastels, and the ham, and the green fig pie. I love Christmas.

After, when we all go out on the veranda, I lean against Ma, and while she speaks with Mummy and Aunty Stella, she keeps hugging me, putting her hand on my head, pulling me closer and rubbing my skin. She doesn't do that with Tara or Diane and Savi. Just with me. I like it. Her hands are soft and warm.

I stay very still so she won't stop. I begin to want to stay here again, and I whisper this to her. She puts her finger to her mouth and shakes her head to say no. Then she bends down and says, Not today, darling. Another time soon, OK?

*

Tara isn't awake, and I don't hear Anil, so he is probably also still asleep. The room is totally dark, but from my bed I can tell that Mummy and Daddy are up and moving about. The door to our room is usually open throughout the night, but someone has shut it. I sit up carefully so as not to awaken Tara, and I look at the space under the door. On the other side, lights are on. Outside the window it is as dark as the darkest night. I want to get out of bed to see what is happening, but I also don't want anyone to know I am awake. I lie down again and remain as still as a broom in a corner. The crickets and frogs are noisier tonight than usual. But I hear Daddy's voice. Maureen is there, too. They are in the kitchen. Minutes pass when I can't tell what's going on, but then the back door is unlocked, and there is the squeak of it as it is opened, then shut. Some minutes later, the engine of the car comes alive. The big gate is opened. The car rolls out, and the gate is dragged closed behind it. I pull up the netting and get out of the bed. I pull open the louvres and see there are thousands and millions of stars in the sky. Maureen's slippers slap up the back stairs. She quietly opens the door of our bedroom and sees me at the window. She puts a forefinger to her lips and with her other hand signals to me to come to her.

Your daddy take your mummy to the hospital. Baby coming, she says as she prepares a cup of Milo for me.

When? I ask.

Some children come one time, bap! Just like that, she says. It could even born in the car self. And some take they time, take they time. And if it don't want to come, they might even have to cut it out. But it don't matter, your mummy will remain in hospital a few days.

For a moment I think that means I should go to my other house on Selvon Street, to be with Ma and Pa. But I also have an odd feeling, unlike any I've had before: I must stay here and make sure everything runs smoothly; I have to stay and protect Tara and Anil. I am not sure from what, nor how things are to be looked after. Perhaps I can make sure Maureen sweeps the stairs at the front of the house and the back, and dusts the inside, wipes down the ledges and the blades of the fan in the living room. I want to ask Maureen what she'll make us for dinner. I imagine Ma speaking to Polly, and Mummy to Maureen: What do we have in the fridge? Is there enough of... this or that... to make something or the other... We'll have this for dinner. Make a salad.

But it all sounds very grown-up in my head, and I don't want to speak to Maureen like that. Even if Maureen were to tell me what ingredients were in the fridge or in the cupboards, I wouldn't know what she could make with them anyway.

Maureen tells me I need to sleep. She walks me back to the bed and tucks me in.

When I awake it's morning and the room is hot, and birds in the jungle are quarrelling and making a lot of noise. Maureen says Daddy phoned from the hospital. The baby hasn't come yet, but it won't be long now. We are not going to school today.

Tara wants to pretend to be a mother. She wants to play with one of her dolls, Annie, to feed Annie and change Annie's diaper. I play with her and with Annie for a few minutes, but it's just too silly feeding a doll. Everything around it gets soaked. With the nipple of the bottle of water in Annie's open mouth, I squeeze hard, and water comes squirting out of Annie's eyes, and Tara gets vexed with me for doing this. I eventually get Tara to put Annie to bed for a nap, and we go down beneath the house and pick marigolds and zinnias, and Maureen helps us thread them into garlands. We make one for Mummy and one for the baby, and Anil wants one, but we can't pick all the flowers or else Mummy will get annoyed. So Anil only has a few flowers. He doesn't mind and is wearing it happily.

We wait and we wait and we wait. And nothing is happening. We have lunch and I get sleepy, but then Mr. Monty arrives at the house in Pa's car. He speaks to Maureen. She hurries us now, bathing and dressing us quickly as if we are going to a birthday party. We go to collect the garlands, but the flowers have wilted and small ants are crawling all over them. We can't take them with us.

Maureen, dressed in a clean, pressed uniform and wearing cologne, gets into the car with Anil, Tara, and me, and we go to the hospital. Pa and Ma and Daddy are there. The baby is lying on Mummy's chest. It's tiny. A girl. She is wrapped tightly in a blanket. She has a lot of hair. I go to the bed, and Mummy tells me I can touch the baby, but to do it gently. I touch her little head with one finger. Her hands are so small, and she mostly keeps them in fists, but she opens out one, stretches her fingers, and quickly makes the fist again. I saw her fingernails and they look like tiny pink shells. She smells like powdered milk.

Daddy brings us back home in his car and we eat dinner together before he leaves for the hospital again to see Mummy and the baby. At the table, I ask him if I was born in the hospital, too. Tara excitedly says, You were born in the Holles Street Maternity Hospital. Like me. And Anil.

We ask him where Mummy was born and he says he doesn't know, but he is sure it would have been at the hospital where she is now, the San Fernando General Hospital. And was he born there, too? we ask. He says, No, I am different. I wasn't born. We don't know what he means so we ask him again and again, and he keeps laughing and saying the same thing, he wasn't born. And then he says, all right, he was found. His parents were walking on a street one day and they heard a baby crying. The sound was coming from a barrel on the side of the road. They went over and saw newspaper on the top of the barrel, and when they removed the newspaper, they found a little baby lying on top of salt fish. He was born, he says, in a barrel of salt fish. We are scornful and sad for him at the same time.

*

They're coming home tomorrow, so Tara and I are cleaning up our bookshelf to surprise Mummy and the new baby. Daddy is not here. Mummy phoned from the hospital to speak with him, but Maureen told her he came, had dinner, and left a good while ago. We are awake even though it is past our bedtime. Mummy phones again.

Maureen is saying, No, I don't know. He say he was going to the hospital. I say it was to see you. No, he didn't phone. Maybe he making a house call.

Mummy doesn't want to speak to any of us. Maureen reads Tara and Anil nursery rhymes. I prefer to watch *Bonanza* on the television. I am Little Joe—brave and strong but quiet, just like him.

We are in bed when the gate opens and the car rolls in. Daddy comes up the stairs. Maureen had been lying on the spare bed in Anil's room. She goes out to meet him. They talk. I know that voice. It's his happy drinking voice. He's had a few. That's what Mummy sometimes says, He's had a few.

*

Mummy and the baby are home. Siri is her name. Pa, Ma, Uncle Sonny, Auntie Stella, Ma's cousin Auntie Rookmin, and Auntie Rookmin's husband, Uncle Sankar, came to see the new baby. Ma held Siri for a long time and fed her, too. Babies do big burps and everyone looks surprised, and even when the baby throws up with the burp, they exclaim happily. I sat next to Ma on the couch and she put Siri on my lap and I got to hold her, but for less than a minute. Tara wriggled her forefinger into Siri's fist and exclaimed how strong her clutch was. Then she told Mummy that Daddy said he was born in a salt-fish barrel and asked her if that was true. Mummy said, in a tired voice, that he was talking nonsense, not to bother with him. But, she added with a weak smile, she didn't actually know for sure.

Auntie Stella brought pastels and a chocolate cake, and Maureen heated the pastels and cut the chocolate cake and brought it all out on a tray with small plates and forks. Mummy sent me for napkins. She told me not to bother to fold them, just to bring them as they were. Daddy came home from his office and opened a bottle of champagne, and everyone had a glass—Tara and I had lime juice with a tiny bit of champagne in it, and Anil had orange juice—and they all talked loudly and everyone was laughing and making a lot of happy noise. Daddy wanted to order Chinese food for everyone, but Mummy said she was tired, and Ma told Daddy, quietly, Thanks, son. Leave that for another time, you hear? Vij should take a rest now. He hugged Ma and she told him the champagne was real nice.

EIGHT

Pupah is Daddy's mother's father. That means he is Daddy's grandfather, and Tara and Anil's great-grandfather, and maybe mine, too. We visit him almost every Saturday, which means on Saturdays we don't go to Selvon Street. For Christmas, in addition to the dollhouse, Ma and Pa gave Tara and me the exact same outfit each. Not even in different colours. But that's OK today, because I am wearing mine on the drive to Pupah's house in Tunapuna, and this way it feels as if they are on the drive with me.

Daddy's parents, Grandma and Granddad, used to live in Trinidad, but they don't now. They live in England. Daddy was a young boy, younger than I am now, when Granddad left him and Grandma in Trinidad while he went to work in England. Trinidad is a British colony—but it won't be anymore when we get independence—and during the Second World War, many colonial subjects went to work in the mother country. Granddad worked there as an airman in the Royal Air Force.

Pupah and Grandma are estranged. To be estranged doesn't mean they are strangers—obviously, he is her father—it just means they don't speak to each other and haven't for a long, long, long time, long before Daddy was born. But when Daddy was a baby, a relative took him to meet Pupah, and Pupah liked

Daddy right away. At the end of the war, Granddad returned to Trinidad, but he didn't want to live here anymore. So he took Grandma and Daddy back to England with him. Although Daddy grew up in England, he would come back here by boat to spend almost all his holidays with Pupah. It is a very long journey, on rough seas sometimes, for a little boy to take on his own, but Daddy is very brave now, and he must have been then, too. Once Grandma and Granddad left, though, they never returned.

It takes forever to get to Pupah's house, and the baby has to be fed. I get to remove the bottle from the bag, shake it, and take off the cover over the nipple, but Mummy feeds her. You have to be careful that she doesn't get too much at one time, or else she could choke.

The drive is long, longer than it takes to get to Port of Spain. Longer than it takes to get to the Maracas Waterfall. Longer than it takes to arrive at Mummy's favourite plant nursery in St. Joseph. From the Marabella house, it takes about two hours to reach his house. That's long. But it's OK, because I like this drive. When we leave Marabella we head north, through smelly Pointe-à-Pierre, and then we go through cane fields on roads with lots of potholes, and then we are on a narrow road with swampy rice fields on either side—there are white egrets in the water here, and red-breasted and yellow-hooded blackbirds—and if another car is coming in the opposite direction, both drivers have to be very careful, otherwise their cars can slip right off the road and into the water, and everyone will drown. Daddy comments all the time on the state of the roads, and of everything. He hopes the new government will widen these roads. Fix the potholes. He says a country that has a pitch lake should never have such bad roads, regardless of where those roads are. This is an oil-rich country, he says, shaking his head. We have pitch and we have money. Traffic lights should be put here, a roundabout would ease the traffic there. I can see what he means.

We cross the long Caroni River, this time in the centre of the island, on a rickety bridge—this bridge should long ago have been upgraded, he says—and after that we're in San Juan. San Juan is always busy. If we had fallen asleep in the car, whenever we get here, we'd definitely wake up because of how noisy it is, and how jerky the drive is, the car moving then stopping all the time. Everywhere you look there is some kind of food or dry goods vendor stall spilling out onto the road. The town smells of car gasoline and pitch oil, and of unwashed vegetables and fruit, and raw fish that has been out in the sun too long. We aren't allowed to turn our windows all the way down, because people begging, and vendors walking past the cars selling bags of limes, or of hot peppers, or chennets, try to put their hands in. But Tara and I, and even Anil, sit up and look out. We don't want to miss anything. Pedestrians run across the street, or they just walk slowly, as if they own the road, without even checking left or right. A drunk man stands in the middle of the road, dancing, and no one can pass until he moves. Cars are parked on the pavement on both sides of the road, and people are selling things out of the open trunks. Donkey carts line the road, too, loaded with bananas, green figs, and coconuts. It's just a big traffic jam, and car horns are honking and angry drivers are shouting.

It's quieter when we leave San Juan. We pass little white huts that are the homes of cane-field workers. For me, this is the best part of the journey to Pupah's house. The huts are built of bricks the people themselves make using cow dung from their own cows or from dung they buy from their neighbours.

Imagine selling your cows' poo. It's funny, but smart, too. And imagine building your house out of something like that. Daddy has been in houses like these when he's made house calls in the South. He assures us they don't smell, and he says the floor in them is just clay packed hard and smoothed so it is shiny. The roofs of the huts are just dried branches from palm trees, woven together. I think about when it rains, especially late in the rainy season when there are tropical storms: surely the people inside get soaked, and the clay floor gets muddy and slippery. Little children run around in the yards naked. Mummy says these people don't go to shops like the ones in San Fernando to buy their clothes. Their clothing is homemade from flour sacks. We see them playing in the clay yards, barefoot. Flags are planted in the corner of their houses, some red, some white, some pink, some yellow. When you see those flags, you know the people who live there are Hindus. Some of the yards have little Hindu temples. The parents here work in the sugar-cane fields, and Mummy tells us that when the children come home from school, they must help their parents plant or pick rice in the fields behind their house, feed the animals, sweep the yard, and some of them even have to cook. Tara asks, Do they have to pick up poo, too? Mummy, her mouth twisted, turns to look at Tara, but seeing that she isn't being funny, she says kindly, You're worried about the children, eh? Don't worry. Girls and women don't have to do that sort of thing.

There are children walking on the road barefoot, some leading cows, others carrying on their backs bundles of grass so big and heavy that the children are bent over. I saw some playing skip with rough frayed ropes, probably the ropes they tied the cows and goats with, and I've seen them play a game using a long stick to push and roll the lid of a can in their yard, and sometimes even down the road, to see who can make it reach the farthest without the lid falling over. Mummy says we must appreciate how lucky we are: we don't have to do yard or house work, only our homework after school; we have shoes, sandals, *and* slippers, and she can go to a store and buy new clothes whenever we need them, or even just want them. And we have all kinds of board and card games and books. We must be thankful for everything we have. Daddy shakes his head. It's a shame there are no proper government-run schools in this area, he says. We must remember that even though we live different lives from these people, we are no different than they are. Remember? He asks. They have the same heart, liver, tummies, and toes like we have. Isn't that right?

Mummy says something and Daddy has to say the opposite. Daddy says something and Mummy has to say the opposite. It's always like that.

When we arrive at Pupah's house, we must go to him and bend down to touch his feet. It's just like in the Indian movies I used to go to with Pa. This is the way we must greet Daddy's older relatives, the ones who don't speak English well. The first time we visited Pupah, we watched Mummy and Daddy do it first. They bent forward and reached their hands toward his feet, but before they could actually touch his feet, Pupah pulled them up by their shoulders and said something softly to each of them. We do it now, too. Everyone watched as we did it the first time, and they made approving sounds. Daddy explained later that this is a gesture of respect for an older person, but the older person must also have respect for us and must always stop us from bending all the way down, from making contact with their feet. If they don't pull you up, it means they are angry with you and have no respect for you. When we're sitting on the floor playing, Mummy often tells us to not point our feet in anyone's direction. It's a sign of disrespect, she says.

Pupah puts his thumb on Siri's forehead, and his lips move. He is saying something but with no sound. He likes Siri. Well, everybody does.

Although Pupah's bedroom has many windows, three on one wall, through which you can see the mountains of the Northern Range, and three on the front wall that look out onto his garden of marigold flowers, his room is smoky from the incense and camphor he burns in poojas. There is a money safe in his room, as tall as me, and on top of that safe are brass plates, one with hibiscus flowers, and the other with Julie mangoes that look ripe enough to eat now. At the side of the plate is a brass vase with mango leaves in it, and behind are framed pictures. The pictures are very colourful. One has a person with a blue face. The person has a child's face, but I don't think it's a child. I'm not sure if it's a he or a she. The person is playing a flute and wears earrings and many necklaces and a crown that looks like a temple, and has four arms. The other one is of a lady who has four arms, too. She plays a musical instrument and sits in a pink flower that has many petals. There is a large white bird in that picture. The first time I saw these pictures, I asked Daddy who they were and if they are people who, like Pupah, are related to us. He said that that set-up is Pupah's altar, and the people in the pictures are a Hindu God and Goddess, and Pupah prays to them. I wonder if Ma knows about them, and if she ever prays to them. Pupah can read a kind of writing called Sanskrit. Not many people can read it. Whenever we go there,

Daddy puts on his stethoscope and listens to Pupah's chest and back, and he takes Pupah's blood pressure. I could have brought my stethoscope. But mine isn't real.

Pupah has a cattle farm. The milk from his cows is sold to a big business called a dairy. They package the milk and sell it in the groceries in Trinidad. So when Mummy buys milk, it's the milk from Pupah's cows we are getting. At Pupah's house, each of us gets a bowl of dahi made from the cows' milk. It is thick and has flakes and chunks like cottage cheese in it, but it is sweet—there is so much sugar in it that the crystals don't melt. You chew *and* drink it.

Pupah speaks mostly Hindi, very little English, so he doesn't speak with us much. But he enjoys watching us sit at the big table in the back, eating—or drinking—the dahi, and cups of dal, and when we eat roti and curried pumpkin with our hands, he nods his head approvingly. He eats like a bird, which means he eats very small amounts of food. No one in his house is allowed to eat meat. We mustn't ever tell him we eat hamburgers and hotdogs. Daddy says Pupah will disown us if he ever finds out that we don't conduct ourselves as proper Brahmins. And also, he mustn't ever find out that Daddy smokes.

After we eat, Tara and I sneak away and go to the long shed with the pens to see the cows. Their heads are huge and so are their soft, kind eyes. They are always making soft moo sounds and chewing, even when there is nothing in their mouths. The workmen let us touch the cows' noses, and sometimes their big fat spitty tongues come out and touch us. We know how to milk a cow, but as we're not supposed to go to the pens, we must never let Pupah know we do this. We are Brahmins, which means we mustn't do anything that makes us dirty. And not only that, but the worker will get in a lot of trouble. The udders are warm and squishy, and they don't feel very good. When we do it, the milk drips into the bucket, but when the worker does it, the milk squirts out and hits the sides of the bucket hard. It bubbles up and smells sweet, like grass. It's also warm.

Next to the house is a big field called a pasture. We have to stay inside the house when they let the cattle out into the pasture, because if there is something called a stampede, we can't be in the way or else we will get trampled. *Stampede* and *trampled*. They sound good together, and their meanings are close: one can cause the other.

By the time we leave Pupah's house, the sun is low in the sky, and even then we still have to return all the way to San Fernando. The whole day is gone by the time we get back home, and it's always too late to speak with Ma and Pa on the phone by then.

As soon as we leave and have passed Pupah's house, Daddy gets his cigarettes from the glove compartment and pretends his cigarette is oxygen and if he doesn't get one in his mouth and suck on it fast-fast, he'll die.

On the way back to Marabella, Mummy and Daddy are talking about Pupah, about how he still won't talk to Daddy's mother, who is his own daughter. He won't even mention her name. I want to listen. I should not interrupt, but I do: I ask why, and Daddy says, You're listening to big people's conversation, darling? But then he answers. He says that Pupah is an old-fashioned Brahmin; he did not approve of Grandma marrying Granddad. Granddad is Catholic.

I don't understand. Daddy explains that people with religious beliefs sometimes don't like, or understand, or respect the beliefs of other people. We ask if he and Mummy don't like

Catholics, too. Because Uncle Phillip, a friend of Daddy's who is a doctor at the hospital, and his wife, Auntie Sally, are Catholics. The parents of Sandy and Sean, who go to the same school as Tara and me, are Mummy and Daddy's friends, and they, too, are Catholic. Daddy says he is not like Pupah. He isn't religious because religion is the root of all evil. Mummy hits his arm and tells him not to tell the children that sort of thing. She turns and says to us, Money is the root of all evil, not religion. Daddy tries again. He explains that Pupah's father was a Hindu pundit, and that Pupah is himself very religious and old-fashioned. I still don't really understand. He says that Pupah is a good man, but that some of his ways aren't the best way to be in life. It is better to be a tolerant person.

We drive in silence and then he says to Mummy, Mama and Daddy are thinking of coming for a holiday. When he speaks to Mummy, that's what he calls his parents. Mummy sharply says, When? I am only now hearing about this. Why didn't you tell me before?

He says, Now, don't start, you, too. Please. They're only thinking. You know them. They're always threatening to return, but they haven't yet, have they? They will change their minds a hundred times before they actually do anything.

*

It was the ringing of the telephone that woke me. Through our open bedroom door, I see the lights are on in the living room. Daddy's voice is coming from the middle room. And there is Maureen's, too. Someone has just pulled in our door, but not shut it. Mummy walks unusually quickly past our room. She is fully dressed. It was the middle of the night, just like this, when they left to go to the hospital for Mummy to have the baby. But I can't think of any reason why they would be awake at this time of the night—outside, through the louvres, it is pitch-dark. When we went to bed, we were all in our pyjamas, Mummy and Daddy, too. Daddy tucked us in, and the lights were all turned off. I didn't fall asleep right away, and the house grew still, dead quiet by the time I did.

Daddy goes past now. Maureen follows in her dressing gown. Her hair isn't combed. She goes past again. The kettle is being filled with water.

Chairs are pulled out from against the table. Cups are being filled. Cups clink against saucers. The chairs scrape the ground again. I want to get up and go out and see what is happening, but it would be easier for me if Tara would come with me. I mustn't wake her, though.

Daddy walks swiftly to their bedroom. The toilet flushes. He's out again. A bunch of keys that live on a hook near the door are lifted off. The back door is opened. He's leaving. A house call maybe? But it sounds as if Mummy is going, too.

The lights have been turned off again, but I make out Maureen as she passes our room. She has gone into Anil's room, where she sleeps. It seems quieter than ever in the house. Such quiet is strange, frightening.

I can't sleep. Mummy went with Daddy. This doesn't make sense. Where would they have gone? I must stop thinking at once. Or just think about the tiny fish, the tadpoles in the drain at the front of the house. When catching them, I mustn't get the dark, slimy, smelly water on my clothes or my hands. Instead of cheese, try bread next time. One one is one. One two is two, two twos are four, two fives equal ten.

One hundred, ninety-nine, ninety-eight, ninety-seven, ninety-six.

Ten green bottles sitting on the wall. If one green bottle should accidentally fall, there'll be nine green bottles sitting on the wall.

Tom Tom the piper's son stole a pig and away he ran, the pig was eat and Tom was beat and Tom went crying down the street.

It is almost light outside. I have barely slept. Every time I dozed off, I awoke with a jolt. The crickets have stopped singing. Noises are coming from the kitchen. Tara isn't awake, and I don't hear Anil.

It's just Maureen tidying up.

Maureen, are Mummy and Daddy here? I ask.

She spins around and looks at me. Our lunch kits are turned over on the draining board. It's a school day, but she hasn't packed them. She looks at me as if she doesn't know me. She hasn't answered. I try again, What happened? Did they come back?

They will come soon. You not going to school today. You want to go and sleep a little more? Don't make noise, I don't want the baby to wake up. Go back in your bed.

I don't go. Instead, I go and sit sideways on the edge of a chair that isn't fully pulled out from the table. She looks at me as if she is about to say something, but she doesn't. She pours a glass of orange juice, takes the sweetbread loaf from the box and cuts a slice, puts it on a plate, and butters it. She puts them in front of me. I tear a piece of sweetbread and put it between my parted lips. But I don't really want to eat.

The sun has come up now, but Anil and Tara are still asleep. Its yellow light angles harshly into the kitchen, and the room is already hot. Maureen has fed Siri and put her in the basinet in the living room.

I hear the car and my heart races. She snaps at me, Go in your room and close the door. And she flies out through the back door to go downstairs.

*

Daddy is struggling to hold Mummy as they come up the back stairs. From behind them Maureen waves her hand to tell me to go back inside. Mummy keeps throwing her head back, as if she wants to look up at the sky, but her eyes are closed, and she is moaning. She doesn't want to come up the stairs. She'll fall if Daddy lets go of her. Is she ill? Maureen looks as if she is crying, too. Daddy is very serious. I have never seen that look on his face.

He's trying to guide Mummy to their bedroom, but she lets out a low howl and collapses on the floor in the doorway. Daddy and Maureen almost trip over her and each other as they reach down to her. Maureen runs to the kitchen and returns with a glass of water and a bowl of ice and a tea towel. Daddy is trying to pick Mummy up, but she is fighting him. She refuses to let herself be picked up. Tara is here now, standing back, covering her mouth with her hands. Anil has come out of his room, too. With a blank look on his face, he stands back against the wall, his hands pressed against his pee pee.

Daddy and Maureen have stooped next to Mummy. Maureen is petting Mummy's head and speaking to her in the tone she uses with Siri. Mummy is just moaning, then she cries out, No, no, no, Mama. Oh God. Mama. I can't bear this. Mama, Mama.

Mama. That's what she calls Ma. Mama.

She grips Daddy's hand and says, Suresh, what to do? I can't go on without her.

*

The house is silent. No one seems to notice I've gone to the desk in my room. I must not let anyone know how I am feeling. I must be patient. Something has happened to Ma. Maybe she took in—which is what Barlow says when she means someone got sick and had to be taken to the hospital. That's it. Mummy is worried because she doesn't want Ma to be ill. I want to go to her and tell her Ma will be all right, Ma is very strong.

I think about birds. Birds on branches. Branches of a mango tree. I open my copybook and begin making drawings and I colour them and silently pray to Jesus, thanking him for beautiful birds and all the fruit trees and for roses and poinsettias, ferns, hummingbirds, red staircases, Solo sweetdrinks, comic books, coconut ice cream, and angel cake. But whenever I think of the night sky and the stars, I don't mean to, but I cry and can't stop. But at least I don't make any sounds when I cry.

*

Mummy is in bed, curled up on her side. The sheet covers her to her neck. Daddy puts his hand out to stop us from entering and comes around and tells us that Mummy isn't well, that we can be helpful by being good, by staying in our rooms and reading, or going downstairs and playing, but we must play quietly. He closes the door. We press our ears to the door; he's turned the air-conditioning unit on so it's hard to hear above its hum. It doesn't sound as if they are talking. The phone rings and is answered on the first ring in Mummy and Daddy's room. It rings again minutes later. Someone is calling at the gate downstairs. We rush onto the veranda. It's Uncle Phillip. Maureen runs down the front stairs to meet him. He hasn't come with Auntie Sally. He has a medical bag, like Daddy's, with him. When he comes up, he has an odd smile that doesn't look real. His eyes are not smiling. He doesn't greet Tara, Anil, or me as he usually does, trying to lift each one of us, then saying we're getting so big and strong that even he—a big strong man himself—can't lift us up. Daddy comes out of the bedroom and pulls the door in behind him, saying without words that we are not to go into the room. He and Uncle Phillip stand on the veranda and chat with their backs to us. Maureen ushers us into the house, so that, I think, we can't hear what Daddy and Uncle Phillip are saying. Then the two of them go straight into the bedroom.

After a while, they come out and walk out to the veranda. Usually, Uncle Phillip tells us riddles and sometimes does magic tricks with coins or matchsticks. But not today. After Uncle Phillip leaves, Daddy comes back in, and we try again to enter the bedroom with him, but he tells us that Mummy is having a little nap, that we'll see her later.

The phone rings again and again and again. Anil is downstairs with Maureen, helping her with the laundry. Siri is down there, too, in her pram. A little while ago I tiptoed down the stairs and asked her, What happened, Maureen? hoping she'd tell me. If only I knew what was happening, no matter how bad it was, at least I would know what or how to feel. She wouldn't look at me. I was about to punch her gently when she said, Hush, child. Hush. Enough happening already. You only going to add to the confusion. She asked if I wanted to go in her room and play on her bed. I wanted to, but I also did not want to be far from Mummy and Daddy. I turned to go back up, and she came behind me and stooped to hug me. She said, Don't mind, you hear? Your daddy will talk to you later.

Standing by the window in the room I share with Tara, I hear no sounds in the house, except for the galvanized roof that pings in the heat. Quiet can actually hurt your ears.

*

It is evening now. Mummy has stayed in bed all day. She's had toast and tea that Maureen took into the room for her. Daddy did not go to work. Some of Mummy's cousins came. Maureen brought the chairs from around the kitchen table and added them to the two armchairs and the rocking chair on the veranda. No children came, only adults. Tara and I are not allowed to go and greet our aunties and uncles. They speak softly, either because they don't want us to hear, or perhaps because they don't want to disturb Mummy. They all look serious, wide-eyed, and daub their eyes and noses with handkerchiefs. No one stays for long.

Tara has managed to slip into the bedroom. She hasn't shut the door. I stand with the door ajar and look. I can't see Mummy's face, as she is lying with her back to the door. But with the covers over her, she seems deeply asleep. Very cold air seeps out through the crack in the doorway. Tara has climbed on the bed and put her face close to Mummy's. I hear Mummy say something, but not what was said. Tara doesn't stay. Then later, Anil goes in and he stays. He hasn't even cried once today. Maureen walks Siri around and around, under the shade of the almond tree in the garden. Siri is a baby, but today it's as if even she knows not to cry or make a fuss.

*

Daddy calls Tara, Anil, and me to sit with him on the couch in the living room. Tara sits on his lap, Anil on the couch leaning against him. I am on the other side of him. He is telling us something, but as he speaks, music comes from the cinema in Marabella and a woman is singing. Usually, from here you can't hear anything that goes on in the town, but her voice floats up to the sky and twirls like a kite and it's all I can hear. Tara has her face in Daddy's chest. His hand is on my shoulder, and he pulls me to him, but I am listening to the woman's high voice. It reminds me of when I used to live in the house with Ma and Pa, and from the bedroom that Ma and I used to sleep in, you could hear music from the cinema up the road. And I am thinking about how I used to walk up the road with Pa, holding his hand. We'd go to the cinema. Ma wouldn't come, but he and I would go. I can taste the sweeties he'd buy me, feel their crunch in my mouth. I don't mean to, but I lean against Daddy. He hugs me tightly, wipes my face, and is saying, I know, I know.

*

Usually, Maureen sits on the closed toilet and reads one of Mummy's fashion magazines while Tara and I shower together. Sometimes she dries me when I finish showering, but this morning she knelt on the rug, bent over the ledge, and pulled me to her. While Tara washed herself, Maureen bathed me. I don't know why she did that, but I was glad, because I felt as if I had no muscles, no strength, as if I didn't know how to do anything. Maybe she saw I had been standing under the water doing nothing. Her clothes got wet, but she didn't quarrel with me like Barlow used to, she just slowly rubbed soap up and down my arms and on my back and tummy and legs, and when she washed my face, she did it gently, her long fingers softly wiping my cheeks, and she kept saying, Don't mind, eh, Anj, shh, shh, don't mind, baby.

Baby. She called me baby. I'm not a baby. I'm almost eight. But I didn't mind. She dried me with the towel, hugging me, pulling me against her body. I put my head on her shoulder, and even though I was wet and naked, I felt I could fall asleep right there. I kept expecting Mummy to come into the bathroom and find Maureen drying me, my face on her, but I didn't care. I felt as if I was spinning and spinning and spinning and would fall.

Daddy wears his blackest suit, with a white shirt and a black tie with a pattern of gold diamond shapes on it. He is wearing a jacket. Mummy wears a black dress with tiny yellow flowers with white centres embroidered around the front part of the neckline. She is wearing black stockings and her shiny black pointed shoes with low heels. Her shoes have velvet bows on the tops of them. Tara and I are dressed in new white dresses, and Maureen made us both wear crinolines, so our dresses stick out. I had pulled off the crinoline, but she shook her head at me, whispering that today was not a day when anyone could just do whatever they wanted. She lifted the skirt of my dress and made me step into the crinoline again. We both have our hair pulled back and wear black velvet bandos to keep our bangs from falling into our faces. We're wearing white socks and white shoes.

Maureen isn't coming. She is staying with Siri and Anil.

*

There are people, men and women, all dressed in black, standing on the concrete play area in the yard, and people standing on the red front stairs, some waiting to go into the house, and some leaning on the railing, just standing there. I don't know these people. Climbing up the stairs, I hear a low buzz of chatter. They're looking at us, stepping apart to allow us to come up, and the chatter goes silent. Although I keep my eyes lowered, it's as if I see everything. Hundreds and hundreds of people. They line the veranda, crowd the living room, come out of the card room to see us, everyone in black, white handkerchiefs in many of the women's hands. The silence is changing to a lot of sniffling.

A woman I've seen once a long time ago, a friend of Ma's, rushes over to Mummy, kisses her cheek and hugs her. The woman's body begins to shake with her weeping. People keep approaching to hug Mummy. She doesn't protest, but she isn't responding to any of them either. She keeps trying to move toward Pa's office. The sniffling has turned to loud crying. It's hot. There is hardly any air in the house.

I want to slip away and go into Ma and Pa's room and hide under the covers of the bed. I want to go across the street to play with Sita. I want Sita's brother to take me under the house and help my mind to drift away. Tara's hand tightens around mine. We are among a sea of black clothing that gives off a stifling heat. All the sad noise and the scent of all kinds of colognes mixed up together make it even hotter inside. People point at me. That is the one they take care of like their own child, they whisper. But she look just like the father, eh? She not living here anymore, you know, she living with them now. I pretend not to hear.

Auntie Sally and Uncle Phillip are here. Auntie Sally kisses Tara and me, and I want to hide myself against her, but she walks off toward the back office. We follow. The bowl of bright red and yellow plastic flowers, anthuriums and calla lilies, has been removed from the dining table, which has been pushed back against the wall.

The large oval photographs—one of Ma and one of Pa, and the hand-coloured one of Ma's father wearing a big heavy chain over his suit because he was a government official, and the rectangular one of Pa when he was a boy, standing with his mother and father and his brother and sisters in a garden—have all been turned to face the wall.

Suddenly, Mummy cries out. Mama, oh Mama. She is sobbing loudly. It is frightening.

People get up and there is a crush to see. In the office Pa's desk has been moved away, and a long sky-blue box lies on a chrome stand in its place.

It looks as if Mummy is fainting. Daddy and other men and some women rush toward her. Someone makes them step away. She is slumped over the box that I know is called a coffin. Pa is on the other side of the box, watching Mummy. His face is red and crumpled. He blows his nose in his handkerchief. He sees me and signals for me to come forward. As I approach him, the moans, groans, and other sounds recede. They are replaced by a heavy drumming in my temples. It is so loud, beating in my head so hard, that my head has begun to hurt. I can't hear anything else, and the light in the room seems to have turned reddish.

Generous amounts of silky, frilly white padding frame my Ma's head. Her eyes are closed. That is not what she looks like when she sleeps. It is as if she is smiling, but the smile doesn't move so it doesn't look real. Her hands are clasped on her chest. Her nails are painted light pink. She is dressed in a pink nightgown I have never seen before. I stare at her, trying to send messages: *Get up, Ma. My ma, get up. Just get up, please.*

The sound of my heartbeats pounding in my head has stopped, replaced by no sound at all, as if I am listening to the place where she is. How long I stand and watch and repeat those words, I don't know. She just lies there, as if she doesn't know I am here, right at her side, speaking to her. Someone has come behind me, pressing against me. Hands are on my shoulders. I don't have to look to know they are Pa's. I turn and bury my face in his belly. He wraps one arm around me; the other hand keeps smoothing down my hair. Tara is also staring into the box. It is as if she isn't seeing anything.

Uncle Sonny and Auntie Stella, Diane, Savi, Sheldon, and Colin emerge from the front room. I hadn't seen them before, didn't know they were there. Uncle Sonny reaches for Mummy, and she falls into his chest and sobs. Sonny, Mama's gone. Sonny, what will I do? He holds her and rubs her back and says, Shhh. Shhh. Don't cry. Don't cry. Look, the children are looking at you. Be strong, darling.

I mustn't draw attention to myself. I am not Ma's daughter. Mummy is Ma's daughter. I wish tears weren't so foolish. You have no control over them. They just do whatever they want—fill up your eyes even though you are not crying, make everything blurry, spill over, run down your cheeks, pool on your lips, salty in your mouth.

I have to keep wiping them away. Someone offers me a handkerchief, but I shake my head. I wish people wouldn't look at me.

Pa's friends are here, the ones he plays cards with. But Uncle John isn't. I glance around to make sure, and I don't see him. I told Ma about him and look at what has happened. But something inside of me says this is not how things work. She did not die because I told her.

Colin comes behind me and pushes me. I spin around in my frilly dress, and he runs off. He turns and waits, and I know he is waiting for me to chase him. I wipe my face and take off after him. I wish I were not wearing this silly white dress. We run through the crowds, into the room with the card table and out onto the veranda. We run the length of the veranda, people pulling their feet in so we do not trip, and everyone looking alarmed and anxious. Sheldon and Tara have joined in the chase, and we are all laughing loudly, as if we want everyone to hear, to stop what they're doing and pay attention to us. I can't see very well, everything is blurred. I am flying through the house, past Sita's mother, who tries to catch me, but I bend my body away from her, sliding, tripping, arching past Miss Fatty and Mrs. Khan, the doily lady, and all the relatives who have come from Port of Spain and Chaguanas and from other places far away. I can tell that people are worried, maybe even upset with us, but I don't care, and neither does Colin, Sheldon, or Tara. Barlow is standing near the front door. She is dressed differently than she usually dresses and wears gold earrings. Our eyes meet. She doesn't try to stop us from chasing each other. I run toward the front room. People are sitting on Ma's and my bed. I fly in and out of the room as if I am an airplane, and down the corridor. I glance through one of the corridor's doors in the direction of Pa's office and see the blue box again. I carry on quickly past people who call my name and tell me to be careful, but I don't answer. I want to stop in the middle room and hide in there, lie on the bed, but there are people in that room, too. Then I reach

Pa and Ma's bedroom. The door is closed. I stop. I hadn't realized no one was chasing me anymore. I can feel people's eyes on me. I turn the doorknob slowly. It clunks open. I peep in. No one is in there. The bed is made. The light is off. It is dark. I enter and close the door behind me. On the other side of the wall is the upstairs office, and in that office is a blue box, a coffin, and in that coffin is Ma, and inside of Ma is me, and inside of me is a

noisy rushing river. I go to the bed, on Ma's side. I touch it, and the wind in the mango tree picks up and scares me. I fly off again, out the back door of the bedroom into Pa's office, the room with the blue box. I don't see Mummy and Daddy. I put my arms out, like the wings of a plane, and I turn around and around. Faster, faster I spin as I would if I were in the yard, getting dizzier and dizzier. The river in me is gurgling, rushing, giggling, laughing loudly. Pa stoops down with his arms wide open, catching me.

He wipes the tears from my face and wraps his arms around me. He smells like his 4711 cologne. He strokes the length of my ponytail down my back. He whispers so that only I, in this hot and stuffy crowded room, can hear, What will we do now, baby? I pull back and look in his eyes. He does not look like Pa. He feels and smells like him, but his face is red and puffy, his eyes are red. It is a serious face, but not angry. He kisses my cheek and puts his hands under my arms and tries to lift me. He grunts and says, Anj, darling, you're getting big, too heavy for your Pa. I want to tell him I am not too heavy, that Pa is big and strong, but when I try to speak I can't. I can part my lips, but hard as I try, no words, no sound, comes out. He calls to Frank, pulls from his pocket some dollar bills and tells Frank to take Colin, Sheldon, Tara, and me to Mr. Tang's shop and buy us whatever we want. He pulls him back and tells him, Don't let go of the girls' hands and don't dilly-dally. You have half an hour. Come back soon.

*

Mummy sleeps a lot. Uncle Phillip comes to visit often. It's depression, Uncle Phillip says to Daddy. She just needs a little time and something to help her in the interim; he's given her tablets for it.

I think I am depressed. Perhaps I should have tablets, too. But I mustn't make trouble. I don't think I should miss Ma as much as Mummy does. Sometimes the feelings go away, but they always sneak up again, they just jump out at me, and I want to fall down really hard and never get up. I want to leave this house, go in the jungle where no one will find me, curl up under a tree, sleep and never wake up. I cry, which is stupid, because only girls and women like Mummy cry, and I don't want to be like them, so even when it is difficult, I am strict with myself and do not allow myself to make any sound at all. Sometimes it's just so horrible that I want to tell Daddy, but I don't. I don't tell Pa either, as I don't want him to worry about me.

In any case, it's very important to be quiet and good so Mummy gets better fast.

She doesn't want Daddy to go out, not even to work. But he has to go to work. She cries a lot. Sometimes her face is still, like a statue. And Daddy sits looking at TV by himself. If I go into her room to see her, she always sends me out to do something—to ask Maureen this, or to do that. But Tara and Anil are allowed to lie on the bed with her.

I know what it is like to miss Ma, too, and I want to tell her this. In my head I practise the words: Mummy, I miss Ma, too. I wish she hadn't died and then you would still be able to go and see her and talk with her, which I know you used to like to do. But whenever there is a chance, I always forget them.

Once, when she was looking sad and as if she didn't even know we were right there beside her, I told her to come out on the patio, I had something to show her. I don't think she really wanted to come, but I was happy that she did. I pointed to the beautiful sunset over the mangroves. The sky was filled with many colours: pink, orange, purple, red, yellow. But it seemed to require the greatest effort for her to look at the sky; she barely glanced up before turning away, as if it had blinded her. I waited, but she said nothing for a long time. And then, as if remembering that I was there, she said in a low voice, Every evening we see a sunset. They are all the same.

LEVER DU SOLEIL EAST

NINE

I was not given any choice. After living in that house in mosquito-infested Marabella for almost a year, they have moved to a house in what is called a residential area in San Fernando. I had to go with them. A hope had leapt up inside me when I learned about the move. I thought it meant I'd be able to move back to Selvon Street, back to Pa. I should have known better. I should have given up this idea by now, but hopes just pop up, all on their own, and then when they get my attention, they laugh and say, Just teasing. Just joking.

Residential means that here in Lever du Soleil East, houses—all concrete—line both sides of the streets and there are no businesses, no empty land, no jungle anywhere. It's a large neighbourhood of houses. We are number 2 Crystal Road, Lever du Soleil East, San Fernando, Trinidad (next to Tobago), West Indies, Caribbean, World, the Milky Way. You can add "Universe" if you want, but that might be silly, because while there may be houses on other planets in the Milky Way, and houses on other planets in other galaxies, all galaxies are in the universe, and as far as astronomers know, this is the only universe that exists. Until they prove themselves wrong, this is it. That's what Daddy says anyway.

He doesn't know that I speak to the stars—no one but Pa knows this, not even Tara—but he does know I love the sky at night. I think he likes it, too, but he likes knowing the names of things. I just like looking at them, twinkling, almost dancing in their own place, and of course I like speaking—in my mind—to them. When he names the stars he knows, he is proud, as if, because he knows their names, they belong to him.

The house is painted dark green, trimmed in white, and much bigger than the Marabella one. The front steps are a red as deep as the dark green house. There are two gates, the back gate and the front one. When we have visitors, they must park their car on the street and enter through the front gate, then walk along a concrete pathway painted that same deep red, to the stairs that lead up to the front door. Tara and I like this house much better than the Marabella house. She, Siri, and I share a room. But I would leave here in a second if Pa would take me back.

This neighbourhood is not far, at least not by car, from where Pa lives all by himself now. This is not a hope, it's just a thought, and I probably shouldn't even think about it, but I do: although it would take a long time to walk to Selvon Street, if I had to, I could. When I close my eyes, I see the route, every house I must pass—some with dogs that go crazy jumping on the fence and barking as if I am going to come into their yard—and outside of this residential area I also know every street corner, traffic light, shop, business building, the many khaki-coloured buildings of the Government School with its green roofs, the steep hill past the school, and the old sprawling mango tree under which sits an old man on his blue bench—he wears colourful cloths tied around his head—selling sweets and fruit chows every school day. It's a long way to walk, so I'd have to stop at that man's blue stand and I'd buy sugar cake for Pa, maybe fudge for Polly, pretend cigarettes for Frank, pink-and-white-striped sour cherry candies for Barlow, and from his large glass jars mango chow and also pommecythere chow for me, and also bene balls for me and maybe salt prunes or preserved plums. Then, after that, from the top of the hill, where I can see buildings far away on the other side of the town—the San Fernando General Hospital and the steeples of the Catholic church and the Anglican church, but I wouldn't have to go as far as those—I'd start going downhill again, and then at the house with the large baskets of ferns hanging from the ceiling all across the veranda I'd turn right and go down that hill, and when I reached Mr. Tang's shop I'd turn left, and our house—Pa's, that is—would be just a few houses away from there, and across from ours would be Sita's. Oh, I'd buy mango chow for Sita, or just share mine with her. It would take a while, and I'd have to look out for cars on the busy roads, but if I had to, I could get to Selvon Street on my own.

The houses on Crystal Road are all fenced off from the road and from each other by low concrete walls from which decorative wrought-iron staves rise. Out of one corner of almost all the yards, including Mummy and Daddy's, rises a fan-shaped traveller's palm.

People here have gardens that are more like Ma's than the ones in Marabella. But when we go to Selvon Street now, the rose bushes at the front don't look as good as they used to. Ma used to clip all the old flowers, but now you see flowers wilted, and browned, dry, all over the plants, and the leaves have bachac holes in them.

Mummy knows the names of almost all the plants we see in this neighbourhood. She likes the shrubs called mussaenda best, with their big floppy salmon-coloured flowers. She's going to get mussaendas from the nursery in St. Joseph and plant them here soon. There are hibiscus shrubs, too, some with red flowers, some with yellow ones, and just like at Pa's house, tall droopy poinsettia form hedges on the insides of the fences—all of Ma's were deep red, and here you see pink ones. All the way down the sidewalk of Crystal Road are small trees whose lumpy branches spread like many-armed ladies dancing, waving their long pointy leaves. This is the frangipani plant. Their flowers bunch up at the tips of the branches, large and cream-coloured with yellow in the centre. They have a very strong smell, one minute like coconut-scented suntan lotion, and the next like overripe bananas, and you can get a headache if you're around them for too long. They are so pretty that you want to pick bunches of them, but they are poisonous. Children and dogs can get really sick, you can fall over in pain, you will drool, your

whole body will itch. You might even die. And yet there is a huge black-and-yellow-striped caterpillar that has a bright red nub of a head that lives on the frangipani tree. The frangipani sphinx caterpillar. Sometimes the trees get covered in these caterpillars, and you don't know which is more beautiful, the flower or the caterpillar. But the caterpillar, too, is poisonous. Why? Because you are what you eat. So we can't keep them as pets to watch them turn into the giant sphinx moths.

Except for the chatter of all kinds of birds, and in the nighttime the piercing note of the crickets, and frogs that sound like old dogs barking, it used to be quiet around the house in Marabella. But here on Crystal Road, all day long and late into the night cars swoosh past, one after the other on the bypass that divides Lever du Soleil East from Pleasantville; people walk in from Pleasantville, past the house, selling vegetables; the fish truck crawls down the road, honking its horn; and just across the way from this house a steel pan player practises scales—doh ray me fa so la ti doh, doh ti la so fa me ray doh. Over and over. It is annoying, you wake up to it in the morning, and he doesn't stop until past dinnertime. Sometimes he plays popular songs, but so slowly that it makes you want to go over to his house and shake him up. He plays calypsos, too, the same way. And a kind of music Maureen says is called classical music.

Every house has a dog—now we have dogs, too, two of them, a young brown-and-white boxer Anil named Bruno who jumps on everybody and everything, and an old dog called Caesar who had belonged to one of Daddy's patients, an old white lady, who couldn't care for him anymore. Caesar is a Rhodesian ridgeback, and he has a line of fur that runs along his spine the length of his body, but it grows in the opposite direction of the rest of his fur. He is the colour of vanilla fudge, and he walks with a limp and pants a lot. Mummy loves Caesar. And I love Caesar, too.

A dog will bark at a pedestrian and interrupt the pan man's music, and that one dog's bark will be followed by two others, then three, and the next thing you know the entire neighbourhood of dogs, including Bruno, will be barking and howling—even old Caesar, grunting with effort, but he looks happy when he does that—and a voice here and there will shout, Be quiet, or Shut up.

A home surgery was built under the house for patients who visit after Daddy's office hours. They always wait for him to leave his office, and they come here before he even has time for dinner. The surgery is supposed to be for emergencies, but the patients who come are not usually having an emergency problem: they just don't want to have to wait with the other patients in his office. This is so ridiculous. That's what Mummy says. She also says there is an emergency department at the hospital with lots of doctors, specialists, too, and nurses, and equipment that a home surgery doesn't have, and Daddy should discourage people from coming to the house. Daddy doesn't like to take money directly from people, so he tells the patients who come here to go to his office when they can and pay the receptionist. But he doesn't check to see if they do this. He says Mummy needs to have more compassion, and she says he has to cultivate a business brain.

Behind the house, for a fence, there is a tall concrete wall. A river flows on the other side of the wall. It's not a real river, but it is wide and deep and looks like a river. The new yardman, Sharma, calls it a gutter and says it's man-made, for the control of rainy-season flooding. Whenever I hear the municipal workers, I run to the window at the back of the dining room upstairs to watch them. Dressed in their tall rubber boots, they balance on the thin ledge that runs along the wall on the other side of the river gutter. They use brooms with extra-long handles to scrub and sweep the concrete-paved sides; they grip the top of the wall with one hand and lean over the river with the broom in the other hand and drag it across the floor of the river. I keep waiting for one of them to fall in, but they are very good at balancing, and they move down the ledge very swiftly, as if they are gliding. They are supposed to clean off the long flowing hair-like strands of bright green moss that sway in the water, but the moss grows back in no time. They drag garbage from the surface of the water, bag it, and haul the bags over the far wall, so the drains don't get blocked and overflow when it rains. All the while, as they twist and turn their bodies, and you think they might fall in, they talk and talk and talk, and they laugh a lot. I can hear them—they don't speak softly—but I don't understand anything they say. They sometimes see me looking at them, but they don't even wave to me. If they waved, I'd wave back, but I'd have to do so without the maid or Mummy seeing, because we're not supposed to be friendly with those kinds of workers. And then they move out of sight, making their way down the row of houses, their sounds gradually fading, and then it's the pan man's music coming from the front that you pay attention to again.

*

Daddy moved his private office again, from Marabella right into San Fernando. Daddy is being employed by oil companies, small ones as well as the big ones, like Texaco and British Petroleum, as the company doctor. He is also now one of the doctors for the United States of America Embassy, doing the medicals for people who are applying to emigrate to the U.S. One day he came home and excitedly told us all that he was appointed the doctor for a big insurance company, which I supposed was almost like a promotion, not only in his field as a doctor but in life, and in front of us he pulled Mummy toward him and kissed her on her mouth—we giggled, and she pulled back, telling him, as she was laughing, too, to behave himself. He said, It's happening, darling. It's beginning to roll in. You will get your Rome before you know it.

She said, My Rome? You mean yours.

And now, Mummy has a car, a green Karmann Ghia with a soft top that can come down. She doesn't drive around with the top down, though, as she doesn't want, she says, to bring attention to herself. Daddy tells her she should do it, she should get a nice scarf and tie it over her head and around her chin—he pretends to place it on her head and tie it for her—and that she'd easily be mistaken for somebody called Audrey Hepburn.

This house is only temporary; they want to live, they say, by the sea. They have been searching for land to buy, on which they will build a house for us, with a swimming pool. That's funny: we will one day live by the sea and still have a swimming pool in our yard. But it will take a few years, we are told. I don't say it aloud, but I do think about it: if a house is to be built, then a room for me, and me alone, can be included in the plan from the very beginning.

There are so many changes, and with every change it feels as if Ma is slipping farther and farther away. Sometimes I have this very strong feeling, a happy feeling, that I must telephone her immediately, that I have something to tell her, or I must see her right away. And then I remember.

She doesn't know this house. If we move to another one, that will make two houses that she doesn't know. Or didn't know. I'm not sure what is the correct way to say this. Anyway, the more things happen, the farther back she is pushed.

*

Almost every night I dream that Mummy has picked us up from school and is driving us to Pa and Ma's house. When we get there, Pa is on the veranda, waiting. I run up the big red front stairs. He doesn't speak, but he points to their bedroom. I run to the bedroom, and something the size and shape of a person is lying on the bed. Even though it doesn't look like Ma, I behave as if it is. She, maybe it, waves me forward and tells me to come and lie down with her. She, or it, has no skin. It is covered in streaks of wet blood that keeps oozing tiny bubbles, thick and shiny, from its flesh. I climb onto the bed, lie next to her, *her* because it has to be her, and I hug her. I run my hand up and down her raw body, trying at the same time not to hurt her. I always wake up at this point, and often I am crying, and I can feel my awake self begging her to come back.

I won't tell Mummy or Daddy about this dream, but I told it to Pa.

He tells me, Shhh, shhh. That's just a dream, darling. You're dreaming about her because you miss her. I miss her, too.

I ask, Why is there so much blood?

He says, That is only in your dream. Maybe you think she died in an accident? There was no blood. Her heart just stopped working.

*

Mornin', madam. Mornin', boss. It's coming from down on the road. Mummy isn't at home. She's gone to the grocery and hairdresser. Daddy is at work.

Mornin', mornin'. The calling is getting closer. Tara and I, curious, run to our louvred windows and peer down. We can't see anyone. Tall hibiscus shrubs along the fence block the view of the sidewalks and part of the road. Bruno is running back and forth along the hedge; he's jumping up, trying to get in between the shrubs; he wants to get at the fence. Caesar is standing on the lawn, trying to bark, but coughing weakly, wheezing.

There it is again, but louder now, and therefore nearer: Mornin', boss. Mornin', madam. A man's voice. Singsong. Not at all demanding. Through the shrubbery, we can see some movement, but still not who the person is. Bruno is going crazy. Hush up, dog, shouts Sharma. Bruno continues barking and now growling, and Sharma is shouting, Dog, keep quiet. Shut up. Then Bruno begins to cry. Sharma must have grabbed him; the clanking of the chain tells us that Sharma is tying him to the post at the foot of the stairs.

And here at the gate now is an old beggar man holding a long stick in one hand and a flour sack in the other. His clothing, a dirty shirt that must have once been white with the sleeves rolled to his elbows, and khaki pants, the hems turned up so that his pale ankles are exposed, hangs off him. He wears open slippers that don't fit his feet. His wild, long hair and the wide, loose beard it runs into look familiar, but I don't think I know anyone like this. The large mass on his head is parted in the middle and falls to below his shoulders. The hair on his face—cheeks, moustache, and beard—are all white, but dirtyish. He grips the gate with a finger through the rigid chain-link, that same hand also holding the stick, as if he is taking a rest. He calls again and glances up toward the windows. He sees us looking at him. Seeming not to really expect a response, he lets go of the gate, puts his weight on the stick, and begins to turn away. Tara whispers, Anj, do you know who that man is? It sounds as if she does, and I think I do, too. But this scares me a little, and I say, No. I think he's hungry.

I call out, Morning. He turns and walks back to the gate. He looks up again. His eyes shine brightly through the white facial hair. I do know who he is.

I whisper, He is the man in the Sunday-school pictures.

Tara says, Yes. Do you remember Ma telling us that he can come dressed as a beggar, to test children?

He turns to leave again. I shout, Wait a minute, please, and say to Tara, Let's pray quickly. We back away from the window and thank God for sending his Only Beloved Son to us. I say a quick prayer to Ma, thanking her, too. I can feel it in my heart that it is she who has made this happen, and I know she is watching.

Tara's job is to keep the man there. Mine is to get him lunch. I run to the kitchen and breathlessly order the new maid, Dolly: There's a man at the gate; make him lunch, please.

As Dolly shouts back at me, I take off down the back stairs. Somewhat brazened by the immense good fortune and wonder at having Jesus at our back gate—and somewhat afraid—I call Sharma and tell him to let the man come in.

Offer him the bench to sit on, I tell Sharma, and tell him we're making him lunch. Sharma, alarmed, says, No, you can't let that man come inside here.

From where I am now, Jesus and Ma can see me, and I know they are seeing the effort we are making. I am nearer to Ma than I have been in a long time.

I tell Sharma softly, It's OK, he's OK. You *can* let him in.

But Sharma doesn't budge. In an instant, I rise up taller than I've ever been in my life, indignant, a demon fighting for good. Sharply, I blurt out that when Mummy and Daddy are not around, I am the boss, and if he doesn't do as I say, he will be fired.

He stares at me. I shout, Do it, Sharma. Sucking his teeth, he goes to the gate and lets Jesus in. I run back upstairs. Dolly and Maureen are both in the kitchen now, aware of what is happening. Dolly says this isn't right. She isn't making food for people she doesn't know. Maureen just looks at me. She doesn't say anything, and I take this to mean she is in agreement with me. I explain to Dolly that how we treat this man is a sign of the kind of people we are, and that as good people, we must give him a proper meal. She says she can't give him our lunch, there is only enough for the family and for the workers. Unsure now, I plead with her to make him a sandwich. She asks Maureen what she should do, and Maureen says, There's enough; no harm in sharing. Reluctantly, Dolly searches the fridge for something to give Jesus—whom I haven't so named to her. From the bread bag she takes out two slices of bread. She cuts a slice of cheese. I ask her to add another. She does and puts them between the bread. I stop her and, hearing myself sound like Mummy, I tell her to add a couple of leaves of lettuce. And a slice of tomato. And to butter the bread and spread mayonnaise on one side. When she prepares to wrap the sandwich in wax paper, I stop her, telling her to remove the crust and cut the sandwich diagonally like she would for us, to put it on a plate, with a knife and fork, a napkin, and place it on a tray with a glass of orange juice. Almost laughing now—but not her usual laugh—she does as I ask. She even carries it down herself to Jesus, who is now sitting on the bench. Tara and I follow her down the back stairs and sit on a step midway down, where we watch through the latticework that runs on that side instead of a railing. We can hardly breathe. Dolly waits until Jesus has taken a bite of the sandwich, then she speaks to him. She is blessed.

Soon, Jesus places his empty plate on the tray and stands, dusting off his clothing. He turns to look at Tara and me through the latticework. My heart thunders. He picks up his stick and walks past the bench toward the lattice. Facing us, he moves his stick under his arm, brings his hands up to his chest, and presses them together like we do when we are praying to him, and looking into our eyes, he bows his head. Tara and I stand and return the gesture. Tears run down my face, and when I look at Tara, she, too, is crying. We, too, are blessed, and I feel close to Ma. We clutch the lattice to better see as he walks away, the gate closing behind him.

Tara and I go immediately into our bedroom, spent. We close the door behind us. We kneel on one side of the bed, and we pray for a long time, letting God know how grateful we are for this opportunity, for blessing us in this way. I thank Ma, too, for getting God to test us, and for having taught us how to pass the test.

Since Jesus's departure, we have not left our bedroom and are admittedly a little worried about what trouble we might face. Mummy and Daddy arrive some hours apart but enter our room together. They sit on the bed, side by side, something they only ever do when trouble is brewing. They tell us they understand we'd had an adventure. I explain quickly that Ma used to feed all the beggars in San Fernando on the first Saturday morning of every month beneath the house on Selvon Street, and she once told us that Jesus usually appears on earth in the guise of a beggar. He sometimes does this, she told us, to see if you are a kind person who treats others with respect and compassion.

I sense we might have made a mistake. Daddy looks stern. That is all well and good, he says, but I hear that when we are not here, you are Sharma's boss?

I knew I was wrong when I said that to Sharma, but it seemed necessary at the time. Neither Tara nor I answer.

When we are not at home, he continues, we have hired people to look after you, and you are to respect them, understood?

We both nod.

Now let me ask you something, he says. Your Ma was a good woman, and she was right about treating people with respect.

Tara added, And compassion.

It looked to me as if he were about to smile, but he said, And compassion, but did your Ma ever tell you that God and Jesus only ever test a person once in their lifetime?

Tara and I shake our heads to say no.

He says he knows this for certain, that you only ever get the test once in your lifetime. And now that we have been given the test in our childhood, and no doubt, from what he and Mummy heard, passed it with a high grade, it is not something we will ever need to do again.

He stands up, and Mummy does, too. As they walk toward the door, Daddy turns and says, By the way, will one of you please ask Dolly to make me a nice cheese sandwich? No tomato, just lettuce, OK?

*

Tara and I have been taken out of Miss Mason's school and are now attending the primary school of the convent near to Daddy's office. We are not Catholics, but you don't have to be a Catholic to go to the convent school. On special school days we do have to attend the church across the street, though, and in between classes we must—even if we're not Catholics—stand and make the sign of the cross and say the Hail Mary. HailMaryfullofgracetheLordiswiththeeblessedartthouamongwomenand-blessedisthefruitofthywombJesusHolyMaryMotherofGod-prayforussinnersnowandatthehourofourdeathamen. We try to see which of us, Tara or I, can say it faster without making a mistake. I can say it very fast, clear, and without a single mistake. She can't even finish it without tumbling over the words and bursting into laughter, as if she is being tickled, tears running down her face, and her laughter makes me begin to laugh also, even when I don't know what she is laughing at.

The seven- and eight-year-old students are to be toy soldiers in a play the convent is putting on at the big theatre in San Fernando at the end of the school year. Which means I am to be a toy soldier. Mummy attends meetings at the convent about rehearsal times, our costumes, and the upcoming performance. The parents have to sell tickets for the show, and she has already sold many tickets. She took me to the dressmaker, who is making the red jackets with gold buttons for all the toy soldiers and the black pants with a shiny black stripe down the sides. And she bought a pair of white boots for me, because there are no children's black boots to be found anywhere on the island, but Sharma painted them black. He did it very neatly.

The only lines we are to learn will be sung—*Toyland, Toyland / Little girl and boy land / While you dwell within it / You are ever happy there.* There are more verses, but after that one, the school choir sings the rest. But we are learning to march in unison, lifting our knees high in time to the beat of the music, swinging our arms in time, our hands open, fingers stiff and tightly held together, pointed at the ground. I love wearing the uniform and marching like this. Pa is coming to the opening. I wish Ma were here. She would have come, too. Pa will be very proud of me. I have been trying to teach him the part of the song the toy soldiers will sing. Uncle Sonny and Auntie Stella and my cousins will also come.

Being a soldier is as good, I think, if not better than being a cowboy. Whenever I try to be a cowboy with Colin and Sheldon, I have to beg, to insist, to almost begin crying, which makes me seem weak and not very much like a real cowboy. But when I wear the soldier's uniform, I march about the house, and it is as if I really am a soldier. Soldiers protect nations. Cowboys tie up and shoot people, rope horses, and make cattle fall to the ground. Not all of them, but many. Everyone says how well I march. No one tells me I can't be a soldier. When we practise onstage, I imagine Sheldon and Colin in the audience, seeing how strong and handsome I am. And I imagine Pa, and I pretend Ma is there and I imagine her, too, smiling and happy to see me like this. Tara is in the play, too, but the students her age sit on the floor of the stage, in the middle of potted plants, and they sing or just look on. They are always waving to other students or teachers in the theatre during rehearsals, even though they have been told a hundred thousand times not to do that.

The leader of the toy soldiers in the play is a man named Tom. He wants to marry the love of his life, a woman named Mary. But all the actors in the play are people from my school, and there are no men in my school. So Tom is really a girl student whose real name is Martina. She is in the highest class at school, doing her Advanced Levels. So is Mary, whose real name is Marilyn. Even when Martina is not rehearsing, she is like a handsome boy. Marilyn is pretty, and very kind.

Tara and I are in the junior part of the school. Rehearsals of the full play are too long for us little children, so we only go to the theatre to rehearse our part, after which we are picked up by parents or drivers as soon as our section is finished, so I have never seen the whole play.

*

Tara didn't come to school today. She has a fever. It's the end of practice time for the toy soldiers and the end of our school day, and I am on my own, waiting with the other soldiers to be picked up. The crowd of soldiers is getting smaller as each is picked up in quick succession by their parents or drivers. I don't see Mummy's car in the line of cars crawling toward us. From out here in the parking lot, you can hear the actors doing their parts onstage but can't see them. I wait and wait, and soon everyone else has been picked up but me. The older student in charge of taking care of me, Shahida, keeps trying to hold my hand. I don't like it. I'm not going to run away, or be grabbed from the parking lot, or get run over by a car. I wish she wouldn't treat me as if I am a baby. I don't want to be rude, so I take my hand away and brush my hair back with it, scratch my other arm, point to a long hanging bunch of orange dates in a grugru palm tree on the grounds, but each time she tries to take it again.

I wonder if Tara had come to school today, if she were waiting with me, if we wouldn't have been forgotten. Shahida takes me into the theatre's office and asks a teacher there to phone my parents and see what's going on. The house line is busy, so they phone Daddy's office. They find out that the driver is supposed to pick me up today in Mummy's car, but he had to run an errand in Port of Spain and should have been back in time to pick me up. Daddy's receptionist does some phoning around and calls the theatre office to say she has learned that a tractor overturned on the highway and traffic has been stalled for hours while that mess is being cleaned up. They will send someone else for me, and we are to look out for a private taxi. A nun comes and tells Shahida to wait with me in the foyer of the building, but when we get to the foyer Shahida asks, You want to go by the entrance doors and wait? We could watch the play from there. She says we will be able to see the taxi from there when it arrives. She hurries me along and keeps looking back, and I think it is to see if any nuns or teachers are noticing that we are going toward the auditorium.

From where we stand, at the back of the auditorium, the entire stage is visible, and we are high up enough to see the orchestra. In the audience, teachers, nuns, and older students are seated, their backs to us. I wish I could have seen, from here, how we looked when we marched. But I am tired now, and hungry, and want to go home. I am sad that all the other toy soldiers have already gone home, and I am still here waiting for someone to come and pick me up. If Pa knew I'd been left like this, he would have sent Mr. Monty for me.

Tom and Mary are onstage. Tom has his arm around Mary. But everyone knows that Tom isn't actually a man. Tom is Martina, and Mary is Marilyn. But when Tom Martina and Mary Marilyn turn to face each other and Tom Martina puts his—but really *her*—arms around Mary Marilyn, I feel the skin on my face begin to burn. The student who is looking after me has her hand on my shoulder. I move a few paces away from her. Then Tom Martina and Mary Marilyn kiss. They kiss. I think they actually kissed on their mouths. The students in the auditorium clap and have begun to laugh out very loudly and make kissing sounds with their mouths and are whistling. Tom and Mary kissed. But no, it was Martina and Marilyn. Martina kissed Marilyn. The cheering and loud laughter and chattering carry on, and Martina and Marilyn are also laughing, but they kiss again. And one of the nuns gets up and claps her hands for the noise in the auditorium to stop and another nun has walked out onstage and is speaking to Tom and Mary, to Martina and Marilyn. I hate Martina.

Well, not hate. The other day, when Colin and Sheldon would not let me be a cowboy and said that if I did not want to be captured or rescued, I should go play dolly house with Tara, I screamed, I hate you. Mummy and Auntie Stella came out on the veranda, and Mummy pulled me by the back of my T-shirt and said, Who did you say that to?

I crouched down, expecting to get a slap. She snapped, I never want to hear you say that to anyone again. Do you hear me? You are never to use the word *hate* again.

I learned later that evening, after Colin and Sheldon had gone home with Auntie Stella, and Daddy came home for dinner before leaving again to attend a meeting, that hate is the cause of a lot of suffering in the world.

That's Daddy. He explains everything. Mummy quarrels with us and Daddy explains. He is usually very reasonable with us, so I made a case, reasonably: I hate sardines with onions, so how does that cause suffering?

He thought about my question and then answered. Words are powerful when they are used properly, and when they are misused, they can actually be dangerous. Lots of words can have similar meanings, but each of those words might have a slightly different weight or stress, or have a different association than the others. I know you won't eat sardines. But do you hate them? Do you hate them as much as you hate it when people, say, kill frogs?

I knew better than to say what was in my mind: that that was a silly question because the answer was obvious, so I answered, No, that's different.

Then what is a way to say those two things differently?

This was difficult. I asked, I hate, not people, but when they kill animals? I don't *like* sardines, because there are too many soft bones in them, but that's not a reason to hate them?

He kissed my forehead and said, That's my girl.

That made me shy.

So, I'm sorry I said that I hate Martina. I don't even dislike her. I just wish I were Tom.

*

The man who lives directly opposite this house, Mr. Ray Scott, has three daughters; two of them, Jen and Julie Scott, are twins. Their house has an open wraparound veranda, and the twins lie on the ledge of the veranda in very short shorts and halter tops, which Mummy says is scandalous. Teenagers, she says, shouldn't wear such clothing, but that just goes to show: white people have different values, even for their children. And then she adds, No wonder so few of them ever go to university or do anything useful with themselves.

Tara and I peep at Jen and Julie Scott from our bedroom window, the louvres opened just enough for us to see them without them seeing us. Their hair is the colour of jungle honey, and they are so beautiful, we wish we could be like them. Well, Tara does: she says when she is their age, she will wear halter tops like those, even if Mummy doesn't like it. And she adds, with annoyance in her voice, that doesn't mean people are not bright.

We think they know we are watching them because it is as if they are posing when they lie on the ledge. They are older than us, by a lot. Maybe they are sixteen. Sweet sixteen. They won't look over our way, and even when we are in the garden and they are downstairs, right in front of us, they don't look at us. I wish they would.

One day, Tara and I hear music coming from their house. We sneak through our room to the window and carefully hide ourselves with the curtains, she on one side, I on the other. We each angle the bank of louvres on our side, opening them just enough to be able to peer across the street. Jen and Julie Scott are dancing on the veranda, slowly, and they seem to glance toward us, then quickly away.

I want to be there with them. I'd dance with the one called Julie, named like the sweetest and most expensive of mangoes. I'd squeeze her oh so tight—like a phrase in the song that is playing. Then the music changes and, facing each other, they jump about and pump their hands in the air and then point their fingers at each other and then pump their fists again but now to the sides—it is as if they are in a crazy-crazy frenzy, but it is always in time to the beat of the music. They have turned that piece of music up really loud. There is a line about a person who is supposed to be high-classed—but the singer makes a mistake and says, *You was high-classed*—which should be *You* were *high-classed*—and they are mouthing the words in an exaggerated way. They lean toward each other and say that line, stressing *high-classed* as if they are taunting each other. I find myself moving to the beat, but Mummy always tells us that good Indian girls don't behave wildly in public, don't make a display of their bodies—I suppose like Julie and Jen are doing right there in the open for all to see—and that it is at home that you practise good behaviour. So I don't move about like Jen and Julie, I just move a tiny bit. In any case, I don't know the music like they do; when the drums do a rapid-fire roll, they both beat the air as if it were an actual drum set right there in front of them. They are fantastic. I slowly raise my hand to the latch of the louvre, to pry it open just a little more so I can better see—the length of the balcony, the balcony framed by the Christmas palms (which grow all year long, so I don't know why they are called by this name), and the two beauties crazy-dancing. But one of the louvres, one that has always been a little loose, slips out of its casing and goes crashing with a horrible sound, like windshield glass in a car accident, onto the concrete driveway below. Tara and I gasp and duck down, my heart thunders, and my skin feels as if it is shot at with a thousand arrows. Mummy is out, but when she returns, she is going to kill us, I'm sure. Stooping low, we both scamper to the far side of the room. We hear the high-classed sweet sixteens opposite laughing out loud.

Tara is shaking. I tell her that when Mummy comes home, she should go to the washroom and stay there. Say she has a tummy ache and has to stay on the toilet, and I'll explain to Mummy that the louvre just fell out on its own, and that all the louvres really should be checked, because what if we had been down there, riding our bicycles when that one fell?

Sharma has already begun to sweep up the broken glass downstairs.

I will never watch Jen and Julie Scott again. I hate them for laughing. I hate Julie Scott. But not really. It's just that if I were a boy and not a girl, or maybe not just a boy, maybe I'd have to be a white boy, they wouldn't laugh at us; they'd wave to us. Julie Scott would laugh with me, not at me, and we could go to birthday parties, and when the lights were turned down low, she'd dance with me.

TEN

Daddy is saying, for the umpteenth time now, that he can't live in this country without doing something for the people. He is standing in the living room, in front of the window. Although the light behind him partially silhouettes him, it looks like stage lighting and he a character on a stage.

It sounds as if Mummy, sitting on the sofa facing him, one minute like an audience of one, the next like a sympathetic friend, is encouraging when she says, But you are a doctor. You *are* helping your people, The People.

I am at the dining table making a drawing, just feet away from them. When they interact like this, him talking about his dreams and wishes, she listening and wanting to know more, I listen—although I pretend not to even be there—and learn things about them both.

But I should have expected it—in no time she becomes terse: Every single evening, every night, every weekend, The People come calling at the back gate, as if they only get sick when you're at home here with us. The People are devious, Suresh. You don't need to do anything more.

It's odd because he sounds like us when he is pleading. Can't you see what I'm talking about? It's not about individuals.

I am talking about the improvement of rural communities. I mean, think about this: A child in a rural area is walking on the road. She is barefoot, walking to her school. On the way she gets bitten by a poisonous snake, or steps on broken glass thrown out of the window of a passing car. Yes, that child is an individual. But do you know that while we have snakebite antivenom in the hospitals in towns like San Fernando—where you'd hardly come across a snake—it is highly unlikely there is any antivenom where that child lives because snake venom has to be kept refrigerated, and there is usually no electricity in her area? There isn't even a full-time doctor in those rural areas. You know how far she would have to travel to get medical attention fast? She would die, she would bleed to death. She is only one person, that's true, but her life depends on the well-being of her entire community.

Daddy turns and faces the garden. I think he is thinking. Mummy says, Well, we are living in San Fernando, and there isn't much you can do about that from here. I am not moving to any rural area.

He says, Oh, come on, pet, use your imagination. This is a political question.

Her words are crisp now when she says, Don't start up with that again. Are you telling me you're getting involved, or asking me? He doesn't answer, and her voice rises when she snaps, Don't turn your back on me, Suresh. We're having a conversation, aren't we? Talk to me. Have you been talking with Robert? What are you not telling me? I'm tired of this. You sound like you want to be the minister of health!

His voice brightens when he says, Perhaps, or minister of finance, education maybe, or, truthfully, something higher.

She stresses her words now. Truthfully, my foot. Look, this is no joking matter. Suresh, listen to me good. When a man is in politics, it is not just him. It is his wife and his children. There'll be no privacy for me, for us, or for the children. I am not giving up my family life. It hasn't even been two years since we returned to Trinidad, and in this short space of time I have lost my mother. I am not losing my husband too. No, I don't want you involved in politics.

I know you lost your mother, he responds, but his voice sounds weak. But everything doesn't stop there. I understand you're grieving. That won't stop now, but we absolutely have no choice but to move forward.

He is waiting for a response. None comes, and moving away from the window, he sits on an armchair facing her and continues in a gentle voice.

That child's parents, Vij, or maybe her grandparents, have likely been in this country for decades, or at the very least for a generation or two. The old people in those kinds of areas, the old sugar-cane farmers, they were among the last to have been brought to Trinidad by the British as indentured servants. And since then, they are no different than when they arrived. Little has changed for them. It is quite possible, he says, they didn't vote in the elections. You know why? Because they can't read or write. So there is no representation in Parliament in these areas.

Well, there are many capable young people in the country, Mummy says. Let them do the kind of work you're talking about. And I don't need a history lesson, or to be lectured. I have said it before and I will say it again: I am not giving up my family life to be the wife of a politician, you hear? Why can't you just listen to what I want, for once, please.

And you listen to me, Vij. I am not looking for a hobby, you know. This is not even my dream, he says, sounding hurt. This is a responsibility.

There is a moment of silence before she says, And now you're saying I'm getting in the way of your dreams?

My God, I never said any such thing, he protests. Look, I can't talk to you if you're not listening to anything I am saying.

He gets up. He is going toward the front door. I can't draw anymore. I put down my pencil and the eraser and look at them.

Mummy has stood up, too, and is following him. So, what? You're going to leave now? Where are you going, Suresh?

He says nothing as he makes his way down the stairs. Mummy turns and marches off to her bedroom and slams the door behind her. Quietly, I tiptoe to the window. I listen for sounds of the back gate being opened, the car. But now I see him. He is walking slowly in the garden with a cigarette in his hand.

*

Daddy has been paying visits to Uncle Robert, the man who was on the truck bed that Sunday before Christmas when we were driving through the neighbourhood on the way to Ma's house for lunch. Mummy isn't happy about this. Uncle Robert was appointed the parliamentary representative for the area we live in. Daddy looks up to him. He hasn't stopped trying to convince Daddy to join his political party, the one currently governing. Mummy says she feels betrayed and as if she has no say in what is going on in her own home. Daddy assures her that he hasn't made any decision yet; he is conflicted. She doesn't want to hear anything about how conflicted he is. He has to stop all this nonsense right away.

But Daddy can't stop talking about the country, so sometimes, when he is home on an evening, at the dinner table in front of Mummy he speaks to Tara and me about the history and politics of Trinidad and Tobago. Mummy just keeps her eyes on the plate in front of her, or she stares straight ahead at the cupboards on the far wall, and he just talks and talks.

Our national anthem, he has told us more than once, says, *Every creed and race finds an equal place*, but that is how it *should* be, not how it is. Every creed and race *should*, ideally, find an equal place. But, he says, politics in Trinidad is race-based. He, however, wants to work for all people regardless of race or creed, but Uncle Robert's party, the People's National Movement, is truly the party of Blacks and doesn't pay attention to the needs of the country's Indian population. The Democratic Labour Party, the traditionally Indian party, has been in disarray for too long now and could do with strong leadership.

He explains that Indians—our ancestors—were brought to Trinidad from India after African slavery was abolished. At the time of abolition, Britain ruled India as well as Trinidad and Tobago, and they brought people from over there to work here on the cocoa and sugar plantations. Our ancestors came as servants—Yes, that's right, he says when he sees the alarm on our faces, servants—under a program known as indentureship.

Dolly has gone home for the day, but Maureen is in the kitchen. If she is listening, she will surely hear all of this lesson we're getting. Mummy doesn't like this. She whispers to Daddy, This can wait until we're in our bedroom. She nods in the direction of the kitchen. Daddy says, in the same volume he has been using, But this is our country's history, there is nothing to be ashamed of. I am not hiding to talk about this. And, after a big inhale of breath, an expression, I think, of exasperation, he carries on. You see, he says, speaking slowly now, the ex-slaves didn't want to do the same kind of work, or to work for the same people under whom they had been slaves. Can you blame them?

I shake my head to say no. He says, Exactly, so a different labour force was needed as a replacement, and that's how come there are Indians here, so very far from India. The people of African origin, the Blacks, they moved far away from the rural plantation areas where they were worked to the bone and mistreated, and they took up jobs in the towns. But the Indians tended to remain, for the most part, as workers on the agricultural estates. And many of them have remained there to this day.

I ask if they were mistreated, too, and he says yes, but they had more freedoms. But he doesn't want to dwell on history, he wants to talk about the present.

Do you know, he tells us, changing the topic, there isn't running water or electricity in the houses like the ones we pass when we go to Pupah? Fifty years after the last shipload of Indian servants arrived in Trinidad, these people, those in the rural areas, are still using pitch oil lamps at night. How could children study for school and compete properly under such conditions?

I am thinking of the answer to this question, but before I can come up with it, I realize he doesn't actually want one from us, because he is already answering it himself. He talks slowly and patiently as he tries to make his thoughts understandable to us.

Schools there, he says, have never been properly funded, and from everything promised during the election season, and everything currently happening with this new government, a government by Blacks for Blacks, you know that nothing will change in these areas. Right now, there aren't any trained teachers assigned to the few primary and elementary schools. And there are no secondary schools in any case. In any community there are bound to be children who are innately bright, bright enough perhaps to attend university one day. But how will they get there if they can't even get a proper primary education?

Another question, but I know now that it's not a true question. It often sounds as if he is practising speeches in front of us, perhaps talking to Maureen, too. Looking past us where we sit at the dining table with him, as if to an audience beyond us, he says, The country is moving in a new direction. With independence just weeks away, Indians will no longer be the lackeys of the British, but we must not now become anyone else's lackey; we have to carve out new roles for ourselves, for all of us—Indians, those of African origin, the once-powerful whites, and everyone else—and capable leaders to guide this are sorely needed.

Daddy gets a funny look on his face when he talks like this. His eyes seem to shine, and he sits up straight and tall. He can see things we can't.

Looking now at Mummy, who still won't look in his direction, he says, Gosh, you all, imagine, just imagine: a prosperous Trinidad where all people—not just one group but all people—are strong, happy, healthy, prosperous Trinidadians. Imagine a Trinidadian identity. You know, he says, even though I am telling you to imagine it, I myself can't—it's a dream. But just think what that will mean for us in the world, how far we can go, together, with the single, focused goal of prosperity for one and for all. And this is what is important: you can't do any of this from within the current ruling party. Their agenda is plain for anyone who is listening. But with a revitalized, strong opposition, we will forge forward and become visible, and when the next election comes, we will rule for everyone.

Mummy finally responds. Everyone? You are so idealistic, Suresh. You want to mix with all kinds of people. Next thing you know, you will be bringing them to our house. You expect me to entertain all those government types, all kinds of people from all over the place? This might be your dream, but it is not mine. Robert is filling your head with all kinds of nonsense. You sound like you're already canvassing. Just stop all this dreaming and wake up. All of this is driving me up a wall.

I am so awake, Vij, he says, and he pushes his chair back as if to leave the table. But he doesn't get up. He looks at her and says, Just try to imagine what I am saying, please.

I imagine. I don't say it, but I wouldn't mind being the child of a politician. I imagine Mummy and Daddy dressed up, and us, too, having our photos taken, and going to events like those we see on the seven o'clock news. We'd have police accompanying us to school, and maybe police on motorcycles riding in front and at the back of our car, and we wouldn't have to wait at stoplights, and we'd get to sit next to Daddy in the front row at the carnival shows at the Savannah and at the Queen's Park Theatre when there are performances there. People are nice to us now, but if he were a member of Parliament or even a prime minister, wherever we went they'd bring us gifts and drinks and sweets.

*

We had to go to the post office to collect two large boxes, both addressed to Misses Anju, Tara, and Siri, and Master Anil Ghoshal. The boxes contain two sets of books sent to us from Daddy's parents in England, whom Tara knows but doesn't remember well. The covers of one set are grey, and inside a rectangular area, which is the colour of Daddy's wine when he holds his glass up to the light, there is gold writing. These books are big, like Daddy's medical textbooks, and the writing in them is tiny. Most of the words are adult words, words I never heard or read before. I asked why these people, Grandma and Granddad, would send such books for Anil, who only knows his ABC and can't yet read, and for Siri, who is a baby. Apparently, these are the kinds of books you grow with. Or grow up with. Or something like that. And one day Siri, too, when she grows up, will discover and treasure them. In the grey set is a book called *World Famous Paintings*, another is *Odhams New Illustrated Atlas of the World*, and the last of that set is *The Children's Bible in Pictures*. The next is a series of four books. One has information about rivers, mountains, and deserts, and another has pictures of famous people, people who invented things like the printing press and engines, and people who were the first ones to do science experiments. Most of the people are men, but there is a woman called Marie Curie who was an important scientist because she discovered radium, which can help patients who have a sickness called cancer. There is an international prize awarded every year to unusually bright people who do great things in the world. It's the Nobel Prize, and mostly men get it. But Marie Curie won it twice. And one of the books shows paintings artists made of themselves—self-portraits—and that same book has a lot of poems in it and short stories, and stories about gods and goddesses who lived in faraway places called Athens and Rome and Egypt, which, if you look at the map of the world in the other book, you see are all quite close together. And then the last one has pictures of people from different countries—it seems that people in different countries dress differently than we do in Trinidad. Some people don't even wear clothes, or just a string around their waists, and you can see everything. I mean EVERYTHING. My favourite of all the books is the one with maps of all the countries of the world, and pictures of the oceans, of the North and South Poles, and of the sky. And the one with the famous paintings.

When I read these books—or try my best to read them, because they are full of words I don't know—or even just look at the pictures, my body is in the chair, but the rest of me, my mind for instance, leaves the room, the house, Crystal Road even, and travels far-far-far away. It makes me want to be an explorer and see the world, and even to leave this world and explore the universe. I can look at the sky with Pa now and tell him that sometimes conjunctions happen, and explain to him that this means that two celestial beings—like two planets, or maybe a planet and a star—are next to each other, almost touching. I tell him about nebulae, which look like little smudges of light against the black sky, and he and I stand on the veranda on Selvon Street at night and search for these.

I have decided to read all the books. It is going to be a slow process, of course. When Daddy was a boy, he used to read the dictionary, and every day he'd make himself memorize one new word. I will begin my own journey by choosing one of the books and reading one page a day for the rest of my life.

*

Every week, news about what is currently going on in the world changes. So Daddy, who likes to know everything, has subscribed to a weekly American magazine called *Time*. It is delivered to our house once a week. He takes the issues to his office when he is finished with them so his patients can look at them while they are waiting. Before that, though, I usually flip through the shiny pages and look at the pictures. Of course I can read the individual words in the magazine, but it is as if you have to already know the topic of the articles in order to understand them. So I hardly ever understand anything. But in our current affairs hour with Daddy on Sundays before Pa comes over for lunch, he tells us what the pictures refer to, and what has happened in the world that week. We learn that there is a war that just began in a place called Yemen, and about an island that is even smaller than Trinidad called Tristan da Cunha, which was almost wiped out recently by a volcano, and all the inhabitants had to be rescued, and we found out about a man named Yuri Gagarin who is a cosmonaut, which means a space pilot, and he is the first human being ever to go into space. He actually orbited the earth in a spaceship. All by himself, for one hundred and eight minutes—almost two hours—on his own. Daddy explains the stories about people in Red China, and tells us about apartheid and the Bantu and Xhosa in South Africa, and about a kind of politics called communism and how the Communist Viet Cong people in the north of Vietnam are trying to convert, by force, the people in the south of Vietnam.

But Daddy is most interested in what is happening in the area of the world called the Middle East, in particular two places there, one called Palestine and the other Israel. Muslims, like we have here in Trinidad, live in Palestine and people called Jews in Israel. The Jewish ones used to live in countries in Europe, but in the Second World War they were persecuted—harassed and treated very badly—by Germans, and millions of them, more than how many people live in Trinidad, were actually killed, all because of their race and their religion. Just because they were Jews. This is shocking to Tara and me. I think about it all the time. I remember the boy Mark killing grasshoppers, stomping on ants, and crushing that poor snail. Killing small helpless creatures is terrible enough. But how can you kill another human being? What kind of person or group of people would kill millions of other people, people who are human beings just like them? What if Trinidadians were Jews? We would all have been killed, people we know, friends, family, and all the people who walk on the streets or go to our school. We, too. Tara, Sita, Colin, all of us.

But not all of the Jews died, thankfully, and after the Second World War, the ones who didn't die no longer wanted to stay in that terrible place, Europe, so they went to the Middle East, specifically to the land of Palestine, and took over a lot of it and made it into their own country and called it Israel. But they didn't ask the Palestine people for permission to do so. So those two sets of people are always quarrelling, always fighting. There is a man called Nostradamus who lived in the sixteenth century and whom Daddy likes to read about, and that man, an astrologer and fortune teller, said there would be a big war that would destroy the entire world, and it is supposed to happen in this century and will start in the Middle East. This is why Daddy pays so much attention to that area. He calls himself a Middle East observer.

Some Jews came to Trinidad after the Second World War. When you see them, even if you are speaking directly to them, you might not know they are Jews. The people who own the store where Daddy buys jewellery for Mummy, and who Mummy bought the Brazilian crystal glasses and bone-china tableware from, are white, but they are Jewish. They just look like ordinary white people to me. I want to ask the owner, Mr. Goldman, what it is like to be persecuted. I could be a journalist; I think maybe I understand what it is like to be left out, to be treated differently than others, to not be allowed to go into a room or to lie on a bed when others can, and I would be a good person to write about these kinds of things. I could write the Goldman family's story maybe, and Daddy could send it to the *Time* magazine people. But Mummy says I am never ever to mention any of this to any of the Goldmans, I am never to ask them anything about that war in Europe.

*

Two things. First, all the hostility between the different racial groups in Trinidad and Tobago would be fixed if Daddy were the leader of this country. When he first announced this some time ago, Mummy asked what his grand plan was for peace between the various races. He didn't look at her when he answered but back and forth between Tara and me, and said with a smile and his eyes wide that he would declare war on the country closest to ours, Venezuela, and that would make all the grown-ups here, regardless of race or occupation, have to pull together to protect our country. All for one and one for all. He likes that phrase, and so do I. Mummy steupsed and said he tells us children so much nonsense and will only confuse us.

Second. From the things he tells us, I, too, am able to imagine myself being the leader. I could be the youngest leader ever. I would be a dictator, which means I would make people keep the country clean—you wouldn't be allowed to throw wrappers and cups out of your car window onto the street. Spitting in public, like on High Street in San Fernando, would be illegal and punishable with jail time. But not just that. If you made the sound called horking, that comes before spitting, the jail time would be even longer. And no one would be allowed to be better or higher than anyone else. You would have to work with your neighbours for the benefit of the country, so there would be no quarrelling with them. All for one and one for all. Everyone would get shoes and be able to attend good schools. And food. There would be no empty stomachs during my leadership. Even poor people would have dessert. But there wouldn't be any poor people anyway, so that doesn't matter. I think about these things all the time, and I am always adding things, and making my ideas better.

*

There is a Negro girl in our class. Her name is Lesley. She is usually one of the first students to arrive at the school. She wears glasses that are thick, and she's very bright. You will always find her sitting by herself at the far end of the room, doing homework, I think, or reading. On mornings, it's as if she doesn't even notice the classroom filling up with the rest of us.

There is a group of girls in my class who use this time before assembly to whisper about Lesley. But I think she knows this, because they gather in their group, watch her, and whisper and laugh with their hands covering their mouths. But they only pretend to whisper, because everyone else is meant to hear, too.

They say that Lesley is a lesbo. Her name clearly tells you this. A lesbo is a girl who is teacher's pet, who knows the answer to everything. They are born with poonkies and yet they stand up to peepee, like boys. They don't wear dresses or skirts, except at school because they have no choice. They don't have birthday parties. They don't look after themselves and can get fat. They wear thick glasses. Lesbos are dirty. They are not Catholic. A lesbo will go to hell no matter how many Hail Marys she says. And when one of them said, It's the feet, look at them, how big, everyone leaned in and bent to watch Lesley's feet.

Once I said loudly, hoping Lesley would hear, She looks to me like someone who has more interesting things on her mind.

One of the horrible girls looked me up and down, moved her hand from her mouth, and responded sharply, Exactly—all she ever does is read. Boys will never find her attractive, which means she wouldn't like boys either. Just look at her, she has no waist; she doesn't even know how to wear a skirt properly.

It's best not to say anything to them. It just makes it all worse.

Lesley doesn't even look up from whatever it is she does back there, she doesn't even look interested in defending herself. She answers questions in class, so I know she can hear and speak.

Another time, I blurted out, We never see Lesley outside of school, so how do any of you know what she wears or what she does when she isn't in school? They turned and looked at me as if they pitied me. I felt foolish. What about Martina and the toy soldiers? I quickly asked, adding, We were all toy soldiers, so what about us?

They looked at one another and rolled their eyes. Someone said, And there is another brilliant observation from Anju Ghoshal. Then she turned to me and said *Babes in Toyland* is just a play, and when you're onstage, you have to act, you must pretend to be someone you're not.

When no one was looking, I have taken glances at Lesley's feet. It's true they are big, and maybe she is a bit odd-looking.

And now, in lunch break, Lesley and I are the only ones who have stayed in the classroom. We are sitting far from one another. My homework is on the desk in front of me, but I'm not really doing it. But I know everything Lesley is doing. She has gone to the globe at the back of the room. I turn my head, as if I am looking off to the side, thinking. I don't look directly at her, of course. She has a tape measure and is measuring something on the globe. I want to know what she is doing. I walk over, but not right up to her, and look at some of the books on the shelf near to the globe. I don't speak to her. She keeps on measuring. She puts one end of the tape on the spot where Trinidad is, holds it there, then tries to spin the globe and put the other end someplace, but the tape keeps slipping. It would be better if she had help. I wonder why she is doing this. It is not part of our homework and has nothing to do with any of our classes.

There is no one around. I slide closer. I put one hand on top of the globe to hold it still. She says, Thanks. She brings the tape, from Trinidad, to someplace that is all the way around to the opposite side of where Trinidad is. She peers toward the back of the globe and whispers: Min da na o.

She writes this name in her notebook.

Then she puts the tape on Trinidad again and this time goes to a spot between Trinidad and the place she just touched, Mindanao. The tape lands on words. She has to look very closely at the globe, probably because she doesn't see very well. Her glasses are really thick. She moves her head close, then back, then close again, trying to see the words because they are written in tiny letters. She chooses a word and says it slowly, and keeps looking from it to her notebook, back and forth, as she tries to write it. I push my head in front of hers and read the word. I call out the letters for her. K I R I B A T I.

I ask her why she is doing this.

I am here in Trinidad, at school, in this classroom, she says. It's our lunchtime. The weather here is nice. Listen, you can hear the traffic, you can hear car horns on High Street. My daddy is at work and my mummy is at her work. I am wondering if a girl in a classroom in these other places halfway, quarter way, around the world, is doing the same things I am doing

right now. I wonder what the weather is like there today, if there's a lot of traffic on the road. What kinds of cars are there. I wonder if there is a girl on the other side of the world thinking about the same things I think about.

I ask her what work her daddy does. He is a policeman. And her mummy? She is a teacher in another school.

The bell rings for the end of lunch, and I hurry back to my desk. But I can't stop thinking about Lesley, and about other countries and islands in the big blue areas of the globe that are so small you can barely see them, and about girls in classes on those islands, and if they are thinking of people like Lesley, and me, and what else they might be doing. I think Lesley is a good person. I think I like her. Well, she is interesting anyway. Probably. I wonder if Lesley's parents will let her come and visit me at home. She might be a good person to play board games with, and maybe to write stories with. Or plays, and to act them out with. Then I think, What if the other girls find out that I have become friends with her? They will not like me either. Or maybe they will think, If Anju and Lesley have become friends, then Lesley is probably a good person, a nice person, and we shouldn't laugh at her anymore. But what if they think instead that I am like Lesley? They will scorn me, too.

*

Miss Hill is English and speaks with an English accent. She has long light brown hair parted in the middle. She teaches us writing and English comprehension and art, and she entered me in an international art competition, and I won a Certificate of Merit and Sister Paul announced it at assembly and everyone clapped. Tara is in a different class, so she was standing in a different line, and she turned around and kept looking at me and smiling and clapping long after all the clapping was finished and her face looked as if it had a light bulb in it. I wished Pa and Mummy and Daddy could have heard. For the competition I drew a jungle with lots of trees with fruit on them—papayas, mangoes, bananas, soursop—and animals—lots of birds, including a toucan and a flock of scarlet ibis, two monkeys, an iguana, and an agouti. I coloured almost every bit of the white paper.

And even though it was daytime in the jungle, in the sky, which I coloured blue and yellow and grey, I drew stars, the sun—the sun is a star—and planets: Venus, Saturn with rings, and Mars, which you have to colour red. The magazine company kept the drawing, but they published it in one of their issues and sent it to Miss Hill and she gave it to me. Mummy shows the magazine to all her friends. She likes my drawings. She has pinned up some of them on the wall above the desk I share with Tara.

Miss Hill is the tallest teacher at school. She may even be taller than Daddy. The skin on her face is thin and it wraps around her jawbone tightly so that her jaw is a thin, sharp line. I like looking at her. Her eyes are glassy, wet like marbles, and her nose is perfectly straight, like on the sculptures of Greek gods and goddesses. Miss Hill likes my essays, too. But she also likes me, I think; she comes sometimes, during lunch break, and sits next to me on the bench near Miss Fong's parlour. Whenever she sits next to me, I feel a bandage wrapped around my forehead, holding back the blood from a cut I recently got in a fight when someone said, or did, something I didn't like. I lick my lips that are dry because of the desert I just rode through on my horse to get here. Or my lips are a bit bloodied because of the fight I just won when I had to defend Miss Hill's honour. But as soon as she begins to speak with me, when I respond and hear myself, my girl's voice too soft, the scar, the blood, the bandage, all evaporate, and I am just me again. I am just Anjula Ghoshal who lives in Trinidad, who has to wear a skirt to school, and white socks and white shoes. Miss Hill has a sister called Celia, and she had a brother, Andrew. She loved Andrew more than anyone in the whole world, but it's really sad, Andrew died when he was just a bit older than me, of leukemia.

She talks to me about things that don't have much to do with school, like her mummy's garden in England and the hummingbird hawk-moths—not a hummingbird, not a hawk, but a moth—that come to a bird feeder there. There are no wild hummingbirds in England, she tells me, but people often mistake that moth for a hummingbird because of the way it hovers in the air over a flower, just like a true hummingbird, and drinks the flower's nectar with its proboscis. I asked her if hummingbird hawk-moths are colourful like Trinidadian hummingbirds. She said they are colourful but not as colourful as hummingbirds found in Trinidad, which, I must understand, is not the same thing as saying Trinidadian hummingbirds. Although Trinidad is known as the Land of the Hummingbird and we have many kinds here, not all hummingbirds found in Trinidad are endemic. Some are migratory. *Endemic. Migratory. Proboscis.* These are good words.

The other students gather some distance away and watch us, but I block them out from my sight. I once told Miss Hill about Ma's garden, that there are roses, yellow and pink ones, and about the large saucers that have a hole in them inside of which the rose bushes are planted, and that the saucers are filled with water to keep red ants and bachacs from getting to the roses because those insects don't swim. I told her that large hummingbirds as iridescent as carnival costumes come to the Antigua Heath flowers, too. I didn't bother to tell her that no one looks after the garden anymore, and hardly any hummingbirds come there now. But she thought I was talking about the garden at Crystal Road, and then I had to explain that it was Ma's garden I was describing, and that I used to live with Ma and Pa. But something happened to me and I couldn't speak anymore. It felt as if I might cry, but no tears came out. She put her arm around me, pulled me closer, and hugged me as if something was wrong with me. I wanted to move away because I didn't want anyone to think something was wrong, or that I am a teacher's pet. But I didn't want to hurt Miss Hill's feelings by pushing her away. Anyway, I liked it. She didn't smell like shampoo or soap, the way some teachers smell. She smelled like a bouquet of cool pink flowers. A strange thing happened: the way she hugged me that day made me miss Ma more than I usually do, and the feeling stayed with me for the rest of that day. I missed her, but what was strange was that it also made me feel strong, as if I didn't need anyone else in the whole world. But this isn't true. I need Pa. I will never not need him. And I think he needs me. So I don't understand why I felt this way.

I am changing my name. Or maybe just adding one to the one I have. But I can't tell anyone. I am replacing the *j* with *d*, and then *r*. Andru. No one needs to know, but I will call myself Andru G from now on.

Miss Hill's dad in England collects stamps. He sends her official first-day covers and she gave one to me as a present. It is my favourite possession.

*

Independence is days away. August 31, 1962. The Queen of England was supposed to come for the celebrations, but she won't be coming. People are disappointed. The Queen has sent her aunt Mary, who is called the Princess Royal, to represent her during the ceremony. Schoolchildren in all the major towns have to line up on the streets in our uniforms and wave to her car when it goes by. The cars, all black, go by very fast, and when they pass on Harris Promenade in San Fernando, I don't know which car she is in, but we wave our little red, white, and black flags, and we get the rest of the day off from school.

*

The day of the ceremony is a holiday, too. During the ceremony, Daddy makes us all sit in the living room with him and watch it on television. When he sees Uncle Robert and his wife, Auntie Margaret, in the audience, he gets very excited. It is as if he himself is there. There is a man called Dr. Rudranath Capildeo, who addresses the Princess Royal. Behind Dr. Capildeo sits a man Daddy knows, Mr. Martin Bahadur. As Daddy watches, he sits at the edge of the seat, and he keeps wiping his mouth as if he is sweating. Mr. Bahadur is shown on the television a lot. His head is bowed, and maybe he doesn't know he is on television because he begins to clean his eyes and then he massages them as if they hurt or are tired. Daddy whispers, Martin, Martin, sit up, man, sit up. There is a man next to Mr. Bahadur fanning himself with the program for the day's events. Daddy says, Look at him. Look at them. How will we get anywhere if our people don't know how to behave themselves? In front of royalty and that is how he is acting?

These images play again and again on the news, and every time Daddy sees the part with Mr. Bahadur wiping his eyes, he sucks his teeth and says, Have they no sense? Had I been there, I would have known how to behave.

ELEVEN

Carnival is around the corner. Carnival happens every year, but this is going to be our first carnival as an independent country, and everyone seems giddy.

All the carnival bands making their way to Skinner Park for the competitions held there pass in front of Pa's house. My cousins and Auntie Stella and Uncle Sonny go to the house each year on carnival Tuesday, and Ma and Pa's friends usually end up there, too. There is food and they drink Scotch and rum and Coke—we, the children, drink red sweetdrink—and the grown-ups dance on the veranda to the music of the steel pans as the bands pass on the street in front. That's how I always spent carnival, before Mummy and Daddy and Tara and Anil came to Trinidad. And that is what we all did last year, too, when Ma was there. That was the first time Tara and Anil ever saw carnival. Daddy took Tara and me—not Anil, he was scared of all the people in costumes and the music and dancing in the street—he took us all the way down the front stairs, and even out the gate and onto the road in front of the house, and we were just inches away from the masqueraders as they shuffled down Selvon Street. It was frightening and wonderful at the same time. The beat of the pans and the brass sections, when they pass by you, inches away from you—your whole body vibrates with sound.

But Mummy doesn't like carnival, all the drinking late into the night and that sort of thing, so she doesn't want to participate this year. That's what she says, but I think it is really because she doesn't want to go to the house when not just my cousins, but people she mightn't know well, Pa's friends, for instance, are there partying, and yet Ma, her mama, isn't there. So she wants us to spend the weekend, including the main mas days, Monday and Tuesday, at the beach in Mayaro. Daddy, however, insists that we, the children, should not only be allowed to participate in this year's carnival when everyone will be celebrating our freedom from British governance, but encouraged, if not actually pushed, to do so. They argue. I agree with him, but I know better than to take sides. Mummy says she has no interest in being caught up in the crowds, especially as people will be drunk with this new sense of liberation, and she doesn't want her children exposed to all the looseness that will be going on. Mummy wins.

The long drive there from Lever du Soleil East, past Mon Repos and the cane fields and sugar factories of Brechin Castle, through busy, noisy Princes Town, the cacao plantations and villages of Tableland and Rio Claro, is quiet. Usually, Daddy gets us to sing *Michael, row your boat ashore, hallelujah,* and we do rounds of *Row, row, row your boat gently down the stream* and *Ten green bottles sitting on the wall.* But we don't sing any songs today. He usually asks us riddles, gives us math quizzes, and we tell him and Mummy jokes from *The Children's Big Book of Jokes*. But not this time.

Siri is sleeping on Mummy's lap, and Mummy keeps her head turned, looking out her window. Tara and Anil sleep for most of the drive. I want to say something, to ask questions, learn things about the places we are driving through, just to hear a happy voice in the car. But I think it is best not to speak. I lean my head against the window and watch the clouds instead and try to see, in each one, or batch of them, animal or people shapes, and when we pass jungles, I search for toucans or monkeys in the trees.

When we arrive at the junction in the village of Plaisance in Mayaro, I decide I must break the quiet in the car, so I ask if we can go to the house I used to go to with Ma and Pa. Daddy says it's already been a long drive and we need to get to the hotel before they stop serving lunch. He promises we'll come back and look for it later. For a second, Mummy seemed interested in finding it, but once Daddy gave his answer, she said nothing.

We are staying at a salmon-coloured hotel that is right on the beach and looks like a castle. We have two rooms with a door that opens from ours into Mummy and Daddy's. Anil, Tara, and I are in one room, and each of us has our own twin bed. Siri will be in the room with Mummy and Daddy, in a crib. We can see the sea from our window. The ocean sounds sometimes as if it is breathing and then you hear the loud boom when the waves break. The sound of wind rustling the branches of the coconut trees never stops, too. There are many people on the beach and in the water.

We are not allowed to go down to the beach by ourselves. We must wait for Mummy and Daddy. I go from the balcony to their room, back and forth, wishing they'd hurry, but Mummy is unpacking our suitcases and bags. She's putting her tops and dresses and Daddy's shirts on hangers. Daddy tells her to leave them, she can finish unpacking when we come back up. She says it won't take a minute; she'd rather do it now because when we return, we'll be tracking sand everywhere. He goes behind her and puts his arms around her waist. I slip further into the room and sit on a wicker chair and unbuckle the sandal on one foot and then buckle it up again. He has pressed his face to her cheek. He says, This is what I love about you. You can make home anywhere.

She doesn't say anything but has slowed in her pace. He turns her to face him and kisses her mouth. She pulls her head back and, as if shy, she says, So that's what you love about me.

It is not a question and she has a smile on her face. I am buckling the other sandal now, but the first one needs to be redone, so I pull that foot up and begin to redo it. I am not looking exactly, but I can see. He has one hand behind her, low down, so I think it must be on her bum. She seems to be pulling him toward her. He says, And that you're always seeing what will happen next. And you're looking very beautiful.

Over his shoulder she looks at me, and I quickly get up, stamp my feet lightly to make sure the troublesome buckles are fine, and go back out onto the balcony. But I am pleased that they are being nice with each other.

*

There is a German family staying here, too, with a girl named Jutta who is my age. You don't pronounce the *J*. It's more like a *Y*. Yutta. Mummy says they should just spell it like that, but I think it's an interesting and different way of pronouncing the *J*. When she asks my name, I tell her, softly, it is Andru.

They are white. Because we are at the beach, I expected them to smell of coconut ice cream, but they don't. Jutta's hair is long and shiny, the colour of brass ornaments.

Ever since we met Jutta, Tara has been calling me Anyu. I poke her tummy and say, An' you, too, and for fun I call her Thara and try to say it the way Miss Hill with her English accent might say it. Jutta asked why my sister calls me Anyu and not Andru, and I said that Anyu is just a nickname, my family likes playing with my name.

It turns out that Jutta's father, Andreas Vogel, works with an oil company that Daddy is the doctor for.

My parents like people who come from other countries, and have had drinks with the German people, Uncle Andreas and Auntie Marta, while Jutta and we children play on the beach and swim in the sea. They keep an eye on us from the hotel's noisy bar where calypso music blasts from speakers.

*

Mayaro Beach is very-very long. If you wanted to walk the whole length of the beach and you started out at one end early in the morning, you'd probably not get to the other end before lunchtime, even if you didn't stop for a swim along the way. You'd have to remember to take a picnic with you because you'd surely get hungry and there are no shops or vendors on the beach. Pa and I used to try to walk all the way. Several rivers flow out to the sea that you can only cross in low tide. He used to lift me when crossing them. But no matter how long we walked for, the end of the beach, which is also the end of Trinidad, would never get any closer.

Whenever I've been to Mayaro before, the beach sloped gradually down to the water, which remained shallow for a far distance. Small weak waves would roll in and splinter far up the sand. But although it is the dry season, it rained a great deal the previous week and the floor of the sea close to the shore in front of the hotel has dropped down steeply. The water is all churned up at the very edge, and when you walk in, the sand is rough and sharp with more broken bits of shell than usual, and then there is an unexpected, steep drop—it's quite deep. Bigger waves than usual crash right at the drop. It is deep enough there that you can stand on the shallow part, just before the drop, and when a wave comes in, dive over the wave just as it crests, into the deep water. Jutta, Tara, and I became braver with each attempt, ending each dive with a glide and a swim far out, only to return and do it again. But on one of these dives, the water receded fast, as if it were sucked back out to sea, leaving the sand in the deep part exposed. Only, I had already dived, and so I crashed my head into the sand. I knew there was a lot of noise all around, but I couldn't hear any of it. There was total silence. I thought I must have broken my head.

In front of everyone, Daddy examined me and said that since I could walk and move my neck—even if it was painful to do so—and tell him how many fingers he was holding up, nothing was broken or fractured, but I was in shock and had sprained my neck quite badly. It was the most hurting I'd ever experienced. He always carries a medical bag in the car, and from it he got me painkillers. He said I would have to have it X-rayed when we get back to San Fernando, and it is likely I'll have to wear a brace around my neck.

It is very painful, and I've had a headache ever since. But everyone is treating me very well.

*

I have a question I really want to ask Jutta, but I know I mustn't ask her in front of my parents, and I don't want to ask her in front of Tara or Anil. So I wait until we are alone on the beach.

I sit still so as not to irritate my neck further, while she builds a sandcastle. The calypso music from the bar is loud. Why did your family kill Jews? I ask. She doesn't answer me. She doesn't even look up. Jutta, I say, and she glances at me and answers, Yes? and carries on sticking shells into the side of her castle.

You're German, right? I say. So your family killed six million Jewish people.

She stops decorating the castle and looks at me with a frown. She tilts her head. She doesn't seem to know what I'm saying. Her English is good enough, so I am confused. I say, Don't you know that?

She answers, My family? We never killed anyone. We don't kill people.

I insist that everyone knows that Germans did kill many, many people, and that since she and her family are German, her parents must have killed some people. Maybe not many, but some. I tell her that she is too young, obviously, to have killed anyone, but not her parents.

She stands up slowly and says again that her family doesn't kill. So I have to explain to her. I tell her about the Second World War and how Germans, not ones like her, and not ones in Trinidad, but the ones in Germany, are very bad people and all the world knows this and that she should know it, too. I do my best to quickly assure her that I can tell *she* isn't bad, and that my parents like hers, so her parents can't be bad. Perhaps *they* didn't kill anyone, but other German people did.

She doesn't want to play on the beach anymore. She gets up, dusts the sand off her hands and off her knees, and leaves me sitting there. I stick more shells into the sides of her castle and wait. I wait for a long time. My ears are hot. I feel a little frightened. I wait, but nothing happens.

*

Jutta's parents have made plans to go on a day trip into the Nariva Swamp to see the wildlife there. Her parents have already hired a guide and they've invited us to go along with them. We will travel, like David Livingstone, up the river in a pirogue, and will see caimans, red-bellied macaws, toucans, and sea cows. We might even see snakes hanging from the trees on the river-banks, or swimming in the water right next to our boat, and might even discover a tribe of people, perhaps naked, who don't speak English and whom no one ever saw before.

It is a beautiful morning. There are no clouds in the sky, and the sky is pale blue. It will be a hot day. We eat breakfast, salt fish and bake, and ham and eggs, and papaya and bananas in the hotel dining room, and when we are finished wait there to meet Mr. and Mrs. Vogel and Jutta. They must already have eaten or haven't yet come down for breakfast. We wait. We are ready and can go as soon as they are ready, too. They are late. Daddy says to Mummy, Strange, these kinds of people are normally very prompt. They can't have left without us.

Mummy says, I'm sure they understood we accepted the invitation to go with them. They agreed to meet us down here. We can call their room.

Daddy says we mustn't rush them, we can wait a little longer.

My face has become very hot. I keep my eyes lowered and hope no one notices.

Some more minutes pass, then Mummy and Daddy go to the front desk. I follow, standing back, but not far, as I need to hear. Daddy asks the receptionist to make the call for him. She tells Daddy the Vogel family left last night. They were supposed to stay for another two nights, she says, but cut short their visit and left. No, they didn't say why. The man had been very friendly all the time, until last night. Suddenly so, he came serious-serious, and said they were leaving and paid their bill. She tells Daddy that the manager came out and asked, but Mr. Vogel said everything was fine with the hotel, but they had had enough and needed to go back to their home. She says they found it strange. Something must have happened, but they don't know what.

Mummy whispers to Daddy that he should ask if they might have left a message for them. I want to say that we should just go to the beach and not worry about the Vogels anymore, but Daddy goes back to the desk and asks the lady. I feel dizzy. But there is nothing from them for us. He asks if there is a way to be in touch with them. The woman says they are so sorry, Dr. Ghoshal, but they can't give out guests' contact information without the guests' permission. She leans across her desk and laughs as she adds, Not even to our favourite guest.

No, Mummy tells Tara when she begs, we won't go to the swamp, we'll just stay at the hotel and spend the day here on the beach.

In my mind, I replay what I said, saying it back to myself in different ways, to see if maybe Jutta might have misunderstood me. Daddy asks why I am so quiet. My neck hurts a lot, I say.

*

Although I am not to go into the water because of my neck, I have changed into my bathing suit along with the others. We are waiting for Mummy and Daddy to go down to the beach when we hear a noise approaching. There is the musical beating of pots and pans, the tinkling sounds of bottles being hit with spoons, and the clanging of the hubs of car wheels being hit with iron wrenches. We run to the balcony and see a procession of people on the beach dancing and making music. It's mostly men. They look as if they are naked, but they are wearing underpants and are covered in black grease and blue paint, even the underpants, and are shuffling down the beach. Daddy pulls Mummy against him and makes her dance with him. She moves slightly, as if she is dancing, even as she pulls away from him. At least she is laughing, and, I think, happily. He says, Let's take the children and go for a little jump up with them. She really pulls away then and, laughing—but not really laughing—asks if he is crazy. They argue, but she gets firm. No, she is not going down there with a bunch of greasy masqueraders. Look at them, she says. You have no idea what kinds of people they are. You want them rubbing up all that grease on us? She is very content, she says, to watch from the balcony. He has gotten quiet, but, looking down at his feet, he shuffles in time to the now fading beat.

Then, hearing a different music, the rhythmic piercing blasts of whistles, Tara, Anil, and I rush to the balcony and lean against the banister—almost over it. There is a group of Midnight Robbers and their entourage heading to the beach-bar patio. We all hurry down, Daddy carrying Siri, I holding Anil's hand, Mummy and Tara following. Tara and I are wringing our hands to show how frightened we are, but we're giggling excitedly at the same time.

There are three Robbers. One is dressed in a bright yellow jacket with a big cape decorated with sequins that spit out sparkly light when he twirls and ducks and jumps about. Another wears a large black-and-white sombrero with tiny white human skulls decorating the brim and long swinging fringes that cover his face. And the third one is wearing a shiny black shirt and a hat that is exactly like a coffin. It bobs forward and backward as if it is too large, too heavy for him. He is wearing gold-coloured cowboy boots. Tara stands close to Mummy. One side of her touches Mummy, as if she is leaning against her. I don't want to be afraid. I don't stand too close to Mummy or to Daddy or to anyone else. I know where Tara and Mummy and Daddy are, I keep them in view, but I don't look at them directly, so it is as if I am on my own.

There are grease devils with the Robbers, beating milk cans with iron rods. Mummy stands back from them, afraid they will get grease on her clothes, or ours. But she doesn't mind the Robbers. She is even tapping her feet to their rhythm. Everyone in the hotel, even the waiters and the barman, are bouncing, some with their hands in the air, to the beat. *Chackalacka chackalacka, chackalaka, chack. Chackalacka chackalacka, chackalaka, chack.* I stay still, not only because of my neck, but I don't want anyone looking at me. *Chackalacka chackalacka, chackalaka, chack.* The beat gets softer and a Robber begins to speak. They take turns reciting endlessly long stories in deep voices meant to frighten us. I am only a little frightened, but I want to hear what they are saying about their history and their adventures around the world, about all their great accomplishments and supernatural powers and how they speak with the devil, and I am not far from where Mummy and Daddy stand. Each time a Robber finishes his story, the beat picks up again, and loudly. The Robbers spin and spin, faster and faster, but they don't seem to get dizzy, and they rush up to people to try to scare them. The women pull back, crossing their arms in front of their chests but laughing at the same time. *Chackalacka chackalacka, chackalaka, chack. Chackalacka chackalacka, chackalaka, chack.* They spin and gyrate and thump the ground with their rods and blow their whistles to the rhythm of the now louder beating of the cans. The whistles are deafening. Then the devils lower their beating again and one of the Robbers bellows, I was born of the bowels of the night, to fight with all my might, all manner of goodness and light. I kill foe and am known to have devoured even a friend. Avoid my wrath, you gawkers, empty your pockets, pay with gold your dividend.

They take turns in deep, trembling voices, chanting their rhyming stories—which remind me of the one we have to recite in class by a man named something-something Coleridge, about a wedding and an old, old ancient mariner, and a special bird that someone shot, God save thee ancient Mariner from the fiends that plague thee thus why lookst thou so with my cross bow I shot the albatross. The Robbers' stories are long, and yet they aren't reading them. I wonder how they remember so many words, all the rhymes, how they can speak so fast and never falter. They will only stop reciting and leave when they are paid. One of the devils turns his can right side up and walks around, holding it out, shaking it at each guest. He even stoops and rattles it at us, the children. But the guests at the hotel take a long time to reach for their money, so the Robbers twist and whirl, their fringes flying almost horizontally now, revealing the black-painted craggy faces of old men, and they carry on about death and the underworld, getting more and more angry, until the can is so full it doesn't rattle anymore.

I am sad when they leave. I carefully climb over the low wall surrounding the patio, on the other side of which is the beach. No one calls me back. I wish Pa were here. If he were, he'd walk with me on the beach. He would let me collect sequins that might have fallen off the costumes. He'd hold my hand and we might follow the Robbers, from a distance, for a little while.

Away from the guests, the whistles and the pan-beating have stopped and calypso music is blaring again. The Robbers and devils talk more quietly now among themselves. They no longer sound like Robbers. They don't look at me. One of them has taken his hat off. He is bald. He looks like Mr. Monty. I want him to look at me, and to see that I am not afraid, I like their stories and dancing and the music. One glances at me, but only for a second, as if I were just a coconut on the beach. He doesn't even smile. They are passing around a bottle of rum and drinking from it. I am not to go beyond the hotel's property, so I can't really follow them. I go down to the edge of the water right in front of the hotel and lower myself onto the sand. I look back; no one is looking for me. I lie on my back, on the hot sand, and stare at the bright blue sky, at the cottony white clouds sliding by. After a few minutes, as the clouds move, I also move, spinning with the earth.

*

From the speakers comes calypso music, all day. Guests are dancing on the patio. Daddy is a little tipsy. You can know this because he looks pleased even though there's nothing in particular to be so pleased about. He doesn't stop smiling, and you can't tell what he is looking at, even if it seems to be you. He dances with some of the women there and gets Mummy to dance with him a few times, too. The women are not simply talking. They are shouting. And everything they say, or rather shout, must be funny, because they are constantly cackling—that last is Mummy's word. They slap their legs and bend forward as if they are going to fall over from so much laughter. There are two who keep going to dance with Daddy. They are behaving scandalously—and that is Mummy's favourite word today. They break away from him, wine up against him, all around him, hugging him close. It makes me uncomfortable—upset, even. Daddy dances, but even when he is dancing with one of them, he looks as if he is dancing by himself, all the while with that strange smile, and looking not at anyone but at the ground. A calypso that is on the radio all the time these days comes on and the people on the patio go crazy. Everyone knows the words and they sing and dance. This one is about a man named Dan in a van, a cow that jumped over the moon, and Tom Tom the piper's son. It is a funny calypso because the lines are from nursery rhymes we know, but I think the singer is mocking the nursery rhymes. Still, everybody likes it. When the chorus comes, they belt it out.

I study Mummy. She has a smile on her face, but it's not a real smile. She sits on a stool at a high table taking turns watching Daddy, glancing down at Siri strapped in the stroller, looking out at the sea, at her bracelet, at a driftwood sculpture that hangs on the wall, and sipping a Bentley. Daddy is on the far side of the room now, among a group of men. There is a woman in between him and another man. She has one arm around the other man and her other arm around Daddy's waist, but only the other man is hugging her back.

I ask Mummy if the stories Midnight Robbers tell are true stories. She watches Daddy now, juts her chin toward him, and says, I don't know. Go and ask your father. I say, It's OK. I don't think they're true, they're just stories.

The other women are shouting out to their friends and to other dancers, and the ones sitting at the bar are dancing even as they sit on the bar stools. There is so much laughter. But Mummy just keeps that same look, with the smile that isn't a smile. And when Daddy comes over and begins to wine next to her, she doesn't respond right away. He whispers in her ear, and she sets her drink aside and gets up to dance with him. She holds herself very close to him. A man pulls her from Daddy to dance with him, and she tries to resist, but Daddy takes his hands off her and makes a gesture suggesting he doesn't mind, so she dances with the man, all the while looking at Tara and me, raising her eyebrows and smiling—a more real smile now—as if to say, Look at me! Can you believe this? I push Siri's stroller, forwards and backwards, and smile back and sip my Bentley nervously. The man, who had been dancing wildly just before with another woman, isn't dancing like that with Mummy. He moves with her more gently. He isn't holding her tightly. Her hands touch him, but barely, it seems.

We have a dinner of mahi mahi caught in the sea in front of the hotel that morning. When Daddy orders himself a rum and Coke, Mummy says, Don't drink anymore. You've already had quite a few. He says, It's carnival weekend, darling. Why don't you have one with me? She does, and we have Bentleys with maraschino cherries in them and paper cocktail umbrellas sticking out of the glasses.

*

Daddy gives me more aspirin as my neck has begun to hurt a lot again. He switches off the lights when we get into bed, making the room darker than a moonless sky. Waves breaking on the

shore and the coconut trees' branches rustling in the constant wind can still be heard, even though the windows are shut because it almost always rains in the night. Every so often I hear a loud but dull thud, a coconut falling from one of the trees nearby. Listening to the waves is hypnotic. I count them—one, two, three, four, five, six, and seven—each getting a little heavier than the last, the seventh making a loud crash, and then the sequence starts again.

I am awakened by the door between our room and Mummy and Daddy's being pulled in and the lock engaged. I am suddenly fully awake. I stay still and listen. I hear nothing for a long while but the waves and the trees in the wind. I begin to fall back asleep. But then I hear the bed in their room. It continues to make sounds, squeaky sounds, and I hear her, Mummy, she is making soft sounds—as if she is crying, but I don't think she is crying—not like she often does—but little sounds almost as if she is being hurt, but not too badly, and then his voice, soft, tender, but then a little loud, as if he gasped—perhaps there is a bat in their room. I listen, worried, wondering if I should knock on the door to make sure everything is OK. But then there is quiet.

I can hear Daddy's soft snoring.

*

Carnival Tuesday, after a dip in the warm salty water, Tara and I pick up our last few shells and some brown pieces of sea-washed glass off the beach. We try to help with packing up the car, but when we store away all the souvenirs we picked up, including some driftwood, we get so much sand on the inside mats that Daddy is irritated with us.

On the road heading back home, I remind Daddy about going to look for the house I used to go to with Ma and Pa. He says it's late, and if we took time looking for it, we would get trapped in the traffic on the way home. Mummy turns to me and says there are so many traces and lanes leading off the main road to the house, and she doesn't remember which we would have to take to get to it. I think I know which one it is. I'm not sure, but I think I know. But I don't bother to say this.

There is already a lot of traffic in the village of Plaisance. The cars stop for a long time and then move only a car length forward, then stop again. Steel pan music comes from some streets away. Our windows are turned down—the doors locked, of course—and we strain to see the bands, but all we see are people. People dressed in costumes walking about in the street as if they own it. Today they do, and cars must give them the right-of-way. Men, women, and children walk through the crowds and weave around the cars, selling little paper windmills, cotton candy, and envelopes of chillibibi and packages of nuts. Throngs of people line the sidewalk waiting for bands to pass. I scan the crowd, looking for the girl I once talked to a long, long time ago when I was on the beach with Ma and Pa and the seine had just come in and children from the village were playing among the fishermen. Angela was her name. Like my other name, almost. She was the only one that day on the beach who tried to play with me. And now I look, imagining that she might be a little taller than I remember, as I am today. I remember her so clearly. I look hard, everywhere. But I don't see her. I have never seen her since that day.

Even though I took more aspirins this morning before we left, my neck hurts a lot. Still, I wish we could park the car and get out, walk among the people, or stand and wait for a band to come by, but I don't like to beg for things. If I wish hard enough, I am sure Tara will ask. It always happens this way. And she does. Daddy, can we stop and see a band? Almost exactly as I would have done. It's as if she reads my mind. Mummy, bouncing Siri on her lap, says, They take a long time to pass through. We don't know when the next one will come, and in any case it's time to get back home. Haven't you had enough already?

Daddy says, Yes, this could take forever. But don't fret. Just trust me.

Mummy looks at him, wondering, I suppose, what we should trust him about. She says nothing, and Tara sits back in her seat, pleased. I am content, too, to see what he is sort of promising us.

The direct route home will take us back through the small towns and villages we passed on our way here, but Daddy, who is driving, doesn't turn left at the crossroad when he has the chance. He turns right and inches down the crammed road, careful not to hit anyone, or another car. That's our first sign that he really does have something in mind. Mummy perks up and says, Where are you going?

He says, Just a minute, I need to concentrate here. I don't want anyone to hit the car.

Mummy says again, in a worried voice, So, why are we going this way?

A little lower down, and he turns left, north, onto the Manzanilla Mayaro Road. There are fewer beach houses here. The road curves out toward the sea, and we come to a narrow bridge over a wide dark green river. *Pludunkpludunk pludunkpludunk.* All the way across. I am sitting straight up and watching to the left, down the black-green water of this river, which looks deep and scary even though the surface glimmers with reflections of blue sky and white clouds. It is a long bridge, and I am terrified that one of the boards making this racket as we slowly pass might break, our car tumbling, with us trapped in it, into the river in which snakes and caimans surely live. I ask Daddy if we should unlock our doors. If the windows of the car should be turned up or kept down. He says, Goodness, you worry about everything. Relax a little, Anyu. This bridge is going nowhere.

I make a small laugh and say, My name is not Anyu.

He says, OK, Anyu was your Mayaro name. You're back to being Anju now.

To the right, with each broken wave the sea rushes into the river. With a particularly loud and frightening *caratakaplakadank-caratakaplakadank*, we're back onto asphalt. And the road follows the coast, sometimes much too close to the water. Now there are no houses. To our left are patches of low mangrove trees and fields of tall grasses, and on the right, beyond a narrow strip of coconut trees and sea grapes and beach, the ocean. The sea looks rougher here than where our hotel was. Huge waves come from the left side of the ocean and the right side at once, and they crash, like cymbals, into each other. It looks scary. A couple of cars, far behind us, are travelling slower than we are, and every so often a car approaches, heading in the direction of Mayaro. Daddy has picked up speed. He hasn't answered Mummy. It's not a good idea to surprise Mummy. He knows this.

There is nothing ahead of us now but coconut trees on either side of the road. They all lean toward the ocean. Mummy's posture has changed. She has become very still, as if she isn't breathing. And yet it also feels as if she is about to explode. Everyone is quiet in the car. Here, towering waves look as if they are being pushed hard and fast toward the shore and will break and race up onto the road.

Mummy continues looking ahead. The turbulent sea to the right is lined with fast-approaching rows of white surf. It's scary, but pretty, too, but she refuses, it seems, to look out. She'd have to watch past Daddy, and it is clear she doesn't want to look in his direction. She's missing the frigate birds above the sea, the diving pelicans and the gulls nipping at the cresting waves. I wonder if she has even seen the committee of vultures in the coconut tree branches hanging over the road. That's what they are called when they gather, so many of them, like that, a committee. There are hundreds of them all the way along. From where I am, behind Daddy, I see Mummy's profile. She isn't even really looking ahead, but rather at the hood of the car. On her side is an endless field of coconut trees—someone's estate probably; you can tell it's not a field of wild trees because they grow in perfect rows and are all the same height, and wide paths cut through the sandy soil for vehicles—donkey carts probably. The ground there is covered in orange crocuses, from the roadway to as far back as it is possible to see. All that orange, and the green and yellow of the coconut trees, with low weeds with tiny purple flowers on the edge of the road, and the blue sky. I want to tell her to look at it all, the sea on the right, the estate to her left. But I don't want to be the one to speak first.

Siri has fallen asleep. I wonder if Mummy isn't speaking because she doesn't want to disturb Siri.

Finally, in a low voice, Daddy says, I'd really like to take in a little carnival. It'll take a little longer to get home, but this way we'll see a few good bands on the road.

Mummy moves. She turns her head to look out toward the coconut trees. I can't see her face anymore.

He says, The kids will get a chance to see carnival in the north.

She still doesn't respond. I sit up. He wants us to see bands, and Mummy wants to head back home, to San Fernando. I have a good idea. We could end the weekend at Pa's house. We'll get there in time to see the last of the bands—and Sheldon and Colin will see that I damaged my neck diving in deep water. Daddy could just turn around and head back that way and we could go to Pa's. I could save us all from an unpleasant drive with my reasonable, excellent idea. I am thinking fast how best to say all of this in fewer words, when Daddy says, So this is my plan. If we head back down south now, by the time we get there, given the traffic we'll encounter in all the towns along the way, it will be almost dark if not fully dark. Think of Rio Claro and Princes Town—it will be sheer madness. Not so? We won't see a thing, but we'll get caught in a sea of cars and people on the streets. By the time we make it to your father's house, the bands will have dispersed. Carnival will be over. There'll only be drunk stragglers on the road. We can get to Sangre Grande, Vij, in less than forty-five minutes.

I see his point. And am happy he said this before I spoke up.

Mummy snaps, Why didn't you tell me this was your plan? Since when did you know you were going to do this? Trust you? Seriously?

And off they go, back and forth. Finally, he says, his voice raised, *You* wanted to go to the beach. It was *you* who wanted to spend the weekend at Mayaro. The entire weekend. You know this is not my speed. Did I get on about it? You got your way. Now I am asking for a couple hours of carnival.

He turns on the radio, trying to find a station that isn't scratchy out here. The reception is bad, but he does find one that, although it, too, comes and goes, has live commentary of the last few bands making their way across the main stage in Port of Spain, where the big carnival competition is held. To the sounds of steel pan music and commentary about costumes and the history of the designers and band leaders in the background, all the way up the coast, I drift into moments of sleepiness, hearing the ghost of their voices playing in my head.

You know *damn* well this is not about the children.

Those women, *wining* up like that against you.

You got what *you* wanted

I'd actually really like

All I'm asking, darling

Don't darling me

You had this planned all along, didn't you

That is *not* true

You always get what you want
Don't bring the children into this
But what are you getting on like this for

Before I can ever really fall asleep, I am pulled awake each time, partly because my neck hurts, and partly because I must be aware of the moment when I might have to intervene.

*

Before we even reach Sangre Grande's town centre, people in costumes with headdresses of tall colourful feathers clog the streets, dancing and waving and twirling bright banners. A band moves slowly, comes to a halt, then moves forward again, and another approaches that one, in the same stop-and-start movement, from yet another street. The three of us in the back seat are now wide awake, sitting up and looking all around us. Siri is awake, and even though she is a baby, she looks as if she knows what is going on. People in ordinary clothes are jumping up wildly in the street to the frantic steel pan music of the two bands playing different tunes. Bare-backed men wave their shirts; men and women wine down on the ground, as if they are crazy. It's exciting. Mummy reminds Daddy that when bands meet like that, they clash and fights break out. He says that that *was* once true, fights *used to* break out in the old days. But nowadays, everyone just wants to have a bit of fun. She tells him to turn down another street quickly or else we'll get trapped, a fight really could break out, and even if we were safe inside the car, the car could get scratched up or dented. Daddy turns off the air-conditioning unit and turns down his window so we can better hear the music from the different bands, and all the singing and shouting. The word *cacophony* comes into my head. It is a cacophony of sound. He tells her to stop being such a worrywart, to relax and have a little fun, let the children see what carnival is like on this side of the island. He has to inch the car forward as hundreds and hundreds more people are dancing on the road in front of us now. He moves his body to the music as he hunches over the steering wheel, drumming his fingers and hands against the wheel, waving to people who, to our surprise, call out: Doc, park up the car, man; come, take a little jump up with us.

Mummy asks how these people, so far from San Fernando, could know him. I can tell he is a little offended by her question. He says, Well, I'm no longer just a San Fernando politician, Vij. I mean, surely you understand this. The upheaval in our party is news, and you've seen it—Martin, Vernon, me, we're in the news, in the papers all the time. In any case, we're on the cusp of a new future in this country, and people all over are paying attention to politics. Everybody is engaged.

He does a little dance in his seat and says, All-a-we-is-one. You can feel it.

He turns back, a huge smile on his face, and says, Not so, kids?

*

We come to an intersection, he turns the car, and we roll down that road slowly. He pulls over, up onto the sidewalk in front of someone's house. He says, Come on, you too, kids, let's all go and have a little jump up.

Mummy shouts angrily, *No*. She does not want us in that crowd. Daddy stares ahead. After some long seconds of silence, he takes the keys out of the ignition and, holding them in his closed fist, rests that hand on the seat between them. Then he opens his fist, the keys fall on the seat, and he moves his hand off them. He opens the car door, steps out, and shuts the door. We in the back seat are still. It is possible, I know, to not breathe and still stay alive. I don't know who is right, who is wrong. I don't know if I want him to go, want to go with him, or want him to stay and take care of us. I should do something, but I'm not sure what. I think I'll tell him—even though it's not true—that I don't want to go with him, my neck hurts too much, he should get back in the car. I try to open my mouth, but all the sound in me has disappeared.

He stoops and looks in the window. He says to Mummy, Go home then. I will find my way back.

Tara sits forward; her fists, placed on the back of the front seat, are clenched. Her voice is very low when she says, Don't go, Daddy. No, don't, please don't. Stay. Don't leave us.

He can't have heard her. I still can't get any sound out of my mouth.

Mummy shouts, her voice high and shaking, How will you find your way back? This is quite the other end of the country. Get back in the car right now and stop being ridiculous. I am not driving in this traffic on carnival Tuesday. Are you out of your head, or what?

He quietly, and calmly, it seems, answers, You can do whatever you want. You can wait here in the hot car, you can come with me, or you can go. I am going to have a little fun.

He doesn't say anything to us in the back seat; he doesn't even look at us. We turn our bodies and follow him with our eyes, but in no time he has disappeared into the crowd at the intersection. People are walking hurriedly up this side street to see the bands. They stare into the car. I see what they are seeing. A car haphazardly parked, blocking part of the sidewalk, in the front passenger seat a distressed woman with a baby on her lap. And three upset children in the back seat looking all around. There is no driver. A woman passing looks at Mummy, whose window is down a crack, and we hear her say, Carnival Tuesday, girl. Soon-soon it will pass—don't mind.

I sit back and try to compose my face so that, to people passing, I don't look upset.

After a while, Mummy, shaking her head side to side, says—I think to herself, but aloud—I can't believe he would do this. Why would he treat me like this?

I am angry with him, but I also feel angry with her, and I'm not sure I can say why. Is it possible for both people in a situation to be wrong?

*

She slides into the centre of the seat, lifts Siri off her, and sets her down again near the door where she had just been sitting. A few minutes pass with her doing nothing but biting her lips. Then she picks up the keys and holds the bundle of them on her lap. From my place in the back, I clutch the front seat, waiting, wondering. She shifts—reluctantly, it seems, and unsure—into place behind the steering wheel, and from there she stares for a long while into the rear-view mirror. Tears are running down her face and she is shaking. I don't know what to do. Not thinking, but panicked that she might drive off while Siri is just on the seat alone like that, I make myself tumble over the seatback. It is an awkward manoeuvre and my neck throbs as I fall into the front. Siri has gotten heavy lately, and I must struggle with her—I think she liked the idea of being on her own in the seat—to pull her onto my lap. She begins to yehn-yeh and I say to her, quietly, but firmly, Stop, be a good child. And she leans back against me, the yehn-yehing stopped immediately.

Mummy says, I don't understand this. Look at what your father has done. I have never driven on these roads before. How am I going to get you all home?

I don't know for how long we sit here, but it seems like no time at all and also long enough for him to have returned. But he hasn't. Mummy starts the ignition. When she pulls off the sidewalk, the car drops down hard onto the street, scaring us. Even though she's been driving us to and back from school, taking us to visit Pa, going to the grocery and hairdresser on her own, I am wondering if she is actually capable of driving us all the way to San Fernando. She'll have to go on highways. I sit up, alert, and wrap my arm around Siri, not too tightly, ready to protect her. My tiredness from our holiday, from swimming under the hot sun this morning, is entirely gone. My neck seems to be getting stiffer and stiffer by the minute, but, oddly, it doesn't hurt anymore. I twist my entire upper body to try to look back before we drive away. Tara is pressed hard against the back seat, her eyes wide open, her face terrified. Anil kneels on the seat, facing the rear window. I don't know if Mummy knows how to take care of herself or us in this situation. Uncle Sonny once said she was a princess before she met Daddy. Or was it before she went to Ireland? Or was she always a princess? I can't remember anything, it seems. But, yes, she is a princess. I will have to look after her, and my sisters and brother. I watch for cars, and for people carelessly, drunkenly spilling off the sidewalks, and for roads where no bands or masqueraders clog them. I point where I think she should go but make sure at the same time to say I'm not sure I'm right.

*

We crawl through traffic jams, and a few times she has to ask someone on the street how to get out of an area and onto the main road. Somehow, we make it, first onto the east-west bypass, and then onto the main north-south highway that winds through the western side of the island. Mummy drives slowly, steadily. Cars pass us, some with people in costumes, flying in both directions.

The weight of Siri on my lap, the effort of holding her tightly on such a long trip, makes me think of Mummy holding her like this on all the drives we take, and also of Mummy being at home with us on weekends when Daddy is at a political meeting, a medical association meeting, a doctors' cricket match, and on afternoons and into the evenings after school when we are waiting to have dinner with him and then end up eating on our own. It must be exhausting for her to always be listening to us, and even if Dolly makes our meals and Maureen cleans up after us, she is still the one making sure everything is properly done for us and around the house. Was Ma like that? I wonder.

I do not once complain about my neck, even when it begins again to throb, and yet, when we arrive in San Fernando, Mummy says, I am taking you to see about that neck. I thought we'd immediately go to Pa's house, but she drives instead to the San Fernando General Hospital. She is more comfortable driving in San Fernando. When we get to the hospital, she says, Your father should be here with you right now.

The emergency room is packed with people. All the chairs are used and people are sprawled on the floor and leaning against the walls. There is blood on some people's clothing, and someone is holding a bloody towel against a man's head. I see two gurneys, each with a person on it. The staff recognize Mummy and come into the waiting room and fuss over me. Siri lets one of the nurses take her from Mummy's arms. I watch the nurse disappear into the nurses' station and expect Siri to begin screaming, but she doesn't make a sound. We don't have to wait. A doctor who knows Daddy, but not Mummy, comes out right away, happy to meet her. He asks where Suresh is today. Mummy tells him Daddy was busy, he had some business with some people. The doctor exclaims, On carnival Tuesday. Suresh is quite the man, isn't he.

I see Tara looking at the ground. I look away. Mummy nods.

The doctor carries on, I hope he doesn't give up his practice if—not if, when—when he becomes the representative for San Fernando, you know. But he is the kind of man, whatever he does he will do it well. OK, let's see what's going on with this young lady.

He walks us through the big doors and puts me to sit on a bed behind a pale blue curtain. He calls for a chair for Mummy. A nurse asks my name, and I whisper, Andru. She looks over to Mummy and says loudly, But that is a boy's name. I say quickly, Sorry, I mean Anju. My embarrassment fades as the doctor holds my head, wraps his hands around my neck, feels my spine, and softly presses here and there. He tells a nurse to bring Mummy, Tara, and Anil something to drink. I am not allowed to have anything until he knows what's wrong with my neck. I feel special.

I am put in a wheelchair—I try hard not to smile—and am wheeled into the X-ray room, where my neck is X-rayed, and in no time I'm wheeled back into the room that isn't a room. Tara is lying on the bed, stretched out fully, her head on the pillow, her feet crossed at the ankles. I want to tell her that it's my bed, to come off. But I think sitting in the wheelchair is better, so I don't. Anil sits on the edge of the bed and crosses his legs as if he is a big man. After a while the doctor returns with several pictures and slaps one after the other, in see-through shades of grey, onto a box on the wall that has a light in it. He shows Mummy the film—the bones in my neck. Nothing to see, he says. It's a sprain, nothing more, just as he had suspected. Children's painkillers will help ease the discomfort. He wraps a brace around my neck. He is gentle and has soft eyes. I will have to wear the brace for several weeks. That means I will go to school with the brace on my neck and will have to explain to everyone that I was in a diving accident. Diving into very deep water. The calm sea suddenly turned rough, unpredictable. The water receded, really, really, really fast, while I was in midair. I crashed into the sand, my head hit it, my neck being both compressed and slightly twisted. I could have drowned but somehow didn't. I was incredibly lucky. Yes, incredibly lucky.

Mummy says it is best we go straight home. I was looking forward to showing Pa the brace around my neck, but she insists she does not want to go there. She says Pa will not like it that Daddy is not with us. I am not supposed to argue with her, so I don't, even though I am disappointed.

*

Daddy returns home before the sun rises Wednesday morning. Tara is awake, too. We listen but cannot hear anything. There is no shouting. He doesn't say, when he sees the brace on my neck, that he is sorry he didn't take me himself to the hospital. He asks Mummy in front of me which doctor saw me at the hospital. She says, So you care now? I should not have had to go there on my own. You should have been there with her.

He says nothing in response but touches my back, my face. I am angry with him, and I want to show him my anger by not speaking a word to him, or perhaps speaking only in short sentences while not looking at him. But when he holds me by my shoulders, his fingers softly wrapped over them, when he examines the brace and asks how my neck feels, I can't help myself; I calm right down, as if everything is as good as ever. I feel shy, but I look directly into his eyes and speak back to him as softly, as kindly, as he has spoken to me, as if I am taking care of him now. I want to tell him that I am happy he has come back home; I want to ask him how he got back. But all I say is, I have to wear this every day until my neck heals. As if none of the previous day had happened at all.

*

Mummy and Daddy haven't spoken much to each other for several days. We have also not been to see Pa. That means he hasn't seen the brace. I think Mummy doesn't want Pa to see her looking sad.

Daddy came home one evening with a little box wrapped in dark green paper and tied with a gold ribbon. When he handed it to her, she said, What is this for? He said, Just take it, na, pet. It's just a gift.

On the midnight-blue box was written *Goldman Jewellers.* Inside was a sparkly pendant with hundreds and hundreds of colourful precious stones in it—so many you can't really count them—and a gold necklace. Daddy said Mr. Goldman told him that Mummy had been in only recently and admired it.

TWELVE

There is something called abortion. I'd never heard of it before. This is big news and it's in the newspaper every day now. Everyone is talking about Daddy and it. Archbishop De Souza says that abortion is evil. It is murder. And that is why it is illegal.

But as an opposition member in the House of Representatives, Daddy has put forward a bill in Parliament to have it legalized. Mummy is embarrassed that people know that her husband wants this illegal, evil, murderous thing made legal.

I ask Daddy to explain what abortion is and why it is causing people to say unkind things about him. Mummy nods her head at him, and says, Eh-heh, let me hear you explain this to your child now.

He stares at me for an uncomfortably long time. Seeming to choose words carefully, he finally speaks, but hesitantly. He says that sometimes bad things happen and a woman who did not intend to have a baby gets pregnant, and sometimes even young girls get pregnant.

How is it possible for a young girl to have a baby? I wonder. Can I get pregnant? How does a person get to be pregnant? This is all confusing.

Young girls? I ask, unable to hide my surprise.

Yes, not all, but some young girls, he says.

Mummy says to him, OK, that's enough, Suresh.

He glances up at her, but he doesn't stop. Who knows why, he says. They just do. But these people often shouldn't have a baby, or at least not at that time. A baby is a big responsibility, and a parent should be capable of taking care of it. A girl shouldn't become a mother when she is still in school. And she shouldn't have to leave school. She should finish school and hopefully go on to university. And a woman who gets pregnant in some unfortunate way should be permitted to end the pregnancy. Abortion is the name of the procedure to do this.

I don't fully understand, but I say, I see.

Encouraged, he says, Sometimes a pregnancy can endanger the life of the woman, too, and she could die. If the pregnancy were ended, she would live. But many people, he says, believe that a baby inside of a woman's tummy, even before it is born, is a person, a human being, life, and this abortion practice is taking the life of a person. It is murder, they believe.

Oh, I say. So then sometimes a choice has to be made? One has to die for the other one to live. How do you decide which one should live?

He nods his head deeply while looking at me. I think that means I got it. These are things I have never thought about before, and it's all very grown-up and interesting.

Daddy carries on: It should be decided by a doctor together with the patient, and perhaps by the law. It is a serious thing to end a pregnancy, and if a person decides to do it—and there has to be a good reason—the procedure, which is dangerous in itself, must be done by a qualified medical practitioner. But because abortion is illegal in our country, doctors aren't allowed to perform such procedures.

Mummy sucks her teeth. This is ridiculous, Suresh. It's time for Anju to go and—

I'm not sure what it is time for me to do, because he interrupts her, saying, Can I speak, please? Can I explain *my* reasoning?

There are people who are not doctors who try to perform abortions, he says. He is now unusually serious. But they do it in rooms that don't have proper sterile medical equipment, and sometimes they use all kinds of tools that can cause life-threatening damage to the women, and to the young girls. Sometimes the abortion is botched, and the baby is damaged but not aborted.

Maybe he sees the horror on my face, because he stops. I am about to leave, but he starts again.

Do you know, Anju, he says, girls from your school have come to me after going to one of these backyard abortion places?

Now I am frightened.

What are you telling her? Mummy asks loudly and more forcefully. That is confidential. There's no need to tell her about girls from—

But he holds up his hand to stop her and says, She is my daughter, too. People will probably ask her why I am proposing legalizing abortion, and she needs to know. Anju is a smart child. She is no shrinking violet. She can take it. And she needs to know that this concerns all classes and levels and ages of people. People like those who work for us, people like us, children like her. I know what I am doing. Let me carry on.

My heart is thumping. I am not comfortable with all this information, but I am smart and capable, and even if I didn't know these things before, I can take it. I try to ask in as neutral a way as possible, Our friends? Girls in my school? I never saw any of them with big tummies. How did they get pregnant? What happened to them? To the babies?

He answers, but not exactly. Once or twice a month I see, in my office, the harm that an illegal abortion attempt caused. I have to pick up the pieces. Let me tell you, it isn't a pretty job. I would quicker amputate a leg than try to repair a woman's insides, or abort a fetus. I am not suggesting giving abortions to anyone just because they want it, but if it is legalized, people who can't afford to leave the country and go to private clinics abroad to safely end a pregnancy that came about because of some terrible situation they were in, or because it could harm them or the baby, could do so legally here, in Trinidad. Professionally. If it is made legal, I wouldn't have to deal with tetanus and all kinds of infections because an attempt to do it was made by someone who was only guessing what to do, in unsanitary conditions, with no proper safe health care afterwards. As a doctor I save individual lives. As a politician, I intend to stand up for all women and children.

These are almost the same words the newspaper quoted. *As a doctor I save individual lives. I am proud to represent San Fernando, but as a politician I intend to stand up for women and children all over this country.*

Mummy breaks in: They shouldn't be getting pregnant in the first place. Archbishop De Souza isn't a foolish man, you yourself have respect for him, so why this now?

Daddy inhales slowly, his eyes blinking fast, hard. His voice is cold when he says, I just explained. I thought you wanted me to stop? But then he adds, Archbishop De Souza isn't concerned with medical issues. I am. Then, directed to me, he says, Do you understand what I'm saying?

I nod that I understand, mostly because I don't want to hear any more. But I am wondering which girl in our neighbourhood, which girl in my school, was or is pregnant. How would it have happened? What happens to a girl after? Will she be OK? There was a girl in a higher class who left school in the middle of the term, and someone said it was because she had to go with her mother to the United States of America, and they decided to stay there for a while. But she never came back to school. Was she one of those? Students were whispering about it. I remember now. Better not to ask.

*

Daddy hasn't come home for dinner. He doesn't usually anymore because his party is trying to reorganize itself, and as its deputy leader and a representative in Parliament, he attends meetings that happen now almost every evening and even on weekends.

The phone rings, and when Mummy answers, she keeps saying, Who is this? Who are you? Where is he?

From the sound of her voice, we know something is wrong and we go and sit with her while she telephones the home of the eye-wiping leader of the party, ready to speak with his wife. We can hear only her side of the conversation, of course.

Eh-eh, Martin, you're back home already? Is Suresh with you? What? I don't understand.

Well, someone just called here and said he's been shot.

Don't tell me to calm down, Martin. I thought there was a meeting in Chaguanas? Weren't you with him? He said he was going there with you.

Then where is he?

But, wherever he is, how am I to find out?

She turns her back to us and lowers her voice, but of course we hear everything.

They said he's dead. Is Suresh OK, Martin? How can I find out? Should I call the police?

As she copies something down on a piece of paper, she says, Yes, but, Martin, all of you think I am a wet blanket, but this is why I have never wanted him involved in any of this. This is not a joke. Politicians and their families, their children, are being threatened, kidnapped, and terrorized, yes, terrorized by these kinds of pranks. And how can you be so sure it is a prank? What if it is true? What should I do right now?

I asked you not to tell me to calm down, Martin. What about that member from the northeast? Ent they shot his wife? This is no joke to make. I suppose I should call the police. Should I call the police?

She is barely off the phone when we hear Bruno whining and the gate downstairs being dragged open. Mummy runs out of the bedroom section and, together with the maids, who have left their room and come into the main part of the house, goes to the windows in the living room and pulls down the louvres. It is his car, it is him, driving through the open gates. Mummy meets him at the back door. We stand back but make sure to be close enough so we can see if there is any blood on him, and hear what happened and how he escaped.

Where were you? she asks him right away.

It is so sad that she speaks to him like that. She should have hugged him and asked him if he was hurt and told him she was happy he was alive. She can be a real wet blanket, in truth.

He laughs and says, What do you mean?

When he tries to kiss her, she pulls away. He sucks his teeth and moves around her, walking further into the house. He sees us, and with concern says, What are you all doing still up?

I smile at him, and he says, Well, someone is happy to see me.

Mummy points her finger sharply at me to direct me to my room, and she follows him. His voice changes again, darkens.

I told you where I was going. I told you I was going with Martin to a meeting in Chaguanas. You should have seen how many people were there. I think we're building a viable party finally.

She hits his chest with her fist and says, I just spoke to Martin. Where the hell were you?

Suddenly, I understand why she is upset. But where was he then? I wonder. They go directly into their bedroom, Mummy calling Maureen before she closes the door, telling her to get us into bed right away. They put on the air-conditioning unit, but above the drone of it we hear shouting, things being thrown, doors slamming, Mummy sobbing.

In the morning, Tara goes into their room as soon as she wakes up. She comes back out immediately. I ask her what they are doing. She says, I am not allowed to be in there, but Anil is. It isn't fair. Daddy had lipstick on his shirt.

I say, Well, it's probably hers.

But I hate Mummy in that moment. Yes, hate. She is so weak. A wet blanket. Always worrying so much that she doesn't even hear when we're trying to speak with her. He even has to tell fibs to her when he wants to go and just have some fun. I don't want to be like her when I grow up, always staying at home, crying, watching him when women speak to him.

And I don't want to be like him either. If I were him, I would take my wife everywhere I went, I would dance with her, even if other women wanted to dance with me. I would hold her hand and go for walks with her, and she would come to all my political meetings with me. If I became the prime minister, I would want her to be the deputy prime minister. And if she didn't want to go out to a meeting with me, but I had to go, well, I'd make sure to come home in time for dinner, or early enough to go to bed with her. Maybe one day we would do what I wanted to do, and then the next we could do what she wanted to do. We'd just take turns.

*

Mummy thinks that just because she opens the bathroom window, we can't tell that she has been smoking. I can smell the matches and the cigarette even when her bedroom door is closed and locked, too. Only men are supposed to smoke, and women who are not nice. She doesn't always smoke. And when she does, she hides in the bathroom to do it. I think she hides from us so we won't know, but she hides from Maureen and from Daddy, too.

These things go together: Mummy smoking in the bathroom, Mummy locking herself in her bedroom and having long conversations on the phone, crying on the phone, and, when she is with us and we try to talk to her, like ask her questions, she just looks at her hands and says, Mhm. Mummy, what is the name of the mayor of San Fernando? Mhm. Mummy, will we go to Mayaro on Sunday like you and Daddy promised? Mhm. Mummy can I have a chocolate? Mhm. That last one is OK, but I don't think she even knows she said yes.

He didn't come home last night. Mummy says it's because he had a meeting in Port of Spain and it ended late and he had another one this morning, so he stayed there. Tara asked if we could phone him to say good morning before we go to school. Mummy's eyes are puffy. Her whole face is puffy. She doesn't answer the question but says we will be late for school and should just finish breakfast and go and brush our teeth and go downstairs and wait for the taxi driver. He'll be here in minutes, and we can't make him wait. Maureen comes and pulls our chairs from the table, one by one. I think Mummy doesn't know where Daddy is. I don't think he is in Port of Spain. Or had a meeting last night. I think when we come home from school there'll be cigarette smoke in the bathroom, lots of tissues in the wastebasket, and lots of mhms. I want to say I am not feeling well, then I'll get to stay at home. But I don't want her to have to worry about me, too. Her face looks long. Puffy and, even so, long, as if it is falling.

*

Auntie Sally and Uncle Phillip, carrying his doctor's bag, are here. Daddy isn't. He hasn't been home for several days. Mummy has closed the accordion door to the living room where they remain, and we aren't allowed to go in there with them. The air-conditioning unit in that section of the house is on, and over its hum not much can be heard from the passageway. But I go into the kitchen a few times and it is from here that I listen. Mummy is crying. She is on the phone, and it sounds as if it might be Daddy she is speaking with. She keeps saying, But this is your home, why are you doing this to me? Please, I'm begging you, come home. Tell me what to do. I'll do anything you want.

And then I hear Uncle Phillip say loudly, So what's going on, man? Yeah. OK. No, no. She's OK. Just a little upset. Yes, I'll give her something to calm her down. Valium. Let her take a little sleep. You want to speak to her again? I hear Mummy say, Yes, let me speak to him. Give it to me. And Uncle Phillip say, OK, take it easy, man. Yeah, yeah. Take care on the road. Don't worry, I'll look after her. Mummy doesn't go back on the phone.

Maureen has caught me listening and pulls me out of the kitchen, saying, Child, you don't want to mind big-people business. She makes me get into bed. I don't know when I fell asleep, when Auntie Sally and Uncle Phillip left, or what time of night it was when Daddy came home. I awoke when he opened our bedroom door. I open my eyes in the dark just enough to see, in the crack of the doorway, his frame darkened by the light of the hallway behind him. I want to jump up and greet him. He's back. Finally, he's back. But I hold my breath and lie still. He must not know I am awake. I hadn't realized that Tara, too, had awakened. She grips my hand, turns to face me, and whispers, Let's put the pillows over our heads, we can relax now.

She places her pillow on her head, but I don't. I lie on my back and try to stay awake and listen. What if one of them needs help? I have to stay awake to be of use, just in case. I hear Daddy go into the washroom. He stays in there a long time, it seems. I keep drifting off to sleep and jerking back awake. I must have fallen asleep before he came back out, because I hear him coughing in the bedroom. But I don't hear Mummy.

THIRTEEN

Tara and I are born almost exactly a year apart—for two weeks every year, we are the same age. At first, when Mummy told Tara and me that she was having this birthday party for us, I felt bad that she would go through such a lot of trouble for me. When she is really angry with me, she snaps, You're just like your father. Sometimes it seems like she is disgusted with him, as if she hates him—not just what he does, but Daddy himself.

People are always saying what a lovely couple they make and how there's so much love between them. Sometimes nothing in this house makes any sense, and there's no one around who can explain any of it. If Pa knew how much Daddy stayed away from home, and if he knew how much Mummy fought with Daddy, he'd be very unhappy. Mummy told us, more than once, that we are never to go and tell tales to Pa about the adult things that happen between her and Daddy.

But when Daddy hugs her, it's as if she can't hear the rest of the world and can't see anything but him.

But I don't cause that kind of reaction in her; she never tries to hug me. Good things I say or do can't make her forget everything. The others—Tara, Anil, Siri—they make her happy. Regardless, I try.

I wonder, if Tara and I did not have birthdays just weeks apart, but maybe months apart, might she just have a party for Tara and not bother with mine? But, as it is, maybe she has no choice.

Then I started to think about all the presents I would get and the children coming over and the fuss that might be made of me. Of the ice cream, chicken puffs, cheese sticks, and sweet-drinks. There would have to be a cake with our names on it, too—maybe we'd each get our own cake. I decided not to worry too much about all the trouble a party would cause. For days before, all I thought of was the party. I became quiet on the outside, helpful around the house, particularly by playing with Siri, and mostly careful not to annoy Mummy or Daddy or cause them to feel I didn't deserve a birthday party. I imagined all the games we'd play. I would be the best in every game. Daddy would have the street in front of our house closed off so we could play cricket in the street, but we'd have to end the match because no one would be able to out me. We could play billiards on Daddy's billiards table, which he keeps in the large paved open area under the living room, beneath the house. Only the boys and Daddy's friends and I would play. I would break the triangle of balls, sinking several at once, and then go on to pocket five in a row.

I've decided I'll wear my favourite outfit: the denim shirt with silver studs on the collar, blue jeans—and maybe I can get Mummy to buy me the holsters and guns we saw at the toy store. And the black felt cowboy hat. I go into the kitchen, where Mummy is leaned over the counter cutting out a picture of a bathroom from *House Beautiful* magazine. As I hover at her side, she tilts the picture toward me and says, Wouldn't it be nice to have a bathroom like this? I point to the marble tiles on the wall and ask if they can be bought in Trinidad. She says, If not, they can be imported. And she tapes it into her scrapbook. It feels like the right time to tell her my plan and so, with some confidence because of this bathroom-picture bonding, I tell her what I want to wear. Turning around to look at me, she says, frowning, That's silly. You are going to wear a dress like all the other girls, and please don't make any fuss about this. In any case, I've already bought what you will both wear. I say only the word *but*, and she stands up straight and snaps, What did I just say? I don't want to hear any more about this.

She's bought Tara and me the exact same yellow dresses that have a big frilly skirt that sticks out all around because they have a cancan built in—it's really scratchy—and you can't remove the cancan without ripping the dress. The only differences between Tara's and mine are hers has a white ribbon woven through the skirt and mine has a black ribbon, and mine is two sizes larger. Often Tara and I are expected to wear the same clothing. It is the worst feeling in the whole wide world having to dress exactly like my little sister. But I am not allowed to say that again. So instead, when Tara comes into our room, I tell her that her dress is ugly and she shouldn't wear it to the party. Tara turns and walks out of our room, and I hear her in the kitchen, saying something in a whiny voice.

I am tidying my shelf of books when Mummy walks into our bedroom and slaps me on my arm. Her long nails, which Daddy is forever saying look so pretty, swish off my skin. I don't cry. My eyes burn and fill up, but I don't cry. She says I am a dishonest child and don't deserve any party and am not to leave my room for the rest of the evening. Anil sticks his tongue out and scrunches his nose up at me, following Mummy out of the room, and they close the door behind them.

I didn't mean to be dishonest. I turn off the light in the room and get into bed. I think of how unfair it is to make me dress exactly like someone else and make me wear a scratchy dress. One day, I think, they will be really happy they are related to me because I will be the greatest. The greatest. The greatest something—maybe a scientist or a doctor, or an artist, or maybe I will become a boy, a stronger boy than Anil. A buddy for Daddy, a son that Mummy will hug and touch.

Mummy also got us the same socks and exactly the same black patent shoes. We will look like twins, except that I am much, much taller than Tara. I'm growing like a string bean, says Maureen.

*

Almost all the children in both our classes, forty in total, have been invited. Some parents and teachers, including Miss Hill, are coming, too. There'll be a magician and lots of games, all of it taking place under the house. We won't be able to play billiards, as there will be a heavy sheet of plywood over the table to protect it and that will be covered with a tie-dye plastic tablecloth and used to set out the party food and the one birthday cake that will have both our names on it.

Daddy has come home early. He and Sharma have tied red, yellow, blue, and white balloons and streamers all around the area where the party will be held. Maureen has on her dark blue dress and her dark blue cap. She, Mummy, Auntie Stella, and Auntie Stella's maid, Corrine, have set all the food from the kitchen in beautiful dishes and brought them downstairs to the table with a cake in the shape of Mary Poppins hanging from an umbrella.

We play catch, hide-and-seek, pin the tail on the donkey, and there is a treasure hunt. A man with a real donkey has been hired to take us on rides in his cart down Crystal Road. Daddy and his friends chat and drink while the mothers arrange the games and prepare the food plates.

Pa is here, of course. Every so often, I run over to him and take a rest from the party. He takes out his big white kerchief, wipes the sweat off my forehead, and tells me not to run so much. These days he seems weak, and I wish I could take care of him, but I can't because I don't live with him. I want him to see that I can feel him. I feel that whatever is in my heart is in his also. Even though there is so much noise at the party, when I am next to him I hear his voice in my mind, singing, *All things bright and beautiful, all creatures great and small.* But there are no words for how I feel. There can't be, for no one ever speaks words that can describe what swims through my heart, and perhaps his, too. My heart is like a river—sometimes the flow of this river gets blocked, as if fallen trees, or even dumped garbage, block the flow. Everything then overflows. That's when I feel as if I will drown, even though I'm not even really in water.

Auntie Stella brings out the cake with the nine candles. Tara goes first because she is the younger. Everyone sings "Happy Birthday"; she makes a wish and blows out the candles. Then comes the sticking of the cake. The boys run away shrieking and giggling, and the grown-ups think this is so cute. One father comments to another on the other's son running from the cake-sticking ceremony by slapping his shoulder, laughing, and saying, He running from girls? That ent your son. You make that boy? You better check with Ann, you hear? And all the grown-ups laugh. We laugh, too, although I don't know what he means. Tara is excited about this part. She allows Auntie Stella to tie the kerchief around her head, covering her eyes. Eventually all the boys get in a circle with Tara in the middle. Auntie Stella turns Tara around three times, then lets her go. She walks forward, and the boys put their hands over their wide-open mouths, as if they are giggling without sound so she can't hear whom she is walking toward. She walks right to Gary Maraj and touches him. She always says that when she gets older, she will marry him, so when she whips off the kerchief and sees him, she blushes. The boys tease him, saying, Gary, you push yourself in front of her, and they make mock kissing sounds. They run up to Gary, tap him on his head, and in singsong voices say, *Gary and Tara sitting in a tree, K-I-S-S-I-N-G.*

First comes love, then comes marriage. Soon comes Gary pushing a baby carriage.

I think the boys are right. He did push himself toward Tara, but now he looks embarrassed. His face has gotten red, and he walks away from everyone. Daddy goes over and convinces him that all the other boys are merely jealous. One father says to Gary's father, Boy, your son could keep Suresh's daughter in all this style? And he guffaws. Mr. Maraj laughs, enjoying the heckling, and says he'd better go and see Mr. Patterson, the bank manager, for a loan.

Then it is my turn. Tara's candles are removed and ten fresh ones replace them. I make three wishes as "Happy Birthday" is sung—that Pa won't die and leave me like Ma did, that when I grow up I will be the best artist that ever existed and books will be made with all my paintings in them, and that I'll be an explorer and travel around the world, to the most remote parts, to Tristan da Cunha, Kiribati, the top of the Himalayas, the North Pole, Antarctica, and I'd like to bicycle from the top of North America to the end of South America. Everyone is shouting, Hurry up, you have too many wishes. But I take my time. I am about to blow out the candles, but some of the boys blow out a few of them before I can, and they have to be lit again.

I was not looking forward to this next part, but it is now my turn to be blindfolded. I look at Miss Hill and feel a tickle in my knees, in my tummy, in my heart, and it's as if the bottom of my stomach has dropped out from me. I know I mustn't say it, but I want to stick the cake with Miss Hill. Blindfolded, I pick Tony, who puffs out his chest and, unlike Gary, looks as if it is only natural that he was chosen. Again, Tara goes first. She and Gary stand in front of the cake, and she gets a knife and Gary a fork. Gary pierces the cake, and Tara cuts a huge chunk around the fork, a piece bigger than a mouth. The whole piece dangles off his fork and he shoves it over Tara's face. Auntie Stella is instantly cleaning off Tara's face. You have to kiss her now, Gary, the other boys call, and Gary goes to her cheek and makes a big smooching noise with his mouth. She pushes him away and wipes her face. Auntie Stella, businesslike, cleans off the knife and fork on a napkin and positions Tony and me. I want to do this quickly. I cut a neat square of cake, and Tony pricks it with his fork and puts it to my mouth. I don't look at Miss Hill. It's over, and I think because I didn't seem excited about this part, and Tony treated it as if it were a serious task, it's a letdown for everyone. I feel silly for not having been more entertaining. I wonder if Miss Hill and others think I'm a wet blanket.

Tara gets a gold bracelet from Pa, and he gives me a gold ring he bought for me on a horse-racing trip to Guyana. There is a heart shape on it, and inside of the heart are my initials in squiggly fancy letters. I put it on straight away and will never take it off, ever.

Between Tara and me, we get twenty-three presents altogether. We like them all, but the ones we are excited about are the Etch-A-Sketch, which we will have to take turns with, a board game called Monopoly, and the Slinky, which is for me. Best of all, though, are Pa's, and then Miss Hill's. She's given me two 45 rpm records. The first one is songs by a band with five men called the Byrds and has a song on one side called "She Don't Care About Time"—I never understand why musicians always speak badly; it should be "*Doesn't* Care"—and on the other side, "Turn! Turn! Turn!" which I have heard on the radio. I lose my breath for a few seconds when I see the second record. On one side is that song with the line about being "high-classed" that caused our louvre to break. It's by a man named Elvis. The other side is "Don't Be Cruel." Do Julie and Jen Scott know Miss Hill? I wonder. Did they tell Miss Hill about Tara and me peeping at them when they were dancing? And did they all laugh at us? I feel light-headed. But it's confusing, too, because I also feel grown-up and special. These are adult records, my first adult records, and it is Miss Hill, my favourite teacher, who I think really likes me, who has given them to me.

*

A seaman on one of the big red oil tankers anchored in the Gulf of Paria is ill. Oil tanker sailors don't normally have visas to come ashore, so when a doctor is needed on one of those ships, the doctor goes to them. Daddy is this shipping company's local doctor, and this is the first time he will make, not a house call, but a ship call. He has to board a tugboat tonight at the Pointe-à-Pierre pier that will take him out into the middle of the gulf to the ship. This sounds like an adventure, and I ask Daddy if I can accompany him. He thinks for a moment, and then agrees it would be an interesting and unusual opportunity for me. But then he says that when he is attending to the patient, I wouldn't be able to be with him. Where would he leave me? he wonders. I, a young girl, will be left on my own with all those sailors—men, likely—and he won't know in advance for how long he will be away from me. Who knows what can happen in that time? I don't ask what he is worried about. I think I know—but I don't think he knows that I know. Mummy, who also, for a minute, thought it would be an adventure for me, says then, No, you're right. What were we thinking? That would be craziness.

I want to insist that I would not dress like a girl, and I would be strong and safe and not let anyone touch me. Something else I don't say, but I think it: I won't be a girl. I will finally be a boy if he takes me with him.

When I lived on Selvon Street, I knew how to get what I wanted. I would scream, or argue with Ma when she was alive, or pretend I couldn't hear what I was being told. But I don't do any of that in this house. Insisting gets you nowhere. In this house it is better to be calm, to seem to be wondering, to be trying to understand.

When Mummy adds, He's going out there after dinner, in the nighttime; what nonsense is this? You're a young girl—do you want to get in trouble, or what? it sounds as if I've been insisting, begging, arguing. But I wasn't. I am about to point this out, but I have learned that sometimes it is best to just be silent.

In any case, I can't believe it. How many children like me have a father who gets to board an oil tanker in the middle of the sea? This is like an adventure you'd read in a book. It seems so unfair not to be able to take part when the opportunity is right here in front of me. But I need to understand something else. I ask in a very straightforward voice, no pleading or arguing, Is it because I am not a boy?

Daddy answers, Young boys are as vulnerable as young girls. Even if you were a boy, it might still be a problem, being left on your own with so many men like that. What I mean is, now that I think about it, I wouldn't take Anil with me either. You've made a good point there, actually.

I haven't made a point at all. I just asked a question. But that is Daddy, always trying to make you feel better. Then, looking at Mummy, he twists his mouth and says, You just can't trust men.

Is what I suspect he is worried about perhaps a common thing, then? Is what Chandra did to me, what Uncle John did, what Clydie tried to do, commonly done by men to little children? Even to boys? Are all men like that? Is he like that? Pa? And Anil, will he grow up to be like that, too? All these questions swim in my head, but I don't want to talk anymore, as I don't want anything horrible to leak out, by mistake, about me. I don't ask again to go with him.

As we have an early dinner together, I look at him in wonder. He is adventurous.

I don't hear when he returns, but in the morning when we wake up, he is sitting up in bed smoking a cigarette. He will go to work later than usual today, as he was on the ship for most of the night. Tara sits on the bed by his side, and I on a chair. He tells us it was pitch-black out on the water, the way ahead—choppy, waves criss-crossing each other—lit by the tugboat's single forward-facing searchlight. To get to the ship from the tugboat, he had to climb up a narrow metal ladder that hung straight down the side of the tanker. That, too, was lit only by the forward-facing light of the tug. When he looked up to try to see the sailors and the captain on the main deck, he had to bend his head all the way back as he stood unsteadily on the tug, and with the harsh light shining up the side of the ship, everything else was in darkness. Yes, it was scary, he says in response to our eyes wide open and our hands over our mouths. The tugboat kept bumping against the ship, then backing away from it, again and again, and the metal ladder was swinging, banging against the ship's side. He couldn't carry his medical bag and climb at the same time, so a sailor climbed down to the tugboat and followed him, carrying the bag up the narrow ladder, the light shifting erratically with the sea motion of the tug, sometimes on the ladder, sometimes away from it. And yes, he felt ill. Before descending again, on his return, he took a Gravol tablet. Just listening to him describe having to climb that ladder makes me feel ill. And I keep thinking, What if he'd allowed me to go and I couldn't climb the ladder? I would have caused a huge problem and embarrassed him and myself.

But there is news: The sick sailor is Norwegian, which means he is from a country called Norway. He is gravely ill and must be admitted to a hospital immediately. The shipping company insists the hospital has to be in Norway, and they insist, too, that for insurance purposes, he must be accompanied on the flight there by the company's doctor. So, in just a couple of days, Daddy is going to Norway.

*

All the way across the Atlantic Ocean, near the top of the map, is Ireland. To the right of Ireland is Great Britain. Go straight over to the right again, past Great Britain, and you come to the Netherlands. Then there is Germany, where Jutta is from, and above Germany is Denmark. On top of Denmark is a sea and across the sea is a long, narrow land mass that curves down and points to Denmark. The top part of that land mass is Norway, the capital of which is Oslo. It is very, very far from Trinidad, so far north on the globe that you will be very near the North Pole if you go there.

Mummy will travel with Daddy, and when Daddy is finished taking care of the man, he and Mummy will tour Europe. Daddy drags his finger on the map in our *Dillingers New Atlas of the World* from Norway down to Denmark, over to Holland, into Germany, and then, finally, to Italy.

Better not to even bother imagining it. They won't take us with them.

And they have a surprise for us: Daddy's parents, the ones who mailed us the big books from England, including the atlas, will come to Trinidad to live with us for the three weeks that Mummy and Daddy are away. They have been threatening, as Daddy says, to come for the last two years, and now they have a good reason. Daddy has booked their airplane tickets, and they will arrive two days after Mummy and Daddy leave; Maureen will be with us before then, of course. Daddy tells us that we know how to behave ourselves, so please behave ourselves. Show them how well we are bringing you up, he says. But Grandma is Hindu, like Pupah, and although she will eat other kinds of meat, there must be no mention at all that we eat beef. Which means, that's right, Anil, no hamburgers for three weeks.

Although I look forward to meeting them—Tara and I want to ask his mother where he was born, and if they really found him in a salt-fish barrel in Port of Spain—I had thought I might be allowed, while they were gone, to go to Pa's house and stay there with him. But I have to stay with Tara, Anil, and Siri, I have to be respectful to Grandma and Granddad, I am not to ask why, not to insist, and not to cause any trouble. Granddad drives, and he and Grandma will take us to the park, the beach, all over the place.

*

Grandma is shorter than Ma, and plump. Her hair is light brown and wavy, almost curly. Ma's was straight, like mine. Grandma wears large tinted glasses that make her eyes look huge. They speak a little like Tara did when she came from Ireland. Grandma smokes and her breath smells like cigarettes. Granddad doesn't like her smoking, but he drinks alcohol, and she doesn't like him drinking, so they are even. They bicker a lot, and it always ends with him laughing and teasing her, and her steupsing, but she never seems to get an angry face. He gets his way sometimes and she gets her way sometimes. They seem to always have something to say to one another, not like Ma and Pa, who seldom spoke unless it was about things that needed them both to organize.

Grandma speaks Hindi, like her father, Pupah. She says *acha* when she means all right. *Chalo* when she wants to say let's go, or it's time to go now, and she has taught me how to say What's your name? and My name is Anju.

Aap ke naam kya hai?

Meera naam Anju hai.

Meera naam Andru G hai.

She can read Sanskrit, like Pupah, and is teaching us to pray in Hindi; at certain times we are to say, along with her, Om Shanti Shanti. She calls God *Bhagwan*.

*

The only time we are ever allowed to drink sweetdrinks is on special occasions, if we have people over, or when we go to Pa's house on Selvon Street. But Grandad sometimes likes a rum and Coke, and now that Mummy and Daddy are gone, there are bottles of Coca-Cola in the fridge. One day, only after Grandma had already poured us each a full cup of Coke did Maureen tell her we aren't supposed to have any. It is now difficult for Grandma to say no to us, so she has made a deal with us: we can only have half a cup of Coke on Saturdays and Sundays. But those are the days they take us to visit Pa, and he gives us either red sweetdrink or Solo Apple J. Grandma doesn't say anything, but she gets this worried look on her face.

When we are with Pa, I try to stay very close to him. But he doesn't pay me too much attention in front of Granddad and Grandma. I think it is because he doesn't want them to think he owns me. I think he is trying to be fair.

We are supposed to be in bed by nine o'clock at night, lights off not a second later. Grandma always gets a very serious look as nine o'clock draws near and we haven't changed into our pyjamas and brushed our teeth, but she doesn't know how to be firm with us. We brush our teeth and change into our pyjamas and then ask for something to drink, and it's as if she gets confused. She asks, But didn't you already brush your teeth, and it is clear that she doesn't want to say no to us. As we walk to the fridge with her, she asks if we aren't afraid that we will be awakened in the middle of the night needing to go to the washroom. Maureen lets her struggle with us for a bit and then tells us to behave ourselves, that if our mummy were here, we wouldn't get away with all of these tricks.

Sometimes when Grandma comes to tuck us in, before she has time to turn off the light, we ask her to help us to pray in Hindi, and to teach us a bhajan. This makes her very happy. She gets in under the mosquito net with us, lies between Tara and me, and we pray, first saying strange words after her, then singing and clapping, and Tara and I watch the little clock in our room go almost to nine thirty before Maureen comes and looks in, which then reminds Grandma that it's now well past our sleeping time. Then we say after Grandma, Now I lay me down to sleep, I pray the Lord my soul to keep, if I should die before I wake, I pray the Lord my soul to take.

When the lights are off and Maureen and Grandma have gone, Tara says, But we're not going to die, right? And I turn and kiss her on her cheek and say what I have heard people say, Don't worry, only the good die young.

*

Granddad is driving Daddy's new black Mercedes. I think people recognize it as his car, because they turn and stare as we go by. Grandma is in the front seat with him, and Tara, Anil, and I are in the back. Siri has stayed back with Maureen. Granddad doesn't like the way people drive in Trinidad. He says Trinidadians are barbarians, that we don't follow rules. And sometimes—but only when he is not talking to us children—he uses bad language. It makes driving with him, even if we're driving to the beach or to the swings in the park, an unpleasant experience. He calls pedestrians and other drivers by their race. If there is an Indian woman crossing the road too slowly, he'll say something like, Come on, Bowhji (or Miss India, or beti), move along now, and if a white driver passes him, he'll say something like, That's right, white-is-might, on your way. When a Chinese person passes by, he calls them by the name of Chinese food dishes. He likes Chinese food and knows the names of many dishes, so each Chinese person gets a different name from him.

But he doesn't like Negroes. On our way to Diego Martin to visit one of Granddad's cousins, a Negro driver on The Coffee whose car was stopped on the side of the road pulls out in front of Daddy's car without signalling. Granddad swerves hard to avoid a collision, which causes him to almost hit a car coming in the other direction. We all scream. He slams on the brake and stops in the middle of the road, blocking the man's car. Granddad yells at the driver and calls him the word we are not supposed to say when speaking about Negroes. I don't even think; I stand up out of my seat and lean over, almost into the front seat, and shout, Granddad, but he just carries on, and he and the man have what Daddy would have called a heated exchange, and Granddad curses at the man and calls him that word again. It is awful and I begin to cry and shout that this is wrong, this is horrible.

When Granddad drives off, we are all silent. I do not want to go with them to his cousin's house. I sit back low in the seat, pressed against the back, my arms folded, refusing to look out. Granddad remains angry, and when we reach the roundabout, he doesn't take the turnoff to Port of Spain that will take us to Diego Martin but goes all the way around and back onto The Coffee, and we head back home to Crystal Road. Once we are in the house, he says, Listen, you, I want to have a word with you. Never contradict me again in front of anyone. Who do you think you are? You are a child, a ten-year-old child. You have no right meddling in adult business.

He is shouting and spittle comes from his mouth. So I lean forward and shout, You were being horrible. You called that man a bad word.

He says, It is a bad word for children to use, but I am your grandfather, and I can use whatever language I want.

I answer back, You spoke to that man as if you hated him.

He says, Yes. So what? Those people are—

And I scream at the top of my voice that I don't want to hear what he has to say and I never want to speak to him ever again, that it is because of people like him that there are wars in the world.

There is sudden silence in the house. Except I am breathing very heavily. Grandma nods to me to go to my room. Tara follows me in. I am shaking with fear. She hugs me. I know I was rude to him. They will tell Daddy when he returns, and I'll get into trouble. Tara won't let go of me, and she whispers, You're so brave, Anju.

He sits in the living room, silent and angry all day; the only sound is the tinkling of the ice in his glass as he shakes it constantly. I don't like him. He doesn't even know us well. This is not his house, he doesn't even live in Trinidad, he is a visitor here, driving Daddy's car, yet he was acting as if this were his country, his house, and his car.

For the rest of the week, I am unable to bring myself to speak with Grandad, and he doesn't speak with me either.

*

Daddy and Mummy return with more suitcases than they left with. Mummy has a new haircut. Her hair is very short. When Grandma sees it, she says, Very chic. Very chic. Granddad, with a wide grin, says, But why did you do that? You look like a boy. I see Daddy poke him in his back, and he spins around laughing and says, What? I am only speaking the truth.

I wonder if they have noticed that Granddad and I aren't speaking to each other and don't even look at one another. I am certain Daddy's parents would have already related to them the incident between him and me, and that I will be punished for talking to an adult, to a visitor, to my grandfather, to Daddy's father, the way I did. A whole day passes, and nothing happens, but I keep waiting. I am worried, but I am also convinced it does not matter that I am a child; I know that how he spoke to the man was wrong, and that is all that matters.

We all stand at the front gate and say goodbye as Grandma and Granddad get into a car one of his cousins has lent him. They are leaving to go back to England in a few weeks' time, but they aren't staying with us any longer; they are going to Granddad's cousin in Diego Martin, and we will go to visit them there. We are still waving when Anil pulls at Mummy's hand and says, OK, now can we please, please, please get hamburgers and chips for dinner tonight?

*

We get trolls and pennants from Norway, a cuckoo clock and pennants from Berlin, clogs and pennants from Holland, and a children's picture history of the Roman Empire from Italy, and pennants from Rome and Venice. And coins and paper money from all the different countries. I decide then to collect things. Pennants and coins.

They have brought back sheets for their bed—not ours, just theirs—and dishes and a vase made of a kind of glass called Murano, from Italy—and Mummy got a necklace of colourful beads, each looking as if it contained a wild and crazy garden inside it, made of that same kind of glass, too. Daddy got pretty, shiny ties from Italy and a doctor's bag from Germany.

Once all the little treasures, as we call these gifts, are unpacked, Daddy calls Tara and me into their bedroom. He sits in the chair I usually sit in, and he tells us—as if he were inviting us—to sit on the bed with Mummy. Tara sits between Mummy and me. His body is almost in silhouette, as the light through the window behind the chair is bright. He says he wants to have a word with me. Tara moves slightly so she is closer to me, close enough that our legs touch. I know what is coming. I can see the cars on The Coffee, the buildings, people on the sidewalks; I can see and feel Daddy's car swerve, Granddad's face, the other car, the other driver's face. I feel myself rise up in the car and shout. But there are no sounds to accompany any of these images.

Daddy, looking only at me, says, I understand you and Granddad have not spoken to each other in almost a week?

My skin has gotten hot, my heart has stopped beating. Very urgently, I need to go to the washroom. I barely nod.

He says, Granddad told me everything. He said he was having an exchange with a driver—Tara interrupts in a very low voice and says, A *heated* exchange. He says, Yes, that's right, a heated exchange. And he used unacceptable language. Is that right?

I can't speak. The pee is so close, so hot. I have to squeeze my legs together very tightly. I see Tara give the slightest nod, enough of one, I think, to try to help me out.

Your grandfather tells me you chastised him, Daddy says, looking from me to Tara and back again. You even shouted at him. Is that true?

I am trying to remember what *chastised* means; the word keeps repeating itself in my head. Too gently, and shortening my name, he says, Anj, I'm talking to you.

I look at him, still in silhouette, everything made worse because my eyes have filled with tears. I still can't answer.

Daddy laughs. He is mocking me, I think, and I look quickly about the room, taking in Tara and Mummy. Mummy doesn't look as angry as the situation seems to call for; her face is serious, but oddly, she looks calm, and even pleased.

He says, You were very correct, you know.

My body is always doing something I don't want it to do, or at the wrong time, or in the wrong place. My cheeks tickle, as if a smile is about to break out without my intending it—and at the same time, I think I am crying. I wait for him to add that I was, however, wrong to speak to an adult, to his father, to Granddad, that way and I will have to apologize.

He is saying, My parents told me exactly what you told Granddad, Anju, and I am very proud of you for trying to stop him.

Mummy adds, She didn't try. Your mother said she actually put a stop to it.

I attempt to say, I'll apologize, but it comes out in the smallest whisper possible.

He says, No, I don't think you need to in this case. Your grandfather agrees that you were very correct in what you were saying to him. It is OK to quarrel with people if they've wronged you or hurt others. But you should always fight with decency. He should never have called that driver, no matter what the man did, such an unacceptable word. He is impressed that almost a week went by and you never backed down. He's surprised that a young girl like you could be so strong. And he said to me that he's very proud to be your grandfather.

I am confused. I say, Then why didn't he try to speak with me?

Daddy says, I guess you are both cut from the same cloth.

That expression is new to me, but it is easy to guess what it means. Tara is looking directly at me, her eyes wide open. She is smiling. I think she is proud of me, too. Then Mummy says, I think it is your father whom you take after, in truth.

This time, she doesn't say that with anger, but as if it were a good thing.

With a happy voice she adds, Clearly, we've taught you well. You're learning to stand up for what's right.

Then, looking back and forth between Daddy and me, she further adds, with a kind of smile I've come to know, You're becoming hard-headed just like your father.

Whenever she says anything that might sound like praise, she always adds something that confuses you and makes you wonder if it really was praise.

FOURTEEN

The artist arrives in a small cream-coloured car. He comes from France and is painting children's portraits to fund his travels through the Caribbean. After seeing the ones he had done of our friends Sandy and Sean, Mummy contacted him to paint our portraits, too.

He is wearing a straw hat and comes up the front stairs carrying a stool in one hand and a thin wooden case in the other. He clutches under his arms several white boards. He sets down everything on the front porch and removes his hat. His hair is light brown and the front of it falls almost to his eyes. He looks like a movie star, and a hippie like the ones we see pictures of in magazines. Mummy doesn't have to ask Sharma to help. He has stopped edging the garden bed at the side of the house and come around, curious. He washes the dirt from his hands and helps the man bring more equipment from the car up to the house. He wants to watch what is happening, but Mummy smiles at him and makes a sideways motion with her head, and he heads back down the stairs.

She calls the artist Antoine but introduces us to him as Mr. Adrien. I want to call him Monsieur Adrien, because I learned that is the word for mister in French. But I'm not sure I'll pronounce it properly, and I don't want to sound silly.

I have never seen an artist make a painting before. He paints with oil paints, which have a strong smell and take a long time to dry, and he doesn't paint on paper but on hard surfaces called canvas boards. I make sure not to be the first one, as I want to watch him draw and fill in colours. The furniture in the living room has been pulled away so he can set up a wooden frame he calls an easel, as well as a stool and a work table, all of which he brought in the small car. He leans a canvas board against the easel, and I recognize what I am seeing: in one of the books that Daddy's parents sent us when they were in England, there is a painting called *The Artist in His Studio* by an artist named Rembrandt. In that painting there is a frame like this, and now I know its name, an easel. And now here is one right in front of me. The artist's paints come in small tubes. He squeezes colours out onto a large round piece of wood he calls a palette. It has a hole in it, and he sticks his thumb through that hole to secure the palette in his hand. Anil is the first to be painted. I position myself behind Monsieur Adrien so I can see what he is doing. He draws first, very faintly, with a fat stick that works like a pencil but doesn't have any wood on it, then he draws over that using a long paintbrush and brown paint. I am watching a real artist make a picture.

Anil's hair is black, but Monsieur Adrien doesn't use pure black paint. He uses brown and red, too, and he even puts a little blue in it, and I am surprised that it looks more real than if he had just coloured it black.

He makes a mixture, in a tiny cup, of a syrupy liquid called linseed oil that has a strong smell, and turpentine. This is what the artist Rembrandt's studio must have smelled like. From the tubes, he squeezes mounds of glistening paint onto the palette, dips his long thin brush in the mixture in the cup and then in the colours on the palette. Sometimes he uses a tool that looks like a knife to mix the paint on the palette, or scrape it off, and he even paints with the knife. The walls of our living room are white, but Monsieur Adrien paints the wall behind us a pale greenish blue.

Each day Monsieur Adrien paints for about three hours. We don't have to sit for the entire time, but we have to remain dressed and not prance around. Whenever we take a break, Mummy—not Maureen—brings him something to drink, something to eat, pastels or chocolate cake. Monsieur Adrien doesn't drink alcohol, so he gets sorrel, lime juice, tea. He likes green tea, which we don't normally have, but Mummy bought a box of it to serve to him. First, they sat on the porch, but as the days have gone by, they go down in the garden and she walks him around, showing him the plants. When they go down, I become a little worried and listen for Daddy's car, for him returning home from his office unexpectedly. I went down once and walked with them for a few minutes. He was telling her about his home in France. His father, like Daddy, is a doctor, and his mother is a painter, like him. Mummy speaks to me differently when he is here. She sent me back upstairs, but she wasn't as strict as she usually is. Very kindly she told me to go back up. I went up and stayed on the porch, looking out onto the road. I wonder if she thinks Monsieur Adrien is handsome. I think so, and I think she does, too. I wish my hair could be like his. And that I had a straw hat.

When he calls us back, we must try to sit exactly as we had before we got up, and he spends some time adjusting us on the chair.

Each day I stand behind Monsieur Adrien, or at his side, and watch. I want to tell him about the beach at Mayaro, and about Maracas, and suggest he paint pictures of those places, too. If I could paint like him, with this kind of paint, I'd make pictures of a river in a jungle, all the dark green trees, and the brown trunks and ground. I'd put red in the browns. And yellow. When Monsieur Adrien leaves, I will make a serious effort to teach myself how to mix the paints in my poster set to get all the different colours, like he does.

To my surprise, without telling me she was going to do this, Mummy brings my sketchpad out during one of the breaks in painting. As she opens the pad to show him my drawings, my first impulse is to grab it from her, but I don't. I am embarrassed, shy, and proud, all at the same time. He spends a long time looking at each picture, especially the one with the sky that is dark blue at the top and blue mixed with red below and that has nothing in it but twenty white stars and twenty red stars and one orange comet, and also the one of a sky that is black with stars I drew with a silver felt pen. He stands close to Mummy. He put his hand on her back once. She didn't move away. My face burns, but I want to know what he thinks of my drawings. He looks at me as he says to Mummy, Ten years old? Very impressive. She has interesting ideas. Talent.

When he says nothing more, I wish she hadn't shown them to him. I want him to talk with me, I want to ask him if he knows the paintings in our big book. If he's seen those paintings in real life. But it is probably silly to ask a real artist that kind of question. The only times he does speak to me are to ask me to hand him this or that from his box, even though the thing he wants is right there, very close to him. It does seem to me that he is aware of me, and that he shifts his body so I am always able to see what he is doing.

On the sixth day my turn comes. Now I am watching the back of the board and the easel against which it leans, and his face whenever it peeps out to study me before disappearing again behind the canvas.

When he is finished, he signs his name, *Antoine Adrien*, on the lower left of each portrait and places them flat to dry on an old bedsheet that has been spread nearby. He closes the tubes of paint, wipes them all with a rag soaked in turpentine, and rests them on the high work table. He then cleans his brushes by swishing them about in a glass jar containing smelly turpentine. He places three brushes beside the tubes and puts the rest in his big box. He closes the linseed oil bottle, uses the rag to wipe it, and sets the bottle beside the brushes. He takes his time doing everything. It is not enough, I see, to make your painting, but when you're finished, you must clean your tools and put everything away properly.

I watch as he folds his easel. It is all coming to an end, and I know he will soon leave the island and we'll never see him again. I wish he lived nearby and could teach me. I want to ask him questions, to speak to him, but I don't know what to ask, what to say. Then he snaps shut the box, forgetting to put into it all the things that are still on the work table. I am about to point out that he needs to pack those up, too, when he picks up the three brushes and presents them to me, as if he were holding a bouquet of flowers. I understand I am to hold them, so I do. He reaches into the large canvas bag and pulls out five small canvases and places them on the work table. He says, As I was painting, I was showing you how I mix the paints with the linseed oil and the turpentine. You were watching. You saw how I washed my brushes and how I cleaned up. Now all of these—the paints, the bottles, brushes and canvases—are yours. All you need is a plate—a Styrofoam plate to use as a palette will do.

I can't speak. Mummy exclaims. Oh no, you can't do that, she says.

And he replies, She has talent. You might as well develop it. Also, this is all so heavy for me. It is a relief to let go of some of it.

Mummy, looking pleased and surprised, says to me, Well, what do you say?

I hold the brushes to my chest and whisper, *Thank you, Monsieur Adrien.* He puts his hand on my head for the most glorious second ever.

He tells Mummy about a series of books that teach people how to mix paints, how to use oil paints, and how to paint people, animals, landscapes, and what he calls still lifes, and although they are meant for adults, he sees in me that they will suit me.

Mummy tells me to wait upstairs, and she walks down the stairs with him, all the way down the path, through the front gate, and stands with him at his car. I watch from the window upstairs as he loads his equipment into the back of his car. There are no neighbours out on their balconies. He opens his car door, and before he steps in, he hugs her. It seems like it's a long hug. When she comes back inside, she doesn't speak to us, but she has an unusual look. She isn't smiling exactly, but her face is alive and bright and soft. At first, she seems far away and doesn't answer when we try to speak with her. Later that day, I ask if we will see Mr. Adrien again, and finally she responds fully. No, he is leaving Trinidad in a couple of days. She speaks gently when she answers me, as if it is not me to whom she is speaking.

*

From his little white van, the salesman unloads boxes of stereo equipment onto a dolly and pulls the dolly through the front gate. He brings the boxes, one at a time, up the front stairs into the living room and lays them out in tidy groupings according to brand. He sets them up in pyramids, as if they are on display in a shop. A corner has been decided on for the inevitable purchase, and whenever he unboxes a system, he sets it up on a shelving unit Daddy has already bought.

Let me get you a drink. What will you have? Daddy says to the man. The man seems to have been caught off guard. He stumbles: I'm. I, er. You mean?—but he doesn't finish. Daddy says, Whatever you'd like. Have a drink with me. How about a Scotch?

Looking at Mummy, as if it was Mummy who had offered him a drink, the salesman answers, Nothing hard for me, thanks, but I wouldn't mind a glass of water, thank you.

Mummy doesn't respond. Daddy answers, Water. Sure. But you won't mind if I help myself to something a little stronger, would you.

It sounds like a question, but it's not. I repeat in my mind, *You won't mind if I help myself to something a little stronger, would you.* A statement.

The man arranges one set and delivers his sales pitch while Daddy hovers, strokes the pieces, turns knobs, and flips switches.

Sitting in one of the new teak armchairs that arrived in crates from Denmark recently, I run my hand back and forth on the slim, silky-smooth arm, and watch. Mummy is on one end of the two-seater sofa. She always showers around four in the afternoon, when Daddy is expected home from work, and changes into a clean, simple, afternoon dress. Today, she is wearing one of her short Italian dresses. Her hair has grown out and she has teased the top to make it look fuller and she wears just a hint of makeup. Even when she is at home, she looks like a princess. Her legs are crossed and angled so as not to invite any unwanted glances. She's always telling me, when I am sitting down, to close my legs, to angle them like that. I do it now, but it feels so girlish. I want to be standing, walking around, inspecting and touching the equipment like Daddy is. But it's best if I just sit and watch.

To illustrate differences between two pieces of equipment that perform the same function, the salesman uses an LP with the name of the singer on it—spelled E-n-g-e-l-b-e-r-t H-u-m-p-e-r-d-i-n-c-k. He asks Mummy if she knows that man's music and hands her the album in its sleeve. She reads the list of songs and hands the album back, pointing to one. He says, Oh, yes, that's a good one. He puts the record on the turntable. He tells Daddy to take note of how quietly the arm disengages from its station. How smoothly it crosses over to the album. How delicately it comes to rest on the record. He lets the record spin and the first few bars of music play before lifting the arm and setting it down on the groove for the song Mummy pointed to, "Yours until Tomorrow." Very quietly, Mummy hums along with the singer. It's a very romantic song.

The man's face has brightened. I look at her and she looks back, smiling, raising her eyebrows, and moving her head slightly in time to the music. This gesture is between her and me and no one else. I am pleased, but a little shy.

Daddy is staring at the arm on the record, his head angled, his ear directed at one of the speakers. He walks to the spot in between the two speakers and listens. The man connects another turntable and begins the process again. Daddy immediately says, Ah, this one is smoother. The other one sounded fine until you put this one on. The record doesn't wobble on this one. You can't even see it spinning.

The man smiles and nods deeply. He says, So, this confirms what I had suspected: you're discerning, a man of taste.

This pleases Daddy. Mummy and I exchange little private smirks that end in smiles.

So I won't bother to show you this one. You won't like it either. You have a good ear. Let's concentrate on these two, the finest turntables available on the island.

Mummy mouths the words of another song on the same record. She looks dreamy when she gets to the words about how hearing someone's name changes a flicker into a flame and makes her whole world turn blue, and I wonder whom she is thinking about. Daddy is right there, but neither of them looks at the other. The man says, Well, I brought the right record with me.

Daddy goes to the buffet bar that is part of the living room set from Denmark and pours himself another drink, dropping ice cubes from the bucket into his glass. The man turns up the volume, blasting the music, dropping it down to barely audible, and then blasting it quite suddenly again.

He turns a knob he calls the bass all the way up, all the way down, and then the one he calls treble. He urgently ushers Daddy with him into different parts of the room and points out what Daddy should be hearing. It's as if they are doing a dance. The man adds two more speakers to the two already set up, and Daddy walks about and stands where the man tells him to and listens. He nods.

The man leaves, and Daddy excitedly discusses with Mummy the one he wants. He seems to have great understanding of something he knew nothing of earlier. She says she can't honestly hear any differences between the systems, and that he should choose the one he wants.

The man returns the following Saturday morning and sets up the chosen system, handing Mummy the Engelbert Humperdinck LP before he leaves. I hear him tell Daddy that he should have known he was dealing with a man of discerning taste, because people speak, so he was at fault for having wasted Daddy's time with two inferior sets. Daddy pats the man on his back and says, Not at all, man. Not at all.

Not at all, man. Not at all.

All weekend long, the LP is played. Daddy reads the manuals and fiddles with the knobs on the amplifier. He turns them in increments all the way down, all the way up, only the bass, only the treble, the two coming together, and every so often there are horrid loud bursts of sound. He presses the tiny levers, pulls the wires from the speakers, then puts them right back, just where he had found them. Mummy remains sitting, watching him. But he is lost in what he is doing. If I were him, I'd play one of the records and ask her to dance. I'd bow and hold my hand out for her to take it. I imagine myself wearing a straw hat, my light brown hair falling down my forehead, but you can still see the bandage over the cut on my forehead that I got in a fight for social justice—a fight that I won. I am tall and thin, and I go to the lady in the Italian dress who is sitting on the sofa. I ask her to dance. She looks at her husband and he nods his assent. When I hold my hand out, she clutches it and stands up to face me.

*

Sunday, Pa comes for lunch. I show him my oil painting of the sea and the beach, and the setting sun. I mixed red and yellow and got lots of shades of orange, all different depending on how much red or yellow I added. Mummy bought me a palette knife, and I made the whole painting with the knife. I didn't use any brushes. Not a single one. And the paint is very thick. It isn't perfectly dry, so, showing it to Pa, I must hold it myself. There are coconut trees in my painting, and a bit of land sticking out on one side. These are all painted black—mixed with a little red—because they are in silhouette. Pa touches my head and says it is exactly like he remembers it from the time when we used to go to Mayaro. Then he asks Mummy quietly, but I hear—because I am listening—Are you sure it is OK she is using paints that smell so strongly?

He and Daddy sit at opposite ends of the table, Mummy on one side of Daddy and I on one side of Pa. I can't take my eyes off Pa, or the smile off my face. He has been shown the record player set-up, and now, throughout the meal, music is played softly, but as one of the speakers is not far from where Pa sits, I worry that the music is too loud. He doesn't say it is, but I feel it might be. On Selvon Street the Rediffusion radio hangs on the wall behind his desk. He listens mostly to the news, and so the only music that comes through—unless it's Christmas—is in advertisements, or announcing the start of the reading of obituaries.

After dinner, Mummy, Daddy, and Pa sit in the living room. Daddy is reading the paper. Tara and I lie on the rug playing Snakes and Ladders. I ask Pa to play with us, but he rubs his tummy and says he is too full to get down on the ground. We offer to play on the dining room table, but he says no again, that he wants to sit and chat with Mummy.

After a while I hear Daddy ask, Pápa, are you OK? Is it too hot in here for you?

Pa is sweating. He says, Bring me a glass of iced water. Daddy tells Mummy to get the water, and he leaves the room and returns with his medical bag. He tells Pa he wants to take his pressure. We have not finished our game, but I sit up and indicate to Tara to wait, that we should see what's going on with Pa. I am scared. I go and stand by him as Daddy takes his pressure. Pa leans his head back and Daddy opens Pa's shirt and listens with his stethoscope to Pa's chest. He tells Pa that everything seems OK, but he wants him to go to his doctor tomorrow for a checkup. He says he'll call and get him an appointment in the morning. Mummy is on one side of Pa, and I am on the other, my hand on his arm. She is asking him if he is feeling OK. He says yes, stop all the fussing. He is just feeling a little hot. He says he gets like that after eating sometimes; he doesn't need to see any doctor. Daddy says there's no harm in having a checkup once in a while. Mummy says, Yes, Papa, listen to Suresh. I'll come and take you tomorrow.

Daddy looks at me, he touches my cheek and tells me to stop worrying; Pa is OK.

So, then, why does he need to see a doctor? I ask. Daddy says, Everybody needs to see a doctor sometime. How else will we make a living?

He gets serious and says, Your Pa isn't a young man, you know. And when people get older, things can go wrong with them. That's why a little checkup now and then is a good idea. To take front before front takes you.

Before Pa leaves, Mummy tells him she'll come for him after she drops us off at our school. He glances around the room. I look at what I think he is seeing: all the new furniture, the portraits of us children, the piano. I think he studies Mummy, and us four children, his grandchildren. Before leaving, he shakes Daddy's hand and says in a small light voice, Everything looks good. You're doing well. I am proud of all of you. Take care of them, you hear?

Before stepping into the car with Mr. Monty, he kisses me on the top of my head. I throw my arms around him, squeezing as tightly as I can. He hugs back tightly when I press my face into his tummy.

FIFTEEN

Daddy is now a senator for the opposition, one of only six, and Pa is very proud of him. You can see it in his face when they are together. Pa used to offer advice about money, land, cars, business. But now he listens to everything, and agrees with everything, Daddy says. Mummy chuckles when she says that Uncle Sonny is not going to like how Pa has become so admiring of Daddy. I think Mummy has become proud of Daddy, too. Letters to him now address him as the Honourable Senator Dr. Ghoshal, and that is how he is introduced when he speaks at public events. People treat us—Tara, Anil, Siri, and me—nicely, too; I think this means that we—and Mummy—are honourable, too. But we get so shy that we are never able to speak up when we are spoken to. It's silly, but we can't help it, we just smile a lot. The Senate meets in Port of Spain once a month, on a Tuesday, at the Red House. For that occasion, Daddy is given an official driver. I imagine being in the back seat of the car with him and Mummy as they are driven to an official function, waving back to people as we pass and they recognize him. Senators get gifts. When new stamps are issued by the post office, each senator gets an official first-day cover before anyone else in the public even sees them. And Daddy gives me the ones he gets. So now, including the one Miss Hill gave me, I have a very good stamp collection.

*

I don't want to wear the white dress with the appliquéd red velvet apples. But I have to. And I didn't want to wear socks and shoes. I'm too old to be wearing socks and shoes if I'm not in my school uniform. But, again, I have to. Mummy herself brushes my long hair back so hard that it hurts, but when she is finished, all of it is caught in the elastic band at the back, not a single hair out of place. Tara's dress is white, with a piece of fabric sewn in the front. I called it a bib and she got upset and pestered Mummy, asking her why she had to wear a bib. Mummy told her it wasn't a bib; it was the design of the dress. I am sorry I made Tara so upset. Siri is wearing a red dress with white frills around the neck. She enjoys dressing up, just like Tara. I don't, because when you dress up, people look at you a lot, and I don't like that. The three of us have big white ribbons in our hair, tied around our ponytails in huge bows. Anil is dressed in a white short-sleeved shirt, with a grey vest that has blue velvet lining the V at the opening. He is also wearing a blue velvet bowtie. The photographer set Siri on her bike on the patio and the three of us behind her, Anil in the middle.

Mummy keeps glancing toward the back gate, which, from where we are, isn't visible, and in between the foliage and fern baskets that surround the patio, out to the roadway. She apologizes again and again to the photographer. She says that Daddy very likely had an emergency house call. As we wait for Daddy, the photographer sets us up in different arrangements in the living room, on the patio, in the garden. He takes one of just me with Caesar, my left arm around Caesar's neck and my right arm on his upper body, that hand on his head. Caesar is breathing heavily. His fur has a sharp, strong smell even though he was bathed just this morning. His eyes are so soft, but a lot of sleep collects on his lids and must be cleaned several times a day. He likes to be hugged. Poor Caesar.

The photographer places an opened-out magazine on the front lawn and has Mummy sit on it with her legs tucked behind her. Her hair has been teased so the top makes what is called a bouffant. She is wearing a shirt printed with large blocks of colour—red, yellow, and white. Neither Mummy nor Daddy ever wears jeans, like the photographer is wearing, or T-shirts. Ladies like Mummy wear slacks and men like Daddy wear trousers. Her slacks are black and shiny. Anil doesn't want to be doing any more posing and he begins his usual constant low crying. He won't look at the camera, doesn't want any part of the whole affair anymore. I think that's good, because his face is tear-stained and his eyes are red and watery. It's a good thing this isn't a movie, because he is also hiccupping and you'd be able to hear that. The photographer gets Mummy to form, he says, a backdrop to her four children. He tells her to sit up high. She doesn't like being told what to do and although she is smiling, under her breath she says, as if for only us, the children, to hear, Unh-unh, and then louder, I am sitting up as much as I can. Tara sits on Mummy's right, and Siri to the left, on Mummy's leg. I watch how he arranges us and see that they form a tight threesome. The photographer puts Anil to kneel behind Siri, but Anil keeps turning his back to the photographer, and he has to be told over and over to face forward. Then there is a gap of grass between that foursome and me. He has angled my body toward them and tells me to turn my face to watch him. I want to move closer to them, to fill the gap between them and me, but when I begin to move, he puts his hand out to stop me. Does he know that I don't really belong to this family? I make my face smile, just as Mummy is doing to my right. I don't know if anyone else can see, but I can: she is trembling. I can't know for sure, but I think she is wondering if a family photo of her with us children is worth all this fuss if the entire family isn't here.

I don't understand how Mummy doesn't know where Daddy is. Or how he could have forgotten about our photography session. She was excited about it and had Daddy organize for the gardeners to come earlier to tidy up and water the plants and sweep the patios. Siri and Tara are all smiles in their crinoline-flared dresses, posing and happy to be at the front, right up against

Mummy. I know that my eyes are looking forward, but I, too, keep listening for the car.

The photographer walks around the garden taking pictures of the plants and of Caesar and Bruno and a few candid shots of us children on the swing set. The sun is setting, and he takes pictures of the birds that sit silhouetted in the evenings on the telephone and electricity wires. But soon it becomes too dark outside for him to take any more pictures, and he apologizes to Mummy, packs up all his bags and his lights and the tripod, and leaves.

We eat dinner with Mummy at the children's table just outside the kitchen. She isn't saying much, but her lips are halfway spread, all the time, as if it is a look that has stuck. Then she tells Maureen to undress us and get us ready for bed. We get into our pyjamas, but we don't want to go into our beds. We all want to be with Mummy.

The room is cool. She is sitting up in their bed, leaning against pillows. She has that look on her face that means she isn't even seeing us, even though we are right there in front of her. A magazine is open on her lap, but she isn't reading, just staring ahead at nothing, it seems. Siri lies on one side of her and Anil on the other. I sit on the wicker chair and try to be as still as an ornament. Tara lies in Daddy's place, and just as he does, her hands are clasped on her chest. We are all quiet, waiting together. Anil and Siri fall asleep, and when Tara's eyes begin to close, Mummy shakes her and tells me to help get us all into our beds. She lifts Anil, I lift Siri, and Tara follows, asking as we leave the room, Daddy hasn't come yet?

*

Mummy and Daddy take Pa, Tara, and me to see a parcel of land on a hill overlooking the sea. It is a corner property. Pa says corner properties are valuable. His three properties, including the two on Selvon Street, are all corner properties. Daddy says it is a great spot in truth, but they need to keep looking. He puts his arm around Mummy as we walk back to the car, Pa and the two of us in tow. I hear Daddy say to her, This really is ideal, but something just as nice will come along, pet, something more affordable.

Pa breaks away from us and walks alongside them; Mummy falls back with us. Cars pass. The people in them appear to be residents of this sparely populated area. All of them are white. They slow down, as if they want to say something, but then they just smile and wave and carry on. They look friendly and are clearly curious.

I hear Pa say to Daddy, What are they asking? Daddy answers, something about a square foot, and something-something about a hectare.

Pa turns back and takes Mummy by her arm, drawing her forward. Something is going on between the three of them.

Tara and I want to hear, but we mustn't appear to be eavesdropping. We pretend to speak to each other but aren't really saying anything.

Pa agrees this would be a very good purchase; the neighbourhood, he says, is a fitting place for a doctor—a man in the public eye, too—for such a man and his wife to live in, and in which to bring up the children—us. He would like to see his daughter and son-in-law live in this kind of an area, and his grandchildren grow up in such a place.

Standing between them both, an arm around Mummy, the other on Daddy's back, he says, There is no traffic here; the children can ride their bicycles in the road and you won't have to worry. Listen. Hear how quiet it is? Look at that view. The land slopes downward, so even if someone were to build in front of this property, it is highly unlikely they would build high enough to block your view. See? You can see the Pointe-à-Pierre pier from here. And Port of Spain. It's faint, but you can see it, and that faint blue, back there, that is the Northern Range. Look to the left. That there is Venezuela. The sun is about to set, and that is the scene you will see every evening from your veranda. I told you before, there is no need to worry about money.

It will be a while before they begin building. I wonder if, as it looks as though I will always have to live with them, I can have a bedroom of my own. Pa says they should hurry; he'd like, before his time is up, he tells them, to see what they did with such a nice property. I don't think he should joke about his time. It's not nice to say that kind of thing. It can make some people scared.

*

Mummy seems happier than I have ever seen her. She needs to have a gold chain repaired, and we are going with her to the jeweller on High Street. She parks in the grocery parking lot, and we walk out onto High Street, where the sidewalks in front of stores are lined with vendors. One of them is selling straw hats. He has children's sizes, and I slow down, looking at them. At first, Mummy tries to hurry me on, but then she stops and lets me look. She asks the man if I can try one on. He wants to show me one that has bunches of cloth flowers around the brim. It might suit Tara, but she doesn't want a hat, and I don't like it at all. I don't answer the man, but Mummy puts a hand on my shoulder. I immediately get frightened, thinking I am doing something wrong, and I step away from the man's tray, and—without asking me—she tells the man that I would prefer a plain hat. I feel my face redden. How does she know that is what I want?

He looks at me and, still holding the flower hat, says, But this one real pretty. It would suit you nice-nice.

Again, Mummy says, laughing this time, No, thanks, just a plain one.

She sees one and reaches for it. The man says, Yes, that one. That one better. You Mummy know you good.

Mummy puts it on my head and, stooping slightly, angles it in some way she thinks makes it look good on me. I think it fits, but she tells me to try on another one. And then another. Finally, she asks the man if I can go inside the clothing store behind him and look at myself in the mirror. He agrees, telling me to take a couple of other styles with me to try on. Mummy comes into the store, and as clerks in the store look on and comment, she sets them on my head, this way, then that, and points at me in the mirror. I don't look at myself, but at her. She is so beautiful.

There is one that puts a stop to all the trying on. It makes my hair feel as if it falls at the front, just to my eyes, and I feel tall and slim and strong, and my yellow shirt and white shorts turn into a plaid shirt and khaki long pants, and my slippers into boots. I can feel the holster on my hips, and I rest my hands on the guns there. A silver star badge is pinned on my shirt. I can hear my horse clip-clopping through town. It whinnies, then neighs.

The man tries to sell Mummy one for herself, but she laughs again and says, Not today. I'll come back for one for myself another day.

The man, laughing too, says, Promise me, you hear. I recognize you, you know. You are the doc's wife. I'll be right here waiting.

As we walk away, he shouts to her, Don't disappoint me, eh.

Mummy holds our hands and pulls us along quickly, but she is smiling broadly.

I wear the hat and ride my horse up High Street. I do not look into the eyes of all the beautiful young women lining the street who want to speak to me, but as we, my horse and I, trot forward, looking straight ahead, I smile and tip my hat to them. But after a few steps forward, I take off the hat, and as we walk beside Mummy, I press it to my chest.

LA PALOMA

SIXTEEN

Lately she's dressed and ready, waiting to go out with him when he gets home from his office. He doesn't even take a rest, just a cup of coffee and a piece of chocolate cake, eclair, or aloo pie, and off they go. They don't tell us where they are going. They come back with their shoes muddy and leave them outside of the house to be cleaned. They have little time for us, it seems.

And now a man has come to visit wielding several long tubes, from which he pulls large sheets of rolled-up paper. On each is drawn pictures; one shows a line drawing of the front of a house, as if you were looking up at it from a road; another shows a side view of that same house, from the street, too. There are squiggly lines that are meant to be plants in the garden. There aren't any colours on the pages. Just very thin, very-very straight black lines that must have been drawn with a ruler. And then on another sheet are lots of lines that I begin to understand are a diagram of the inside of the drawn house. Where we live now, there is only one bathroom, but I can see the symbol for the toilet and sink, and there are four of those. There are lots of rooms with drawings of beds in them. The beds have what look like pillows on them. Understanding now what these drawings are, I interrupt as they pore over the sheets of paper to ask with excitement where I will sleep. Mummy points to one room, says, Here, you and Tara. This is your room. And then gently pushes me aside as she listens to Daddy and the man, an architect, speak.

I want to suggest that they have the opportunity, before the house is actually built, to add another room in the bedroom section. Tara doesn't like the smell of the linseed oil and turpentine I use when I am painting. It would be good to have a place where I could paint and no one would be bothered by the odours. I can see where that room, my room, could go. The architect and Mummy and Daddy are discussing the height of a front wall. I tap the paper in the area of the bedrooms, trying to get their attention. Finally, under my breath, I say, several times, Another room can be added *here*. Mummy brushes my hand from the drawing, saying, Anju, please. We're speaking, don't interrupt—go outside and play. And she and Daddy keep talking to the man, while the man stares at me.

*

The words we hear these days are odd and some are funny. Parquet, terrazzo, mahogany. Clerestory. Check throat. Scuncheon.

Uncle Sonny and Auntie Stella and our cousins come for lunch one Sunday, bringing Pa with them. Daddy shows them the drawings. Uncle Sonny studies them and says, But that is going to cost you a fortune. An architect? Why you need an architect? You wasting good money. Between us we could have designed a good little house and had a draughtsman do up the drawings.

I look at Pa, thinking he will say there is no need to worry about money. Mummy, Daddy, and Pa keep quiet. I am about to say to everyone that the land was a gift from Pa, but something tells me to keep my mouth shut. Uncle Sonny points in the air with his forefinger and carries on explaining how they could save money: Put a porch here, look, here, put it here facing the sea so you get the sunset and the sea breeze. He stabs the plans on the table with the same forefinger and says, And you right by the sea; why you want a swimming pool? Suppose it crack with the shifting land? You know we have earthquakes here. I hope you all have your heads on and don't end up losing one set of money. Money, land, and limb—down the drain.

Auntie Stella says, There is only one other house in all of San Fernando with a swimming pool. Yours will be the second. You see, Sonny? All the time, I am telling you we can build a swimming pool for the children in the backyard.

After Uncle Sonny moves away from the plans, she bends over them and names what she sees: Home surgery. Maid's room. Guest room. What, four bathrooms? Well, if you are building from scratch, why not? Utility room. Billiards room? A whole room for the billiards table? Hmm. And this terrazzo floor. I have never seen that in a house. Only in hotels. But, Vijay, you good, yes. You have it all around, on the patio and in the kitchen and in the utility room, too?

Mummy smiles, but she doesn't say anything. Auntie Stella remains bent over the plans. After some seconds of quiet study, she says, Eh-eh, but so many sliding doors. You not afraid, having so many doors? You will have to remember to lock each and every one of them at night. What is this here? A stone garden? A garden for stones? Well, that is unusual.

Mummy laughs and says, Yes, it's just a garden feature.

Auntie Stella says, Oh-ho. Yes.

I am listening, too. And getting answers to questions she and Daddy don't answer when we ask them directly. The foundation of the house is already being built. And that swimming pool. We will have a swimming pool. Like the swimming pools at the private clubs in Pointe-à-Pierre and La Brea, and the ones at the country club in Port of Spain that we can't go to unless we go as guests of the white-members-only. It is all very exciting, and, if I am to continue living with them, I want to ask again if I can have my own bedroom, but I wonder if it is too late for them to make changes to these beautiful drawings. If I had my own room, I would turn it into an art studio like the one in the painting called *The Artist in His Studio*, and I could have an easel like Monsieur Adrien's.

We get used to Mummy and Daddy going to see the progress of the new house. We are not allowed to go with them because it is unsafe. We could fall into an excavated area, we could step on nails and get tetanus and our legs would have to be amputated and we'd have to live like that for the rest of our lives, or an unsecure beam could fall on our heads and kill us dead-dead.

Finally, after begging and begging, Tara, Anil, and I are taken to the property. We do really have to be careful; there are lots of boards, bags and bags and bags of concrete and bales of wire and lengths of rebar all around and loose nails and pieces of wood with nails in them and splinters we can't easily see. If we trip on anything, we can get from a small scratch to something so serious that we end up having to go to emergency at the hospital. Tara and I look at Daddy when he tells us this, and we say to him very seriously, and in unison, And it could kill us dead-dead, and we burst out laughing.

One day, Mummy tells us, a landscape architect will come and smooth out the ground around the house and build patios, one at the front, and one on each side of the house, and grass will be planted and shrubs and trees, and yes, there will be a stone garden right outside the dining room windows. I whisper, The garden feature. She nudges Daddy with her elbow, a large smile making her look happy. She looks really happy every day now and has eyes that look as if they are constantly thinking and doing business.

A man is emptying bags of stones and of powdered cement and water into a large, tilted metal bucket that is slowly spinning. Clouds of chalky-smelling grey dust float through the air. It is very noisy; the man wears muffs on his ears and eye protectors, and we stand back and press our hands against our ears. After a while he stops the machine and shovels the mixture onto the ground. He spreads the lumpy mixture about with something that looks like a giant garden rake. Water fills in the lines made by the tines of the rake. It makes a loud back-and-forth scraping noise as he spreads it. Another man hoses down an area that has already been spread and dried. He wears tall rubber boots and even though his khaki pants are tucked into the boots, they are soaked above the boots. Then one of the men comes in an even noisier tractor-like machine with a large flat round wheel under the front. It is a giant floor polisher. Round and round the polisher man drives, and the concrete and stones beneath his machine are ground down, getting smoother and smoother, shinier and shinier. It's noisy, so we leave and go exploring, but every time I return to see where he has reached in this task, the floor looks different. First it's a riverbed with pebbles, then it's the coral reef in Barbados with anemones and shells of many colours.

Then it is like the sky at night, with stars sparkling in every colour that could possibly exist in the universe.

The area under construction is so big and there are so many large rooms, so many doors through which to enter and exit, we get lost. We laugh at first but then shout for help. Inside, you can tell there is a room here and another one there, but they don't have floors. We cross from one area to the next on wide springy beams. We are not allowed to go by ourselves anywhere near the area with the big open hole that will be the swimming pool. It hasn't yet been paved with cement. Sometimes, when we visit the property after there has been a heavy rainfall and stand near the edge, holding Pa's hand or Daddy's, of course, we see frogs down there sitting on the boards, discarded paint cans, cement bags, and makeshift ladders that have landed on the bottom, and we see tadpoles darting about in the dirty water on the bottom. How will the frogs, and the tadpoles when they become frogs, get out? Pa says, Exactly how they found their way in is how they will find their way out.

I asked Mummy if Pa will come and live with us when the house is built. He is always so happy when he comes to see how the building is progressing. She said she asked him, but he doesn't want to leave Selvon Street, as the ice factory is there; even though Uncle Sonny manages it now, Pa still wants to be close by daily. But we all see how bright he gets when he walks about the property and discusses the plans and progress with Daddy and Mummy.

*

Maureen goes with Tara, Anil, Siri, and me to spend the weekend at Pa's house. Mummy and Daddy stay at Crystal Road in the daytime, but they come to Selvon Street at night to sleep there with us. On the first night, Tara and I sleep in Pa's bed with him. But she gets out of bed in the middle of the night and goes in the front room, where Mummy and Daddy are sleeping with Anil and Siri. Pa snores, Tara says, and it keeps her awake; after that she sleeps in the front room. I stay with him, though. I like being alone with him. I want to hug him, like how Ma used to hug him sometimes, but I stay on Ma's side of the bed, and it feels as if there is a big empty hole inside of me. Once he stopped snoring, and I listened for a long while. I couldn't tell if he was breathing. I put my hand, very softly, on his back. There was movement, up and down, up and down, up and down, slowly but evenly.

Then we move straight into the new house. 110 Paria Drive, La Paloma, La Romain, Trinidad (and Tobago), West Indies, Caribbean, World, the Milky Way.

All our Crystal Road furniture is here in the La Paloma house, and there are boxes upon boxes piled up in all the rooms. The walls outside and at the front of the house are painted white. The ceiling of the entire house is made of thin strips of gleaming wood. The patio, kitchen, utility room, and corridor floors are all in that shiny night-sky terrazzo, but the living room, dining room, and all the bedroom floors are parquet.

Although we can live in the house, some parts remain unfinished, and workers still come. I watch two men working on the floor. They have several boxes of very small strips of hardwood, all the pieces the exact same size and shape, and they glue each one to the plain wood, five in one direction, and then perpendicular to that little block of five, they glue another five. When they are finished, the entire floor has been turned into a perfect zigzag pattern, which the man calls a chevron design. He asks what made me such a curious child. I don't know what to say, and he gives me one of the strips to keep.

For days after we have moved into the house, we aren't able to find our way through it. We scream for help, but no one answers. Then, when we find ourselves where Mummy and Daddy are, they laugh at us.

For a while, containers filled with furniture—a carved liquor cabinet, crystal chandeliers, sconces, carved curtain rods, a kind of chair-bed called a recamier, patio furniture, garden statues for the garden feature—arrive regularly at the wharf. At first, the house is filled almost every day of the week with workers installing or touching up this and that, redoing something or the other. And then there are fewer workers, then longer periods when we have the house to ourselves, and then, finally, it is as if we have lived here always, on the corner of Seaview and Paria Drives.

*

We are the most popular children in our area. All the neighbours' children come on Saturdays and Sundays to swim in the pool. Mummy has made a rule. On Sundays, between the hours of 1:00 and 4:00 p.m., we can't have friends over, and most importantly no one is allowed, in that time, in the pool.

I didn't get the room I wanted—I have to share one with Tara—but my favourite place in the house is the study. Each of us has a desk of our own here. To fill the shelves of the study, Daddy bought a hundred million million books, all cream-coloured, with gold writing on them, from a salesman from America. They are called the *Encyclopædia Britannica*. There is also a collection called Great Books of the Western World. In them are essays. These books are not for children, and we're not supposed to take them down off the shelves. But when Mummy is in her room and not paying us attention, only worrying about where Daddy is and when he will come home, I sometimes take one down and have a look. I didn't, at first, understand what I read, but I *can* read, so I knew it meant that I just had to take my time, look up in the new dictionary the words I didn't know or understand, and if I still didn't understand what they meant, I just had to read it over, again and again, until it made sense. And almost always, this works. Some of the books have poems in them. There are plays by a man named William Shakespeare, who writes using strange English; sometimes his sentences don't make any sense. For instance, someone called Hermia in a play called *A Midsummer Night's Dream* says, *I would my father look'd but with my eyes.* And the other person, named Theseus, says, *Rather your eyes must with his judgment look.* I think I know what they mean, but not exactly. I can't read the whole play because it is too difficult to make sense of it, but still, I like the words in the parts I do read.

Therefore, fair Hermia, question your desires;
Know of your youth, examine well your blood,
Whether, if you yield not to your father's choice,
You can endure the livery of a nun,
For aye to be in shady cloister mew'd,
To live a barren sister all your life,
Chanting faint hymns to the cold fruitless moon.

Livery means uniform. But a special uniform worn by a special person, like a nun. He could have said *habit*, which is what we call the clothing the nuns at school wear, but maybe that word didn't exist in olden days. Or he just didn't like that word. Or that word has other meanings—as it does—that could confuse what he is trying to say.

I like the line where he tells fair Hermia to question her desires. That's interesting. I will always ask myself—question myself, that is—why I want something, and also why I don't want something. I think even when you get an answer to a question, you can still, again, ask *why*. I don't entirely understand the rest of the words, but I love the last line, and I say it in my mind all the time. *I chant faint hymns to the cold fruitless moon*. The cold fruitless moon.

It is only a matter of time, and persistence, before I am able to understand anything, and maybe even everything, which is what Daddy tells us whenever we have to learn anything new. You just take it one word at a time. Then two, and you may have to use the dictionary, and sometimes you even just have to not think about it anymore, and then suddenly, magically, the meaning dawns on you.

We also have books written by someone named René Descartes, and someone else named Jean-Jacques Rousseau, and another person named Emmanuel Kant. I can read the words of these books, and sometimes a line or two make sense, and this is exciting. In the essay by the Emmanuel person there is a lot of writing about the numbers five and seven, and I think maybe I have the same problem as that person. I know that five pens plus seven pens make twelve pens. But I don't understand how you can just add two numbers of nothings and expect them to add up to something that doesn't exist. I am not sure that is what the writer is saying, but when I read his words—I think it's a man, but maybe not—I get excited and wish I could talk to the writer and say what I think. When I read the pages, they sort of make sense, but afterwards I can't really say back out loud what is in the book. I don't mind this, though, as it is like dreaming and then when you wake up you only sort of remember the dream, or it's like doing a jigsaw puzzle, or just disappearing into an ocean of interesting words and sentences that are like different kinds and colours of shells and fish. I like the thin, light pages and the small letters. When I turn the pages, I feel as if I am going to find out a secret on the next page, or learn something big and important, even if I can't say back what it is, which is all right, because no one ever asks me about any of it.

I make drawings and dream of one day explaining to Mummy where and how the house can be expanded so a room can be built for me alone. For now, I have to share the bedroom with Tara, and even with Siri. Our room is painted pink. I don't mean to be ungrateful, but I wish we had been asked and that it was painted a different colour. The pink makes me feel weak, and as if I can't hear myself when I speak. Anil has his own room. His is painted bluish grey. Three of us share one room, but he is only one person, younger than Tara and I, and yet he gets his own room. Just because he is a boy. Maybe when I am bigger, or older, I will be able to speak up and be listened to.

*

Things are changing. I am getting used to living here. I like this house because there are so many rooms that sometimes you can go to one section of the house, go into a room, and even if you're not hiding, still be all alone. I've never been comfortable just opening the fridge and taking anything I want from it the way Tara and Anil do. I always ask first. But Mummy shouted at me with exasperation the other day when I asked if I could have a glass of orange juice. What do you mean *if*? she asked. Why do you always ask? You are not a guest in the house, you know. You *live* here. Whatever is in the fridge is yours as much as it is your sisters' and brother's. Look, please stop acting like a stranger in the house. Don't ask me this again. Just go and help yourself.

It was so odd. I felt embarrassed, and yet I wanted to laugh, but I also wanted to cry with—with something. Can you cry with happiness? Laugh and cry?

*

Pa brings apples and bananas and boxes of barbecue chicken and chips when he comes over. He usually comes about four in the afternoon, after we arrive from school. Once, just when he arrived, Mummy told me to go finish my homework. It was one of the few times I disobeyed her. With some trepidation, I told

her I needed to spend time with Pa first, and then I would do all my homework. She didn't respond. She just stared at me, but she wasn't annoyed. And then she turned away. I'm afraid to jinx the way things are these days, but it seems as if she is understanding and accepting me a bit more now.

Pa likes to sit by the pool, and I sit with him, my hand on his bony warm arm, or I lean against him, inhaling the faint scent of Vicks. When the sun sets, we do not have to prompt each other. It is as if we were both waiting for this time. We look up. We search the fast-darkening sky in the direction where we know the first star will appear at any minute. He kisses my head, and with his lips close to my ear, he asks, You made your wish?

SEVENTEEN

The house on Selvon Street has lost its lustre. The crucifix I remember from Ma's coffin leans against the fish-shaped green vase in the centre of the table. Little rough bubbles of rust that look like barnacles seem to be sprouting on it.

Clear plastic covers have been thrown over the sitting room chairs, so when we visit Pa we don't even go into that room that was once bright and welcoming. The front room, where Ma and I used to sleep, is closed up now, making it musty and stiflingly hot. The bedspread is dusty and faded. The ornaments that were on the dresser are gone. There used to be a shiny ceramic statue of a lady in a pink dress holding a basket of flowers. She wore a pink bonnet with long thin ribbons that, although made of ceramic, looked as if they were billowing in a wind. The pink lady stood on a bed of flowers, all made of ceramic, too. I was not allowed to play with her, but I would lean against the dresser and stare at her. There were also two very small ceramic Scottie dogs. They were painted green, which doesn't really make sense, and yet they were perfect and beautiful. They had shiny wavy fur—ceramic, of course—and very small tails that stuck up in the air, like their ears. Ma kept a jewellery box that was inlaid with smooth abalone shells. It was a gift to her from

Pa; he'd brought it back from one of his trips to Barbados. She kept Barbadian dollar bills and coins from other countries all around the world in it. It's all gone. Everything. Only the crocheted doilies remain, including, until the other day, the pink one Mummy gave me a long time ago. We were visiting Pa, and I went into the room when no one was around to see, and I scrunched it up and stuffed it into my pocket. I worried that I was stealing, but how could that be? It's mine. Back in La Paloma, I didn't know what to do with the doily I had removed without asking. I folded it into a tiny triangle and put it in my box of secret treasures.

Even the armoire is empty, except for the last drawer, which, full of bedding and towels once, now has only two pillowcases in it. Some time ago, I stuck my head in a drawer and sniffed, hoping for scents that would help me remember. Even the smell of camphor balls, dried sargasso grass, and cedar wood has gone.

Mummy often speaks about this, and it seems as if she suspects different people of having taken various things. She asks Pa if he knows what happened to this dish or that ornament, but he seldom knows what she is talking about. He doesn't seem to really know what was in any of the cupboards.

I am deeply sad I don't own any objects I associate with Ma. I clutch at the tiniest clues about her because she's fading in my mind. I have that dream of her still, regularly. In the dream I am so happy she is there, but within seconds of being with her, I realize her body is lacerated, her flesh in ribbon-like strips, and I want both to stay with her, to take care of her, and to get away from the horrible sight. I smell the blood, and it overwhelms me in sadness and fear. When I awaken, the smell of blood is still in my nostrils and mind.

Pa's Christmas presents from last year remain unopened on his dressing table. He doesn't change out of his pyjamas anymore unless he's going out, and he always smells now as if he has a cold. Mummy worries about him. She complains to Daddy that he seems to have lost interest in everything.

Mr. Monty brings him to visit us. As usual, he brings sikiya bananas for me, apples for Tara, and choc ice for us all. I reach him by his chest now that I am eleven and quite tall for my age. He is a little stooped and moves about slower than usual. His clothes seem big for him, and his cheeks have sunken in.

*

Daddy is good at many things. He is a doctor. He is a politician. He plays cricket, billiards, and golf. And he is even a member of the International Brotherhood of Magicians. He is adventurous, but he isn't a show-off. Mummy always says nice Indian girls don't bring notice to themselves. But I would like to be like Daddy, to be good at many different things and to have all kinds of adventures. And an opportunity has arisen.

Today is the day of the school talent show. When it was first announced, I had no idea how I could contribute. Daddy said he believed I would make a good magician and with a little training could put on a very fine show. I don't know why he thought I could do this, but once he announced it, I wanted to try. It would be a matter of practice, but if I could manage being onstage, it would surely be an adventure—and more than that, it might show my classmates and all the teachers that, like him, I am worthy of respect and admiration.

For several days before the show at school, he came straight home from work, which made Mummy very happy, and he taught me tricks. But I really wanted to be able to perform one I'd seen him do, called the Dagger Chest. It's a very grown-up one that requires a lot of practice and ability, but it's scary and effective if you don't know how it is done. And he agreed to teach it to me.

A magician needs a helper, and my helper is Lesley. Ever since she and I became friends, the mean students have stopped teasing her. I don't think it is because they like me. Actually, I don't think they do. Though today might change this. Lesley is bright and she helps me with my schoolwork, and I am creative and I help her with her art assignments. We are a good team. Miss Hill has even said that to the class. So Lesley is my assistant onstage.

Lesley's mother dropped her off at our house several evenings after school so we could practise with Daddy. The very first thing we had to do was swear an oath. Daddy made us both hold our right hand to our heart, and our left up, palm open and facing him, and repeat after him some funny words that made us double over in laughter, but then we had to solemnly swear loyalty and secrecy to the art and craft of the performance of magic for the sole and noble purpose of entertainment. We practised our set several times. When our motions were faultless, Daddy kept saying to us, to Lesley's mother, and to Mummy how proud he was of us. I know now that there is no such thing as magic; it's all what is known as sleight-of-hand, and anyone can do it if they practise hard. But when he said he was proud of us, it made me want to grow up to be a famous magician.

Now, onstage at school, wearing Daddy's too-big black magician's top hat, looking out at the sea of students and teachers, I am shy and a little bit scared. I mustn't let them see this, so I think of Daddy giving speeches and imagine myself like him. I take a deep breath and begin. I surprise myself with this strange and loud voice I am able to muster. I tell my audience I have the easiest recipe for a delicious chocolate cake. You could go home this evening and I bet you would find all the ingredients in your kitchen. Just follow my directions—you don't even have to take notes, it's so easy you won't need help and certainly not supervision, and everyone will be very impressed. I don't think I have their full attention, but I carry on as if I do. Allow me to demonstrate, I say.

I ask my assistant to pass around a baking pan to the audience for their inspection. It is so hot in the room that with both hands I raise my magician's black top hat off my head, wipe the imaginary sweat off my forehead, and delicately position the hat on a raised platform on my work table. Then, while Lesley is still in the audience showing off the pan, I begin.

Pay attention, I say in the manner of one of our teachers. It works. They are listening. It's logical really, I say, and therefore very easy to remember: one full glass of milk.

I pull a carton of milk out of my box of equipment. I look around for a bowl, I look under the table, in my toolbox, I walk to the back of the stage and rummage about, and, finding none, I make myself appear despondent. But then I look at my hat, and an idea comes to me. I turn the hat upside down and with a cloth I wipe its inside. I glance around my area for a measuring cup and shout out to Lesley, asking if she brought it. She says no, she forgot. I shrug.

Do not allow obstacles to deter you, I say. We must make do with what we have and have not.

With a pair of very large scissors, I clip the milk carton, lift it high, and pour all the milk into my hat. I pick up two eggs and make a show of cracking one and throwing the contents, and the two halves of the shell, into my hat. The second one, I stand back and toss it, whole, into the hat. Flour, I say. How much? someone calls. I hear Daddy's voice in my head, and I say after him, Exactly enough, not more, not less. And I put the entire unopened bag of flour into the hat.

And now, most importantly, chocolate. I empty a paper bag full of wrapped chocolate bars into the hat. Now you will need a nice hot fire, I say, so I light a match and drop it into the hat, and then I leap away and shriek, searching the auditorium for Lesley. Oh no, I say, I was supposed to have emptied the contents of this here hat-bowl into the pan. My hat, oh my hat.

The form-one students are giggling. I look toward the row of sitting teachers in the auditorium. They are grinning. Miss Hill is beaming, and I feel more encouraged than ever. The students are shouting directions at me. And my assistant, Lesley, comes racing down the aisle and up onto the stage with the pan, which I grab from her and toss over the hat. I wave and wave and wave my wand, looking worried and pretending to be praying. I circle the table, twirling the wand frantically around the hat, saying in a loud, deep, and urgent voice, Abracadabra, abracadabra, abracadabra. I stop and hesitantly remove the baking pan. From deep inside the hat I slowly pull up a real and beautiful chocolate cake, which I hand to Lesley to display. Students clap and shout, begging for cake. Lesley cuts it up into thin slices and puts the slices on paper plates, placing them, with napkins, on a tray, and she passes the tray around to the teachers while the students scream, Not fair, not fair. They are chanting, We want cake, we want cake. They settle down when I send around a basket of chocolate bars.

But it is the last trick, the more complicated one, that makes all the students and teachers gasp, the one with the daggers. I select two of the daggers from the collection on the table, and holding them up for all to see, I clack the stiff blades against each other, causing them to make a noisy racket. There is on my table a fire-engine-red box about the size of a large grocery box, with slits all along its sides. I say, while poking the daggers into the slits, pulling them out and poking them in again, that I need, from the audience, someone who will be a guinea pig for a trick I will perform in public for the first time in my life. Several people stand and try to run down the aisles toward the stage, but a teacher who has been alerted to help in this moment holds all but one student back. This student had, a day earlier, to take the oath, given to her by Lesley and me. I give her one of the daggers and she runs her fingers along the blade and says, Ouch! This is sharp, man. I whisper to her, Very good, thank you. She sits on a stool as I lift up a panel at the front of the box and one at the back, walking across the stage with the open box, showing it off. Then I set the box over her head. It rests on her shoulders. With a sweep of my hand in which I hold a dagger, I point the blade to the open box, showing the audience that the volunteer's head is indeed within the space of the box. I slide the back panel down. She is still visible to the audience. Working so that the audience doesn't see what I am doing, pretending to stroke the box, I smoothly slide together two black-painted panels that are located inside the box and therefore not visible to the audience. My daggers clank and make a gloriously loud metallic sound, blade run against blade, as I sharpen them. I call out, Are you OK? No one can hear how she responds, so Lesley says, She said it's dark in there. I say, Of course it is dark in there, but does she trust me? Lesley says to the audience that the student wants to know what I am going to do because she is now afraid.

Without answering, I slam the first dagger into the side of the box, piercing it, and she screams long and loud and suddenly stops. The audience shrieks. I can see teachers and students with their hands over their mouths. Some students stand up. The teacher who helped control the hopeful volunteers is standing at the front of the audience, conducting them with both hands to sit and to be quiet. The box tilts precariously to the side. I call out to the volunteer. There is no answer from her, and the audience is restless. I must settle them by assuring them that I might be their classmate, but I am always also a magician—they saw my previous trick, didn't they? This one, I say, is just more difficult, more dangerous, risky, but although there are a few magicians—very few, but nevertheless some—who have successfully done this trick, and many who have not completed it well, I myself, in private practice sessions with the Grand Master (meaning Daddy, of course—but I don't tell them that), performed it, and it always went well. What is crucial is silence. Of course, there's a first time for everything, but I feel confident, I say, that the universe is on my side, and that they, every one of them, must place all their trust in me. If a single person disbelieves, we may never see our schoolmate again. Silence is all I ask. I thrust another dagger, and again my fellow students scream. Then I frenziedly thrust all the other daggers into the box from all sides. When there are no more, I walk around the volunteer, dagger handles sticking out of the box at every angle possible. With some fanfare, I pull up the front panel to reveal a space of pure blackness save for the criss-crossing of gleaming silver blades. The gasp from the audience is loud, but no one speaks.

I pull the panel down. I gently tap the volunteer's shoulders with my wand, and wave the wand above the box as I very solemnly say, I am chanting faint hymns to the cold fruitless moon. An Advanced Level English teacher claps her hands and bursts into laughter in the midst of the silence. The other teachers on either side of her lean in to ask her what that was about. I begin to slowly draw the daggers out, none of which come with the ease with which they went in. I wipe the blades with a tea towel and bang each on the table to remind all of the firmness of the metal. I walk around my volunteer, stroking the box and asking if she is OK, but what I'm really doing is sliding back the interior panels. Then, with some drama, I slide the front panel all the way up, and there is the volunteer, alive, a nervous look turning into a large smile. I swiftly lift the box from her head, and she performs antics with her upper body to show she is unharmed. Students jump to their feet, stomping and clapping. It is deafening, grand. Even the teachers, not just Miss Hill but all of them, are standing and clapping. Convent girls are not allowed to whistle, but girls have put their thumb and forefingers between their lips and are whistling. Mother Evangeline stands and presses her forefinger to her lips, trying hard not to show too much displeasure with all that unladylike whistling.

When I relay to Daddy how it went, he is delighted and ready to show me other tricks, and I want to learn everything from him. Our friends love him because he pulls coins from behind their ears, and he is always telling us jokes.

*

I come to the last line of the book just as the blue-grey tanagers and kiskadees in the neighbours' pomerac tree behind our house begin their first chirps of the day. Yesterday, mid-morning, I began reading *Voices in the Wind.* I barely touched lunch because it was hard to tear myself away from the story. And then, the instant we were allowed to leave the dinner table, instead of watching the few minutes of television we're usually allowed, I went into bed to continue reading. Tara came in eventually; she was chattering away as usual, but, buried in the book, I didn't look up, answering only, appropriately or not, Mhm. After the ceiling light had been turned off, I continued reading by the light of the bedside table lamp.

I am tired now. But I can't stop thinking about Robyn, the girl in the book who is, I think, about my age. She and her friends solve a mystery that was plaguing her seaside home, and, after many dangerous adventures, it is she who leads the police to capture some very bad people. She is a hero. A girl, but a stargirl. I don't want these feelings to fade away. I would like to be as brave, as capable, smart, and adventurous as Robyn.

It is quite possible that at the bottom of the hill on which our house stands, down on the waterfront, a smuggling operation is, at this very moment, taking place. It is so quiet in our neighbourhood that no one would ever suspect such a thing could be happening. This would be the perfect place to commit a crime.

I slip out of bed, shove my feet into my slippers, and tiptoe out of our room. I scurry down the dark hallway. Tiptoeing past the doorway of my parents' bedroom, I hear only Daddy's light snoring. By way of steadying myself in the unlit passageway, I slide my forefinger against the wall of the study and descend the two steps to the kitchen hallway, pausing beside the children's dinner table to listen. The wall clock in the kitchen ticks loudly. The green glow of a light on an appliance lets me see the time:

4:45. Maureen is usually up well before anyone else in the house, but it is too early still for her. I continue quietly into the dining room. The curtains have not been tightly closed and a shaft of yellow street light cuts across the room. Remaining close to the wall, I descend the stairs into the living room. Heavy gold-and-white curtains are drawn across the sliding doors that open onto the main patio. I stand still and listen. All is quiet. The curtains fall neatly to the floor. There are no unusual bulges; no one is hiding there. I slip my fingers between the curtains, no more than an inch apart, but it is too dark to identify anything. There are no lights on in the houses across the road. I know where the shrubs and plants in the yard are, but I can't make out if anyone lurks among them. What if I open the door only to find that someone is standing there, or behind the young poui tree, or in the heliconia clump? I scan to the left in between the fronds of the philodendron in the stone garden, and then inch by inch across the righthand side of the patio, then toward the gulf, only a sliver of which I see from where I am. I know to look for dim lights being flashed intermittently, an indication that codes are being transmitted. But as carefully as I look, I see no such thing.

I unlock the sliding door and push it apart, an inch at a time so as not to awaken anyone inside the house, or alert anyone outside, and just wide enough for me to squeeze through. And out I slip, not closing the door behind me, in case I need a speedy retreat.

Caesar usually spends the night here on the patio. He likes stretching his body out on the cool terrazzo, his hind legs splayed out long behind him. But he isn't here. He is our only dog now. Bruno had started having seizures and it would have cost a lot to give him all the medication he needed, so the vet offered to take him from us to care for him. Otherwise, he would already have awakened the entire neighbourhood with his usual barking. I whisper Caesar's name, but he doesn't answer. My first thought is he's been poisoned by the smugglers who used the patio, our yard, our house situated on a hill, as a lookout. As far as I can tell, they have left nothing behind—no dropped piece of paper with a list scribbled illegibly on it, no piece of clothing, no cigarette butts. I call again, comforting myself that he is probably in his next-favourite place, on the mat by the back gate leading to the garage. But I don't feel as courageous as I did a short while ago. From right where I am, I should be able to see any unusual activity in the area, so there is no need to traipse around in the cool and damp.

I lower myself into the covered patio swing, intending to keep watch, particularly over the water at the foot of the hill. I am jolted by the voices of people on the road, not yards away from me. I crouch and peer at them through the fronds of the ferns. They talk loudly, making no attempt to hide themselves. But I recognize them—I've seen two of them pushing the prams of babies and walking children. They work in the area.

Light comes up, I see, as fast and sudden as day switches to night. Kiskadees swoop across the patio squawking loudly, as if to alert other birds that a human is occupying their morning space.

I'm surprised and peeved that Caesar still hasn't come to greet me. When he does, he'll lick me, rub his nose against me, and his spittle will be thick and slimy, but I won't mind. I call him again, softly. I step off the patio onto the damp grass, my feet getting wet, and walk along the side of the house toward the back. As I pass shrubs, hitting their extended arms, dew shatters off their finger-like leaves onto my skin and wets my pyjamas. I whistle and, still in a low voice, call again. Then I see him in the garage, in front of one of the cars, lying on his side. But his tongue hangs out of his mouth in a mound of white froth pooled on the asphalt. His eyes are open, but they don't move. Something is wrong with him. His eyes are dull and he is just staring, but at nothing, it seems. He does not even try to turn his head to look at me. I say his name again, as a question

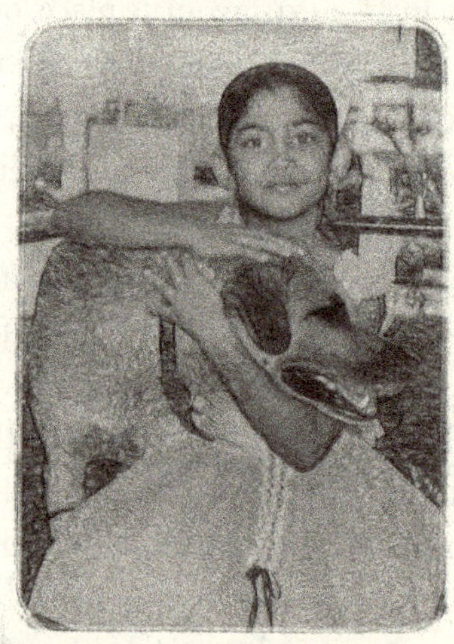

this time. Still, he does not move. There is a thundering in my temples. Moving closer, I can smell him. The usual sharpness is stronger than ever. Almost nauseating. I stoop and, even though I am scared to do so, place my hand against his tummy. He is oddly cool, much cooler than I've ever felt him to be. I hold his front paw and try to lift it, but it doesn't budge. It's a bit stiff. Something is wrong with him. I want to hug him, but he is smelling quite bad.

I rub Caesar's forehead, the shaft just above his nose—his fur is oily and beneath it is cold. I smell my hand. Tears begin to run down my face, and mucus pools on my upper lip.

Caesar. This is Caesar. Our Caesar. I am looking at him. But it doesn't seem as if he is there, inside his body. Where did he go? Is it bad, am I a bad person, for not hugging him? He smells, and his eyes, they frighten me. Is this what happens to the body of a person, or an animal, or someone you love—to everyone and everything—when they die? Ma, her skin. Her body, did she get cold and stiff? Can we make Caesar come back? I don't want to leave him, but I know I must go back inside and awaken Mummy. Perhaps there is still time to do something.

*

A hole will be dug, he will be put in the hole and the hole will be filled up, dirt will be dumped on top of him, flattening him. We will never see him again. Or hear his gentle old-dog bark. He always used to look as if he were saying he was sorry, but with a little smile. Caesar used to smile. That's what I used to say, and Mummy said I was right, he smiled. I am sorry, Caesar. I should have hugged you, and walked around the garden with you, and spoken to you lots more.

We'll put flowers on top of his grave, but soon grasses and weeds will grow over him. Before long, we'll talk about him in the past tense, and then we'll talk less about him, and then days will go by when we won't even mention his name.

EIGHTEEN

We are having a three-in-one party. Number one: It will be the first big party at this house, so the house has to be spic and span. The garden has to be in tip-top shape, not just the lawn and the beds, but the large pots that hold dwarf bougainvillea. The pots edging the patio at the front are being painted white, and we just got white wrought-iron chairs and matching tables for two of the patios. Number two: It will also be the first party since Daddy's appointment in the Senate. And number three: Carnival is around the corner and so it can't just be an ordinary party, it has to be a carnival fete, which means there'll be dancing and lots of food all night long.

Invitations, seventy-three of them, have already been sent out. At this time of year, all catering, bands, barmen, and security have to be booked well in advance, as the closer it gets to carnival itself, the busier and more booked up these businesses become. Six weeks ago, Mummy, sitting at her secretaire in their bedroom, wrote with her fountain pen the names of the invitees, then addressed each envelope in her neat and flowery handwriting. Tara and I got to lick the stamps and paste them on the envelopes. Then the driver took the stack of invitations to the mailbox down on the corner where the road into and out of this residential area meets the highway that takes us into San Fernando.

The barman and his team have been hired, stemware ordered, tables and chairs for the lawn, tablecloths and decorations. There'll be a band—a guitarist, a man who plays the electric piano, a drummer, and a steel pan player, and their singer is a woman named Alana. And a DJ has also been hired to fill in when the band takes breaks.

The days are rolling by, but there hasn't been a single response to the mailed invitations. Mummy began speaking with caterers about the different kinds of menus suitable for the evening: hors d'oeuvres, a buffet dinner, and after-dinner snacking, and about hiring their kitchen and serving staff, but she needs to know how many guests plan to attend before she finalizes any of this.

Daddy is mentioned in the papers almost every day now. He has presented to Parliament two bills to be discussed—one that will legalize prostitution, and the other that will do away with capital punishment. The abortion one went nowhere. Again, as a medical doctor, he feels that, when it becomes legal, better health care will be provided to women who work as prostitutes. Mummy reminds him of his failure with the abortion bill and says he's beating his head against a wall in this Catholic country.

To which he answers, Are you Catholic? Are Pundit Maharaj and his family Catholic? Is the Muslim family across the road Catholic? Are Catholics even Catholic?

To which she answers, Everything to you is a joke.

But the truth is, neither of these causes is popular with the majority of people in the country, and the papers have something to say about this and about Daddy every day. In letters to the editors, some people support him, but the majority condemn him. Mummy wonders, therefore, if there haven't been responses to her invitations because most of the invitees are Catholics and other kinds of Christians and because, as she has said, everyone in this country is religious when they want to be. I admit that I feel ashamed he is doing something so many people disagree with, even teachers at school and the parents of students in my class, and yet I also feel proud of him because after he explains to us again why he wants abortion, and now prostitution, legalized, and why capital punishment is wrong, I want him to win all of these causes.

Mummy and Daddy wonder if they should phone around and ask people if they are coming to the party or not, but they always decide against this, as they think it crass to do so.

But we're approaching two weeks now before the date scheduled for the party, and the food and drinks haven't even been ordered. Not a single person has responded.

Mummy decides, without Daddy's knowledge, to phone one of their friends and see what the reason for their silence is. I hear her gasp on the phone. There is confusion in her voice, then laughter, then surprise. She calls another person on the invitation list, and then another. She seems to be getting the same response. She calls Daddy and tells him that not a single person she spoke with has received an invitation.

Daddy calls the postmaster general, and a postal employee is sent to open the box down the road from our house. We receive a call right away from the postmaster general: He is horrified to say that all the invitations are still in the box, along with about three months' worth of mail posted by other residents. The postal worker who was assigned to that box doesn't like the turnoff from the highway, thinks it too treacherous to cross the highway to enter the residential area and then have to turn around and negotiate the exit. After a while, he simply forgot about that box.

*

A man comes with hundreds of pink and white balloons and a helium tank. He ties the filled balloons into the shrubs and places them on the huge broad leaves of the stone garden philodendron, and he totally covers the pool with pink balloons that throb against each other in the currents created by the filter jet systems. There are people making flambeaux with bamboo poles in which are stuck bottles of kerosene with wicks of cloth stuffed in them. The flambeaux are placed at even intervals all around the fencing of the house, on the two streets that corner the house. The band came earlier and set up, and had a small practice session. It was loud, and sometimes you had to cover your ears quickly because of a horrible piercing screech coming out of the microphones.

Daddy comes home early. He doesn't go back to work after lunch. When he sees the tables on the lawn, set with tablecloths and all the dishes, cutlery, and napkins, and he hears the DJ setting up and trying out his speakers in this spot and that spot, when he smells the food being uncovered in the kitchen, being put on the caterer's heating elements, and sees the balloons, he holds Mummy close, kisses her on her mouth. He tells her that no one makes a place as beautiful and welcoming as she. She is so proud. Still, she says to him, And all you have to do is show up. He says, I am a lucky man. In any case, how else will all of this get paid for?

She says, Well, that is true.

He has hired security for the night; they will show guests where to park and then accompany those who have had to park far away to the house.

We have to dress up, as usual, even though there are no other children at the party. And for this party we don't have to leave and come inside and go to bed early. We wouldn't be able to sleep if we did anyway, because the music is loud and won't stop until the last guest has left. Daddy dresses in white trousers and a purple shirt with yellow and green flowers and Mummy in a short, shiny, mauve strapless dress and matching high-heeled shoes, and her hair is all done up and she looks more beautiful than I've ever seen her.

Pa doesn't come. He's been tired these days. This is just as much his house as it is Mummy and Daddy's, and Tara and Anil and Siri's. I guess it's mine, too, but I still think of the one on Selvon Street as my true house. If it weren't for him, we might not be living on this particular piece of land. That's what I think. And he's never seen this house decorated like this. So, earlier in the afternoon I phoned and begged him, telling him all about how beautiful the house is looking, and about all the music and food. I love his voice. But it was soft. He said he is too old now for late nights. His dancing days are behind him. I asked him if he used to be a dancer. He said there was a time when he could have danced Daddy under the table in a competition. I wanted to ask if Ma liked to dance, but I don't like to mention her to him, because it might make him sad.

Now I want to phone him and tell him to listen through the phone to the music and to all the noise of the people chatting and laughing and singing to the music, but Maureen stops me, saying he'll probably be asleep by now, and I mustn't awaken him. He would have been proud of Mummy, though, I think.

Everyone keeps saying that this is *the* fete of the season. That everything is perfect. Mummy loves all the praise, and Daddy tells them he had nothing to do with any of it. I overhear one of the people who are in politics with him, standing away from Mummy, say, But, Suresh, you know how lucky you are, boy? Why you like to play the fool so? And Daddy says, Play the fool? What are you talking about? I am as clean as an archbishop, man. And yes, you're right, I am a lucky man. I am married to my biggest asset. The root of all my achievements.

And when the man, laughing and poking his hand in Daddy's stomach, says, And you, boy, like you are the root of all evil, Daddy slaps him on his back, both of them laughing, and responds, It takes one to know one, boy. What you say, what you say?

They, Mummy and Daddy, dance together, the band playing popular top-forty tunes and current calypsos, with no screeches thankfully, and they slide through the crowd, talking with the guests, Mummy dipping inside every so often to make sure the servers are bringing this and that out on time.

We don't even have to ask the head barman—three times for the night, he just makes Bentleys for Tara and me. He puts umbrellas on the side of the glasses and sets the glasses on a tray. Just those two glasses. And he sends a waiter to hand them to us with napkins, as if we are guests. I look over at him, nod and smile, not a big friendly smile, but a quick, tiny one, the way I see guests do it, but he never smiles back. He just nods deeply and returns to his work.

Just before the last stragglers leave, Tara, Anil, Siri, and I, exhausted, change into our pyjamas on our own and get into bed. I didn't dance. I just watched, and I fall into sleep recalling every detail of the evening, and the beautiful voice of Alana, the singer.

*

Some of Daddy's family who live in Port of Spain are coming to visit. The leaf is put into the centre of the table in the guest dining room, as there will be eleven of us. I don't want to let Mummy know I don't remember everything she has taught me, so I take the etiquette book to my room and study the map of the table. We don't need the four glasses for each person, and only the adults will have wine. Dolly brings the glasses from the cabinet and sets them where I tell her. Mummy comes and studies what I've done. She nods. Very good.

I blush and my heart beats so fast I feel dizzy.

Do you want to cut some flowers and put them in a vase? she asks.

I will do anything that pleases her.

Grandma's cousin Auntie Jasso, Auntie Jasso's daughter Auntie Cammie and Auntie Cammie's husband, Uncle Bal, and their little daughter arrive. Daddy loves this side of his family, too. They laugh a lot together, and they are not serious like Uncle Sonny and Auntie Stella. They are always teasing each other and telling jokes I don't understand and don't think I'm supposed to understand.

The little girl's name is Shylana; she is four and a little bit fat because she likes food *too bad*. With great pleasure, that is what her grandmother says. They like to feed her and watch her eat. That side of the family thinks we are too thin.

Shylana wants to play on the swing set. I offer to look after her. She is very talkative. She has a horse, but she can't ride it because she is too small and the horse is too big. When she gets taller, she will take lessons and learn to ride it. As I hold her, I push the swing very gently, and when she slides down the slide, I hold her hand.

They are Hindus. Vegetarians. Mummy told us, before they arrived, that we won't be having meat today, and to please not ask for it in front of our guests. During dinner, Daddy tells Shylana's mother about the courses at his college in Ireland. They all speak for a long time about first-year courses, and then about specializing later. He tells them about the billiards club and championship competitions with the other universities, and how he was the college's billiards champion for three years in a row. He tells them a story we have heard before, about a time before he and Mummy were married: the college's basketball team was going on tour, playing through Europe. Daddy was too short to play so he was not on the team. But he and most of the players were good friends, known for getting themselves into "good trouble."

When he says this, Auntie Cammie, Uncle Bal, and Auntie Jasso interrupt him, all speaking at the same time and teasing him, wanting to know the details of this "good trouble."

The other basketball players, Daddy carries on, ignoring the aunties and uncle with a sort of shy, guilty, and apologetic look on his face, wanted him to go on the tour with them and decided they would bandage his arm after they arrived in France and put it in a sling, so it would seem that although he was part of the team, he had been injured in a game in France and was now unable to play. It worked. He travelled with them on a bus to many countries, even to Communist countries.

This impresses Uncle Bal and Auntie Cammie.

He fell in love with a girl in Romania, he says. Yes, that's right, he'd just met her, that's right, but it was love at first sight.

Auntie Cammie and Uncle Bal tease Daddy and say that that is just like him, a girl in every port.

Then Daddy says yes, but it was past the curfew in the town, and he and the girl, sitting on a park bench, were caught by the police. They were both taken to the police station, and it wasn't only that it was past the curfew, but they were underaged, and Daddy was accused of trying to seduce the girl. We hadn't heard that part of the story before. Auntie Cammie gasps. Her mother twists her mouth and smiles at the same time, but Uncle Bal throws his head back and laughs. When adults are speaking, we're not supposed to enter their conversations, so I can't ask what *seduce* means. In any case, I have a feeling I shouldn't ask. I'll look it up in the dictionary later. The girl's father came down to the police station, and although they didn't speak the same language, Daddy understood the man was threatening to kill him, and the police struggled to hold him back from beating up Daddy. Daddy says he was such a skinny fellow in those days, and the man was solid, like a tank, that one lash from him and Daddy would have been down for

the count. As the man was wrestling with the police, Daddy shouted to the father that he was in love with his daughter and promised to marry her right away.

Auntie Cammie says, But, Suresh, you real good for yourself, yes.

Just at that time, his teammates arrived at the station, intervened, and stopped him from getting married or killed.

Mummy says how she used to take Tara in her pram for walks along the Liffey while Daddy was at the college. She talks about spending time in St. Stephen's Green with Tara and Anil. I look at Tara; she was lucky. I sit up, smile bravely, eat my dinner, and take sips of my lime juice. I picture Tara's mummy walking, pushing the pram with Anil in it, and Tara walking alongside, holding her mummy's dress, or the arm of the pram, or one of her mummy's hands.

I am not in any of their photographs from Ireland. No one looks at me as Mummy tells her stories, but I feel they are seeing that I wasn't there. I want to tell them I was in Trinidad living with Ma and Pa at the time, but instead I work at making my face pleasant, and try to show I am enjoying what Mummy is saying.

Daddy says little children used to run up to him on the street and touch his arm, as if wiping it, and then run off while looking at their fingers, expecting the colour of his skin to have come off on them.

I am understanding that Auntie Cammie, Uncle Bal, and Shylana are going to Ireland. I think Auntie Cammie and Uncle Bal are both going to attend the same college that Daddy went to. Both of them will become doctors, like Daddy.

Mummy says they lived in a flat on Adelaide Street and had a landlady who liked Daddy a lot. He flirted with her, of course, even though she was an old lady, Mummy says, shaking her head and pursing her lips. Once, the lady made Daddy a tomato sandwich, not knowing that Daddy didn't like tomatoes. Mummy rolls her eyes when she relates how Daddy, typically, told the lady the sandwich was so delicious, and he went on and on about how much he enjoyed it. But the truth was, he didn't really like it. The bread was tasteless white bread, it wasn't buttered, there was no salt or pepper on the tomato. But he'd been so effusive in his praise and appreciation that every day for the rest of the term the lady waited with a soggy tomato sandwich for Daddy to return from the college.

We leave the adults at the table talking about Ireland and medical college and go to play in our bedroom. Tara and Shylana sit on Tara's bed and dress and undress Annie, Tara's old favourite doll, and then they dress her all over again. They put water in the doll's bottle and feed her. As usual, water squirts out of the doll's eyes, and everything gets wet. Maureen is going to quarrel with Tara when she has to change the sheet before we go to bed. Not me. I wasn't playing with the doll, and I told them several times not to play with water on the bed.

*

We are standing on the patio, inching our way toward the front stairs. The adults are having one of those very long goodbyes before they head down to the car. Tara is already walking with Shylana, holding her hand and going slowly down the stairs. Shylana is a chatterbox. Tara has met her match. I am with the adults, listening to their adult conversation. Auntie Jasso, Auntie Cammie's mother, says to Mummy that Shylana spends so much time with her at her house that she thinks Shylana will not miss Cammie and Bal too much when they go. No, Auntie Jasso answers a question Mummy has asked her, Shylana doesn't yet know anything. They are not going to tell her until just before they leave. No point. No point in upsetting her now.

My heart has stopped beating. I want to join the conversation, but all I can think of saying is, Excuse me, excuse me. But then I don't know what I would say.

Auntie Cammie is telling Daddy that she and Uncle Bal likely won't be coming back until they have qualified. I hear her say they will miss Shylana, and hope she remembers them when they return so many years from now.

I have made a fist with one hand and hold that fist with my other hand, the knot of them clutched under my chin.

Auntie Cammie's face has gotten all crooked, and tears fill her eyes. Uncle Bal chuckles nervously, and Daddy reaches in and hugs Auntie Cammie. Auntie Jasso rubs Auntie Cammie's back as she says, Shylana couldn't be in better hands. She appeals to Daddy, Not so, Suresh? I will take care of her, she says, like she is my own.

I am standing between my parents and Shylana's parents and I am hopping from one foot to the next. My whole body is tickling, my thoughts are jumbled.

I leave them and catch up with Tara and Shylana. I bend down and hug Shylana. She is such a sweet little girl. She is loving, too. She throws her arms around my neck and, even though we met each other only today, holds on as if we have known each other forever. In my mind I say, Don't let them leave you here, Shylana. You have to go with them. If you don't, if you stay here, you will love your Ma and Pa more than anything in the whole world. Then, one day, these strangers who are your parents will return, but you won't know who they are, and they will take you away from your Ma and Pa. Then your Ma will die, and you'll be all alone. Even when you're with your parents, you'll be all alone. You have to, you must, go with them.

I hold on to her and press my lips to her head and try to make my thoughts go right into her brain.

After they leave, Mummy goes into their washroom to undress. I feel an urgency I have never felt before. Mummy lets the other children go into that room with her when she is undressing but doesn't like me to see her undressed. But I can't waste time and must speak to her right now.

I go in as she is removing her eye makeup. She turns around to tell me to get out, but I quickly say, Mummy, I wonder if you can speak to Auntie Cammie, please?

She says, What? Did something happen?

I say, You have to call them right away. You have to call them today. You must tell her not to leave Shylana in Trinidad when they go to Ireland.

Mummy stares at me. She is paying attention, and I feel she understands how urgent this message is.

She won't know who they are when they come back, I say. It won't be good for her. They have to understand. They must take her with them.

Mummy turns back to face the mirror. She holds a cotton ball in one hand, but she isn't attending to her makeup anymore. Even though she doesn't say anything, she is watching me in the mirror. She is listening, she is thoughtful. For the first time since I've come to live with them, I feel as if I am having a serious conversation with Mummy, although she hasn't spoken yet.

Seeing that she is listening and taking my worry seriously, I ask more directly, Will you phone them and tell them right away, before it's too late?

She bites her lips and is wiping her face with the cotton ball. She hasn't responded, though. Perhaps I'm not explaining myself well, I think. I feel as if I'm not making sense. I ask again, Please? Will you tell them?

Her face is obscured by her hand, and I can't see her expression, but I see her nod. She pulls the door open wider, and I understand that I am to leave now.

I am so proud of myself. I have just intervened in a huge mistake and saved everyone a lot of future trouble, especially a little girl who otherwise will grow up to be very lonely. And I saw, too, that Mummy listened. It took her a few minutes, but she understood, and agrees. I feel quite grown-up and responsible.

*

Not long after, I am down in the living room with Tara. We are playing the piano. I play bass, she plays treble. We are like jazz musicians; she plays all the high tinkly notes, and I follow with a beat. We just move up and down in our sections. It's noisy and not at all harmonious, but we are enjoying pretending we're great musicians. I can do that and at the same time think about Shylana. I bang the keys out fast and loud.

Suddenly, Daddy rushes down the stairs from the guest dining room into the living room toward us; he comes to me and spins me around on the piano bench.

What did you just say to your mother?

I don't know what he is talking about, because Tara and I have been at the piano for a while now.

But he is firm and angry. He shakes me hard, and says, What did you tell her? She won't come out of the bathroom, and she is crying. She said you spoke to her. Come here, right now.

I try to think what I did that was wrong. The last thing I said to her was important, but not mean. Just urgent. Frightened, I follow him through the house and into their room. She is sitting on her side of the bed.

Apologize to your mother right now. Tell her you didn't mean what you said.

I say, I'm sorry, I didn't mean it. But I am confused, unsure of what I am apologizing for. Is it that I meddled in adult business? I am now wondering.

Then he says, Let me explain something. We had no choice. I was at college and your mother was having another baby and wasn't well with that pregnancy.

Now I understand. We have never spoken about why I wasn't in Ireland with them, about why I was with Ma and Pa, and why, when they returned, they took me away from Ma and Pa to live with them when I didn't know who they were. This is the first time. And it is getting clear that I shouldn't have brought it up. I don't feel grown-up and responsible anymore. What I said to Mummy was wrong. I am ungrateful and stupid. I hurt her. And I've made a fool of myself. Daddy isn't finished.

We didn't leave you with your grandparents because we were bad people. We didn't leave you with strangers. We didn't leave you because we didn't love you. We left you with people who cared about you, who loved you, too. Every day we thought about you. Instead of just thinking about yourself, you should think about the sacrifices we have made to give you—all of you—a good life. Whatever we do, it is because we love each one of you. Now go back outside and don't let us hear any more about any of this. Look at how upset you've made your mother.

My face burns. I never meant to hurt Mummy. I think she thinks I am blaming her for something. Was I? I didn't mean to. I am sorry I made her cry, and now I want to cry, but I mustn't. I try to hold my breath, but it's awful because I have no choice but to breathe, and when I breathe, my chest moves in and out very fast, and everyone in the world can see my body—as if I have no clothes on—and my chest is exposed and they can see how it moves, so fast, as if I am a frightened dog.

I go and touch her hand that clutches a wad of tissues. Her eyes and her nose are red, and her face puffy. She glances at me and then back down at her hands. Although I already said it, I whisper, I'm sorry. I didn't mean it. I don't know if words actually left my mouth or, if they did, whether they were loud enough to be heard. She folds her lips into her mouth, so they disappear. She has a frown, and it seems she will cry again. She nods. I turn to leave, my back to them, and I feel as if my back is bare, as if I am naked, for all the world to see. I tiptoe out of the room.

I don't think she is going to phone Auntie Cammie. People might be different from one another, but all people have problems. A person's problems can begin when they are very little. As little as Shylana. You can't see another person's troubles, but that doesn't mean they have none, no matter what age they are, how little they are. You can try to help other people, but that doesn't mean you'll be able to. In any case, you don't die because of your problems. They can press against your chest and make you feel as if you can't breathe, but even if you want to, you don't die. Sometimes I feel as if I can't get my chest to open up, can't get air inside me. But I haven't died. I am alive. And I love the sky, and birds and dogs, and flowers. The sunsets. Trees that lose all their leaves in the dry season and then get covered in flowers. I love the sea. The sand, and wind and waves. Even if you're sad, all of these things still exist, and they are beautiful even if you are not. You can look at them and let them look back at you, and you'll feel happy.

You just have to learn how to live with problems, how to carry them around, as if in a schoolbag hanging at your side, off your shoulder. You have to learn how to carry them. On your own.

The first rule is that you shouldn't bother to tell people your problems and mustn't show your feelings to anyone. Second is that you mustn't meddle in other people's business. And last—at least last for now—it's best to keep your mouth shut and take care of your own self. Everybody, I suppose, eventually learns these things, like how I am learning them now.

I won't think of Shylana anymore. I hope I never see her again. She'll find out everything on her own. She'll be all right. She has no choice. We have no choice. Realizing this makes me feel a lot better—even though I should, I know, I know, I know, I should try to stop all this feeling.

*

Sunday morning. Daddy is home. He'll be home all day. Pa will come and have lunch with us. I am tidying my desk in our room so he can see how well I am doing. I'll go polish my bicycle, and around the time we expect Mr. Monty to arrive with him, I will go ride it on the street just in front of the garage gates. He'll be very impressed.

Daddy has put on a new record he recently bought. I can't pronounce it, but on the album jacket is spelled T-C-H-A-I-K-O-V-S-K-Y's and then there are the words *1812 Overture*. It is what is known as classical music and it is, apparently unusually, played on the pan. He intends to play it during lunch. Music to dine by, he said with authority. I smiled, repeating to myself, *Music to dine by*.

The cherry pie is ready, but we aren't allowed to touch it. We have to wait until after lunch. I helped by crushing the graham crackers with the rolling pin, but Mummy made the Philadelphia Cream Cheese filling. She put condensed milk in it, and after she had scraped out the tin, she gave me the spoon to lick. The cherries come from a can, and she puts some alcohol in it, but not enough to get children sick or drunk. For lunch she is making her special Irish dish called shepherd's pie, and the smell of the lamb, onions, garlic, and the Spanish thyme from the garden cooking away on the stovetop makes me hungry. Dolly is peeling potatoes for the topping, and Maureen is folding washed clothing in the backroom. No matter what Mummy is cooking, Pa always brings Man Ten barbecued chicken for us. So we will have shepherd's pie and barbecued chicken. And, of course, a hand of bananas. He never comes with his hands swinging.

Pa always calls us just before he leaves his house, and when the phone rings I run to the kitchen. I am ready and waiting. In about ten minutes, I will run out and get on my bike. Dolly wipes her hands on her apron and answers the phone. She holds it away from her, looks at Mummy, then at Daddy, and says, Is Mr. Sonny. He say tell Doctor take the phone quick-quick. Daddy lunges forward and grabs it. There are prickles, like pins and needles all over my body, even on my face.

Mummy and Daddy leave the house not minutes after that call. Mummy, her face rigid, her eyes wide, as if she is terrified, doesn't even say goodbye to us or tell us where they are going. But I know.

They are gone well past lunchtime. The ground lamb is cooked, but it sits on the stovetop, covered. Dolly sets the children's table for us and serves us the mashed potatoes, with chicken sausages from a tin. I eat one sausage and one spoonful of the potatoes. She gives us cherry pie afterwards, but I can't eat mine. She is being very gentle, with me in particular. No one has to tell me what is happening. I know. It's Pa. He isn't coming here any time today. I keep thinking we will go and see him later this evening, but I have this feeling that's not going to happen. I go to the metal trinket box on our dresser and from it I take the gold ring with the heart and my initials engraved in it, the ring he gave me two years ago on my tenth birthday, and I put it on. My chest is expanding and expanding on its own, getting so big that I think it will burst.

I hear the metal gates sliding open and the car slowly coming into the driveway. I want to race to the back door, to open it. For the tiniest fraction of a second, I am sure Pa will be with them, but just as quickly, I stop myself from thinking.

I walk instead, slowly, tiptoeing. Maureen unlocks and opens the door, holding me back behind her. She presses me between her and the wall as Mummy enters the house. Maureen asks Daddy if she should get dinner for them. He says, No, I'll eat later, but I don't think madam will eat anything right now. Make me a cup of tea. And bring a glass of water in for madam. I am going to give her a sedative. Keep the children away from the bedroom section.

I mustn't be sadder than Mummy. Don't make such a fuss that you have to be taken care of, I tell myself. Don't bring attention to yourself. Don't ask, because you don't want to know. The words *dil deke dekho, dil dekho* come into my mind. I try to whisper them to the tune from the Indian cinema, but it's all crackly and I can't finish it.

I remember Caesar lying on his side in the garage, his tongue hanging out, white froth around his mouth. Once something dies, it doesn't come back. When Ma died, I kept hoping a mistake had been made. That the next time I went to Selvon Street, she'd be there, walking around and talking, like always. All things die—animals, flowers, and people, too—and once they do, that's it. Don't ask. You don't want to hear.

Later that evening, above the sound of a strong wind howling, waves crashing in my ears, as if they are floating in from the horizon, Daddy casts words, like shells scattering on sand, *Your Pa, heaven, Ma.* He keeps wiping my cheeks with his hand. No tune, just the words, *dil deke dekho, dil dekho, dil deke dekho, dil dekho,* hammer inside my chest.

*

Maureen says I am clammy. She keeps rubbing my back and hugging me. She gives me ice to suck. My face and neck are covered in beads of perspiration, and yet I am cold. She fans me with the folded newspaper. The scent of Pa's hair oil fills my head. His 4711 aftershave lotion. His cream-coloured shirt with the tiny blue-and-brown arrows, the Vicks VapoRub when I would rest my face against his belly. His smile. Sometimes he doesn't shave right away. I can feel the scratchiness against my cheeks when I press my face against his. His eyes—I can see them as if he is right here looking at me. His eyes smile even when his mouth doesn't. I see him studying the horse-racing paper. I want to go to Selvon Street and save everything in the drawer of his dresser—the penknife, his pens, the tie pin box, the cigarette holder, the money clip—before someone else takes it all.

The girl Angela—she will remember him. I'm sure she will. He was there with me, watching us on the beach. I want to fly over the roads and trees and the river with the wood bridge, past Rio Claro, to the village in Mayaro. I need to find Angela. Anjula with a g. She might be on the beach. She will want to know. Can I ask if Mr. Monty can take me? But we are to be quiet. I mustn't make any trouble.

The coconut man. The oyster man and the mauby man. Do they know? Someone has to tell them. They will want to know. I haven't seen them—or Angela—in a long time, but it is certain now that I will never again see any of them. They will wonder why no one came and said anything to them.

I am standing still, but my body is twisting, this way and that way, it wants to go, and yet I am as still and heavy as a sack of cement. Pa's hand, it is splayed, all five fingers on my head, like a cap. He is here, even though I can't see him. I am standing still and yet I am spinning around and around.

*

Tomorrow is the funeral. It's late, but the only person asleep right now is Siri. The rest of them are in the bedroom section. Except Maureen. She is in the laundry room ironing. I slip out of the house and stand alone by the pool. It is a moonless night, but had there been a moon, I am sure it would have been cold and fruitless. Of all nights to have missed the first star. The vast black sky sparkles with millions and millions of them. Far, far, far away, deep into the blackness, are tiny indistinct smudges of light, nebulae.

The jets in the pool spurt, a low, steady pulse, and a gurgling. For a second, I think Pa is standing there with me. I don't know how everything inside of me isn't falling out of the hole in my chest. An owl hoots in a tree at the back of the yard, and some seconds later there is a commotion, as if it has tumbled, fallen. And then it has risen again, flapping its wings wildly as it rights itself before flying off.

I should be afraid of this dark night—was it really an owl I heard? Is the noise of the pool's jets masking danger?

But I am not afraid. It is a still, warm night, and yet I am trembling. But I'm not afraid.

If everything dies, why does it all have to go through the whole of living to get to dying? Living just tricks you. Because you fall in love with everything all around you, you want to know everything, you love everything, and then one day, you will have to leave it all and go. But go where? No matter how much you love someone, how much someone loves you, they will die. And you will, too. You will trick someone who loves you, because one day, you won't even say goodbye to them. You will just leave them.

It's best not to love anyone, and not to let anyone love you.

There, right there, Ursa Minor, Ursa Major, and Cassiopeia. And there, Mercury and Saturn, large silver dots, bright, bold, and unblinking.

I fix my eyes to the brightest star, one in Ursa Major. That star is Pa. I love you. I remain back here, but I will always love you, only you, and you will always be with me.

I am afraid to blink, lest the star fade, lest he disappear. I meant to be strong, not to cry. And now I can't stop. I wish the sky had long hands that would reach down, lift me, and carry me up into its blackness.

But in all the time I stand there waiting, no hands reach for me.

I am as flimsy as a ghost.

I turn and go back in, pulling the sliding door shut.

*

Rock of ages, cleft for me, let me hide myself in thee.

At the graveside, Reverend Seepersad says, Ashes to ashes, dust to dust.

Nothing about stars.

ACKNOWLEDGEMENTS

Propping up a book like this is a world of people who fleshed out its story and made the person who would one day write it. They are unnamed in the list that follows, but it can only have been my good fortune to have been placed among them, and I am grateful beyond words.

Kathryn Kuitenbrouwer and Marlene McCallum, thank you for reading the early drafts, for the many ways in which your encouragements continue to come, and for our stimulating friendship. It is not hyperbole to say that you, Shelagh Hurley, have, from the first few pages, when it was the length of a short story, read every draft of this novel, thoroughly editing each along the way. The details you caught, and offered—like the hummingbird hawk moth, which is not a hummingbird, and not a hawk, but a moth. And so much more that makes my heart soar with gratitude and awe.

Vahli Mahabir, Ramesh Mootoo, Indrani Mootoo, and Kavir Mootoo—no matter what I write, my siblings are all always there with me. I couldn't, I wouldn't, do any of this without you. Regarding starry nights and more, Vahli and Indrani gently burnished the edges of my memory, generously mined theirs on my behalf, and granted me all the rein a writer needs. Thank you, and thank you again.

Dearest Mia Raani Wingson, your artwork, the paintings and drawings, are absolutely perfect, and I am delighted to be able to use them here. Arini and Brett, thanks tons for permitting me to use this young artist's work in mine.

It was a great pleasure, yet again, watching the brilliant Mike Gaudaur of Quinte Photo Services work his photography skills and magic, manipulating my old photos into just what was needed for this book.

Thank you, Samantha Haywood and Eva Oakes of Transatlantic Agency, for helping me to find a home for the book. Jay and Hazel Millar of Book*hug Press took every care with this book, and I am deeply pleased to have worked with them yet again. They put the book in the hands of Anne Horowitz, who at once "caught" Anju's voices as she grew up, and only helped strengthen each stage of her development on the page. I am eternally grateful for Anne as the book's editor. And for Ingrid Paulson, whose cover design perfectly captured the tenor and mood of this book. Book*hug's team includes Stuart Ross, with his enviable ability to spot that unnecessary or overused word, and yet respect the various raced and classed accents of an oh-so-long-ago time and place. Proofreader Laurie Siblock must also be well-lauded for the final shine she put on the work. Thank you Laurie. Included are Reid Millar and Brittany Landry, who diligently and beautifully work to lay the book's path onward. I am ever so grateful for this publishing home and family.

I am pleased to have been able to write this book with the generous support of the Canada Council for the Arts. Thank you, CCA.

The ability to write a novel like *Starry Starry Night* depends on a number of conditions being met, not least of which is having someone who travels alongside you, believing in you and in the work, who is there, always there, ready to catch both when the inevitable stumbles occur. Deborah Root, you are that silky net, my rock—my first, second, third...last reader, my joy to talk with, walk with, and to mind our little flock of birds with.

PHOTO: DARREN RAMPERSAUD

SHANI MOOTOO is the author of six novels, three collections of poetry, and one short story collection. She is a four-time Giller Prize nominee, and her work has been longlisted and shortlisted for the Booker Prize, the Lambda Literary Prize, and the IMPAC Dublin Literary Award. She has been awarded the Doctor of Letters honoris causa degree from Western University, is a recipient of Lambda Literary's James Duggins Outstanding Mid-Career Novelist Prize, the Writers' Trust Engel Findley Award, and Library and Archives Canada Scholar Award. Mootoo was born in Ireland, raised in Trinidad, and lives in Southern Ontario, Canada.

COLOPHON

Manufactured as the first edition of
Starry Starry Night
in the fall of 2025 by Book*hug Press

Edited for the press by Anne Horowitz
Copy Edited by Stuart Ross
Proofread by Laurie Siblock
Type + design by Ingrid Paulson
Cover image: ©iStockPhoto/Esteban David Saavedra Del Rayo

Printed in Canada

bookhugpress.ca